John

The Tailor of Panama

John

Also by John le Carré

Call for the Dead
A Murder of Quality
The Spy Who Came In From the Cold
The Looking-Glass War
A Small Town In Germany
The Naive and Sentimental Lover
Tinker Tailor Soldier Spy
The Honourable Schoolboy
Smiley's People
The Little Drummer Girl
A Perfect Spy
The Russia House
The Secret Pilgrim
The Night Manager
Our Game

le Carré

The Tailor of Panama

Hodder & Stoughton

Copyright © David Cornwell 1996

First published in 1996
by Hodder and Stoughton
A division of Hodder Headline PLC

The right of David Cornwell to be identified as the Author of
the Work has been asserted by him in accordance with the
Copyright, Designs and Patents Act 1988.

10 9 8 7 6 5 4 3 2 1

A CIP catalogue record for this title is available from the British Library

ISBN 0 340 68478 X

Typeset by Rowland Phototypesetting Ltd,
Bury St Edmunds, Suffolk

Printed and bound in Great Britain by
Clays Ltd, St Ives plc

Hodder and Stoughton Ltd
A division of Hodder Headline PLC
338 Euston Road
London NW1 3BH

In memory of
Rainer Heumann,
literary agent, gentleman and friend

'Quel Panamá!'

Expression current in France
in the early years of this century.
Describes an insoluble mess.

(See David McCullough's admirable
The Path Between the Seas)

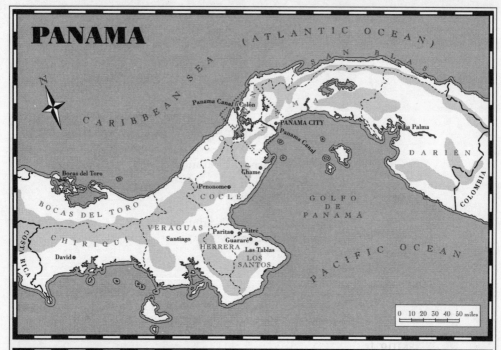

PANAMA

CARIBBEAN SEA (ATLANTIC OCEAN)

SAN BLAS

Panama Canal · Colón

· PANAMA CITY

Panama Canal

Ghame

La Palma

DARIÉN

Bocas del Toro

Penonome

COCLÉ

COLOMBIA

BOCAS DEL TORO

GOLFO DE PANAMÁ

VERAGUAS

Santiago

Parita · Chitré

Guararé

HERRERA

Las Tablas

LOS SANTOS

CHIRIQUÍ

David

COSTA RICA

PACIFIC OCEAN

0 10 20 30 40 50 miles

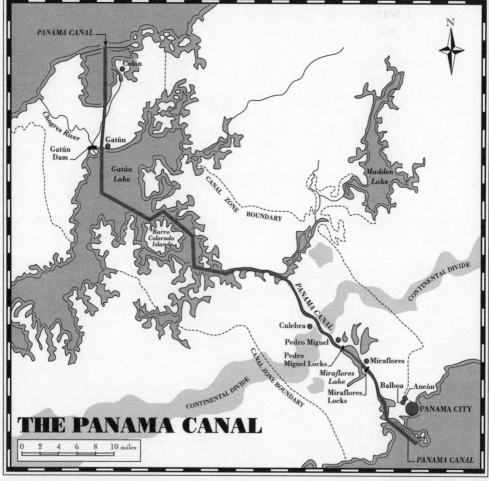

PANAMA CANAL

Colón

Chagres River

Gatún

Gatún Dam

Gatún Lake

CANAL ZONE BOUNDARY

Madden Lake

Barro Colorado Island

CONTINENTAL DIVIDE

PANAMA CANAL

Culebra

Pedro Miguel

Pedro Miguel Locks

Miraflores

Miraflores Lake

Miraflores Locks

Balboa

Ancón

PANAMA CITY

CONTINENTAL DIVIDE

CANAL ZONE BOUNDARY

THE PANAMA CANAL

0 2 4 6 8 10 miles

PANAMA CANAL

CHAPTER ONE

It was a perfectly ordinary Friday afternoon in tropical Panama until Andrew Osnard barged into Harry Pendel's shop asking to be measured for a suit. When he barged in, Pendel was one person. By the time he barged out again Pendel was another. Total time elapsed: seventy-seven minutes according to the mahogany-cased clock by Samuel Collier of Eccles, one of the many historic features of the house of Pendel & Braithwaite Co., Limitada, Tailors to Royalty, formerly of Savile Row, London and presently of the Vía España, Panama City.

Or just off it. As near to the España as made no difference. And P & B for short.

*　　　*　　　*

The day began prompt at six when Pendel woke with a jolt to the din of bandsaws and building work and traffic in the valley and the sturdy male voice of Armed Forces Radio. 'I wasn't there, it was two other blokes, she hit me first and it was with her consent, Your Honour,' he informed the morning, because he had a sense of impending punishment but couldn't place it. Then he remembered his eight-thirty appointment with his bank manager and sprang out of bed at the same moment that his wife Louisa howled 'No, no, *no*,' and pulled the sheet over her head because mornings were her worst time.

'Why not "yes, yes, yes," for a change?' he asked her in the mirror while he waited for the tap to run hot. 'Let's have a bit of optimism round the place, shall we, Lou?'

Louisa groaned but her corpse under the sheet didn't stir so Pendel amused himself with a game of cocky repartee with the news reader in order to lift his spirits.

'*The Commander in charge of US Southern Command last night again insisted that the United States will honour its treaty obligations to Panama, both in the principle and in the deed,*' the news reader proclaimed with male majesty.

'It's a con, darling,' Pendel retorted lathering soap onto his face. 'If it wasn't a con you wouldn't go on saying it, would you, General?'

'*The Panamanian President has today arrived in Hong Kong for the start of his two-week tour of South-East Asian capitals,*' said the news reader.

'Here we go, here's your boss!' Pendel called, and held out a soapy hand to command her attention.

'*He is accompanied by a team of the country's economic and trade experts, including his Forward Planning advisor on the Panama Canal, Dr Ernesto Delgado.*'

'Well done, Ernie,' said Pendel approvingly, with an eye to his recumbent wife.

'*On Monday the presidential party will continue to Tokyo for substantive talks aimed at increasing Japanese investment in Panama,*' said the news reader.

'And those geishas aren't going to know what hit them,' said Pendel in a lower tone, as he shaved his left cheek. 'Not with our Ernie on the prowl.'

Louisa woke up with a crash.

'Harry, I do not wish you to speak of Ernesto in those terms even in jest, please.'

'No, dear. Very sorry, dear. It shall not happen again. *Ever*,' he promised while he navigated the difficult bit just under the nostrils.

But Louisa was not appeased.

'Why can't Panama invest in Panama?' she complained, sweeping aside the sheet and sitting bolt upright in the white linen nightdress she had inherited from her mother. 'Why do we have to have *Asians* do it? We're rich enough. We've got one hundred and seven banks in this town *alone*, don't we? Why can't we use our own drug money to build our own factories and schools and hospitals?'

The 'we' was not literal. Louisa was a Zonian, raised in the Canal Zone in the days when by extortionate treaty it was American territory for ever, even if the territory was only ten miles wide and fifty miles long and surrounded by despised Panamanians. Her late father was an Army engineer who, having been seconded to the Canal, took early retirement to become a servant of the Canal Company. Her late mother was a libertarian Bible teacher in one of the Zone's segregated schools.

'You know what they say, dear,' Pendel replied, holding up an earlobe and shaving beneath it. He shaved as others might paint, loving his bottles and brushes. 'Panama's not a country, it's a casino. And we know the boys who run it. You work for one of them, don't you?'

He had done it again. When his conscience was bad he couldn't help himself any more than Louisa could help rising.

'No, Harry, I do not. I work for Ernesto Delgado and Ernesto is not one of *them.* Ernesto is a straight arrow, he has ideals, he cherishes Panama's future as a free and sovereign state in the community of nations. Unlike *them* he is not on the take, he is not carpetbagging his country's inheritance. That makes him very special and very, very rare.'

Secretly ashamed of himself, Pendel turned on the shower and tested the water with his hand.

'Pressure's down again,' he said brightly. 'Serves us right for living on a hill.'

Louisa got out of bed and yanked her nightdress over her head. She was tall and long-waisted, with dark tough hair and the high breasts of a sportswoman. When she forgot herself she was beautiful. But when she remembered herself again, she stooped her shoulders and looked glum.

'Just one good man, Harry,' she persisted as she rammed her hair inside her showercap. 'That's all it takes to make this country work. One good man of Ernesto's calibre. Not another orator, not another egomaniac, just one good Christian ethical man is all it takes. One decent capable administrator who is not corrupt, who can fix the roads and the drains and the poverty and the crime and the drugs and preserve the Canal and not sell it to the highest bidder. Ernesto sincerely wishes to be that person. It does not behove you or anybody else to speak ill of him.'

Dressing quickly, though with his customary care, Pendel hastened to the kitchen. The Pendels, like everyone else who was middle-class in Panama, kept a string of servants, but an unspoken puritanism dictated that the master of the family make breakfast. Poached egg on toast for Mark, bagel and cream cheese for Hannah. And passages by heart from *The Mikado* quite pleasantly sung because Pendel loved his music. Mark was dressed and doing his homework at the kitchen table. Hannah had to be coaxed from the bathroom where she was worrying about a blemish on her nose.

Then a helter-skelter of recrimination and farewells as Louisa, dressed but late for work at the Panama Canal Commission Administration Building, leaps for her Peugeot and Pendel and the kids take to the Toyota and set off on the school rat-run, left, right, left down the steep hillside to the main road, Hannah eating her bagel and Mark wrestling with homework in the bouncing four-track and Pendel saying sorry about the rush today, gang, I've got a bit of an early pow-wow with the money-boys, and privately wishing he hadn't been cheap about Delgado.

Then a spurt on the wrong carriageway, courtesy of the morning *operativo* that allows city-bound commuters to use both lanes. Then a life-and-death scramble through charging traffic into small roads again, past American-style houses very like their own to the glass-and-plastic village with its Charlie Pops and McDonald's and Kentucky Fried Chicken and the funfair where Mark had his arm broken by an enemy bumper car last Fourth of July, and when they got to the hospital it was full of kids with firework burns.

Then pandemonium while Pendel rummages for a spare quarter to give the black boy selling roses at the lights, then wild waving from all three of them for the old man who's been standing at the same street corner for the last six months offering the same rocking-chair at two hundred and fifty dollars written on a placard round his neck. Side roads again, it's Mark's turn to be dropped first, join the stinking inferno of Manuel Espinosa Batista, pass the National University, sneak a wistful glance at leggy girls with white shirts and books under their arms, acknowledge the wedding-cake glory of the del Carmen Church – good morning, God – take your life in your hands across the Vía España, duck into the Avenida Federico Boyd with a sigh of relief, duck again into Vía Israel onto San Francisco, go with the flow to Paitilla airport, good morning again to the ladies and gentlemen of the drugs trade who account largely for the rows of pretty private aeroplanes parked among the trash, crumbling buildings, stray dogs and chickens, but rein back now, a little caution, please, breathe out, the rash of anti-Jewish bombings in Latin America has not passed unnoticed: those hard-faced young men at the gate of the Albert Einstein mean business, so watch your manners. Mark hops out, early for once, Hannah yells, 'Forgot this, goofy!' and chucks his satchel after him. Mark strides off, no demonstrations of affection allowed, not even a flap of the hand lest it be misinterpreted by his peers as wistful longing.

Then back into the fray, the frustrated shriek of police sirens, the grunt and grind of bulldozers and power drills, all the mindless hooting, farting and protesting of a third world tropical city that can't wait to choke itself to death, back to the beggars and cripples and the sellers of hand towels, flowers, drinking mugs and cookies, crowding you at every traffic light – Hannah, get your window down and where's that tin of half-balboas? – today it's the turn of the legless white-haired senator paddling himself in his dog cart, and after him the beautiful black mother with her happy baby on her hip, fifty cents for the mother and a wave for the baby and here comes the weeping boy on crutches again, one leg bent under him like an over-ripe banana, does he weep all day or only in the rush hour? Hannah gives him a half-balboa as well.

Then clear water for a moment as we race on up the hill at full speed to the María Inmaculada with its powdery-faced nuns fussing around the yellow school buses in the forecourt – *Señor Pendel, buenos días!* and *Buenos días* to you, Sister Piedad! And to you too, Sister Imelda! – and has Hannah remembered her collection money for whichever saint it is today? No, she's goofy too, so here's five bucks, darling, you've got plenty of time and have a great day. Hannah who is plump gives her father a pulpy kiss and wanders off in search of Sarah who is this week's soulmate while a smiling very fat policeman with a gold wristwatch looks on like Father Christmas.

And nobody makes anything of it, Pendel thinks in near contentment as he watches her disappear into the crowd. Not the kids, not anyone. Not even me. One Jewish boy except he's not, one Catholic girl except she's not either, and for all of us it's normal. And sorry I was rude about the peerless Ernesto Delgado, dear, but it's not my day for being a good boy.

*   *   *

After which, in the sweetness of his own company, Pendel rejoins the highway and switches on his Mozart. And at once his awareness sharpens, as it tends to as soon as he is alone. Out of habit he makes sure his doors are locked and keeps half an eye for traffic muggers, cops and other dangerous characters. But he isn't worried. For a few months after the US invasion gunmen ruled Panama in peace. Today if anybody pulled a gun in a traffic jam he would be met with a fusillade from every car but Pendel's.

A scorching sun leaps at him from behind yet another half-built highrise, shadows blacken, the clatter of the city thickens. Rainbow washing appears amid the darkness of the rickety tenements of the narrow streets he must negotiate. The faces on the pavement are African, Indian, Chinese and every mixture in between. Panama boasts as many varieties of human being as birds, a thing that daily gladdens the hybrid Pendel's heart. Some were descended from slaves, others might as well have been, for their forefathers had been shipped here in their tens of thousands to work and sometimes die for the Canal.

The road opens. Low tide and low lighting on the Pacific. The dark grey islands across the bay are like far-off Chinese mountains suspended in the dusky mist. Pendel has a great wish to go to them. Perhaps that's Louisa's fault because sometimes her strident insecurity wears him out. Or perhaps it's because he can already see straight ahead of him the raw red tip of the bank's skyscraper jostling for who's-longest among its equally hideous fellows. A dozen ships float in ghostly line above the invisible horizon, burning up dead time while they wait to enter the Canal. In a leap of empathy Pendel endures the tedium of life on board. He is sweltering on the motionless deck, he is lying in a stinking cabin full of foreign bodies and oil fumes. No more dead time for me, thank you, he promises himself with a shudder. Never again. For the rest of his natural life, Harry Pendel will relish every hour of every day and that's official. Ask Uncle Benny, alive or dead.

Entering the stately Avenida Balboa he has the sensation of becoming airborne. To his right the United States Embassy rolls by, larger than the Presidential Palace, larger even than his bank. But not, at this moment, larger than Louisa. I'm too grandiose, he explains to her as he descends into the bank's forecourt. If I wasn't so grandiose in my head I'd never be in the mess I'm in now, I'd never have seen myself as a landed baron and I'd never be owing a mint I haven't got and I'd stop sniping at Ernie Delgado and anybody else you happen to regard as Mister Morally Impeccable. Reluctantly he switches off his Mozart, reaches into the back of the car, removes his jacket from its hanger – he has selected dark blue – slips it on and adjusts his Denman & Goddard tie in the driving mirror. A stern boy in uniform guards the great glass entrance. He nurses a pump-action shotgun and salutes everyone who wears a suit.

'Don Eduardo, Monseñor, how are *we* today, sir?' Pendel cries in English, flinging up an arm. The boy beams in delight.

'Good morning, Mr Pendel,' he replies. It's all the English he knows.

* * *

For a tailor Harry Pendel is unexpectedly physical. Perhaps he is aware of this because he walks with an air of power restrained. He is broad as well as tall with grizzled hair cropped short. He has a heavy chest and the thick sloped shoulders of a boxer. Yet his walk is statesmanlike and disciplined. His hands, at first curled lightly at his sides, link themselves primly behind the sturdy back. It is a walk to inspect a guard of honour or face assassination with dignity. In his imagination Pendel has done both. One vent in the back of the jacket is all he allows. He calls it Braithwaite's Law.

But it was in the face which at forty he deserved that the zest and pleasure of the man were most apparent. An unrepentant innocence shone from his baby-blue eyes. His mouth, even in repose, gave out a warm and unobstructed smile. To catch sight of it unexpectedly was to feel a little better.

* * *

Great Men in Panama have gorgeous black secretaries in prim blue bus-conductress uniforms. They have panelled, steel-lined bulletproof doors of rainforest teak with brass handles you can't turn because the doors are worked on buzzers from within so that Great Men can't be kidnapped. Ramón Rudd's room was huge and modern and sixteen floors up with tinted windows from floor to ceiling looking onto the bay and a desk the size of a tennis court and Ramón Rudd clinging to the far end of it like a very small rat clinging to a very big raft. He was chubby as well as short, with a dark blue jaw and slicked dark hair with blue-black sideburns and greedy bright eyes. For practice he insisted on speaking English, mainly through the nose. He had paid large sums to research his genealogy and claimed to be descended from Scottish adventurers left stranded by the Darién disaster. Six weeks ago he had ordered a kilt in the Rudd tartan so that he could take part in Scottish dancing at the Club Unión. Ramón Rudd owed Pendel ten thousand dollars for five suits. Pendel owed Rudd a hundred and fifty thousand dollars. As a gesture Ramón was adding the unpaid interest to the capital which was why the capital was growing.

'Peppermint?' Rudd enquired, pushing at a brass tray of wrapped green sweets.

'Thank you, Ramón,' Pendel said, but didn't take one. Ramón helped himself.

'Why are you paying a *lawyer* so much money?' Rudd asked after a two-minute silence in which he sucked his peppermint and they separately grieved over the rice farm's latest account sheets.

'He said he was going to bribe the judge, Ramón,' Pendel explained with the humility of a culprit giving evidence. 'He said they were friends. He said he'd rather keep me out of it.'

'But why did the judge postpone the hearing if your lawyer bribed him?' Rudd reasoned. 'Why did he not award the water to you as he promised?'

'It was a different judge by then, Ramón. A new judge was appointed after the election and the bribe wasn't transferable from the old one to the new one, you see. Now the new judge is marking time to see which side comes up with the best offer. The clerk says the new judge has got more integrity than the old one, so naturally he's more expensive. Scruples are expensive in Panama, he says. And it's getting worse.'

Ramón Rudd took off his spectacles and breathed on them, then polished each lens in turn with a piece of chamois leather from the top pocket of his Pendel & Braithwaite suit. Then settled the gold loops behind his shiny little ears.

'Why don't you bribe someone at the Ministry of Agricultural Development?' he suggested, with a superior forbearance.

'We did try, Ramón, but they're high-minded, you see. They say the other side has already bribed them and it wouldn't be ethical for them to switch allegiance.'

'Couldn't your farm manager arrange something? You pay him a big salary. Why doesn't he involve himself?'

'Well now, Angel's a bit lapsadaisy, frankly, Ramón,' said Pendel, who sometimes chose unconsciously to improve on the English language. 'I think he may be more use not being there, not to put too fine a point on it. I'm going to have to screw myself up to say something, if I'm not mistaken.'

Ramón Rudd's jacket was still pinching him under the armpits. They stood at the big window face-to-face while he folded his arms across his chest, then lowered them to his sides, then linked his hands behind his back while Pendel attentively tugged with his fingertips at the seams, waiting like a doctor to know what hurt.

'It's only a tad, Ramón, if it's anything at all,' he pronounced at last. 'I'm not unpicking the sleeves unnecessarily because it's bad for the jacket. But if you drop it in next time we'll see.'

They sat down again.

'Is the farm producing any rice?' Rudd asked.

'A little, Ramón, I'll put it that way. We're competing with the globalisation, I'm told, which is the cheap rice that's imported from other countries where there's subsidisation from the government. I was hasty. We both were.'

'You and Louisa?'

'Well, you and me, really, Ramón.'

Ramón Rudd frowned and looked at his watch, which was what he did with clients who had no money.

'It's a pity you didn't make the farm a separate company while you had the chance, Harry. Pledging a good shop as surety for a rice farm that has run out of water makes no sense at all.'

'But Ramón – it was what you insisted on at the time,' Pendel objected. But his shame already undermined his indignation. 'You said that unless we jointly accounted the businesses you couldn't take the risk on the rice farm. That was a condition of the loan. All right, it was my fault, I should never have listened to you. But I did. I think you were representing the bank that day, not Harry Pendel.'

They talked racehorses. Ramón owned a couple. They talked property. Ramón owned a chunk of coast on the Atlantic side. Maybe Harry would drive out one weekend, buy a plot perhaps, even if he didn't build on it for a year or two, Ramón's bank would provide a mortgage. But Ramón didn't say bring Louisa and the kids although Ramón's daughter went to the María Inmaculada and the two girls were friendly. Neither, to Pendel's immense relief, did he find it appropriate to refer to the two hundred thousand dollars Louisa had inherited from her late father and handed to Pendel to invest in something sound.

'Have you been trying to shift your account to a different bank?' Ramón Rudd asked, when everything unsayable had been left thoroughly unsaid.

'I don't think there's a lot would have me at this particular moment, Ramón. Why?'

'One of the merchant banks called me. Wanted to know all about you. Your credit-standing, commitments, turnover. A lot of things I don't tell anybody. Naturally.'

'They're daft. They're talking about someone else. What merchant bank was that?'

'A British one. From London.'

'From *London?* They called *you?* About *me?* Who? Which one? I thought they were all broke.'

Ramón Rudd regretted he could not be more precise. He had told them nothing, naturally. Inducements didn't interest him.

'*What* inducements, for Heaven's sake?' Pendel exclaimed.

But Rudd seemed almost to have forgotten them. Introductions, he said vaguely. Recommendations. It was immaterial. Harry was a friend.

'I've been thinking about a blazer,' Ramón Rudd said as they shook hands. 'Navy blue.'

'This sort of blue?'

'Darker. Double-breasted. Brass buttons. Scottish ones.'

So Pendel in another gush of gratitude told him about this fabulous new line of buttons he'd got hold of from the London Badge & Button Company.

'They could do your family coat-of-arms for you, Ramón. I'm seeing a thistle. They could do you the cufflinks too.'

Ramón said he'd think about it. The day being Friday, they wished each other a nice weekend. And why not? It was still an ordinary day in tropical Panama. A few clouds on his personal horizon perhaps but nothing Pendel hadn't coped with in his time. A fancy London bank had tele-phoned Ramón – or there again, maybe it hadn't. Ramón was a nice enough fellow in his way, a valued customer when he paid, and they'd downed a few jars together. But you'd have to have a doctorate in extra-sensory perception to know what was going on inside that Spanish-Scottish head of his.

*　　*　　*

To arrive in his little side street is for Harry Pendel a coming into harbour every time. On some days he may tease himself with the notion that the shop has vanished, been stolen, wiped out by a bomb. Or it was never there in the first place, it was one of his fantasies, something put in his imagination by his late Uncle Benny. But today his visit to the bank has unsettled him and his eye hunts out the shop and fixes on it the moment he enters the shadow of the tall trees. You're a real house, he tells the rusty-pink Spanish roof-tiles wink-ing at him through the foliage. You're not a shop at all. You're the kind of house an orphan dreams of all his life. If only Uncle Benny could see you now:

'Notice the flower-strewn porch there?' Pendel asks Benny with a nudge, 'inviting you to come inside where it's nice and cool and you'll be looked after like a pasha?'

'Harry boy, it's the maximum,' Uncle Benny replies, touching the brim of his black Homburg hat with both his palms at once which was what he did when he had something cooking. 'A shop like that, you can charge a pound for coming through the door.'

'And the painted sign, Benny? P & B scrolled together in a crest, which is what gives the shop its name up and down the town, whether you're in the Club Unión or the Legislative Assembly or the Palace of Herons itself? "Been to P & B lately? – There goes old so-and-so in his P & B suit." That's the way they talk round here, Benny!'

'I've said it before, Harry boy, I'll say it again. You've got the fluence. You've got the rock of eye. Who gave it you I'll always wonder.'

His courage near enough restored, and Ramón Rudd near enough forgotten, Harry Pendel mounts the steps to start his working day.

CHAPTER TWO

Osnard's phone call, when it came around ten-thirty, caused not a ripple. He was a new customer and new customers by definition must be put through to Señor Harry or, if he was tied up, invited to leave their number so that Señor Harry could call them back immediately.

Pendel was in his cutting room, shaping patterns out of brown paper for a naval uniform to the strains of Gustav Mahler. The cutting room was his sanctuary and he shared it with no man. The key lived in his waistcoat pocket. Sometimes for the luxury of what the key meant to him he would slip it in the lock and turn it against the world as proof he was his own master. And sometimes before unlocking the door again he would stand for a second with his head bowed and his feet together in an attitude of submission before resuming his good day. Nobody saw him do this except the part of him that played spectator to his more theatrical actions.

Behind him in rooms equally tall, under bright new lighting and electric punkahs, his pampered workers of all races sewed and ironed and chattered with a liberty not customarily granted to Panama's toiling classes. But none toiled with more dedication than their employer Pendel as he paused to catch a wave of Mahler then deftly closed the

shears along the yellow chalk-curve that defined the back
and shoulders of a Colombian Admiral of the Fleet who
wished only to exceed in fineness his disgraced predecessor.

The uniform Pendel had designed for him was particularly splendid. The white breeches, already entrusted to his
Italian trouser-makers ensconced a few doors down the corridor behind him, were to be fitted flush against the seat,
suitable for standing but not sitting. The tailcoat which Pendel was this minute cutting was white and navy blue with
gold epaulettes and braid cuffs, gold frogging and a high
Nelsonian collar crusted with oak leaves round ships'
anchors – an imaginative touch of Pendel's own that had
pleased the Admiral's private secretary when Pendel faxed
the drawing to him. Pendel had never entirely understood
what Benny meant by rock of eye, but when he looked at
that drawing he knew he had it.

And as he went on cutting to the music his back began
to arch in empathy until he became Admiral Pendel
descending a great staircase for his inaugural ball. Such
harmless imaginings in no way impaired his tailor's skills.
Your ideal cutter, he liked to maintain – with acknowledgements to his late partner Braithwaite – is your born imper-
sonator. His job is to place himself in the clothes of whoever
he is cutting for and become that person until the rightful
owner claims them.

*   *   *

It was in this happy state of transference that Pendel received
Osnard's call. First Marta came on the line. Marta was his
receptionist, telephonist, accountant and sandwich-maker,
a dour, loyal, half-black little creature with a scarred, lopsided face blotched by skin grafts and bad surgery.

'Good morning,' she said in Spanish, in her beautiful
voice.

Not 'Harry' not 'Señor Pendel' – she never did. Just good
morning in the voice of an angel, because her voice and eyes
were the two parts of her face that had survived unscathed.

'And good morning to you, Marta.'

'I've got a new customer on the line.'

'From which side of the bridge?'

This was a running joke they had.

'Your side. He's an Osnard.'

'A *what?*'

'Señor Osnard. He's English. He makes jokes.'

'What sort of jokes?'

'You tell me.'

Setting aside his shears, Pendel turned Mahler down to nearly nothing and slid an appointments book and a pencil towards him in that order. At his cutting table, it was known of him, he was a stickler for precision: cloth here, patterns there, invoices and order book over there, everything ship-shape. To cut he had donned as usual a black silk-backed waistcoat with a fly front of his own design and making. He liked the air of service it conveyed.

'So now how are we spelling that, sir?' he enquired cheerily when Osnard gave his name again.

A smile got into Pendel's voice when he spoke into the telephone. Total strangers had an immediate feeling of talking to somebody they liked. But Osnard was possessed of the same infectious gift, apparently, because a merriment quickly developed between them which afterwards accounted for the length and ease of their very English conversation.

'It's O-S-N at the beginning and A-R-D at the end,' said Osnard, and something in the way he said it must have struck Pendel as particularly witty because he wrote the name down as Osnard dictated it, in three-letter groups of capitals with an ampersand between.

'You Pendel or Braithwaite, by the by?' Osnard asked.

To which Pendel, as often when faced with this question, replied, with a lavishness appropriate to both identities: 'Well, sir, in a manner of speaking, I'm the two in one. My partner Braithwaite, I'm sad to tell you, has been dead and gone these many years. However I *can* assure you that his standards are very much alive and well *and* observed by the house to this day, which is a joy to all who knew him.'

Pendel's sentences when he was pulling out the stops of

his professional identity had the vigour of a man returning to the known world after long exile. Also they possessed more bits than you expected, particularly at the tail end, rather like a passage of concert music which the audience keeps expecting to finish and it won't.

'Sorry to hear that,' Osnard replied dropping his tone respectfully after a little pause. 'What d'he die of?'

And Pendel said to himself: funny how many ask that, but it's natural when you remember that it comes to all of us sooner or later.

'Well they did *call* it a stroke, Mr Osnard,' he replied in the bold tone that healthy men adopt for talking of such matters. 'But myself, if I'm honest, I tend to call it a broken heart brought on by the tragic closing down of our Savile Row premises as a consequence of the punitive taxation. Are we resident here in Panama, Mr Osnard, may I ask without being impertinent, or are we merely passing through?'

'Hit town couple o'days ago. Expect to be here quite a while.'

'Then welcome to Panama, sir, and may I possibly have a contact number for you in case we get cut off which I'm afraid is quite a usual event in these parts?'

Both men, as Englishmen, were branded on the tongue. To an Osnard, Pendel's origins were as unmistakable as his aspirations to escape them. His voice for all its mellowness had never lost the stain of Leman Street in the East End of London. If he got his vowels right, cadence and hiatus let him down. And even if everything was right, he could be a mite ambitious with his vocabulary. To a Pendel, on the other hand, Osnard had the slur of the rude and privileged who ignored Uncle Benny's bills. But as the two men talked and listened to each other it seemed to Pendel that an agreeable complicity formed between them, as between two exiles, whereby each man gladly set aside his prejudices in favour of a common bond.

'Staying at the El Panama till my apartment's ready,' Osnard explained. 'Place was *supposed* to have been ready a month ago.'

'Always the way, Mr Osnard. Builders the world over. I've said it many times and I'll say it again. You can be in Timbuctoo or New York City, I don't care where you are. There's no worse trade for inefficiency than a builder's.'

'And you're quietish round five, are you? Not going to be a big stampede around five?'

'Five o'clock is our happy hour, Mr Osnard. My lunchtime gentlemen are safely back at work and what I call my pre-prandials have not yet come out to play.' He checked himself with a self-deprecatory laugh. 'There you are. I'm a liar. It's a Friday so my pre-prandials go home to their wives. At five o'clock I shall be delighted to offer you my full attention.'

'You personally? In the flesh? Lot o' you posh tailors hire flunkeys to do their hard work for 'em.'

'I'm your old-fashioned sort, I'm afraid, Mr Osnard. Every customer is a challenge to me. I measure, I cut, I fit, and I never mind how many fittings it takes me to produce the best. No part of any suit leaves these premises while it's being made and I supervise every stage of the making as it goes along.'

'Okay. How much?' Osnard demanded. But playfully, not offensively.

Pendel's good smile widened. If he had been speaking Spanish, which had become his second soul and his preferred one, he would have had no difficulty answering the question. Nobody in Panama is embarrassed about money unless he has run out of it. But your English upper classes were notoriously unpredictable where money was concerned, the richest often being the thriftiest.

'I provide the best, Mr Osnard. Rolls Royces don't come free, I always say, and nor does a Pendel & Braithwaite.'

'So how much?'

'Well, sir, two and a half thousand dollars for your standard two-piece is about normal, though it could be more depending on cloth and style. A jacket or blazer fifteen hundred, waistcoat six hundred. And since we tend to use the lighter materials, and accordingly recommend a second pair of trousers to match, a special price of eight hundred for the second pair. Is this a shocked silence I'm hearing, Mr Osnard?'

'Thought the going rate was two grand a pop.'

'And so it was, sir, until three years ago. Since when, alas, the dollar's gone through the floor, while we at P & B have been obliged to continue buying the very finest materials, which I need hardly tell you is what we use throughout, irregardless of cost, many of them from Europe, and all of them –' He was going to come out with something fancy like 'hard-currency-related' but changed his mind. 'Though I am *told*, sir, that your top-class off-the-peg these days – I'll take Ralph Lauren as a benchmark – is pushing the two thousand and in some cases going beyond even that. May I also point out that we provide aftercare, sir? I don't think you can go back to your average haberdasher and tell him you're a bit tight round the shoulders, can you? Not for free you can't. What was it we were thinking of having made exactly?'

'Me? Oh, usual sort of thing. Start with a couple o' lounge suits, see how they go. After that it's the full Monty.'

'*The full Monty*,' Pendel repeated in awe, as memories of Uncle Benny nearly drowned him. 'It must be twenty years since I heard that expression, Mr Osnard. Bless my soul. The full Monty. My goodness me.'

Here again, any other tailor might reasonably have contained his enthusiasm and returned to his naval uniform. And so on any other day might Pendel. An appointment had been made, the price acknowledged, social preliminaries exchanged. But Pendel was enjoying himself. His visit to the bank had left him feeling lonely. He had few English customers and fewer English friends. Louisa, guided by her late father's ghost, did not encourage them.

'And P & B are still the only show in town, that right?' Osnard was asking. 'Tailors to Panama's best and brightest fatcats and so forth?'

Pendel smiled at fatcat. 'We like to think so, sir. We're not complacent but we're proud of our achievements. It wasn't all roses these last ten years, I can assure you. There's not a lot of *taste* in Panama to be frank. Or there wasn't until *we* came along. We had to educate them before we could sell to them. All that money for a suit? They thought we were mad or worse. Then gradually it took on till there was no stopping it, I'm pleased to say. They began to understand we don't just throw a suit at them and ask for the money, we provide maintenance, we alter, we're always there when they come back, we're friends and supporters, we're human beings. You're not a gentleman of the press by any chance are you, sir? We were rather tickled recently by an article that appeared in our local edition of the *Miami Herald*, I don't know whether it chanced to catch your eye.'

'Must have missed it.'

'Well, let me put it this way, Mr Osnard. I'll be serious, if you don't mind. We dress presidents, lawyers, bankers, bishops, members of legislative assemblies, generals and admirals. We dress whoever appreciates a bespoke suit and can pay for it irregardless of colour, creed or reputation. How does that sound?'

'Promising, actually. Very promising. Five o'clock, then. Happy hour. Osnard.'

'Five o'clock it is, Mr Osnard. I look forward to it.'

'Makes two of us.'

'Another fine new customer then, Marta,' Pendel told her when she came in with some bills.

But nothing he ever said to Marta was quite natural. Neither was the way she heard him: mauled head cocked away from him, the wise dark eyes on something else, curtains of black hair to hide the worst of her.

*   *   *

And that was that. Vain fool that he afterwards called himself, Pendel was amused and flattered. This Osnard was evidently a card and Pendel loved a card the way Uncle Benny had, and the Brits, whatever Louisa and her late father might say about them, made better cards than most. Perhaps after all these years of turning his back on the old country it wasn't such a bad place after all. He made nothing of Osnard's reticence about the nature of his business. A lot of his customers were reticent, others should have been who weren't. He was amused, he was not prescient. And on putting down the telephone he went back to his Admiral's uniform until the Happy Friday midday rush began, because that was what Friday lunchtime was called until Osnard came along and ruined the last of Pendel's innocence.

*   *   *

And today, who should be heading the parade but the one and only Rafi Domingo himself, billed as Panama's leading playboy, and one of Louisa's pet hates.

'Señor Domingo, sir!' – opening his arms – 'Superb to see you, and looking shamefully youthful with it, if I may say so!' – a quick lowering of the voice – 'and *may* I remind you, Rafi, that the late Mr Braithwaite's definition of our *perfect* gentleman' – deferentially pinching at the lower sleeve of Rafi's blazer – 'is a thumb-knuckle's width of shirt cuff, never more?'

After which they try on Rafi's new dinner jacket, which needs trying for no reason except to show it off to the other Friday customers who by this time have started to gather in the shop with their mobile telephones and cigarette smoke and bawdy chatter and heroic stories of deals and sexual conquests. Next in line is Aristides the *braguetazo*, which means he married for money, and is for this reason regarded by his friends as something of a male martyr. Then comes Ricardo-call-me-Ricki, who in a short but profitable reign in the upper echelons of the Ministry of Public Works awarded himself the right to build every road in Panama from now until eternity. Ricki is accompanied by Teddy, alias the Bear, Panama's most hated newspaper columnist and undoubtedly its ugliest, bringing his own lonely chill with him, but Pendel is not affected by it.

'Teddy, fabled scribe and keeper of reputations. Give life a pause, sir. Rest our weary soul.'

And hot on their heels comes Philip, sometime Health Minister under Noriega – or was it Education? 'Marta, a glass for His Excellency! And a morning suit, please, also for His Excellency – one last fitting and I think we're home.' He drops his voice. 'And my congratulations, Philip. I hear she's highly mischievous, very beautiful and adores you,' he murmurs in a graceful reference to Philip's newest *chiquilla*.

These and other brave men pass blithely in and out of Pendel's emporium on the last Happy Friday in human history. And Pendel, as he moves nimbly among them, laughing, selling, quoting the wise words of dear old Arthur Braithwaite, borrows their delight and honours them.

CHAPTER THREE

It was entirely appropriate, in Pendel's later opinion, that Osnard's arrival at P & B should have been accompanied by a clap of thunder and what Uncle Benny would have called the trimmings. It had been a sparkly Panamanian afternoon in the wet season till then with a nice splash of sunshine and two pretty girls peering into the window of Sally's Giftique across the road. And the Bougainvilia in next door's garden so lovely you wanted to bite it. Then at three minutes to five – Pendel had somehow never doubted that Osnard would be punctual – along comes a brown Ford hatchback with an Avis sticker on the back window and pulls into the space reserved for customers. And this easy-going face with a cap of black hair on top of it, planted like a Hallowe'en pumpkin in the windscreen. Why on earth Pendel should have thought Hallowe'en he couldn't fathom but he thought it. It must have been the round black eyes, he told himself afterwards.

At which moment the lights go out on Panama.

And all it is, it's this one perfectly defined raincloud no bigger than Hannah's hand getting in front of the sun. And the next second it's your six-inch raindrops pumping up and down like bobbins on the front steps and the thunder and lightning setting off every car alarm in the street and the drain covers bursting their housings and slithering like discuses down the road in the brown current and the palm fronds and trash-cans adding their unlovely contribution, and the black fellows in capes who always appear out of nowhere whenever there's a downpour, flogging you golf umbrellas through your car window or offering to push you to higher ground for a dollar so that you don't get your distributor wet.

And one of these fellows is already putting the hard word on pumpkin-face as he sits inside his car fifteen yards from the steps waiting for Armageddon to blow over. But Armageddon takes its time on account of there being very little wind. Pumpkin-face tries to ignore black fellow. Black fellow doesn't budge. Pumpkin-face relents, delves inside his jacket – he's wearing one, not usual for Panama unless you're *somebody* or a bodyguard – extracts his wallet, extracts a banknote from said wallet, restores said wallet to inside pocket left, lowers window enough for black fellow to poke brolly into car and pumpkin-face to exchange pleasantries and give him ten bucks without getting soaked. Manoeuvre completed. Note for the record: pumpkin-face speaks Spanish although he's only just arrived here.

And Pendel smiles. Actually smiles in anticipation, beyond the smile that is always written on his face.

'Younger than I thought,' he calls aloud to Marta's shapely back as she crouches in her glass box anxiously checking through her lottery tickets for the winning numbers that she never has.

Approvingly. As if he were gazing upon extra years of selling suits to Osnard and enjoying Osnard's friendship instead of recognising him at once for what he was: a customer from hell.

*   *   *

And having ventured this observation to Marta and received no reply beyond an empathetic lifting of the dark head, Pendel arranged himself, as always for a new account, in the attitude in which he wished to be discovered.

For just as life had trained him to rely on first impressions, so he set a similar value on the first impression he made on other people. Nobody, for instance, expects a tailor to be sitting down. But Pendel had long ago determined that P & B should be an oasis of tranquillity in a bustling world. Therefore he made a point of being discovered in his old porter's chair, most likely with a copy of the day-before-yesterday's *Times* spread on his lap.

And he didn't mind at all if there was a tray of tea on the table in front of him, as there was now, perched among old copies of *Illustrated London News* and *Country Life*, with a real silver teapot on it, and some nice fresh cucumber sandwiches extra thin which Marta had made to perfection in her kitchen where, at her own insistence, she was confined for the first nervous stages of any new customer's appearance lest the presence of a badly scarred woman of mixed race should prove threatening to white male Panamanian pride in the throes of self-adornment. Also she liked to read her books there, because he had finally got her studying again. Psychology and Social History and another one he always forgot. He had wanted her to do Law but she had refused point blank on the grounds that lawyers were liars.

'It is not appropriate,' she would say, in her carefully-honed, ironic Spanish, 'that the daughter of a black carpenter should debase herself for money.'

*   *   *

There are several ways for a large-bodied young man with a blue-and-white bookmaker's brolly to get out of a small car in pelting rain. Osnard's – if it was he – was ingenious but flawed. His strategy was to start opening the umbrella inside the car and reverse buttocks-first in an ungainly crouch, at the same time whisking the brolly after and over him while opening it the rest of the way in a single triumphant flourish. But either Osnard or the brolly jammed in the doorway so that for a moment all Pendel saw of him was a broad English bum covered by brown gabardine trouser cut too deep in the crotch and a twin-vented matching jacket shot to rags by rainfire.

Ten-ounce summerweight, Pendel noted. Terylene mix, too hot for Panama by half. No wonder he wants a couple of suits in a hurry. Thirty-eight waist if a day. The brolly opened. Some don't. This one shot up like a flag of instant surrender, to descend at the same pace over the upper part of the body. Then he vanished, which was what every customer did between the carpark and the front door. He's coming up the steps, thought Pendel contentedly. And heard his footsteps above the torrent. Here he is, he's standing in the porch, I can see his shadow. Come on, silly, it's not locked. But Pendel remained seated. He had taught himself to do that. Otherwise he'd be opening and closing doors all day. Patches of sodden brown gabardine, like shards in a kaleidoscope, were appearing in the transparent half-halo of letters blazoned on the frosted glass: PENDEL & BRAITHWAITE, Panama and Savile Row since 1932. Another moment and the whole bulky apparition, crabwise and brolly first, lurched into the shop.

'Mr Osnard, I presume' – from the depths of his porter's chair – 'come in, sir. I'm Harry Pendel. Sorry about our rain. Have a cup of tea or something a little stronger.'

Appetites was his first thought. A quick brown fox's eyes. Slow body, big limbs, one of your lazy athletes. Allow plenty of spare cloth for expansion. And after that he remembered a bit of music hall banter that Uncle Benny never tired of, to the insincere outrage of Auntie Ruth:

'Big hands, ladies, big feet, and you all know what *that* means – big gloves and big socks.'

*   *   *

Gentlemen entering P & B were presented with a choice. They could sit down, which was what the cosy ones did, accept a bowl of Marta's soup or a glass of whatever, trade gossip and let the place work its balm on them before the drift to the fitting room upstairs, which took them casually past a seductive display of pattern books strewn over an applewood side-table. Or they could make a beeline for the fitting room, which is what the fidgety ones did, mostly the new accounts, barking orders to their drivers through the wood partition and making phone calls on their cellulars to mistresses and stockbrokers and generally setting out to impress with their importance. Till with time the fidgety ones became the cosy ones and were in turn replaced by brash new accounts. Pendel waited to see which of these categories Osnard would conform with. Answer, neither.

Nor did he betray any of the known symptoms of a man about to spend five thousand dollars on his appearance. He wasn't nervous, he wasn't cast down by insecurity or hesitation, he wasn't brash or garrulous or over-familiar. He wasn't guilty, but then guilt in Panama is rare. Even if you bring some with you when you come, it runs out pretty fast. He was disturbingly composed.

And what he did was, he propped himself on his dripping umbrella, with one foot forward and the other parked squarely on the doormat, which explained why the bell was still ringing in the rear corridor. But Osnard didn't hear the bell. Or he heard it and was impervious to embarrassment. Because while it went on ringing he peered round him with a sunny expression on his face. Smiling in a recognising kind of way as if he had stumbled on a long lost friend:

The curved mahogany staircase leading to the gents' boutique on the upper gallery: my goodness me, the dear old staircase... The foulards, dressing gowns, monogrammed house slippers: yes, yes, I remember you well... The library steps artfully converted to a tie-rack: who'd have thought *that's* what they'd do with it? The wooden punkahs swinging lazily from the moulded ceiling, the bolts of cloth, the counter with its turn-of-the-century shears and brass rule set along one edge: old chums, every one... And finally the scuffed leather porter's chair, authenticated by local legend as Braithwaite's very own. And Pendel himself sitting in it, beaming with benign authority upon his new account.

And Osnard looking back at him – a searching, unabashed up-and-down look, beginning with Pendel's face, then descending by way of his fly-fronted waistcoat to his dark blue trousers, silk socks and black town shoes by Ducker's of Oxford, sizes six to ten available from stock upstairs. Then up again, taking all the time in the world for a second scrutiny of the face before darting away to the recesses of the shop. And the doorbell ringing on and on because of his thick hind leg planted on Pendel's coconut doormat.

'Marvellous,' he declared. 'Perfectly marvellous. Don't alter it by a brushstroke.'

'Take a seat, sir,' Pendel urged hospitably. 'Make yourself at home, Mr Osnard. Everyone's at home here or we hope they are. We get more people dropping in for a chat than what we do for suits. There's an umbrella stand beside you. Pop it in there.'

But far from popping his brolly anywhere Osnard was pointing it like a wand at a framed photograph that hung centre-stage on the back wall, showing a Socratic, bespectacled gentleman in rounded collars and black jacket frowning on a younger world.

'And that's *him*, is it?'

'What's who, sir? Where?'

'Over there. The Great One. Arthur Braithwaite.'

'It is indeed, sir. You have a sharp eye, if I may say so. The Great One himself, as you rightly describe him. Pictured in his prime, at the request of his highly admiring employees, and presented to him on the occasion of his sixtieth.'

Osnard leapt forward to have a closer look, and the bell at last stopped ringing. '"Arthur G.,"' he read aloud from the brass plate mounted on the base of the frame. '"1908–1981. Founder." Well I'm damned. Wouldn't have recognised him. Hell did the G stand for?'

'George,' said Pendel, wondering why Osnard thought he should have recognised him in the first place but not going so far as to enquire.

'Where d'he come from?'

'Pinner,' said Pendel.

'I meant the picture. Did you bring it with you? Where was it?'

Pendel allowed himself a sad smile and a sigh.

'A gift from his dear widow, Mr Osnard, shortly before she followed him. A beautiful thought that she could ill afford considering the cost of shipping all the way from England, but she would do it, irregardless. "It's where he'd like to be," she said, and nobody could talk her out of it. Not that they wanted to. Not if she'd set her heart on it. Who would?'

'What was her name?'

'Doris.'

'Any kids?'

'I'm sorry, sir?'

'Mrs Braithwaite. Did she have children? Heirs. Descendants.'

'No, alas, their union was not blessed.'

'Still, you'd think it would be Braithwaite & Pendel, wouldn't you? Old Braithwaite, senior partner after all. Ought to be first, even if he's dead.'

Pendel was already shaking his head. 'No, sir. Not so. It was Arthur Braithwaite's express wish at the time. "Harry, my son, it's youth before age. From now on we're P & B, and that way we won't be mistaken for a certain oil company."'

'So who are these royals you've been dressing? "Tailors to Royalty." Saw it on your sign. Busting to ask.'

Pendel allowed his smile to cool a little.

'Well, sir, I'll put it this way, and I'm afraid that's as far as I'm allowed to go, owing to laze majesty. Certain gentlemen *not* a great distance from a certain royal throne *have* seen fit to honour us in the past, and up to the present day. Alas, we are not at liberty to divulge further details.'

'Why not?'

'Partly by reason of the Guild of Tailors' code of conduct, which guarantees *every* customer his confidentiality, be he high or low. And partly I'm afraid these days for reasons of security.'

'Throne of England?'

'There you press me too hard, Mr Osnard.'

'Hell's the crest o' the Prince of Wales hanging outside for then? Thought you were a pub for a moment.'

'Thank you, Mr Osnard. You have noticed what few have

noticed here in Panama, but further than that my lips are sealed. Sit yourself down, sir. Marta's sandwiches are cucumber if you're interested. I don't know whether her renown has reached you. And there's a very nice light white I can recommend. Chilean, which one of my customers imports and has the grace to send me a case of now and then. What can I tempt you with?'

For by now it was becoming important to Pendel that Osnard should be tempted.

*   *   *

Osnard had not sat down but he had accepted a sandwich. Which is to say he had helped himself to three from the plate, one to keep him going and two to balance in the ample cushions of his left palm while he stood shoulder to shoulder with Pendel at the applewood table.

'Now these aren't us at *all,* sir,' Pendel confided, dismissing at one gesture a swatch of lightweight tweeds, which was what he always did. 'Can't be doing with these either – not for what I call the mature figure – all right for your beardless boy or your beanstalk but not for the likes of a you or a me, I'll put it that way.' Another flip. 'Now we're getting somewhere.'

'Prime alpaca.'

'It is indeed, sir,' said Pendel, much surprised. 'From the Andean Highlands of South Peru, appreciated for its soft touch and variety of natural shades, to quote *Wool Record,* if I may make so bold. Well, I'm blessed, you *are* a dark horse, Mr Osnard.'

But he only said this because your average customer didn't know the first thing about cloth.

'My dad's favourite. Swore by it. Used to. Alpaca or bust.'

'Used to, sir? Oh dear.'

'Dead. Up there with Braithwaite.'

'Well, all I can say is, Mr Osnard, with no disrespect intended, your esteemed father knew whereof he spoke,' Pendel exclaimed, launching upon a favourite subject. 'Because alpaca cloth is in my fairly informed judgment the finest lightweight in the world bar none. Ever was and ever shall be, if you'll pardon me. You can have all your mohair-and-worsted mixes in the world, I don't care. Alpaca is dyed in the thread, hence your variety of colour, hence your richness. Alpaca is pure, it's resilient, it breathes. Your most sensitive skin is not bothered by it.' He laid a confiding finger on Osnard's upper arm. 'And what did our Savile Row tailor use it for, Mr Osnard, to his eternal and everlasting shame until the scarcity prevented him, I wonder?'

'Try me.'

'Linings,' Pendel declared with disgust. 'Common linings. Vandalism, that's what it is.'

'Old Braithwaite would have boiled over.'

'He did, sir, and I'm not ashamed to quote him. "Harry," he said to me – it took him nine years to call me Harry – "Harry, what they're doing to the alpaca, I wouldn't do to a dog." His words and I can hear them to this day.'

'Me too.'

'I beg your pardon, sir?'

If Pendel was all alertness, Osnard was the reverse. He seemed unaware of the impact of his words and was studiously turning over samples.

'I don't think I quite got your meaning there, Mr Osnard.'

'Old Braithwaite dressed m'dad. Long ago, mind. I was just a nipper.'

Pendel appeared too moved to speak. A rigidity came over him and his shoulders lifted in the manner of an old soldier at the Cenotaph. His words, when he found them, lacked breath. 'Well I never, sir. Excuse me. This *is* a turn-up for the book.' He rallied a little. 'It's a first, I don't mind admitting. Father to son. The two generations both, here at P & B. We've not had that, not in Panama. Not yet. Not since we left the Row.'

'Thought you'd be surprised.'

For a moment Pendel could have sworn the quick brown fox's eyes had lost their twinkle and become circular and smoky-dark, with only a splinter of light glowing in the centre of each pupil. And in his later imagination the splinter was not gold, but red. But the twinkle was quickly there again.

'Something wrong?' Osnard enquired.

'I think I was marvelling, Mr Osnard. "A defining moment" I believe is the expression these days. I must have been having one.'

'Great wheel o'time, eh?'

'Indeed, sir. The one that spins and grinds and tramples all before it, they say,' Pendel agreed, and turned back to the samples book like one who seeks consolation in labour.

But Osnard had first to eat another cucumber sandwich, which he did in one swallow, then brushed the crumbs off his palms by bringing them together in a slow slapping movement several times until he was satisfied.

*   *   *

There was a well-oiled procedure at P & B for the reception of new customers. Select cloth from samples book, admire same cloth in the piece – since Pendel was careful never to display a sample unless he had the cloth in stock – repair to fitting room for measurement, inspect Gentleman's Boutique and Sportsman's Corner, tour rear corridor, say hullo to Marta, open account, pay deposit unless otherwise agreed, come back in ten days for first fitting. For Osnard, however, Pendel decided on a variation. From the samples desk he marched him to the rear corridor, somewhat to the consternation of Marta who had retreated to the kitchen and was deep in a book called *Ecology on Loan*, being a history of the wholesale decimation of the jungles of South America with the hearty encouragement of the World Bank.

'Meet the real brains of P & B, Mr Osnard, though she'll kill me for saying it. Marta, shake hands with Mr Osnard. O-S-N then A-R-D. Make a card for him, dear, and mark it old customer because Mr Braithwaite made for his father. And the first name, sir?'

'Andrew,' said Osnard, and Pendel saw Marta's eyes lift to him, and study him, as if she had heard something other than his name, then turn to Pendel in enquiry.

'*Andrew?*' she repeated.

Pendel hastened to explain: 'Temporarily of the El Panama Hotel, Marta, but shortly to be moving, courtesy of our fabled Panamanian builders, to –?'

'Punta Paitilla.'

'Of course,' said Pendel with a pious smile, as if Osnard had ordered caviar.

And Marta, having very deliberately marked the place in her tome and pushed the tome aside, grimly noted these particulars from within the walls of her black hair.

'Hell happened to that woman?' Osnard demanded in a low voice as soon as they were safely back in the corridor.

'An accident, I'm afraid, sir. And some rather summary medical attention after it.'

'Surprised you keep her on. Must give your customers the willies.'

'Quite the reverse, I'm pleased to say, sir,' Pendel replied stoutly. 'Marta is by way of being a favourite among my customers. And her sandwiches are to die for, as they say.'

After which, to head off further questioning about Marta, and expunge her disapproval, Pendel launched himself immediately upon his standard lecture on the tagua nut, grown in the rainforest and now, he assured Osnard earnestly, recognised throughout the feeling world as an acceptable substitute for ivory.

'My question being, Mr Osnard, what are the current uses of your tagua today?' he demanded with even more than his customary vigour. 'Ornamental chess sets? I'll give you chess sets. Carved artefacts? Right, again. Our earrings, our costume jewellery, we're getting warm – but what else? What possible other use is there which is traditional, which is totally forgotten in our modern age, and which we here at P & B have at some cost to ourselves revived for the benefit of our valued clients and the posterity of future generations?'

'Buttons,' Osnard suggested.

'Answer, of course, our buttons. Thank you,' said Pendel, drawing to a halt before another door. 'Indian ladies,' he warned, dropping his voice. 'Cunas. Very sensitive, if you don't mind.'

He knocked, opened the door, stepped reverently inside and beckoned his guest to follow. Three Indian women of indeterminate age sat stitching jackets under the beam of angled lamps.

'Meet our finishing hands, Mr Osnard,' he murmured, as if fearful of disturbing their concentration.

But the women did not seem half as sensitive as Pendel was, for they at once looked up cheerfully from their work and gave Osnard broad, appraising grins.

'Our buttonhole to our tailormade suit, Mr Osnard, is as our ruby to our turban, sir,' Pendel pronounced, still at a murmur. 'It's where the eye falls, it's the detail that speaks for the whole. A good buttonhole doesn't make a good suit. But a *bad* buttonhole makes a *bad* suit.'

'To quote dear old Arthur Braithwaite,' Osnard suggested, copying Pendel's low tone.

'Indeed, sir, yes. And your tagua button, which prior to the regrettable invention of plastic was in wide use across the continents of America and Europe and never bettered in my opinion is, thanks to P & B, back in service as the crowning glory of our fully tailored suit.'

'That Braithwaite's idea too?'

'The concept was Braithwaite's, Mr Osnard,' said Pendel, passing the closed door of the Chinese jacket-makers and deciding for no reason except panic to leave them undisturbed. 'The putting it into effect, there I claim the credit.'

But while Pendel was at pains to keep the movement going, Osnard evidently preferred a slower pace for he had leaned a bulky arm against the wall, blocking Pendel's progress.

'Heard you dressed Noriega in his day. True?'

Pendel hesitated, and his gaze slipped instinctively down the corridor towards the door to Marta's kitchen.

'What if I did?' he said. And for a moment his face stiffened with mistrust, and his voice became sullen and toneless. 'What was I supposed to do? Put up the shutters? Go home?'

'What did you make for him?'

'The General was never what I call a natural suit-wearer,

Mr Osnard. Uniforms, he could fritter away whole days pondering his variations. Boots and caps the same. But resist it how he would, there were times when he couldn't escape a suit.'

He turned, trying to will Osnard into continuing their progress down the corridor. But Osnard did not remove his arm.

'What sort o' times?'

'Well, sir, there was the occasion when the General was invited to deliver a celebrated speech at Harvard University, you may remember, even if Harvard would prefer you didn't. Quite a challenge he was. Very restless when it came to his fittings.'

'Won't be needing suits where he is now, I dare say, will he?'

'Indeed not, Mr Osnard. It's all provided, I'm told. There was also the occasion when France awarded him its highest honour and appointed him a *Légionnaire*.'

'Hell did they give him that for?'

The lighting in the corridor was all overhead, making bullet holes of Osnard's eyes.

'A number of explanations come to mind, Mr Osnard. The most favoured is that, for a cash consideration, the General permitted the French Airforce to use Panama as a staging point when they were causing their unpopular nuclear explosions in the South Pacific.'

'Who says?'

'There was a lot of loose talk around the General sometimes. Not all his hangers-on were as discreet as he was.'

'Dress the hangers-on too?'

'And still do, sir, still do,' Pendel replied, once more his cheerful self. 'We did endure what you might call a slight low directly after the American invasion when some of the General's higher officials felt obliged to take the air abroad for a time, but they soon came back. Nobody loses his reputation in Panama, not for long, and Panamanian gentlemen don't care to spend their own money in exile. The tendency is more to recycle your politician rather than disgrace him. That way, nobody gets left out too long.'

'Weren't branded a collaborator or whatever?'

'There weren't a lot left to point the finger, frankly, Mr Osnard. I dressed the General a few times, it's true. Most of my customers did slightly more than that, didn't they?'

'What about the protest strikes? Join in?'

Another nervous glance towards the kitchen where Marta was by now presumably back at her studies.

'I'll put it this way, Mr Osnard. We closed the front of the shop. We didn't always close the back.'

'Wise man.'

Pendel grabbed the nearest doorhandle and shoved it. Two elderly Italian trouser-makers in white aprons and gold-rimmed spectacles peered up from their labours. Osnard bestowed a royal wave on them and stepped back into the corridor. Pendel followed him.

'Dress the new chap too, don't you?' Osnard asked carelessly.

'Yes, sir, I'm proud to say, the President of the Republic of Panama numbers today among our customers. And a more agreeable gentleman you couldn't wish to meet.'

'Where d'you do it?'

'I beg your pardon, sir?'

'He come here, you go there?'

Pendel adopted a slightly superior manner. 'The summons is always to the Palace, Mr Osnard. People go to the President. He doesn't go to them.'

'Know your way around up there, do you?'

'Well, sir, he's my third president. Bonds are formed.'

'With his flunkeys?'

'Yes. Them too.'

'How about Himself? Pres?'

Pendel again paused, as he had done before when rules of professional confidence came under strain.

'Your great statesman of today, sir, he's under stress, he's a lonely man, cut off from what I call the common pleasures that make our lives worth living. A few minutes alone with his tailor can be a blessed truce amid the fray.'

'So you chat away?'

'I would prefer the term soothing interlude. He'll ask me

what my customers are saying about him. I respond – not naming names, naturally. Occasionally, if he has something on his chest, he may favour me with a small confidence in return. I do have a certain reputation for discretion, as I have no doubt his highly vigilant advisors have informed him. Now, sir. If you please.'

'What does he call you?'

'One to one or in the presence of others?'

'Harry, then?' said Osnard.

'Correct.'

'And you?'

'I never presume, Mr Osnard. I've had the chance, I've been invited. But it's Mr President, and it always will be.'

'How about Fidel?'

Pendel laughed gaily. He had been wanting a laugh for some time. 'Well, sir, the Comandante does *like* a suit these days, and so he should, given the advance of corpulence. There's not a tailor in the region wouldn't give his eye teeth to dress him, whatever those Yanquis think of him. But he will adhere to his Cuban tailor, as I dare say you have noticed to your embarrassment on the television. Oh dear. I'll say no more. We're here, we're standing by. If the call comes, P & B will answer it.'

'Quite an intelligence service you run, then.'

'It's a cut-throat world, Mr Osnard. There's a lot of competition out there. I'd be a fool if I didn't keep an ear to the ground, wouldn't I?'

'Sure would. Don't want to go old Braithwaite's route, do we?'

*   *   *

Pendel had climbed a step-ladder. He was balanced on the folding platform that he normally stopped short of, and he was busying himself with a bolt of best grey alpaca that he had coaxed from the top shelf, brandishing it aloft for Osnard's inspection. How he had got up there, what had impelled him, were mysteries he was no more disposed to contemplate than a cat that finds itself at the top of a tree. What mattered was escape.

'The important thing, sir, I always say, is hang them while they're still warm and never fail to rotate them,' he announced in a loud voice to a shelf of midnight blue worsteds six inches from his nose. 'Now here's the one we thought might be to our liking, Mr Osnard. An excellent choice if I may say so and your grey suit in Panama is practically de rigger. I'll bring you down the bolt and you can have a look and a feel. Marta! Shop, please, dear.'

'Hell's rotate?' asked Osnard from below where he was standing with his hands in his pockets, examining ties.

'No suit should be worn two days running, least of all your lightweight, Mr Osnard. As I'm sure your good father will have told you many a time and oft.'

'Learned it from Arthur, did 'e?'

'It's your chemical dry cleaner that kills the real suit, I always say. Once you've got the grime and sweat embedded in it, which is what happens if you overwork it, you're on your way to the chemical cleaner, and that's the beginning of the end. A suit that isn't rotated is a suit halved, I say. Marta! Where *is* that girl?'

Osnard remained intent upon the ties.

'Mr Braithwaite even went so far as to advise his customers to abstain from cleaners altogether,' Pendel ran on, his voice rising slightly. 'Brush their suits only, the sponge if necessary, and bring them to the shop once a year to be washed in the River Dee.'

Osnard had ceased to examine the ties and was staring up at him.

'Owing to that river's highly prized cleansing powers,' Pendel explained. 'The Dee being to our suit somewhat of your true Jordan to the pilgrim.'

'Thought that was Huntsman's,' Osnard said, his eyes steadfastly on Pendel's.

Pendel did hesitate. And it did show. And Osnard did watch him while it showed.

'Mr Huntsman is a very fine tailor, sir. One of the Row's

greatest. But in this case, he followed in the footprints of Arthur Braithwaite.'

He probably meant footsteps, but under the intensity of Osnard's gaze he had formed a clear image of the great Mr Huntsman, like King Wenceslas' page, obediently tracing Braithwaite's pugmarks across the black Scottish mud. Desperate to break the spell, he grabbed the bolt of cloth and, with one hand for the ship and the other clutching the bolt like a baby to his breast, he groped his way down the step-ladder.

'Here we are, sir. Our mid-grey alpaca in all its glory. Thank you, Marta,' as she belatedly appeared below him.

Her face averted, Marta grasped her end of the cloth in both hands and marched backwards towards the door, at the same time tilting it for Osnard to inspect. And somehow she caught Pendel's eye, and somehow he caught hers, and there was both question and reproach in her expression. But Osnard was mercifully unaware of this. He was studying the cloth. He had stooped over it, hands behind his back like visiting royalty. He was sniffing it. He pinched an edge, sampling the texture between the tips of his thumb and forefinger. The ponderousness of his movements spurred Pendel to greater efforts, and Marta to greater disapproval.

'Grey not right for us, Mr Osnard? I see you favour brown yourself! It becomes you very well, if I may say so, brown. There's not a lot of brown being worn in Panama today, to be frank. Your average Panamanian gentleman seems to consider brown unmanly, I don't know why.' He was already halfway up the ladder again, leaving Marta clutching her end of the cloth, and the grey bolt lying at her feet. 'There's a mid-brown up here I could see you in, not too much red. Here we go. I always say it's the too-much-red that spoils a good brown, I don't know if I'm right. What's our preference today, sir?'

Osnard took a very long time to reply. First the grey cloth continued to hold his attention, then Marta did, for she was studying him with a kind of medical distaste. Then he raised his head and stared at Pendel up his ladder. And Pendel might as well have been a trapeze artist stuck in the big top without his pole, and the world beneath him a whole life away, to judge by the cold dispassion that was displayed in Osnard's upturned face.

'Stick with grey, if you don't mind, ol' boy,' he said. '"Grey for town, brown for country." Isn't that what he used to say?'

'Who?'

'Braithwaite. Hell d'you think?'

Pendel slowly descended the ladder. He seemed about to speak but didn't. He had run out of words: Pendel, for whom words were his safety and comfort. So instead he smiled while Marta brought her end of the cloth to him and he reeled it in, smiling till his smile hurt and Marta scowling, partly because of Osnard and partly because that was the way her face had set after the doctor had done his terrified best.

CHAPTER FOUR

'Now, sir. Your vital statistics if I *may*.'

Pendel had removed Osnard's jacket for him, observing as he did so a fat brown envelope slotted between the two halves of his wallet. The heat rose from Osnard's heavy body like heat from a wet spaniel. His nipples, shaded by chaste curls, showed clearly through his sweat-soaked shirt. Pendel placed himself behind him and measured back collar to waist. Neither man spoke. Panamanians in Pendel's experience enjoyed being measured. Englishmen did not. It had to do with being touched. From the collar again, he took the full length of the back, careful as ever to avoid contact with the rump. Still neither man spoke. He took the centre back seam, then centre back to elbow, then centre back to cuff. He placed himself at Osnard's side, touched his elbows to raise them and passed the tape beneath his arms and across his nipples. Sometimes with his bachelor gentlemen he navigated a less sensitive route but with Osnard he felt no misgivings. From the shop downstairs they heard the bell ring out and the front door slam accusingly.

'That Marta?'

'It was indeed, sir. Going home, no doubt.'

'She got something on you?'

'Certainly not. Whatever made you ask that?'

51

'Vibe, that's all.'

'Well I'm blessed,' said Pendel, recovering.

'Thought she had something on me, too.'

'Good heavens, sir. What could that possibly be?'

'Don't owe her money. Never screwed her. Your guess as good as mine.'

The fitting room was a wooden cell about the regulation twelve by nine, built at one end of the Sportsman's Corner on the upper floor. A cheval mirror, three wall mirrors and a small gilt chair provided the only furnishings. A heavy green curtain did duty for a door. But the Sportsman's Corner was not a corner at all. It was a long, low timbered attic hideaway with a suggestion of lost childhood about it. Nowhere in the shop had Pendel worked harder to achieve his effect. From brass rails mounted along the wall hung a small army of half-finished suits awaiting the final bugle. Golf shoes, hats and green weatherproofs gleamed from ancient mahogany shelves. Riding boots, whips, spurs, a pair of fine English shotguns, ammunition belts and golf clubs lay about in artful confusion. And in the foreground, in pride of place, loomed a stately hide mounting horse like a horse in a gymnasium, but with a tail and head, on which a sporting gentleman could test the comfort of his breeches, confident that his mount would not disgrace him.

Pendel was racking his brains for a topic. In the fitting room it was his habit to chatter incessantly as a means of dispelling intimacy, but for some reason his customary material eluded him. He resorted to reminiscences of My Early Struggle.

'Oh, my, did we have to get up early in those days! The freezing dark mornings in Whitechapel, the dew on the cobble, I can feel the cold now. Different today, of course. Hardly a young one going into the trade, I'm told. Not in the East End. Not real tailoring. Too hard for them, I expect. Quite right.'

He was taking the cape measurement, across the back again but this time with Osnard's arms hanging straight down and the tape going round the outside of them. It was not a measurement he would normally have taken but Osnard was not a normal customer.

'East End to West End,' Osnard remarked. 'Quite a shift.'

'It was indeed, sir, and I never had cause to rue the day.'

They were face to face and very close. But whereas Osnard's tight brown eyes seemed to pursue Pendel from every angle, Pendel's were fixed on the sweat-puckered waistband of the gabardine trousers. He placed the tape round Osnard's girth and tugged at it.

'What's the damage?' Osnard asked.

'Let's say a modest thirty-six plus, sir.'

'Plus what?'

'Plus lunch, put it that way, sir,' said Pendel, and won a much needed laugh.

'Ever pine for the old country at all?' Osnard enquired, while Pendel discreetly recorded thirty-eight in his notebook.

'Not really, sir. No, I don't think so. Not so's you'd notice. No,' he replied, slipping the notebook into his hip pocket.

'Bet you hanker for the Row now and then.'

'Ah well, the *Row*,' Pendel agreed heartily, succumbing to a wistful vision of himself safely consigned to an earlier century, measuring for tailcoats and breeches. 'Yes, the Row's a different thing again, isn't it? If we had more of Savile Row as it used to be and less of some of the other things we've got today, England would be a lot better off. A happier country altogether, we'd be, if you'll pardon me.'

But if Pendel thought that by mouthing platitudes he could divert the thrust of Osnard's inquisition, he was wasting his breath.

'Tell us about it.'

'About what, sir?'

'Old Braithwaite took you on as an apprentice, right?'

'Right.'

'Aspiring young Pendel sat on his doorstep day after day. Every morning when the old boy clocked in, there you were. "Good morning, Mr Braithwaite, sir, how are we today? My name's Harry Pendel and I'm your new apprentice." Love it. Love that sort o' chutzpah.'

'I'm very glad to hear that,' Pendel replied uncertainly as he tried to shake off the experience of having his own anecdote retold to him in one of its many versions.

'So you wear him down and you become his favourite apprentice, just like in the fairy tale,' Osnard went on. He didn't say which fairy tale, and Pendel didn't ask him. 'And one day – how many years is it? – old Braithwaite turns round to you and says, "All right, Pendel. Tired o' having you as an apprentice. From now on, you're crown prince." Or words to that effect. Give us the scene. Mustard for it.'

A frown of ferocious concentration settled over Pendel's normally untroubled brow. Placing himself at Osnard's left flank, he looped the tape round his rump, coaxed it to the amplest point and again jotted in his notebook. He stooped for the outside leg measurement, straightened and, like a failing swimmer, sank again until his head was at the height of Osnard's right knee.

'And we dress, sir –?' he murmured, feeling Osnard's gaze burning the nape of his neck. 'Most of my gentlemen seem to favour left these days. I don't *think* it's political.'

This was his standard joke, calculated to raise a laugh even with the most sedate of his customers. Not with Osnard apparently.

'Never know where the bloody thing is. Bobs about like a windsock,' he replied dismissively. 'Morning, was it? Evening? What time o' day did 'e pay you the royal visit?'

'Evening,' Pendel muttered after an age. And like an admission of defeat: 'A Friday like today.'

Assuming left but taking no chances, he conveyed the brass end of his tape into the right side of Osnard's fly, studiously avoiding contact with whatever lay within. Then with his left hand he drew the tape downward as far as the upper sole of Osnard's shoe, which was of the heavy, officer-off-duty type and much repaired. And having subtracted an inch and written down his finding, he bravely stood his full height, only to discover the dark round eyes so tightly upon him that he had the illusion of having walked into the enemy's guns.

'Winter or summer?'

'Summer.' Pendel's voice was running out of power. He took a brave breath and started again. 'Not many of us young ones fancied working Friday evenings in the summertime. I suppose I was the exception, which was one of the things about me that commended me to Mr Braithwaite's attention.'

'Year?'

'Well, yes, my goodness, the year.' Rallying, he shook his head and tried to smile. 'Oh dear me. A whole generation ago. Still, you can't sweep back the tide, can you? King Canute tried it and look where he ended up,' he added, not at all sure where Canute did end up, if anywhere.

All the same, he was feeling the artistry coming back to him, what Uncle Benny called his fluence.

'He was standing in the doorway,' he resumed, striking a lyrical note. 'I must have been absorbed in a pair of trousers I'd been entrusted with, which is what happens to me when I'm cutting, because it gave me a start. I looked up and there he was, watching me, not saying anything. He was a big man. People forget that about him. The big bald head, big eyebrows – he was imposing. A force. A fact of life –'

'You've forgotten his moustache,' Osnard objected.

'Moustache?'

'Bloody great big bushy job, soup all over it. Must've shaved it off by the time they took that picture of him downstairs. Frightened the daylights out o' me. Only five at the time.'

'There was no moustache in my day, Mr Osnard.'

' 'Course there was. I can see it as if it was yesterday.'

But either stubbornness or instinct told Pendel to give no ground.

'I think your memory is playing tricks on you there, Mr Osnard. You're remembering a different gentleman and awarding his moustache to Arthur Braithwaite.'

'Bravo,' said Osnard softly.

But Pendel refused to believe that he had heard this, or that Osnard had tipped him the shadow of a wink. He ploughed on:

' "Pendel," he says to me. "I want you to be my son. As

soon as you've got the Queen's English, I propose to call you Harry, promote you to the front of shop and appoint you my heir and partner –"'

'You said it took him nine years.'

'What did?'

'To call you Harry.'

'I started as an apprentice, didn't I?'

'My mistake. On you go.'

'– "and that's all I've got to say to you, so now get back to your trousers and sign yourself into nightschool for the elocution."'

He had stopped. Dried up. His throat was sore, his eyes hurt and there was a singing in his ears. But somewhere in him there was also a sense of accomplishment. I did it. My leg was broken, I had a temperature of a hundred and five, but the show went on.

'Fabulous,' Osnard breathed.

'Thank you, sir.'

'Most beautiful bullshit I've ever listened to in my life and you socked it to me like a hero.'

Pendel was hearing Osnard from a long way off, among a lot of other voices. The Sisters of Charity at his North London orphanage telling him Jesus would be angry with him. The laughter of his children in the four-track. Ramón's voice telling him that a London merchant bank had been enquiring about his status and offering inducements for the information. Louisa's voice telling him that one good man was all it took. After that he heard the rush-hour traffic heading out of town and dreamed of being stuck in it and free.

'Thing is, old boy, I know who you are, you see.' But Pendel saw nothing at all, not even Osnard's black gaze boring into him. He had put up a screen in his mind and Osnard was the other side of it. 'Put more accurately, I know who you aren't. No cause for panic or alarm. I love it. Every bit of it. Wouldn't be without it for the world.'

'I'm not anybody,' Pendel heard himself whisper from his side of the screen, and after that, the sound of the fitting room curtain being swept aside.

And he saw with deliberately fogged eyes that Osnard was peering through the opening, making a precautionary survey of the Sportsman's Corner. He heard Osnard speaking again, but so close to his ear that the murmur made it buzz.

'You're 906017 Pendel, convict and ex-juvenile delinquent, six years for arson, two-and-a-half served. Taught himself his tailoring in the slammer. Left the country three days after he had paid his debt to society, staked by his paternal Uncle Benjamin, now deceased. Married to Louisa, daughter of Zonian roughneck and Bible-punching schoolteacher, who dogsbodies five days a week for the great and good Ernie Delgado over at the Panama Canal Commission. Two kids, Mark eight, Hannah ten. Insolvent, courtesy o' the rice farm. Pendel & Braithwaite a load o' bollocks. No such firm existed in Savile Row. There was never a liquidation because there was nothing to liquidate. Arthur Braithwaite one of the great characters o' fiction. Adore a con. What life's about. Don't give me that swivel-eyed look. I'm bonus. Answer to your prayers. You hearing me?'

Pendel heard nothing at all. He stood head down and feet together, numb all over, ears included. Rousing himself, he lifted Osnard's arm until it was level with the shoulder. Folded it so that the hand rested flat against the chest. Pressed the end of the tape to the centre point of Osnard's back. Led it round the elbow to the wrist-bone.

'I asked you who else is in on it?' Osnard was saying.

'In on what?'

'The con. Mantle o' Saint Arthur falling on the infant Pendel's shoulders. P & B, tailor to the royals. Thousand years o' history. All that crap. Apart from your wife, of course.'

'She isn't in on it at all,' Pendel exclaimed in naked alarm.

'Doesn't know?'

Pendel shook his head, mute again.

'*Louisa* doesn't? You're conning her too?'

Keep *shtumm*, Harry boy. *Shtumm*'s the word.

'How about your little local difficulty?'

'Which one?'

'Prison.'

Pendel whispered something he himself could barely hear.

'Is that another no?'

'Yes. No.'

'*She doesn't know you did time? She doesn't know about Uncle Arthur?* Does she know the rice farm's going down the tube?'

The same measurement again. Centre-back to wrist-bone, but with Osnard's arms straight down. Passing the tape over his shoulder with wooden gestures.

'No again?'

'Yes.'

'Thought it was joint-ownership.'

'It is.'

'But she still doesn't know.'

'I look after the money matters, don't I?'

'I'll say you do. How much are you in for?'

'Pushing a hundred grand.'

'I heard it was nearer two hundred and rising.'

'It is.'

'Interest?'

'Two.'

'Two per cent quarterly?'

'Monthly.'

'Compound?'

'Could be.'

'Set against this place. Hell d'you do that for?'

'We had something called the recession, I don't know if it ever came your way,' said Pendel, incongruously recalling the days when, if he only had three customers, he would book them back-to-back at half-hour intervals in order to create an air of flurry.

'What were you doing? Playing the Stock Exchange?'

'With the advice of my expert banker, yes.'

'Your expert banker specialise in bankruptcy sales or something?'

'I expect so.'

'And it was Louisa's lolly, right?'

'Her dad's. Half her dad's. She's got a sister, hasn't she.'

'What about the police?'

'What police?'

'Pans. Local whoosies.'

'What's it to them?' Pendel's voice had finally unlocked itself and was running free. 'I pay my taxes. Social Security. I do my worksheets. I haven't gone bust yet. Why should they care?'

'Thought they might have dug up your record. Invited you to fork out a little hush-money. Wouldn't want 'em chucking you out because you couldn't pay your bribes, would we?'

Pendel shook his head, then laid his palm on the top of it, either to pray or to make sure it was still on his body. After that he took on the posture dinned into him by his Uncle Benny before he went to gaol.

'You've got to *drucken* yourself, Harry boy,' Benny had insisted, using an expression Pendel never heard before or since from anyone but Benny. 'Press yourself in. Go small. Don't *be* anybody, don't *look* at anybody. It bothers them, same as being pathetic. You're not even a fly on the wall. You're *part* of the wall.'

But quite soon he grew tired of being a wall. He lifted his head and blinked round the fitting room, waking up in it after his first night. He remembered one of Benny's more mystifying confessions and decided that he finally understood it:

Harry boy, my trouble is, everywhere I go, I come too and spoil it.

'What are *you*, then?' Pendel demanded of Osnard with a stirring of truculence.

'I'm a spy. Spy for Merrie England. We're reopening Panama.'

'What for?'

'Tell you over dinner. What time d'you close the shop on Fridays?'

'Now, if I want. Surprised you had to ask.'

'What about home? Candles. *Kiddush.* Whatever you do?'

'We don't. We're Christian. Where it hurts.'

'You're a member of the Club Unión, right?'

'Just.'

'Just what?'

'I had to buy the rice farm before they'd make me a member. They don't take Turco tailors but Mick farmers are all right. Long as they've got twenty-five grand for the membership.'

'Why did you join?'

To his amazement Pendel found he was smiling beyond what was normal to him. A crazy smile, forced out of him by astonishment and terror maybe, but a smile for all that, and the relief it brought him was like discovering he still had the use of his limbs.

'I'll tell you something, Mr Osnard,' he said with a rush of companionability. 'It's a mystery to me yet to be resolved. I'm impetuous and sometimes I'm grandiose with it. It's my failing. My Uncle Benjamin you mentioned just now always dreamed of owning a villa in Italy. Perhaps I did it to please Benny. Or it could have been to give two fingers to Mrs Porter.'

'Don't know her.'

'The Probation Officer. A very serious lady who thought I was destined for the bad.'

'Go to the Club Unión for dinner ever? Take a guest?'

'Very rarely. Not in my present state of economic health, I'll put it that way.'

'If I'd ordered ten suits instead o' two and I was free for dinner, would you take me there?'

Osnard was pulling on his jacket. Best to let him do it for himself, thought Pendel, restraining his eternal impulse to be of service.

'I might. It depends,' he replied cautiously.

'And you'd ring Louisa. "Darling, great news, I've flogged ten suits to a mad Brit and I'm buying him dinner at the Club Unión."'

'I might.'

'How would she take it?'

'She varies.'

Osnard slipped a hand into his jacket, drew out the brown

envelope that Pendel had already glimpsed and handed it to him.

'Five grand on account o' two suits. No need for a receipt. More where it came from. Plus a couple o' hundred extra for the nosebag.'

Pendel was still wearing his fly-fronted waistcoat so he slipped the envelope into the hip pocket of his trousers where his notebook was.

'In Panama everyone knows Harry Pendel,' Osnard was saying. 'Hide somewhere, they'll see us hiding. Go somewhere you're known, they won't think twice about us.'

They were face to face again. Seen closer, Osnard's was lit with suppressed excitement. Pendel, always quick to empathise, felt himself brighten in its glow. They went downstairs so that he could call Louisa from his cutting room while Osnard tested his weight on a furled umbrella marked 'as carried by the Queen's Brigade of Guards'.

*　　*　　*

'You and you alone know, Harry,' Louisa said into Pendel's hot left ear. Her mother's voice. Socialism and Bible School.

'Know *what*, Lou? What am I supposed to know?' – jokey, always hoping for a laugh. 'You know me, Lou. I don't know anything. I'm dead ignorant.'

On the telephone she could hand out pauses like prison time.

'You alone, Harry, know what it is worth to you to desert your family for the night and go to your club and amuse yourself among other men and women instead of being a presence to those who love you, Harry.'

Her voice dropped into tenderness and he nearly died for her. But as usual she couldn't do the tender words.

'Harry?' – as if she were still waiting for him.

'Yes, darling?'

'You have no call to blandish me, Harry,' she retorted, which was her way of saying 'darling' back. But whatever else she was proposing to say, she didn't say it.

'We've got the whole weekend, Lou. It's not as if I was

doing a bunk or something.' A pause as wide as the Pacific. 'How was old Ernie today? He's a great man, Louisa. I don't know why I tease you about him. He's right up there with your father. I should be sitting at his feet.'

It's her sister, he thought. Whenever she gets angry, it's because she's jealous of her sister for putting herself about.

'He's given me five thousand dollars on account, Lou' – begging her approval – 'cash in my pocket. He's lonely. He wants a bit of company. What am I supposed to do? Shove him out into the night, tell him thank you for buying ten suits from me, now go out and find yourself a woman?'

'Harry, you don't have to tell him anything of the kind. You are welcome to bring him home to us. If we are not acceptable, then please do what you must do and don't punish yourself for it.'

And the same tenderness in her voice again, the Louisa that she longed to be rather than the one who spoke for her.

'No problems?' Osnard asked lightly.

He had found the hospitality whisky and two glasses. He handed one to Pendel.

'Everything hunkydory, thank you. She's a woman in a million.'

*   *   *

Pendel stood alone in the stockroom. He took off his day suit and out of blind habit hung it on its hanger, the trousers from the metal clips, the jacket nice and square. To replace it he chose a powder blue mohair, single-breasted, that he had cut for himself to Mozart six months ago and never worn, fearing it was flashy. His face in the mirror startled him with its normality. Why haven't you changed colour, shape, size? What else has to happen to you before something happens to you? You get up in the morning. Your bank manager confirms the end of the world is at hand. You go to the shop and in marches an English spy who mugs you with your past and tells you he wants to make you rich and keep you as you are.

'You're Andrew, right?' he called into the open doorway, making a new friend.

'Andy Osnard, single, Brit Embassy boffin on the political treadmill, recently arrived. Old Braithwaite made suits for m'dad and you used to come along and hold the tape. Cover. Nothing like it.'

And that tie I always fancied, he thought. With the blue zigzags and a touch of Leander pink. Osnard looked on with a creator's pride while Pendel set the alarm.

CHAPTER FIVE

The rain had stopped. The fairy-lit buses that bounced past
them over the pot-holes were empty. A hot blue evening sky
was disappearing into night but its heat remained behind
because in Panama City it always does. There is dry heat,
there is wet heat. But there is always heat, just as there is
always noise: of traffic, power drills, of scaffolding going
up or down, of aeroplanes, air-conditioners, canned music,
bulldozers, helicopters and – if you are very lucky – birds.
Osnard was trailing his bookie's umbrella. Pendel, though
alert, was unarmed. His feelings were a mystery to him. He
had been tested, he had come out stronger and wiser. But
tested for what? Stronger and wiser how? And if he had
survived, why didn't he feel safer? Nevertheless re-entering
the world's atmosphere he appeared to himself reborn if
apprehensive.

'Fifty thousand bucks!' he yelled to Osnard, unlocking his
car.

'What for?'

'What it costs to hand-paint those buses! They hire real
artists! Takes two years!'

It was not something Pendel had known till this moment,
if he knew it now, but something inside him required him
to be an authority. Settling into his driving seat he had

an uncomfortable feeling that the figure was nearer fifteen hundred, and it was two months, not two years.

'Want me to drive?' Osnard asked with a sideways glance up and down the road.

But Pendel was his own master. Ten minutes ago he had persuaded himself he would never walk free again. Now he was sitting at his own steering wheel with his jailer at his side and wearing his own powder blue suit instead of a stinking jute tunic with Pendel on the pocket.

'And no pitfalls?' Osnard asked.

Pendel didn't understand.

'People you don't want to meet – owe money to – screwed their wives – whatever?'

'I don't owe anyone except the bank, Andy. I don't do the other either, though it's not something I confess to my customers, Latin gentlemen being what they are. They'd think I was a capon or a poofter.' He laughed a little wildly for both of them while Osnard checked the driving mirrors. 'Where are you from, Andy? Where's home then? Your dad features large in your life unless he's a figment. Was he a famous person at all? I'm sure he was.'

'Doctor,' said Osnard, without a second's hesitation.

'What sort? Major brain surgeon? Heart-lung?'

'GP.'

'Where did he practise then? Somewhere exotic?'

'Birmingham.'

'And the mother, if I may ask?'

'South o' France.'

But Pendel couldn't help wondering whether Osnard had consigned his late father to Birmingham and his mother to the French Riviera with the same abandon with which Pendel had consigned the late Braithwaite to Pinner.

*   *   *

The Club Unión is where the super-rich of Panama have their presence here on earth. With appropriate deference, Pendel drove under a red pagoda arch, braking almost to a halt in his anxiety to assure the two uniformed guards that he and his guest were white and middle class. Fridays are disco-nights for the children of gentile millionaires. At the brightly lit entrance glistening four-tracks disgorge scowling seventeen-year-old princesses and thick-necked swains with gold bracelets and dead eyes. The porch was bordered with heavy crimson ropes and guarded by big-shouldered men wearing chauffeurs' suits and identity tags for buttonholes. Bestowing a confiding smile on Osnard, they glowered at Pendel but let him pass. Inside, the hall was wide and cool and open to the sea. A green-carpeted slipway descended to a balconied terrace. Beyond it lay the bay with its perpetual line of ships pressed like men-of-war under banks of black stormcloud. The day's last light was quickly vanishing. Cigarette smoke, costly scent and beat music filled the air.

'See the causeway there, Andy?' Pendel yelled, flinging out a proprietorial arm while he proudly signed his guest into the book with the other. 'Made from all the rubble dug out of the Canal. Stops the rivers from silting up the navigation channel. Those Yanqui forefathers of ours knew a thing or two,' he declared, though he must have been identifying with Louisa, for he had no Yanqui forefathers. 'You should have been here when we had our open-air movies. You wouldn't think it was possible, open-air movies in the wet season. Well it is. Know how often rain falls in Panama between six and eight of an evening, wet or dry? Two days *per year* average! I see you're surprised.'

'Where do we get a drink?' Osnard asked.

But Pendel still had to show him the Club's newest, grandest acquisition: a silent, gorgeously panelled lift to raise and lower geriatric heiresses nine feet from floor to floor.

'It's for their cards, Andy. Night and day, some of those old ladies play. I suppose they think they can take it with them.'

*   *   *

The bar was in Friday-night fever. At every table revellers waved, beckoned, slapped each other on the shoulders, argued, sprang about and shouted one another down. And some took time off to wave to Pendel, press his hand or make some ribald joke about his suit.

'Allow me to present my good friend Andy Osnard, one of Her Majesty's favourite sons recently arrived from England to restore the good name of diplomacy,' he yelled to a banker called Luis.

'Just say Andy next time. No one gives a toss,' Osnard advised when Luis had rejoined the girls. 'Any heavy hitters out tonight? Who's all here? No Delgado, that's for sure. He's in Japan playing hookey with Pres.'

'Correct, Andy, Ernie's in Japan, and giving Louisa a nice rest into the bargain. Well I never! Who have we here? Well, that *is* a turn-up for the book.'

Gossip is what Panama has instead of culture. Pendel's eye had fallen on a distinguished-looking, moustachioed gentleman in his mid-fifties in the company of a beautiful young woman. He wore a dark suit and silver tie. She wore tresses of black hair over one naked shoulder and a diamond collar big enough to sink her. They were sitting side by side and upright, like a couple in an old photograph, and they were receiving the congratulatory handshakes of well-wishers.

'Our gallant top judge, Andy, back among us,' Pendel replied in answer to Osnard's prompting, 'just one week after all charges against him were dropped. Bravo, Miguel.'

'Customer o' yours?'

'Indeed he is, Andy, and a highly valued one. I've got four unfinished suits plus a dinner jacket invested in that gentleman, and until last week they were destined for our New Year's sale.' He needed no further prodding. 'My friend Miguel,' he went on, exercising the kind of pedantry that persuades us that a person is being most particular about the truth, 'came to the conclusion, a couple of years ago, that a certain lady friend whose welfare he had made his personal responsibility was bestowing her favours on another. The said rival being a fellow lawyer, naturally. In Panama they always are, and mostly American-educated, I regret to say. So Miguel did what any of us would do in the circumstances, he hired an assassin who duly put an end to the nuisance.'

'Bully for him. How?'

Pendel recalled a phrase of Mark's culled from a lurid comic that Louisa had confiscated. 'Lead poisoning, Andy. The professional three shots. One to the head, two to the body, and what was left of him all over the front pages. The assassin was arrested, which in Panama is highly unusual. And he duly confessed which, let's face it, isn't.'

He paused, allowing Osnard an appreciative smile and himself an extra moment for artistic inspiration. Picking out the hidden highlights, Benny would have called it. Giving his fluence its head. Juicing up the story for the benefit of your wider audience.

'The basis of the arrest, Andy – *and* of the confession – being a cheque for one hundred thousand dollars, drawn by our friend Miguel in favour of the alleged assassin and banked here in Panama on the somewhat risky assumption that banking confidentiality would provide immunity from prying eyes.'

'And that's the lady in the case,' Osnard said, with quiet appreciation. 'Looks as though she'd put on quite a turn.'

'The same, Andy, and now joined to Miguel in very holy matrimony though they do say she resents the limitation. And what you are seeing tonight is a triumphant demonstration of Miguel and Amanda's return to grace.'

'Hell did he swing it?'

'Well, first of all, Andy,' Pendel continued, very excited by an omniscience that stretched well beyond his knowledge of the case, 'there is a backhander of seven million dollars spoken of, which our learned judge can well afford seeing he owns a trucking business which specialises in the informal importation of rice and coffee from Costa Rica without troubling our overworked officials, his brother being a very high official in Customs.'

'Second of all?'

Pendel was loving everything: himself, his voice, and the sense he had of his own triumphant resurrection.

'Our highly judicial committee appointed to examine the

evidence against Miguel came to the wise conclusion that the charges lacked credibility. One hundred thousand dollars was regarded as a grossly inflated price for a simple assassination here in Panama, one thousand being more the appropriate figure. Plus name me the trained top judge who signs a personal cheque to a hired assassin while being of sound mind. It was the committee's considered opinion that the charges were a crude attempt to frame a highly honourable servant of his party and country. We have a saying here in Panama. Justice is a man.'

'What did they do with the assassin?'

'Andy, those interrogators had another word with him, and he obliged them with a second confession confirming that he had never met Miguel in his life, having taken his instructions from a bearded gentleman in dark glasses that he met once only in the lobby of the Caesar Park Hotel during a power cut.'

'Nobody protest?'

Pendel was already shaking his head. 'Ernie Delgado plus a group of fellow saints in the human rights area had a go but as usual their protests fell on stony ground, owing to a certain credibility gap,' he added, before he had even thought what this might be. But he rolled straight on like a driver in a runaway truck. 'Ernie being not *always* what he's cracked up to be, which is known.'

'Who to?'

'Circles, Andy. Informed circles.'

'Mean he's on the take like the rest o' them?'

'It has been said,' Pendel replied mysteriously, lowering his eyelids for greater veracity. 'I'll say no more, if you don't mind. If I'm not careful, I'll say something contrary to Louisa's best interests.'

'What about the cheque?'

Pendel noticed with discomfort how the little eyes, as in the shop, had become black pinholes in the bland surfaces of Osnard's face.

'A crude forgery, Andy, as you suspected all along,' he replied, feeling his cheeks heat up. 'The bank teller concerned has been duly relieved of his post, I'm pleased to say, so it won't happen again. Then of course there's the white suits, white playing a very big part in Panama, bigger than a lot of people understand.'

'Hell's that mean?' Osnard asked, the eyes still bearing in on him.

It meant that Pendel had caught sight of an earnest Dutchman named Henk who habitually bestowed strange handshakes and talked in confidential murmurs about mundane matters.

'Masons, Andy,' he said, now seriously bent upon deflecting Osnard's gaze. 'Secret societies. Opus Dei. Voodoo for the upper classes. Reinsurance in case religion doesn't do the job. Very superstitious place, Panama. You should see us with our lottery tickets twice a week.'

'How d'you know all this stuff?' Osnard said, giving his voice a downward trajectory that made it carry no further than the table.

'Two ways, Andy.'

'Which are?'

'Well, there's what I call the grapevine, which is when my gentlemen get together of a Thursday evening, which they like to, quite by chance, and have a heart-to-heart and a glass of something in my shop.'

'Second way?' The close, hard stare again.

'Andy, if I told you that the walls of my fitting room hear more confessions than a priest in a penitentiary, I'd still be underselling them.'

*   *   *

But there was a third way and Pendel didn't mention it. Perhaps he was not conscious of being in its thrall. It was tailoring. It was improving on people. It was cutting and shaping them until they became understandable members of his internal universe. It was fluence. It was running ahead of events and waiting for them to catch up. It was making people bigger or smaller according to whether they enhanced or threatened his existence. Downsize Delgado. Upsize Miguel. And Harry Pendel on the water like a cork.

It was a system of survival that Pendel had developed in prison and perfected in marriage, and its purpose was to provide a hostile world with whatever made it feel at ease with itself. To make it tolerable. To befriend it. To draw its sting.

'And of course, what old Miguel is doing *now*,' Pendel ran on, deftly slipping loose of Osnard's gaze and smiling across the room, 'he's having what I call his last spring. I see it all the time in my profession. One day they're your normal nine-till-fivers, good fathers and husbands and a couple of suits a year. Next day they turn fifty, they're coming in for the two-tone buckskins and canary jackets and their wives are ringing up asking whether I've seen them.'

But Osnard, for all Pendel's efforts to divert his interest elsewhere, had not ceased his watch. The quick brown fox's eyes were aimed at Pendel's, and his expression, if anybody in that mayhem had troubled to study it, was of a man who had struck true gold and didn't know whether to run for help or dig it alone.

*   *   *

A phalanx of revellers descended. Pendel loved every one of them:

Jules, my goodness, lovely to see you, sir! Meet Andy, chum of mine – *French bondseller, Andy, problems with his bill.*

Mordi, what a joy, sir! – *young wheeler-dealer from Kiev, Andy, came in with the new wave of Ashkenazis, reminds me of my Uncle Benny* – Mordi, say hullo to Andy!

Handsome young Kazuo and child bride from the Japanese Trade Centre, prettiest couple in town – Salaams, sir! Madam, my sincere respects! – *three suits with extra trousers and I still can't do his other name for you, Andy.*

Pedro, young lawyer.

Fidel, young banker.

José-María, Antonio, Salvador, Paul, infant sharedealers, witless white-arse princelings known otherwise as *rabiblancos*, bug-eyed traders of twenty-three worrying about their manhood and drinking themselves impotent. And somewhere between handshakes and backslaps and see-you-Thursday-Harrys, Pendel's murmured commentary, about who their fathers were and how much who was worth and how their brothers and sisters were tactically distributed among the political parties.

'Jesus,' Osnard marvelled devoutly, when they were finally alone again.

'What's Jesus got to do with it, then, Andy?' Pendel demanded a little aggressively, for Louisa did not permit blaspheming in the house.

'Not Jesus, Harry, old boy. You.'

*   *   *

With its teak thrones and scrolled silver cutlery the restaurant of the Club Unión was designed to be a feast of opulence, but the curiously low ceiling and emergency lighting make it more like a deep shelter for errant bankers on the run. Seated at a corner window, Pendel and Osnard drank Chilean wine and ate Pacific fish. From each candlelit encampment diners priced each other with discontented eyes: how many millions have *you* got – how did *he* get in here? – where does she think *she*'s going in those diamonds? Outside the window the sky was by now pitch black. In the lighted pool below them a four-year-old girl in a gold bikini was being walked gravely through the deep end on the shoulders of a brawny swimming instructor in a skullcap. Beside him waded an overweight bodyguard, hands tensely outstretched to catch her if she fell. At the pool's edge the girl's bored mother, dressed in a designer trousersuit, painting her fingernails.

'Louisa's what I call the *hub*, Andy, not wishing to boast,' Pendel was saying. Why was he talking about her? Osnard must have mentioned her. 'Louisa is a one-in-a-million top secretary of incredible potential not yet fully realised in my opinion.' It was a pleasure to him to make things right with her after their bad telephone conversation. 'Dogsbody doesn't cover it at all. Officially, as of three months ago, she's PA to Ernie Delgado, previously of the law firm of

Delgado & Woolf, but he's given up his interests for the sake of the people. Unofficially, the Canal administration is in such a flux from the handover, what with your Yanquis going out one door and your Panamanians coming in the other, that she's one of the few with a clear head who can tell them the score. She greets, she covers, she papers over the cracks. She knows where to find it if it's there, and who's nicked it if it's not.'

'Sounds like a rare find,' said Osnard.

Pendel swelled with marital pride.

'Andy, you are not wrong. And if you want my personal view, Ernie Delgado is a very fortunate man. One moment it's your high-level shipping conference to be prepared for, and where's the minutes of the last one? The next it's your foreign delegation wanting to be briefed, and where on earth have those Japanese interpreters got to?' Yet again he felt an irrepressible urge to chip at Ernie Delgado's pedestal: 'Plus she's the only one can speak to Ernie when he's got a hangover or is suffering the serious criticism of his lady wife. Without Louisa, old Ernie would be belly up and his very shiny halo would be acquiring quite a lot of rust-spots.'

'*Japanese*,' said Osnard in a trailed, contemplative sort of voice.

'Well, they could be Swedish or German or French, I suppose. But it's more your Japanese than most.'

'What sort o' Japanese? Local? Visiting? Commercial? Official?'

'I can't say I know, Andy.' A silly, over-excited giggle. 'They're all a bit alike to me, I suppose. Bankers a lot of them, I expect.'

'But Louisa knows.'

'Andy, those Japs eat out of her hand. I don't know what it is about her, but to see her with her Jap delegations, doing her bowing and her smiling and her come-this-way-gentlemen – it's a privilege, is what it is.'

'Bring work home, does she? Weekend work? Evenings?'

'Only when she's pressed, Andy. Thursdays mostly, so that she can get herself clear for the weekend and the kids while I'm entertaining my customers. There's no overtime paid and they exploit her something rotten. Though they do pay her the American rates, which makes a difference, I'll admit.'

'What does she do with it?'

'With the work? Work on it. Type it.'

'The lolly. Jack. Pay.'

'It all goes into the joint account, Andy, which is what she considers right and proper, being a very high-minded woman and mother,' Pendel replied primly.

And to his surprise he felt himself blush scarlet, and his eyes filled with hot tears until he somehow persuaded them to go back to where they had come from. But Osnard wasn't blushing and no tears flooded his boot-button black eyes.

'Poor girl's working to pay off Ramón,' he said relentlessly. 'And doesn't even know it.'

But if Pendel was mortified by this cruel statement of hard fact, his expression no longer showed it. He was peering excitedly down the room, his face a mixture of joy and apprehension.

*　　*　　*

'Harry! My friend! Harry! I swear to God. I love you!'

An enormous figure in a magenta smoking jacket was lumbering towards them, crashing against tables, drawing cries of anger and turning over drinks along his path. He was a young man still and the vestiges of good looks clung to him despite the ravages of pain and dissipation. Seeing him approach, Pendel had already risen to his feet.

'Señor Mickie, sir, I love you back, and how are you today?' he enquired anxiously. 'Meet Andy Osnard, chum of mine. Andy, this is Mickie Abraxas. Mickie, I think you're a touch refreshed. Why don't we both sit down?'

But Mickie needed to show off his jacket and he couldn't do it sitting down. Knuckles to his hips, fingertips outward, he executed a grotesque rendering of a fashion-model's pirouette before grabbing the edge of the table to steady himself. The table rocked and a couple of plates crashed to the floor.

'You like it, Harry? You proud of it?' He was speaking American English very loud.

'Mickie, it's truly beautiful,' said Pendel earnestly. 'I was just saying to Andy here, I never cut a better pair of shoulders and you show them off a treat, didn't I, Andy? Now why don't we sit down and have a natter?'

But Mickie had focused on Osnard.

'What do *you* think, Mister?'

Osnard gave an easy smile. 'Congratulations. P & B at their best. Centre runs right down the middle.'

'Who the fuck are you?'

'He's a customer, Mickie,' said Pendel, working hard for peace, which with Mickie he always did. 'Name of Andy. I told you but you wouldn't listen. Mickie was at Oxford, weren't you, Mickie? Tell Andy which college you were at. He's also a very big fan of our English way of life and some-time president of our Anglo-Panamanian Society of Culture, right, Mickie? Andy's a highly important diplomat, right, Andy? He works at the British Embassy. Arthur Braithwaite made suits for his old dad.'

Mickie Abraxas digested this, but not with any great pleasure, for he was eyeing Osnard darkly, not much liking what he saw.

'Know what I would do if I was President of Panama, Mr Andy?'

'Why don't you sit down, Mickie, and we'll hear all about it?'

'I'd kill the lot of us. There's no hope for us. We're screwed. We've got everything God needed to make para-dise. Great farming, beaches, mountains, wildlife you wouldn't believe, put a stick in the ground you get a fruit tree, people so beautiful you could cry. What do we do? Cheat. Conspire. Lie. Pretend. Steal. Starve each other. Behave like there's nothing left for anyone except me. We're so stupid and corrupt and blind I don't know why the earth doesn't swallow us up right now. Yes, I do. We sold the earth to the fucking Arabs in Colón. You gonna tell that to the Queen?'

'Can't wait,' said Osnard pleasantly.

'Mickie, I'm going to get cross with you in a minute if you don't sit down. You're making a spectacle of yourself and embarrassing me.'

'Don't you love me?'

'You know I do. Now sit yourself down like a good lad.'

'Where's Marta?'

'At home, I expect, Mickie. In El Chorillo where she lives. Doing her studies, I expect.'

'I love that woman.'

'I'm glad to hear it, Mickie, and so will Marta be. Now sit down.'

'You love her too.'

'We both do, Mickie, in our separate ways, I'm sure,' Pendel replied, not blushing exactly, but suffering an inconvenient clotting of the voice. 'Now sit yourself down like a good lad. Please.'

Grabbing Pendel's head in both hands, Mickie whispered wetly in his ear. 'Dolce Vita for the big race on Sunday, hear me? Rafi Domingo bought the jockeys. All of them, hear me? Tell Marta. Make her rich.'

'Mickie, I hear you loud and clear, and Rafi was in my shop this morning but you weren't, which was a pity, because there's a nice dinner jacket there waiting for you to try it on. Now sit down, *please*, like a good friend.'

Out of the corner of his eye Pendel saw two large men with identity tags advancing purposefully towards them along the edge of the room. Pendel reached a protective arm halfway across Mickie's mountainous shoulders.

'Mickie, if you make any more trouble I'll never cut another suit for you,' he said in English. And in Spanish to the men: 'We're all fine, thank you, gentlemen. Mr Abraxas will be leaving of his own accord. Mickie.'

'What?'

'Are you listening to me, Mickie?'

'No.'

'Is your nice driver Santos outside with the car?'

'Who cares?'

Taking Mickie's arm, Pendel led him gently through the dining room under a mirrored ceiling to the lobby, where

Santos the driver was anxiously waiting for his master.

*   *   *

'I'm sorry you didn't see him at his best, Andy,' Pendel said shyly. 'Mickie is one of Panama's few real heroes.'

With defensive pride, he volunteered a brief history of Mickie's life till now: father an immigrant Greek ship-owner and close chum of General Omar Torrijos, which was why he agreed to neglect his business interests and devote himself full time to Panama's drug trade, turning it into something everyone could be proud of in the war against Communism.

'He always talk like that?'

'Well, it's not all *talk*, Andy, I will say. Mickie had a high regard for his old dad, he liked Torrijos and didn't like We-Know-Who,' he explained, observing the oppressive local convention of not mentioning Noriega by name. 'A fact which Mickie felt obliged to declare from the rooftops to all who had ears to listen, till We-Know-Who popped his garters and had him put in prison to shut him up.'

'Hell was all that about Marta?'

'Yes, well you see, that was the old days, Andy, what I'd call a hangover. From when they were both active together in their cause, you see. Marta being a black artisan's daughter and him a spoiled rich boy, but shoulder to shoulder for democracy, as you might say,' Pendel replied, running ahead of himself in his desire to put the topic behind him as fast as possible. 'Unusual friendships were made in those days. Bonds were forged. Like he said. They loved each other. Well they would.'

'Thought he was talking about you.'

Pendel rode himself still harder.

'Only, your prison here, Andy, it's a bit more prison than what it is back home, I'll put it that way. Which is not to put down the home variety, not by any means. Only what they did, you see, was they banged Mickie up with a large quantity of not very sensitive long-term criminals, twelve to a cell or more, and every now and then they'd move him to another cell, if you follow me, which didn't do a lot for Mickie's health, on account of him being what you might call a handsome young man in his day,' he ended awkwardly. And he allowed a moment of silence, which Osnard had the tact not to interrupt, to commemorate Mickie's lost beauty. 'Plus they beat him senseless a few times, for annoying them,' he added.

'Look him up at all?' Osnard enquired carelessly.

'In prison, Andy? Yes. Yes, I did.'

'Must have made a change, being t'other side o' the bars.'

Mickie scarecrow thin, face lopsided from a beating, eyes still fresh from hell. Mickie in frayed orange rags, no bespoke tailor available. Wet red blisters round his ankles, more round his wrists. A man in chains must learn not to writhe while he is beaten but learning this takes time. Mickie mumbling: 'Harry, I swear to God, give me your hand, Harry, as I love you, get me out of here.' Pendel whispering: 'Mickie, listen to me, you've got to drucken yourself, lad, don't look them in the eye.' Neither man hearing the other. Nothing to be said except hullo and see you soon.

'So what's he up to now?' Osnard asked, as if the subject had already lost its interest for him. 'Apart from drinking himself to death and being a bloody nuisance around the place?'

'Mickie?' Pendel asked.

'Who d'you think?'

And suddenly the same imp that had obliged Pendel to make a scallywag of Delgado obliged him also to make a modern hero of Abraxas: *If this Osnard thinks he can write Mickie off, then he's got another think coming, hasn't he? Mickie's my friend, my winger, my oppo, my cellmate. Mickie had his fingers broken and his balls crushed. Mickie was gangbanged by bad convicts while you were playing leapfrog in your nice English public school.*

Pendel shot a furtive glance round the dining room in case they were being overheard. At the next table a bullet-headed man was accepting a large white portable telephone from the head waiter. He spoke, the head waiter removed the phone, only to bestow it like a loving cup on another needy guest.

'Mickie's still at it, Andy,' Pendel murmured under his breath. 'What you see isn't what you get, not with Mickie, not by a long chalk, never was and isn't now, I'll put it that way.'

What was he doing? What was he saying? He hardly knew himself. He was a muddler. Somewhere in his overworked mind was an idea that he could make a gift of love to Mickie, build him into something he could never be, a Mickie redux, dried out, shining bright, militant and courageous.

'Still at what? Don't follow you. Talking code again.'

'He's *in there.*'

'In where?'

'With the Silent Opposition,' said Pendel, in the manner of a mediaeval warrior who hurls his colours into the enemy ranks before plunging in to win them back.

'The *what?*'

'Silently opposing. Him and his tightly-knit group of fellow believers.'

'Believers in *what*, Christ's sake?'

'The sham, Andy. The veneer. The beneath the surface, put it that way,' Pendel insisted, giddily ascending to hitherto unscaled heights of fantasy. Half-remembered recent dialogues with Marta were speeding to his aid. 'The phoney democracy that is the new squeaky-clean Panama, ha ha. It's all a pretence. That's what he was telling you. You heard him. Cheat. Conspire. Lie. Pretend. Draw aside the curtain and it's the same boys that owned We-Know-Who waiting to take back the reins.'

Osnard's pinhole eyes continued to hold Pendel in their black beam. It's my range, thought Pendel, already protecting himself from the consequences of his rashness. That's all he wants to hear. Not my accuracy, my range. He doesn't care whether I'm reading notes or playing from memory or improvising. He's probably not even listening, not as such.

'Mickie's in touch with the people the other side of the bridge,' he forged on bravely.

'Hell are they?'

The bridge was the Bridge of the Americas. The expression was once more Marta's.

'The hidden rank and file, Andy,' said Pendel boldly. 'The strivers and believers who would rather see progress than take bribes,' he replied, quoting Marta verbatim. 'The farmers and artisans who've been betrayed by lousy greedy government. The honourable small professionals. The decent part of Panama you never get to see or hear about. They're organising themselves. They've had enough. So's Mickie.'

'Marta in on this?'

'She could be, Andy. I never ask. It's not my place to know. I have my thoughts. That's all I'm saying.'

Long pause.

'Had enough of *what* exactly?'

Pendel cast a swift, conspiratorial glance round the dining room. He was Robin Hood, bringer of hope to the oppressed, dispenser of justice. At the next table, a noisy party of twelve was tucking into lobster and Dom Pérignon.

'*This,*' he replied in a low, emphatic voice. '*Them. And all that they entail.*'

*   *   *

Osnard wanted to hear more about the Japanese.

'Well now, your *Japanese*, Andy – you met one just now, which I expect is why you asked – are what I call highly present in Panama, and have been for many years now, I would say as many as twenty,' Pendel replied enthusiastically, grateful to be able to put the subject of his only true friend behind him. 'There's your Japanese processions to amuse the crowds, there's your Japanese brass bands, there's a Japanese seafood market they presented to the nation, and there's even a Japanese-funded educational TV channel,' he added, recalling one of the few programmes his children were allowed to watch.

'Who's your top Jap?'

'Customerwise, Andy? Top I don't know. They're what I call enigmatic. I'd have to ask Marta probably. It's one to be measured and six to bow and take his picture, we always say, and we're not far wrong. There's a Mr Yoshio from one of their trade missions who throws his weight around the shop a bit, and there's a Toshikazu from the Embassy, but whether we're talking first or second names here, I'd have to look it up.'

'Or get Marta to.'

'Correct.'

Conscious again of Osnard's blackened stare, Pendel vouchsafed him an endearing smile in an effort to deflect him, but without success.

'You ever have Ernie Delgado to dinner?' he asked while Pendel was still expecting further questions about the Japanese.

'Not as such, Andy, no.'

'Why not? He's your wife's boss.'

'I don't think Louisa would approve, frankly.'

'Why not?'

The imp again. The one that pops up to remind us that nothing goes away; that a moment's jealousy can spawn a lifetime's fiction; and that the only thing to do with a good man once you've pulled him low is pull him lower.

'Ernie is what I call of the hard right, Andy. He was the same under We-Know-Who, although he never let on. All piss and mustard when he was with his liberal friends, if you'll pardon me, but as soon as their backs were turned it was pop next door to We-Know-Who and "Yes sir, no sir, and how can we be of service, Your Highness?"'

'Not generally known, though, is it, all the same? Still a white man to most of us, Ernie is.'

'Which is why he's dangerous, Andy. Ask Mickie. Ernie's an iceberg. There's a lot more of him below the water than what there is above, I'll put it that way.'

Osnard scrunched a roll, added a spot of butter and ate with slow, ruminative circular movements of the lower jaw. But his chip-black eyes wanted more than bread and butter.

'That upstairs room you've got in the shop – Sportsman's Corner.'

'You like it, do you, Andy?'

'Ever thought o' turning it into a clubroom for your customers? Somewhere they can let their hair down? Better than a clapped out sofa and an armchair on the ground floor on a Thursday night, isn't it?'

'I have thought along those lines many times, Andy, I'll admit, and I'm quite impressed you've hit on the same idea after just one look. But I always bump up against the same immoveable objection, which is where would I put my Sportsman's Corner?'

'Show a good return, that stuff?'

'Quite. Oh yes.'

'Didn't make *me* horny.'

'Sports articles are more what I call my loss leader, Andy. If I don't sell them, someone else will, and they'll grab my customers at the same time.'

No wasted body movements, Pendel noticed uneasily. I had a police sergeant like you once. Never fidgeted his hands or scratched his head or shifted his arse about. Just sits and looks at you with these eyes he's got.

'Are you measuring me for a suit, Andy?' he asked facetiously.

But Osnard was not required to answer, for Pendel's gaze had once more darted away towards a far corner of the room where a dozen or so noisy new arrivals, men and women, were taking their places at a long table.

'And there's the other half of the equation, as you might say!' he declared exchanging over-energetic hand signals with the figure at the head of the table. 'Rafi Domingo himself, no less. Mickie's other friend, beat that!'

'What equation?' Osnard asked.

Pendel cupped a hand to his mouth for discretion. 'It's the lady *beside* him, Andy.'

'What about her?'

'She's *Mickie's wife.*'

Osnard's furtive gaze made a quick raid to the far table while he busied himself with his food.

'One with the tits?'

'Correct, Andy. You do wonder how people get married sometimes, don't you?'

'Give me Domingo,' Osnard ordered – like, give me a middle C.

Pendel drew a breath. His head was spinning and his mind was tired but nobody had called intermission so he played on.

'Flies his own aeroplane,' he began arbitrarily.

Scraps he had picked up in the shop.

'What for?'

'Runs a string of very fine hotels no one stays in.'

Tittle-tattle from more than one country.

'Why?'

The rest fluence.

'The hotels belong to a certain *consortium* which has its headquarters in Madrid, Andy.'

'So?'

'*So*. Rumour has it that this *consortium* belongs to some Colombian gentlemen not totally unconnected with the cocaine trade, doesn't it? The consortium is doing nicely, you'll be pleased to hear. A posh new place in Chitré, another going up in David, two in Bocas del Toro and Rafi Domingo hops between them in his plane like a cricket in a frying-pan.'

'Hell for?'

A silence of spies while the waiter replenished their water glasses. A chink of ice cubes like tiny church bells. And a rush like genius in Pendel's ears.

'We may only guess, Andy. Rafi doesn't know the hotel business from his elbow, which is not a problem because like I told you the hotels don't take guests. They don't advertise and if you try and book a room you'll be politely told they're full up.'

'Don't get it.'

Rafi wouldn't mind, Pendel told himself. Rafi's a Benny. He'd say, Harry boy, you tell that Mr Osnard whatever keeps him happy, just as long as you haven't got a witness.

'Each hotel banks five thousand dollars a day cash, right? A financial year or two from now, as soon as the hotels have notched up a healthy set of accounts, they'll be sold off to the highest bidder who by coincidence will be Rafi Domingo wearing a different company hat. The hotels will be in excellent order throughout, which is not surprising seeing they haven't been slept in, and there's not one hamburger been cooked in the kitchen. And they'll be legitimate businesses because in Panama three-year-old money is more than just respectable, it's antique.'

'And he screws Mickie's wife.'

'So we are told, Andy,' said Pendel, wary now, since this part was true.

'Told by Mickie?'

'Not as such, Andy. Not in as many words. It's what the eye doesn't see in Mickie's case.' The fluence again. Why was he doing it? What was driving him? Andy was. A performer is a performer. If your audience isn't with you it's against you. Or perhaps, with his own fictions in tatters, he needed to enrich the fictions of others. Perhaps he found renewal in the remaking of his world.

'Rafi's one of them, you see, Andy. Rafi's one of the absolute biggest, frankly.'

'Biggest *what?*'

'The Silent Opposers. Mickie's boys. Waiters-in-the-wings, I call them. Those that have seen the writing on the wall. Rafi's a bitser.'

'Hell's that?'

'A bitser, Andy. The same as Marta. The same as me. Part-Indian, in his case. There's no racial discrimination in Panama, you'll be pleased to learn, but they don't care for Turcos a lot, specially not new ones, and faces do get whiter as you go up the social ladder. What I call altitude sickness.'

It was a brand new joke and one that he intended to include in his material, but Osnard didn't see it. Or if he did, he didn't find it funny. In fact, to Pendel's eye, he looked as though he would prefer to be watching a public execution.

*   *   *

'Payment by results,' Osnard said. 'Only way. Agreed?' He

had lowered his head into his shoulders, and his voice with it.

'Andy, that has been a principle of mine ever since we opened shop,' Pendel replied fervently, trying to think when he had last paid anyone by results.

And feeling light-headed from the drink and a general sense of unreality, his own and everybody else's, he almost added that it had been a principle of dear old Arthur Braithwaite's too, but restrained himself on the grounds that he had done enough with his fluence for one evening, and an artist must ration himself even when he feels he could go on all night.

'Nobody's ashamed o' mercenary motive any more. Only thing that makes anybody tick.'

'Oh, I do agree, Andy,' said Pendel, assuming that Osnard was now lamenting the parlous state of England.

Osnard cast round the room in case he was being overheard. And perhaps the sight of so many head-to-head conspirators at nearby tables emboldened him, for his face stiffened in some way Pendel was not at all at ease with, and his voice, though muted, acquired a serrated edge.

'Ramón's got you over a barrel. If you don't pay him off, you're screwed. If you do pay him off, you're stuck with a river with no water and a rice farm that can't grow rice. Not to mention the hairy eyeball from Louisa.'

'It's a worry to me, Andy. I'll not deny it. It's been putting me off my food for weeks.'

'Know who your neighbour is up there?'

'He's an absentee landlord, Andy. A highly malicious phantom.'

'Know his name?'

Pendel shook his head. 'He's not a person, you see. More a corporation registered in Miami.'

'Know where he banks?'

'Not as such, Andy.'

'With your chum Ramón. It's Rudd's company. Rudd owns two-thirds, Mr X owns t'other third. Know who X is?'

'I'm reeling, Andy.'

'How about your farm manager chap? What's-his-face?'

'Angel? He loves me like a brother.'

'You've been conned. Case o' the biter bit. Think about it.'

'I am doing, Andy. I haven't thought like this for a long time,' said Pendel as another part of his world keeled over and sank beneath his gaze.

'Anybody been offering to buy the farm off you for peanuts?' Osnard was asking, from behind the wall of mist that had somehow gathered between them.

'My neighbour. Then he'll put back the water, won't he, and have a nice viable rice farm worth five times what he gave for it.'

'And Angel running it for him.'

'I'm looking at a circle, Andy. With me in the middle.'

'How big's your neighbour's farm?'

'Two hundred acres.'

'What's he do with it?'

'Cattle. Low upkeep. He doesn't need the water. He's just keeping it away from me.'

The prisoner is giving one-line answers while the officer writes them down: except that Osnard doesn't write anything down. He remembers with his quick brown fox's eyes.

'Did Rudd put you onto buying your farm in the first place?'

'He said it was cheap. An executors' sale. Just the place for Louisa's money. I was green is what I was.'

Osnard drew his balloon glass to his lips, perhaps to mask them. Then he took a suck of air and his voice flattened itself for speed.

'You're God's gift, Harry. Classic, ultimate listening post. Wife with access. Contacts to kill for. Chum in the resistance. Girl in the shop who runs with the mob. Behaviour pattern established over ten years. Natural cover, local language, gift o' the gab, quick on your feet. Never heard anyone pitch the tale better. Be who you are but more of it and we'll have the whole o' Panama stitched up. Plus you're deniable. You on or not?'

Pendel smirked, partly from the flattery, partly in awe of his predicament. But mostly because he was aware of witnessing a great moment in his life which, though terrible and cleansing, appeared to be taking place without his participation.

'I've been deniable ever since I can remember, if I'm honest, Andy,' he confided, while his mind cruised erratically round the outer edges of his life so far. But he hadn't said yes.

'Down side is, you'll be in up to your neck from day one. That going to bother you?'

'I'm up to my neck already, aren't I? It's a question of where I'd sooner not be.'

The eyes again, too old, too steady, listening, remembering, smelling, doing all the jobs at once. And Pendel recklessly asserting himself despite them or because of them.

'Though what you're going to do with a bankrupt listening post is slightly beyond my powers of comprehension,' he declared with the boastful pride of the condemned. 'There's no way out that *I* know of to save me, short of a mad millionaire.' A needless glance around the room. 'See a mad millionaire at all, Andy, among the crowd? I'm not saying they're all sane, mind. Just not mad in my direction.'

Nothing changed in Osnard. Not his stare, not his voice, not his heavy hands that sat uncurled and fingers down on the rich white tablecloth.

'Maybe my outfit's mad enough,' he said.

Casting round for relief, Pendel's gaze selected the gruesome figure of the Bear, Panama's most hated columnist, treading his inconsolable path towards a solitary table in the darkest part of the room. But he still hadn't said yes, and with one ear he was listening desperately to Uncle Benny: *Son, when you meet a con, dangle him. Because there's nothing a con likes less than being told to come back next week.*

'You on or not?'

'I'm thinking, Andy. I'm pondering is what I'm doing.'

'Hell about?'

About being a sober adult making up my mind, he replied truculently in his head. About having a centre and a will instead of a bunch of stupid impulses and bad memories and an excessive dose of fluence.

'I'm weighing my options, Andy. Looking at all sides,' he said loftily.

*   *   *

Osnard is denying accusations nobody has levelled against him. He is doing this in a low wet murmur that perfectly suits his bungy body, but Pendel finds no continuity in his words. It's a different evening. I was thinking of Benny again. I need to go home to bed.

'We don't put the hard word on chaps, Harry. Not chaps we like.'

'I never said you did, Andy.'

'Not our style. Hell's the point o' leaking your criminal record to the Pans when we want you the way you are and more so?'

'There's no point at all, Andy, and I'm pleased to hear you say it.'

'Why blow the whistle on old Braithwaite, make a fool o' you to your wife and kids, break up the happy home? We want *you*, Harry. You've got a hell of a lot to sell. All we want to do is buy it.'

'Sort out the rice farm for me and you can have my head on a charger, Andy,' says Pendel to be companionable.

'No sale, old boy. Need your soul.'

Aping the example of his host, Pendel has taken his brandy glass in both hands and is leaning across the candlelit table. Weighing his decision still. Holding out, even though most of him would like to say 'yes', just to end the embarrassment of not saying it.

'I haven't heard you on job description yet, have I, Andy?'

'Listening post. Told you.'

'Yes, but what do you want me to *hear*, Andy? What's the bottom line?'

The eyes again, needle-sharp. The red sparks back inside. The slouchy jaw, absently masticating while he ruminates. The slumped fat-boy's body. The trailed, damped-down voice spoken from one corner of the crooked mouth.

'Not a lot. Balance o' global power in the twenty-first

century. Future o' world trade. Panama's political chess-board. Silent opposers. Chaps from the other side o' the bridge, as you call 'em. What's going to happen when the Yanks pull out? If they do. Who'll be laughing, who'll be crying, come midday December 31st 1999? Shape o' things to come when one o' the world's two greatest gateways goes under the hammer and the auction's run by a bunch o' wide boys? Piece o' cake,' he replied, but ending on a question mark, as if the best were yet to come.

Pendel grins in return. 'Oh, well, there's no problem then, is there? We'll have it all packed and ready for your collection by lunchtime tomorrow. If it doesn't fit, bring it back as often as you like.'

'Plus a few things that aren't on the menu,' Osnard adds even more quietly. 'Or not yet, shall we say.'

'What are they then, Andy?'

A shrug. A long slow complicitous, insinuating, unnerving policeman's shrug, expressing false ease, terrible powers and an immense store of superior knowledge.

'Lot o' different ways to skin a cat, this game. Can't learn 'em all in a night. That a "yes" I heard, or you doing a Garbo?'

Astonishingly, if only to himself, Pendel still contrives to prevaricate. Perhaps he knows that indecision is the only freedom left to him. Perhaps Uncle Benny is once more plucking at his sleeve. Or perhaps he has some hazy notion that, according to prisoner's rights, a man selling his soul is entitled to a period of reflection.

'It's not a Garbo I'm doing, Andy. It's a Harry,' he says, bravely rising to his feet and pulling back his shoulders. 'I'm afraid that when it comes to life-altering decisions, you'll find Harry Pendel somewhat of a highly calculating animal.'

*   *   *

It was after eleven when Pendel switched off the engine of his car and coasted to a halt twenty yards below the house in order not to wake the children. Then used both hands to open the front door, one to shove it and one to turn the key. Because if you shoved it first the lock worked smoothly, otherwise it went off like a pistol shot. He went to the kitchen and rinsed his mouth out with Coca-Cola in the hope that it would take away the brandy fumes. Then he undressed in the hall and laid his clothes on the chair before tiptoeing into the bedroom. Louisa had opened both windows which was how she liked to sleep. Sea air wafted in from the Pacific. Drawing back the sheet he saw to his surprise that she was naked like himself and wide awake and staring at him.

'What's wrong?' he whispered, dreading a row that would wake the children.

Reaching out her long arms she clutched him fiercely against her, and he discovered that her face was sticky with tears.

'Harry, I'm really sorry, I want you to know that. Really, really sorry.' She was kissing him and not letting him kiss her in return. 'You're not to forgive me, Harry, not yet. You're a good fine man and a fine husband, and you're earning great, and my father was right, I'm a cold, mean-hearted bitch and I wouldn't know a kind word if it got up and bit me in the butt.'

It's too late, he thought as she took him. This is who we should have been before it was too late.

CHAPTER SIX

Harry Pendel loved his wife and children with an obedience that can only be understood by people who have never belonged to a family themselves, never known what it is to respect a decent father, love a happy mother, or accept them as the natural reward for being born into the world.

The Pendels lived on the top of a hill in a neighbourhood called Bethania in a fine, two-storey modern house with front and back lawns and Bougainvilia galore and lovely views down to the sea and the Old City and Punta Paitilla in the distance. Pendel had heard that the hills around were hollow, full of American atom bombs and war rooms, but Louisa said we should all feel safer for them and Pendel, not wishing to argue with her, said perhaps we should.

The Pendels had a maid to mop the tiled floors and a maid to do the washing and a maid to babysit and do the routine shopping, and a grizzled black man with white stubble and a straw hat who hacked at the garden, grew whatever came into his head, smoked illegal substances and cadged from the kitchen. For this small army of servants they paid a hundred and forty dollars a week.

When Pendel lay in bed at night it was his secret pleasure to enter the troubled sleep of prison, with his knees drawn up and his chin down and his hands cupped over his ears to keep out the groans of fellow prisoners, then wake himself and establish by cautious reconnaissance that he wasn't in prison at all but here in Bethania under the charge of a loyal wife who needed and respected him and happy children sleeping just across the corridor, which was a blessing every time, what Uncle Benny called a *mitzvah*: Hannah his nine-year-old Catholic princess, Mark his eight-year-old rebel Jewish violinist. But while Pendel loved his family with dutiful energy and devotion, he also feared for it and trained himself to regard his happiness as fool's gold.

When he stood alone on his balcony in the darkness, which was what he liked to do each evening after work, maybe with one of Uncle Benny's small cigars, and scented the night smells of luscious flowers on the damp air and watched the lights swimming in the rainy mist and glimpsed through fitful clouds the queue of boats at anchor in the mouth of the Canal, the abundance of his good luck instilled in him a keen awareness of its fragility: you know this can't last, Harry boy, you know the world can blow up in your face, you've watched it happen from this very spot, and what it's done once it can do again whenever it feels like it, so look out.

Then he would stare into the too-peaceful city, and very soon the flares and the red and green tracer and the hoarse tattoo of machineguns and the jackhammer rattle of cannons would start to create their own mad daytime in the theatre of his memory, just as they had on that December night in 1989, when the hills blinked and shuddered huge Spectre gunships flew in unopposed from the sea to punish the mostly wooden slums of El Chorillo – as usual it was the poor who were to blame for everything – bludgeoning the burning hovels at their leisure, then going off to replenish themselves and coming back to bludgeon them again. And probably the attackers never meant it to be that way. Probably they were fine sons and fathers, and all they meant to do was take out Noriega's *comandancia* until a couple of shells strayed off course, and a couple more followed. But good intentions in wartime do not easily communicate themselves to the subjects of them, self-restraint passes unnoticed, and the presence of a few fugitive enemy snipers in a poor suburb does not explain its wholesale incineration. It's not much help saying, 'We used the minimum force' to terrified people running barefoot for their lives over blood and smashed glass, dragging suitcases and children with them on their way to nowhere. It's not much help to maintain that the fires were started by vindictive members of Noriega's Dignity Battalions. Even if they were, why should anyone believe you?

So the screams were soon coming up the hill, and Pendel, who had heard screams in his time and uttered a few, would never have supposed that one human scream would be able to assert itself above the sickening drone of armoured vehicles or the hump-clump of state-of-the-art ordnance, but it really could, particularly when there were a lot of screams together, and they were delivered by the lusty throats of children in terror and accompanied by the porky stink of burning human flesh.

'Harry, come inside. We need you, Harry. Harry, come back from there. Harry, I do not understand what you are doing out there.'

But that was Louisa screaming, Louisa wedged upright in the broom cupboard under the stairs, with her long arched back braced into the joinery for the greater protection of her children: Mark nearly two who was hugged into her belly, soaking her through his nappy – Mark, like the American soldiers, seemed to have unlimited supplies of ammunition – Hannah kneeling at her feet in her Yogi bear dressing gown and slippers, praying to somebody she insisted on calling Jovey, who was afterwards perceived to be an amalgam of Jesus, Jehovah and Jupiter, a sort of divine cocktail run up from the dregs of spiritual folklore that Hannah had assembled in her three years of life.

'They know what they're doing,' Louisa kept repeating in a high military bark unpleasantly reminiscent of her father's. 'This is not a one-off thing. They have it all figured out. They never, *never* hit civilians.'

And Pendel, because he loved her, felt it kindest to leave her with her faith, while El Chorillo sobbed and glowed and fell apart under the repeated onslaughts of whatever weaponry the Pentagon needed to try out next.

'Marta lives down there,' he said.

But a woman fearing for her children fears for no one else, so when morning came Pendel took a stroll down the hill and heard a silence that in all his time in Panama City he had never heard before. It was suddenly clear to him that, under the terms of the ceasefire, all parties had agreed there would never again be air-conditioning or construction work or digging or dredging; and that all cars, lorries, school buses, taxis, garbage trucks, police cars and ambulances would be henceforth banished from God's sight for ever more; and that no babies or mothers would be permitted to scream again on pain of death.

Not even the immense and stately column of black smoke rising out of what had once been El Chorillo made the smallest sound as it emptied itself into the morning sky. Only a few malcontents were refusing as usual to recognise the ban, and they were the last remaining sharpshooters in the compound of the *comandancia*, who were still potting at American emplacements in the surrounding streets. But soon they too, with a little encouragement from the tanks installed on Ancón Hill, fell silent.

Not even the telephone in the forecourt of the petrol station was exempt from the self-denying ordinance. It was intact. It was able. But Marta's number refused to ring.

*   *   *

Clinging defiantly to his newly assumed mantle of Solitary Mature Man Facing a Life Decision, Pendel rode his familiar seesaw of devotion and chronic pessimism with a wildness of indetermination that threatened to unseat him. From the accusing internal voices of Betania he bolted to the sanctuary of the shop, and from the accusing voices of the shop he bolted to the sanctuary of home, and all in the name of calmly weighing his alternatives. Not for one minute would he allow himself to think – not even in his most self-accusing moments – that he was alternating between two women.

You're rumbled, he told himself, with the triumphalism that seizes us when our worst expectations are fulfilled. Your grandiose visions have come home to roost. Your fabricated world is crashing round your ears and it's your own stupid fault for building a temple without foundation. But no sooner had he flailed himself with these doomsday predictions than cheering counsel came running to his rescue:

'So a few home truths make a *Nemesis* already' – using Benny's voice – 'when a fine young diplomat is asking you to stand up and be a man for England, you think you're a doomed corpse in a morgue? Does a Nemesis offer to play mad millionaire for you, slip you an inch of fifties in a plain envelope and tell you there's plenty more where they came from? Call you God's gift, Harry, which is more than some have done? A classic? A *Nemesis?*'

Then Hannah needed the Great Decider to decide which book she should read for the school reading competition, and Mark needed to play 'Lazy Sheep' for him on his new violin so that they could decide whether he was good enough to sit his exam, and Louisa needed his opinion on the latest outrage at the Headquarters Building so that they could decide what to think about the future of the Canal, although Louisa's views upon that subject had been decided long ago: the peerless Ernesto Delgado, American-approved straight arrow and Preserver of the Golden Past, was incapable of fault:

'Harry, I do not understand. Ernesto only has to leave the country for ten days in order to escort his President, and his staff immediately sanction the appointment of no fewer than five attractive Panamanian women as Public Relations Officers on full American scale, when their sole qualifications are that they are young, white, drive BMWs, wear designer dresses, have large breasts and rich fathers, and refuse to speak to the permanent employees.'

'Shocking,' Pendel decided.

Then back to the shop where Marta needed to go through overdue bills and uncollected orders with him so that they could decide who to chase and who to leave another month.

'How are the headaches?' he asked her tenderly, noticing she was even paler than usual.

'It's nothing,' Marta replied from behind her hair.

'Has the lift stopped again?'

'The lift is now permanently stopped' – granting him a lopsided smile – 'the lift is officially declared stopped.'

'I'm sorry.'

'Well please don't be. You are not responsible for the lift. Who is Osnard?'

Pendel was at first appalled. Osnard? *Osnard?* He's a customer, woman. Stop shouting his name around!

'Why?' he said, sobering completely.

'He's evil.'

'Aren't all my customers?' he said, harping playfully upon her preference for the people the other side of the bridge.

'Yes, but they don't know it,' she replied, not smiling any more.

'And Osnard knows it?'

'Yes. Osnard is evil. Don't do what he is asking you to do.'

'But what's he asking me to do?'

'I don't know. If I did I would prevent him. Please.'

She would have added 'Harry', he could feel his name forming on her frayed lips. But in the shop it was her pride never to prey upon his indulgence, never to show by word or sign that they were joined to each other in eternity, that each time they saw each other, they saw the same thing through different windows:

Marta in her ripped white shirt and jeans lying like uncollected refuse in the gutter while three members of Noriega's Dignity Battalions, known affectionately as Dingbats, take turns to win her heart and mind with the aid of a bloodied baseball bat, starting with her face. Pendel staring down at her with his arms twisted up his back by two more of them, yelling his heart out first in fear, then in anger, then in supplication, begging them to let her be.

But they don't. They force him to watch. Because what is the point of making an example of a rebellious woman if there's nobody around to take the point?

It's all a mistake, captain. It's sheer coincidence that this lady is wearing the white shirt of protest.

Compose yourself, señor. It won't be white much longer.

Marta on the bed in the makeshift clinic to which Mickie Abraxas has bravely taken them; Marta naked and covered in blood and bruises while Pendel desperately plies the doctor with dollars and assurances, and Mickie stands at the window keeping guard.

'We are better than this,' Marta whispers through bloodied lips and smashed teeth.

She means: there is a better Panama. She is talking about the people from the other side of the bridge.

The next day, Mickie is arrested.

*   *   *

'I'm thinking of turning the Sportsman's Corner into a bit of a clubroom,' Pendel told Louisa, still in his quest for a Decision. 'I see a bar.'

'Harry, I do not understand why you need a bar. Your Thursday evening gatherings are riotous enough as it is.'

'It's about pulling people in, Lou. Whipping up more custom. Friends bring friends, the friends get their knees under the table, feel at ease, start looking at a few materials, full order books result.'

'Where will the fitting room go?' she objected.

Good question, Pendel thought. Even Andy couldn't tell me the answer to that one. Decision deferred.

*   *   *

'For the customers, Marta,' Pendel explained patiently. 'For all the people who come to eat your sandwiches. So that they increase and multiply and order up more suits.'

'I wish my sandwiches would poison them.'

'And then who would I dress? All those hotheaded student friends of yours, I suppose. The world's first tailormade revolution, courtesy of P & B. Thank you very much.'

'Since Lenin used Rolls Royces, why not?' she retorted with equal spirit.

*   *   *

I never asked him about his pockets, he thought, working late in the shop cutting a dinner jacket to the strains of Bach. Or his turn-ups or his preferred width of trouser. I never lectured him on the advantage of braces over belts in a humid climate, specially for gentlemen whose waistline is what I call a moveable feast. Equipped with this excuse, he was on the point of reaching for the telephone when it rang for him, and who should be there but Osnard saying how about a nightcap?

They met in the panelled modern bar of the Executive Hotel, a clean white tower a stone's throw from Pendel's shop. A huge television set was showing basketball to two attractive girls in short skirts. Pendel and Osnard sat apart from them and heads together, in cane chairs that wanted them to sit back instead of forward.

'Made up your mind yet?' Osnard asked.

'Not as such, Andy. Working on it, you might say. Deliberating.'

'London likes everything it's heard. They want to clinch the deal.'

'Well, that's nice, Andy. You must have given me quite a write-up, then.'

'They want you up and running soonest. Fascinated by the Silent Opposition. Want the names o' the players. Finances. Links with the students. Have they got a manifesto? Methods and intent.'

'Oh, well, good. Yes. Right, then,' said Pendel, who among his many worries had rather lost sight of Mickie Abraxas the great freedom-fighter, and Rafi Domingo his egregious paymaster. 'I'm glad they liked it,' he added politely.

'Thought you might pump Marta: sidelights on student activism. Bomb factories in the classroom.'

'Oh. Good. Right.'

'Want to get the relationship on a formal basis, Harry. So

do I. Sign you up, brief you, pay you, show you a couple o' the tricks. Don't like the trail getting cold.'

'It's any day now, Andy. It's like I said. I'm not the rash sort. I reflect.'

'They're upping the terms by ten per cent. Help you concentrate your mind. Want me to run 'em by you?'

Osnard ran 'em by him anyway, mumbling through his cupped hand like someone working on his teeth with a toothpick, this much down, this much set against your loan each month, cash bonuses payable depending on the quality o' the product, London's sole discretion, gratuity o' so much.

'Should be out o' the woods in three years max,' he said.

'Or less if I'm lucky, Andy.'

'Or smart,' said Osnard.

* * *

'*Harry.*'

It is an hour later but Pendel is too estranged to go home, so he is back in his cutting room with his dinner jacket and Bach.

'*Harry.*'

The voice that is addressing him is Louisa's from the first time they went to bed together, really went, not just fingers and tongues and listening for her parents' car coming back from the movie, but completely naked in Harry's bed in his grotty attic flat in Calidonia where he's tailoring at night after selling ready-mades all day for a clever Syrian haberdasher called Alto. Their first effort has not been blessed by success. Both are shy, both late-developers, held back by too many household ghosts.

'*Harry.*'

'Yes, darling.' Darling never came naturally to either of them. Not at the beginning, not today.

'If Mr Braithwaite gave you your first break, and took you into his house, and put you through night school, and won you away from that wicked Uncle Benny of yours, he has my vote alive or dead.'

'I'm very glad you feel that, darling.'

'You should honour and revere him and tell our children about him as they grow up, so that they know how a good Samaritan can save a young orphan's life.'

'Arthur Braithwaite was the only moral man I knew until I met your father, Lou,' Pendel assures her devoutly in return.

And I meant it, Lou! Pendel implores her frantically in his mind, as he closes the shears on the shoulder of the left sleeve *Everything in the world is true if you invent it hard enough and love the person it's for!*

'I'll tell her,' Pendel announces aloud as Bach elevates him to a plane of perfect truthfulness. And for a dreadful moment of self-indulgence he seriously contemplates throwing aside every wise precept he has lived by and making a full confession of his sins to his life's partner. Or nearly full. A quorum.

Louisa, I've got to tell you something which is frankly a bit of a facer. What you know about me is not strictly kosher as regards all the details. It's more in the line of what I'd like to have been, if all things had been a bit more equal than they were.

I haven't got the vocabulary, he thinks. I've never confessed anything in my life, except the once for Uncle Benny. Where would I stop? And when would she ever believe me again, about anything? In horror he paints the war party in his imagination, one of Louisa's Trust-in-Jesus sessions but full dress, with the servants banished from the house and the family nucleus gathered round the table with its hands together and Louisa with her back stiff and her mouth shrunk with fear because deep down the truth scares her more than it does me. Last time it was Mark who had to own up to spraying 'bollocks' on the gatepost of his school. The time before it was Hannah who had poured a can of quick-drying paint down the sink as an act of vengeance against one of the maids.

But today it's our own Harry in the hot seat, explaining to his beloved children that Daddy, for the entire length of his marriage to Mummy and for all the time the children have been old enough to listen to him, has been telling some highly ornamented porky-pies about our great family hero and rôle model, the non-existent Mr Braithwaite, rest his soul. And that, far from being Braithwaite's favoured son, your father and husband devoted nine hundred and twelve formative days and nights to an in-depth study of the brickwork of Her Majesty's houses of correction.

Decision taken. Tell you later. Much later. Like in another life entirely. A life without fluence.

*   *   *

Pendel brought his four-track to a halt just a foot from the car in front and waited for the car behind him to smash into him but for some reason it refused. How did I get here? he wondered. Maybe it hit me and I'm dead. I must have locked up the shop without noticing. Then he remembered cutting the dinner jacket and laying the finished pieces flat on his workbench to consider them, a thing he always did: took a creator's farewell of them until they came back to him, basted into semi-human form.

Black rain was hurtling onto the bonnet. A lorry was slewed across the road fifty yards ahead of him, its wheels shed like cowpats in its path. Nothing else was visible through the waterfall except lines and lines of clogged traffic going to the war or trying to get away from it. He switched on his radio but couldn't hear it over the thunder of artillery. Rain on a Hot Tin Roof. I'm here for ever. Banged up. In the womb. Doing time. Turn off engine, turn off air-con. Wait. Cook. Sweat. Another salvo coming. Hide under the seat.

Sweat pouring off him, heavy as the rain. Running water gurgling under his feet. Pendel floating, upriver or down. The entire past that he has buried six feet deep, crashing in upon him: the unexpurgated, unsanitised, un-Braithwaited version of his life, starting with the miracle of his birth as related to him in prison by his Uncle Benny and ending with the Day of Absolutely No Atonement thirteen years ago when he invented himself to Louisa on an immaculate all-American lawn in the officially abolished Canal Zone with the Stars & Stripes flapping in the smoke of her daddy's barbecue and the band playing hope-and-glory and the black men watching through the wire.

He sees the orphanage he refused to remember and his Uncle Benny resplendent in his Homburg hat leading him away from it by the hand. He had never seen a Homburg before and wondered whether Uncle Benny was God. He sees the wet grey paving stones of Whitechapel jolting beneath his feet as he trundles trolley-loads of swaying garments through the honking traffic on his way to Uncle Benny's warehouse. He sees himself twelve years later, the same child exactly, just larger, standing spellbound among pillars of orange smoke in the same warehouse and the rows of ladies' summer frocks like convent martyrs and the flames licking at their feet.

He sees Uncle Benny with his hands cupped to his mouth yelling, 'Run, Harry boy, you stupid tart, where's your imagination?' to the accompaniment of ringing bells and the clatter of Benny's hastily departing footsteps. And himself locked in a quicksand, can't move hand or limb. He sees blue uniforms wading towards him, seizing him, dragging him to the van, and the kindly sergeant holding up the empty paraffin can, smiling like any decent father. 'Is this yours, by any chance, Mr Hymie, sir, or did you just happen to have it in your hand?'

'I can't move my legs,' Pendel explains to the kindly sergeant. 'They're stuck. It's like a cramp or something. I ought to run away but I can't.'

'Don't worry, son. We'll soon put that right,' the kindly sergeant says.

He sees himself standing bone-thin and naked against the brick wall of the police cell. And the long slow night-time while the blue uniforms take it in turns to hit him, the way they hit Marta but with more deliberation, and more pints of beer under their belts. And the kindly sergeant, who is such a decent father, urging them on. Until the water covers him over and he drowns.

The rain ends. It never happened. Cars sparkling, everybody happy to go home. Pendel tired to death. Starts the engine and the slow crawl forward, propping both forearms

on the wheel. Watches out for dangerous débris. Starts to
smile, hearing Uncle Benny.

*   *   *

'It was an explosion, Harry boy,' Uncle Benny whispered
through his tears. 'An explosion of the flesh.'

Without the weekly prison visits Uncle Benny would never
have been so forthcoming about Pendel's origins. But the
sight of his nephew seated to attention before him in his
box-pleated denims with his name on the pocket is more
than Benny's good guilty heart can bear, never mind how
many cheesecakes and books on keeping fit Auntie Ruth
sends along with him, or how many times Benny chokes
out his thanks that Pendel has kept faith through all the
circumstances. He means, kept *shtumm*.

*It was my own idea, Sergeant... I did it because I hated the
warehouse, Sergeant... I was highly angry with my Uncle Benny
for all the hours he made me work and didn't pay me for, Sergeant...
Your Honour, I have nothing to say except I greatly regret my wicked
actions and the grief I have caused to all who loved me and have
brought me up, my Uncle Benny specially...*

Benny is very old – to a child as ancient as a willow tree.
He comes from Lvov, and Pendel by the time he is ten knows
Lvov as if it were his own home town. Benny's relations
were humble peasants and artisans and little tradesmen and
cobblers. For many of them, the trains that took them to
the camps provided them with their first and last sight of
the world beyond the shtetl and the ghetto. But not for
Benny. The Benny of those days is a smart young tailor with
dreams of the big time and somehow he talks himself out
of the camps and all the way to Berlin to make uniforms
for German officers, though his real ambition is to train as
a tenor under Gigli and buy a villa on the hills of Umbria.

'That Wehrmacht *shmatte* was number one, Harry boy,'
says the democrat Benny, for whom all cloth is *shmatte*, never
mind the quality. 'You can have your best Ascot suit, your
finest quality hunting breeches and the boots. They were

never a patch on our Wehrmacht, not till after Stalingrad when it all went downhill.'

From Germany Benny graduates to Leman Street in the east of London, to set up a sweatshop with his family, four to a room and take the garment industry by storm so that he can go to Vienna and sing opera. Benny is already an anachronism. By the late 'forties most of the tailoring Jews have risen to Stoke Newington and Edgware and are plying less humble trades. Their places have been taken by Indians, Chinese and Pakistanis. Benny is not deterred. Soon the East End is his Lvov and Evering Road the finest street in Europe. And it is in Evering Road a couple of years later – so much Pendel has been allowed to know – that Benny's elder brother Leon joins them with his wife Rachel and their several children, the same Leon who, due to the said explosion, impregnates an eighteen-year-old Irish house-maid who calls the bastard Harry.

*   *   *

Pendel driving to eternity. Following with exhausted eyes the smudged red stars ahead of him, tailgating his own past. Nearly laughing in his sleep. Decision consigned to oblivion while every syllable and cadence of Uncle Benny's anguished monologue is jealously remembered.

*   *   *

'Why Rachel ever let your mother across the threshold I'll never know,' says Benny, with a shake of the Homburg. 'You didn't have to be trained in the scriptures to see she was dynamite. Innocent or virtuous was not the issue. She was a highly nubile, very stupid shicksa on the brink of woman-hood. The slightest shove, she'd be over. It was all written down in advance.'

'What was her name?' Pendel asks.

'Cherry,' sighs his uncle, like a dying man parting with his last secret. 'Short for Cherida, I believe, though I never saw the certificate. She ought to have been Teresa or Bernadette or Carmel but had to be Cherida. Her Dad was a brickie from County Mayo. The Irish were even poorer than we were so we had Irish maids. Us Yids don't like to grow old, Harry boy. Your father was no different. It's the not believing in Heaven that gets us. A lot of time standing in God's long corridor, but for God's main room with all the furbishments we're still waiting, and there's a good few of us doubt it will ever come.' He leans across the iron table and clutches Pendel's hand. 'Harry, listen to me, son. Jews ask forgiveness of man, not God, which is rough on us because man is a harder con than God any day. Harry, I'm looking at you for that forgiveness. Redemption, I can get it on my deathbed. Forgiveness, Harry, it's you who signs the cheque.'

Pendel will give Benny whatever he asks, if only he will go on about the explosion.

'It was the smell of her, your father told me,' Benny resumes. 'Pulling at his hair he was, with the remorse. Sitting before me as you're sitting now except for the uniform. "For the sake of her smell I brought down the temple on my head," he told me. Your father was a religious man, Harry. "She was kneeling at the grate and I smelt the sweet womanhood of her, not soap and scrubbing, Benny, but the natural woman. The smell of her womanhood overcame me." If Rachel hadn't been having a knees-up with the Daughters of Jewish Purity on Southend Pier your father would never have fallen.'

'But he did,' Pendel prompts him.

'Harry, amid the mingled tears of Catholic and Jewish guilt, amid Ave Marias and Oi veys and what-will-become-of-me's on both sides, your father plucked the cherry. See it as an act of God I can't, but the Jewish chutzpah is yours and so is the Irish blarney, if you could only ditch the guilt.'

'How did you get me out of the orphanage?' Pendel demands, nearly shouting now, he cares so much.

Somewhere among his muddy memories of childhood before Benny rescued him there is a picture of a dark-haired woman like Louisa on her hands and knees while she scrubs a stone floor as big as a playground, watched by a statue of a blue-robed Good Shepherd and His Lamb.

* * *

Pendel driving the homeward stretch. Familiar houses long asleep. The stars washed clean by rain. A full moon outside his prison window. Bang me up again, he thinks. Prison's where you go when you don't want to take decisions.

* * *

'Harry, I was magnificent. Those nuns were French snobs and thought I was a gentleman. I wore the full Monty, a grey suit out of the window, a tie selected by your Auntie Ruth, socks to match, the shoes hand-made by Lobb of St James's which was always my indulgence. No swagger, hands to my sides, my Socialism nowhere to be seen.' For Benny amid his myriad accomplishments is a passionate supporter of the Workers' Cause and believer in the Rights of Man. '"Mothers," I say to them, "I promise you this. Little Harry will have the good life if it kills me. Harry shall be our *mitzvah*. You tell me the wise men to take him to and he'll be there on the dot with a white shirt for his instruction. A fee-paying education at the school of your choice I guarantee, the finest music on the gramophone and a home life any orphan child would give his eyes for. Salmon on the table, idealistic conversation, his own room to sleep in, a down mattress." I was on the way up in those days. No more *shmatte* for me, it was all golf clubs and footwear and the palace in Umbria just round the corner. We thought we'd be millionaires in a week.'

'Where was Cherry?'

'Gone, Harry boy, gone,' says Benny dropping his voice for tragedy. 'Your mother fled the coop and who can blame her? One letter from an aunt in County Mayo saying her poor sad Cherry was worn out from all the opportunities the Sisters gave her to wash away her sins.'

'And my father?'

Benny falls back into despair. 'In the soil, son,' he says,

wiping away fresh tears. 'Your father, my brother. Where I should be for making you do what you did. Died of the shame in my opinion, which is what I nearly do every time I look at you here. It was those summer frocks that did for me. There's no more depressing sight on earth than five hundred unsold summer frocks in autumn, as every shlemiel knows. Each day that passed, the insurance policy became a temptation of the devil. I was a slave to convention, is what I was, Harry, and what's worse, I made you carry the torch for me.'

'I'm doing the course,' Pendel tells him to cheer him up as the bell goes. 'I'm going to be the best cutter in the world. Look at this then.' And he shows him a panel of prison cloth that he cadged from stores and cut to measure.

It is on his next visit that Benny in his guilt presents Pendel with a tin-framed icon of the Virgin Mary that he says reminds him of his childhood in Lvov on the days he crept out of the ghetto to watch the goyim pray. And she is with him now, next to the wake-up clock on the rattan table at his bedside in Bethania, watching with her vanished Irish smile as he drags off his sweat-drenched prison uniform and creeps into bed for a share of Louisa's blameless sleep.

Tomorrow, he thought. I'll tell her tomorrow.

*   *   *

'Harry, that you?'

Mickie Abraxas, the great underground revolutionary and secret hero of the students, lucid drunk at two-fifty a.m., swearing to God that he would kill himself because his wife had thrown him out.

'Where are you?' Pendel said, smiling in the dark, because Mickie for all the trouble he caused was a cellmate for life.

'Nowhere. I'm a bum.'

'Mickie.'

'What?'

'Where's Ana?'

Ana was Mickie's reigning *chiquilla*, a sturdy, practical-minded childhood friend of Marta's from la Cordillera who seemed to accept Mickie as found. Marta had introduced them.

'Hi, Harry,' said Ana cheerfully, so Pendel said 'Hi' cheerfully too.

'How much has he had, Ana?'

'I don't know. He says he went to a casino with Rafi Domingo. Did some vodka, lost some money. Maybe did a little coke, he forgets. He's sweating all over. Do I call a doctor?'

Mickie was back on the line before Pendel could answer her.

'Harry, I love you.'

'I know that, Mickie, and I'm grateful, and I love you too.'

'Did you do that horse?'

'I did, Mickie, yes, I have to say I did that horse.'

'I'm sorry, Harry. Okay? I'm sorry.'

'No problem, Mickie. No bones broken. Not every good horse wins.'

'I love you, Harry. You're my good friend, hear me?'

'Then you won't need to kill yourself, will you, Mickie,' said Pendel kindly. 'Not if you've got Ana and a good friend.'

'You know what we do, Harry? We make a weekend together. You, me, Ana, Marta. Go fishing. Fuck.'

'So you have yourself a good night's sleep, Mickie,' said Pendel firmly, 'and tomorrow in the morning you come round for your fitting and a sandwich and we'll have a nice natter. Yes? Right, then.'

'Who was it?' Louisa said as he rang off.

'Mickie. His wife's locked him out of the house again.'

'Why?'

'Because she's having an affair with Rafi Domingo,' said Pendel, wrestling with life's ineluctable logic.

'Why doesn't he punch her in the mouth?'

'Who?' said Pendel stupidly.

'His *wife*, Harry. Who do you think?'

'He's tired,' said Pendel. 'Noriega beat the spirit out of him.'

Hannah climbed into their bed, to be followed by Mark and the giant teddy bear he had given up years ago.

It was tomorrow, so he told her.

I did it to be believed, he told her, when she was safely back to sleep.

To prop you up when you get wobbly.

To give you a real shoulder to lean on, instead of just me.

To make me someone better for a Zonian roughneck's daughter who blurts a bit and goes ballistic when she's threatened and forgets to take short steps after twenty years of being told by her mother that she'd never get married like Emily if she didn't.

And thinks she's too ugly and too tall while everyone around her is the right size and glamorous like Emily.

And who would never in a million years, not even in her most vulnerable and insecure moment, not even to spite Emily, set fire to Uncle Benny's warehouse as a favour to him, starting with the summer frocks.

Pendel sits in the armchair, pulls a coverlet over himself, leaves his bed to the pure in heart.

* * *

'I'll be out all day,' he tells Marta, arriving in the shop next morning. 'You'll have to do front of shop.'

'You've got the Bolivian Ambassador at eleven.'

'Put him off. I need to see you.'

'When?'

'Tonight.'

* * *

Until now they had gone as a family, picnicking in the shade of the mango trees, watching the hawks and ospreys and vultures lazing on the burning breeze and the riders on white horses looking like the last of Pancho Villa's army. Or they'd haul the inflated rubber dinghy across the flooded paddies with Louisa at her happiest as she waded through the water in her shorts playing Katharine Hepburn in *The African Queen* to Pendel's Bogart, and Mark pleading for caution and Hannah telling Mark not to be a drip.

Or they'd drive the four-track down cloudy yellow dust-tracks that stopped dead when they reached the forest's edge, at which point to the huge delight of the kids Pendel would let out one of Uncle Benny's wonderful wails of despair pretending they were lost. Which they were, until the silver towers of the mill rose out of the palm trees fifty yards ahead of them.

Or they'd go at reaping time, ride in pairs on huge tracked harvesters, the flails hanging out in front of them, beating the rice and raising clouds of bugs. Sticky hot air pressed under hard low sky. Table-flat fields fading into mangrove swamps. Mangrove swamps fading into sea.

But today as the Great Decider drove his solitary path everything he saw bothered him, everything was an omen: the I-hate-you razor wire of the American ammunition dumps, reminding him of Louisa's father, the reproachful signs saying 'Jesus is the Lord', the squatters' cardboard villages on every hillside: any day now and I'll be joining you.

And after the squalor, the lost paradise of Pendel's ten-minute childhood. Rolling tracts of red Devon earth from holiday school at Okehampton. English cows that stared at him from banana groves. Not even Haydn on the cassette player could save him from their melancholy. Entering the farm's drive he demanded only to know how long it was since he had told Angel to get these bloody pot-holes fixed. The sight of Angel himself in boned riding boots, straw trilby and gold neck-chains only quickened his anger. They drove to the spot where the corporate neighbour from Miami had cut his trench into Pendel's river.

'You know something, Harry, my friend?'

'What?'

'What that judge did is immoral. Here in Panama when we bribe somebody we expect loyalty. You know what else we expect, my friend?'

'No.'

'We expect a deal to be a deal, Harry. No top-ups. No pressure. No comebacks. I say the guy is antisocial.'

'So what do we do?' Pendel said.

Angel gave the contented shrug of a man whose favourite news is bad.

'You want my advice, Harry? Straight? As your friend?'

They had reached the river. On the opposite bank, the neighbour's henchmen refused to notice Pendel's presence. The trench had become a canal. Below it, the river bed was dry.

'My advice, Harry, is negotiate. Cut your losses, do a deal. You want me to feel these guys out? Start a dialogue with them?'

'No.'

'So go to your banker. Ramón's a tough guy. He'll do the talking for you.'

'How come you know Ramón Rudd?'

'Everybody knows Ramón. Listen, I'm not just your manager, okay? I'm your friend.'

But Pendel has no friends, except for Marta and Mickie, and just possibly Mr Charlie Blüthner who lives ten miles up the coast and is expecting him for chess.

*   *   *

'Blüthner like piano?' Pendel asked the living Benny centuries ago as they stood on the rainswept dockside at Tilbury, studying the rusted freighter that will convey the released convict on the next stage of his life's toil.

'The same, Harry boy, and he owes me,' Benny replied, adding his tears to the rain. 'Charlie Blüthner is the *shmatte* king of Panama and he wouldn't be where he is today if Benny hadn't kept *shtumm* for him just like you did for me.'

'Did you burn his summer frocks for him?'

'Worse, Harry boy. And he's never forgotten.'

For the first and last time in their lives, they embraced. Pendel wept too but wasn't sure why, because all he could think as he trotted up the gangway was: I'm out and I'll never come back.

And Mr Blüthner had been as good as Benny's word. Pendel had scarcely set foot in Panama before the maroon chauffeur-driven Mercedes was whisking him from his pitiful lodgings in Calidonia to the stately Blüthner villa, set in its own manicured acres overlooking the Pacific, with its tiled floors and air-conditioned stables and paintings by Nolde and illuminated testimonials from impressive-sounding, non-existent American universities appointing Mr Blüthner their well-beloved Professor, Doctor, Regent, etc. And an upright piano from the ghetto.

Within weeks Pendel had become in his own eyes Mr Blüthner's cherished son, taking his natural place among the raucous, gingery children and grandchildren, the stately aunts and podgy uncles and the servants in their pastel-green tunics. At family festivals and *Kiddush* Pendel sang badly and nobody minded. He played lousy golf on their private golf course and didn't bother to apologise. He splashed around on the beach with the children and rode the family buggies at breakneck speed over sand-black dunes. He fooled with the sloppy dogs and threw fallen mangoes for them, and watched the squadrons of pelicans crank themselves across the sea, and believed in all of it: their faith, the morality of their wealth, the Bougainvilia, the thousand different greens, and their respectability which far outglowed whatever little blazes Uncle Benny might have started in the days of Mr Blüthner's struggle.

And Mr Blüthner's kindness didn't stop in the home, because when Pendel took his first steps into bespoke tailoring it was Blüthner Compañia Limitada who gave him six months' credit on their huge textile warehouse in Colón, and the Blüthner word that sent him his first customers and opened early doors for him. And when Pendel tried to thank Mr Blüthner, who was small and wrinkled and shiny, he only shook his head and said, 'Thank your Uncle Benny,' adding his habitual advice: 'Find yourself a good Jewish girl, Harry. Don't leave us.'

Even when Pendel married Louisa, his visits to Mr Blüthner did not cease but they acquired a necessary furtiveness. The Blüthner household became his secret paradise, a shrine that he could only ever visit alone and under a pretext. And Mr Blüthner, by way of reciprocation, preferred to ignore Louisa's existence.

* * *

'I've got a bit of a liquidity problem, Mr Blüthner,' Pendel confessed, as they sat over chess on the north verandah. There was a verandah on each side of the headland so that Mr Blüthner could always be protected from the wind.

'Liquidity at the *rice farm?*' Mr Blüthner asked.

His little jaw was made of rock until he smiled, and he wasn't smiling. His old eyes spent a lot of time asleep. They were sleeping now.

'Plus the shop,' said Pendel, blushing.

'You have mortgaged the shop to finance the *rice farm*, Harry?'

'Only in a manner of speaking, Mr Blüthner.' He tried humour. 'So naturally I'm looking for a mad millionaire.'

Mr Blüthner always spent a long time thinking, whether he was playing chess or being asked for money. He sat quite still while he thought, and seemed not to breathe. Pendel remembered old lags who were the same.

'Either a man is mad or he's a millionaire,' Mr Blüthner replied at last. 'Harry boy, it's a law. A man's got to pay for his own dreams.'

* * *

He drove to her nervously, as he always did, by way of 4th July Avenue that had once formed the boundary of the Canal Zone. Low to his left, the bay. High to his right, Ancón Hill. Between them lay the reconstructed El Chorillo with its patch of too-green grassland marking the spot where the *comandancia* had stood. A cluster of gimcrack highrises had been built by way of reparation and painted in pastel bars. Marta lived in the middle one. He climbed the filthy staircase cautiously, remembering how the last time he had come here he had been pissed on from the pitch darkness above him while the building convulsed itself with prison catcalls and wild laughter.

'You are welcome,' she said solemnly, having unlocked the door to him, four locks.

They lay on the bed where they always lay, dressed and separated from each other, Marta's small dry fingers curled in Pendel's palm. There were no chairs, there was very little floor. The flat consisted of one tiny room divided by brown curtains: a cubicle to wash in, another to cook in and this one to lie in. At Pendel's left ear stood a glass case crammed with china animals that had belonged to Marta's mother, and at his stockinged feet a three-foot-high ceramic tiger that her father had given to her mother for their twenty-fifth wedding anniversary three days before they were blown to smithereens. And if Marta had gone with her parents to visit her married sister that night instead of lying in bed nursing her smashed face and beaten body, she would have been blown to smithereens as well, because her sister had lived in the first street to be hit, though today you wouldn't find it: any more than you would find Marta's parents, sister, brother-in-law or six-month-old baby niece or their orange cat called Hemingway. Bodies, rubble and the whole street had been swept into official oblivion.

'I just wish you'd move back to your old place,' he said to her as usual.

'I can't.'

Can't because her parents had lived where this building now stood.

Can't because this was her Panama.

Can't because her heart was with the dead.

They spoke little, preferring to contemplate the monstrous secret history that joined them:

A young, idealistic, beautiful female employee has been taking part in a public demonstration against the tyrant. She arrives at her place of work breathless and afraid. Come evening, her employer offers to drive her home with the undoubted aim of becoming her lover, because in the tension of recent weeks they have become irresistible to each other. The dream of a better Panama is like the dream of a shared life together, and even Marta agrees that only the Yanquis can cure the mess the Yanquis have created, and that the Yanquis must act soon. On the way, they are stopped at a roadblock by Dingbats who wish to know why Marta is wearing a white shirt, which is the symbol of resistance to Noriega. Receiving no satisfactory explanation, they obliterate her face. Pendel lays the freely-bleeding Marta in the back of his car and drives in blind panic and at breakneck speed to the university – Mickie is a student too in those days – and by a miracle finds him in the library, and Mickie is the only person Pendel can think of who is safe. Mickie knows a doctor, calls him, threatens, bribes him. Mickie drives Pendel's four-track, Pendel sits in the back with Marta's head bleeding all over his lap, soaking his trousers and messing up the family upholstery for ever. The doctor does his worst, Pendel informs Marta's parents, gives money, showers and changes clothes at the shop, goes home by cab to Louisa and for three days is prevented by guilt and fear from telling her what has happened, preferring to regale her instead with a cock-and-bull story about some idiot driving into the side of the four-track, total write-off, Lou, have to get a whole new one, I've spoken to the insurance boys, doesn't seem to be a problem. Not till day five does he find the courage to explain deprecatingly that Marta got herself mixed up in a student riot, Lou, facial injuries, long recuperation necessary, I've promised to take her back when she's recovered.

'Oh,' says Louisa.

'And Mickie's gone to prison,' he goes on inconsequentially, omitting to add that the craven doctor has informed on him, and would have informed on Pendel also, if he had only known his name.

'Oh,' says Louisa a second time.

*　　　*　　　*

'Reason only functions when the emotions are involved,' Marta announced, holding Pendel's fingers to her lips and kissing each in turn.

117

'What does that mean?'

'I read it. You seem to be puzzling about something. I thought it might be useful.'

'Reason is supposed to be logical,' he objected.

'There's no logic unless the emotions are involved. You want to do something, so you do it. That's logical. You want to do something and don't do it, that's a breakdown of reason.'

'I suppose that's true then, isn't it?' said Pendel, who distrusted all abstracts except his own. 'I must say, those books do give you the lingo, then, don't they? Proper little professor you sound like, and you haven't even taken your exams.'

She never pressed him, which was why he was not afraid to come to her. She seemed to know that he never spoke the truth to anyone, that he kept it all inside himself for politeness. The little he told her was therefore precious to them both.

'How's Osnard?' she asked.

'How should he be?'

'Why does he think he owns you?'

'He knows things,' Pendel replied.

'Things about you?'

'Yes.'

'Do I know them?'

'I don't think so.'

'Are they bad things?'

'Yes.'

'I'll do whatever you want. I'll help you, whatever it is. You want me to kill him, I'll kill him and go to jail.'

'For the other Panama?'

'For you.'

*   *   *

Ramón Rudd had shares in a casino in the Old City and liked to go there to relax. They perched on a plush bench looking down on bare-shouldered women and puffy-eyed croupiers seated at empty roulette tables.

118

'I'm going to pay off the debt, Ramón,' Pendel told him. 'The principal, the interest, the lot. I'm going to wipe the slate clean.'

'What with?'

'Let's say I've met a mad millionaire.'

Ramón sucked some lemon juice through a straw.

'I'm going to buy your farm from you, Ramón. It's too small to make money and you're not there for the farming. You're there to rip me off.'

Rudd examined himself in the mirror and was unmoved by what he saw.

'Have you got another business going somewhere? Something I don't know about?'

'I only wish I had, Ramón.'

'Something unofficial?'

'Nothing unofficial either, Ramón.'

'Because if you have, I need a piece of it. I lend you money, so you tell me what your business is. That's morality. That's fair.'

'I'm not in a moral mood tonight, Ramón, to be frank.'

Rudd considered this and it seemed to make him unhappy.

'You've got a mad millionaire so you pay me three thousand an acre,' he said, citing another immutable moral law.

Pendel got him down to two thousand and went home.

*   *   *

Hannah had a temperature.

Mark wanted best of three at ping-pong.

The clothes-washing maid was pregnant again.

The floor-mopper was complaining that the gardener had propositioned her.

The gardener was insisting that at seventy he was entitled to proposition whomever he damn well chose.

The saintly Ernesto Delgado had arrived home from Tokyo.

Entering his shop next morning, Harry Pendel glumly inspects his lines, starting with his Cuna finishing hands, proceeding to his Italian trouser-makers, his Chinese coat-makers and ending with Señora Esmeralda, an elderly mulatto lady with red hair who does nothing but make waist-coats from dawn till dusk and is content. As a great commander on the eve of battle he exchanges a comforting word with each of them, except that the comfort is for Pendel because his troops are not in need of it. Today is payday and they are in jolly mood. Locking himself in his cutting room, Pendel unrolls two metres of brown paper onto the table, props his open notebook on its wooden stand and, to the melodious lament of Alfred Deller, begins delicately sketching the contours for the first of Andrew Osnard's two alpaca suits by Messrs Pendel & Braithwaite Co., Limitada, Tailors to Royalty, formerly of Savile Row.

The Mature Man of Affairs, the Great Weigher of Arguments and Cool Assessor of Situations is voting with his shears.

CHAPTER SEVEN

Ambassador Maltby's mirthless announcement that a Mister Andrew *Osnard* – was that some sort of bird? he rather wondered – would shortly be added to the strength of the British Embassy in Panama struck disbelief then apprehension into the good heart of the Head of Chancery, Nigel Stormont.

Any normal Ambassador would have taken his Head of Chancery aside, of course. Courtesy alone required it: 'Oh, Nigel, I thought you should be the first to know...' But after a year of one another they had passed the stage where courtesy could be taken for granted. And anyway Maltby prided himself on his droll little surprises. So he held back the news until his Monday morning Ambassadorial meeting, which Stormont privately regarded as the low point of every working week.

His audience of one beautiful woman and three men including Stormont sat before his desk in a crescent of chrome chairs. Maltby faced them like the creature of a larger, poorer race. He was late forties and six feet three, with a mangy black forelock, a First Class Honours degree in something useless and a permanent smirk that should never be mistaken for a smile. Whenever his gaze settled on the beautiful woman, you knew it would like to be there all the time and didn't dare, for no sooner had it settled than it darted shamefully away to the wall and only the smirk remained. The jacket of his suit hung over the back of his chair and the dandruff on it twinkled in the morning sun. His taste in shirts was flamboyant and this morning he was nineteen stripes wide. Or so reckoned Stormont, who hated the ground he loped on.

*   *   *

If Maltby did not conform with the imposing image of British officialdom abroad, neither did his Embassy. No wrought-iron gates, no gilded porticos or grand staircases to instil humility in lesser breeds without the law. No eighteenth-century portraits of great men in sashes. Maltby's patch of Imperial Britain was suspended quarter of the way up a skyscraper owned by Panama's biggest law firm and crowned with the insignia of a Swiss bank.

The Embassy's front door was of bulletproof steel lined with a veneer of English oak. You attained it by touching a button in a silent lift. The royal crest, in this air-conditioned stillness, suggested silicone and funeral parlours. The windows like the doors had been toughened to frustrate the Irish and tinted to frustrate the sun. Not a whisper of the real world penetrated. The silent traffic, cranes, shipping, old town and new town, the brigade of women in orange tunics gathering leaves along the central reservation of the Avenida Balboa, were mere specimens in Her Majesty's inspection chamber. From the moment you set foot in British extra-territorial airspace, you were looking in, not out.

*   *   *

The meeting had discussed, in short order, Panama's chances of becoming a signatory to the North American Free Trade Agreement (negligible in Stormont's view), Panama's relations with Cuba (seedy trade alliances, Stormont reckoned, mostly drug-related) and the impact of the Guatemalan elections on the Panamanian political psyche (nil, as Stormont had already advised Department). Maltby had dwelt – as he invariably did – on the rebarbative topic of the Canal; on the omnipresence of the Japanese; and of Mainland Chinese disguised as representatives of Hong Kong; and on certain bizarre rumours in the Panamanian press of a Franco-Peruvian consortium that proposed to buy up the Canal with the aid of French know-how and Colombian drug money. And it was somewhere around this point, most likely, that Stormont, partly out of boredom and partly in self-defence, drifted off into a troubled review of his life till now:

Stormont, Nigel, born too long ago, educated not very well at Shrewsbury and Jesus, Oxford. Second in History like everybody else, divorced like everybody else: except that my little escapade happened to make the Sunday newspapers. Married finally to Paddy, short for Patricia, peerless ex-wife of *cher collègue* at British Embassy, Madrid, after he tried to immolate me with a silver wassail bowl at the All Ranks Christmas party; and currently serving a three-year sentence in Sing Sing, Panama, local population 2.6 million, quarter of it unemployed, half of it below the poverty line. Personnel undecided what to do with me after this, if anything at all apart from chuck me on the scrap heap, see their crabbed reply of yesterday to mine of six weeks ago. And Paddy's cough a continuing anxiety – when will those bloody doctors find a cure for it?

'Why can't it be a wicked *British* consortium for a change?' Maltby was complaining in a thin voice delivered mostly through the nose. 'I'd *adore* to be at the centre of a fiendish British plot. I never have. Have you, Fran?'

The beautiful Francesca Deane smiled blandly and said, 'Alas.'

'Alas *yes?*'

'Alas no.'

Maltby was not the only man Francesca drove mad. Half Panama was after her. A body to kill for, the brains to go with it. One of those creamy blond English complexions that Latin men go crazy over. Stormont would catch sight of her at parties, surrounded by Panama's most eligible studs, every one of them begging for a date with her. But by eleven she'd be home in bed with a book, and next morning at nine sitting at her desk wearing her legal black powersuit and no make-up, all set for another day in Paradise.

'Don't you think a *terrifically* secret British bid to turn the Canal into a trout farm would be fun, Gully?' Maltby asked with elephantine facetiousness of the tiny, immaculately rigged Lieutenant Gulliver RN, retired, the Embassy's Procurement Officer. 'Baby fish in the Miraflores locks, bigger chaps in the Pedro Miguel, grown-ups in Gatún Lake? *I* think it's a marvellous idea.'

Gully let out a boisterous laugh. Procurement was the last of his concerns. His job was to offload as many British weapons as he could on anybody with enough drug money to pay for them, landmines a speciality.

'Marvellous idea, Ambass, marvellous,' he boomed with his habitual messroom heartiness, pulling a spotted handkerchief from his sleeve and vigorously dusting his nose with it. 'Bagged a jolly good salmon over the weekend, by the by. Twenty-two pounder. Had to drive two hours to catch the bugger, but worth every mile.'

Gulliver had taken part in the Falklands Thing and won a gong for it. Since when, so far as Stormont knew, he had never left this side of the Atlantic. Occasionally when he was drunk he would raise a glass to 'a certain patient little lady across the pond' and heave a sigh. But it was a sigh of gratitude rather than deprival.

*   *   *

'*Political* Officer?' Stormont echoed.

He must have spoken louder than he realised. Perhaps he had nodded off. After sitting up with Paddy all night, he wouldn't be surprised.

'*I'm* the *Political* Officer, Ambassador. Chancery's the *political* section. Why isn't he being posted to Chancery where he belongs? Tell 'em no. Dig your toes in.'

'I'm afraid one couldn't possibly tell them anything of

the sort, Nigel. It's a done thing,' Maltby replied. His donn-
ish neigh set Stormont's teeth on edge every time. 'Within
parameters, of course. One did fax a guarded objection to
Personnel. Open-line stuff, one can't say much. The cost of
coded signals these days is astronomic. All those machines
and clever women, I suppose.' His smirk gave way to another
downtrodden smile for Francesca. 'But one fights one's
corner, naturally. Their response very much as you'd expect.
Sympathetic to one's point of view but unyielding. Which in
a way one can understand. After all, if one were in Personnel
Department oneself, that's how one would respond. I mean
they've no more choice than we have, have they? Given the
circumstances.'

It was the word 'circumstances' attached as a postscript
that provided Stormont with his first hint of the truth, but
young Simon Pitt got in ahead of him. Simon was tall and
flaxen and impish and wore a pony tail which Maltby's
imperious wife had vainly ordered him to cut off. He was a
new entrant, currently responsible for everything nobody
else wanted: Visas, Information, Embassy computers on the
blink, local British nationals and points below.

'Perhaps he could take over some of my stuff, sir,' he
volunteered cheekily, one hand draped aloft to make the
bid. 'How about "Dreams of Albion" for openers?' he
added, referring to a touring collection of early English
watercolours presently rotting in a Panamanian Customs
shed to the shrill despair of the British Council in London.

Maltby picked his words with even more than his customary fastidiousness. 'No, Simon, I'm afraid I *don't* think he'll
be able to take over "Dreams of Albion", thank you,' he
replied, selecting a paper clip with his spidery fingers and
unfolding it while he deliberated. 'Osnard's not strictly
speaking one of *us*, you see. Rather more one of *them*, if you
follow me.'

Even then, amazingly, Stormont failed to take the obvious
inference. 'I'm sorry, Ambassador, I don't read you. One of
whom? Is he a contract man or something?' A frightful
thought struck him. 'He's not drafted from industry, is he?'

Maltby bestowed a forbearing sigh on his paper clip. 'No,

Nigel, he is not, so far as I know, drafted from industry. He *may* be drafted from industry. I don't *know* that he is not. I know nothing about his past and very little about his present. His future is also a closed book to me. He's a Friend. Not, I hasten to say, a real friend, although we shall all naturally live in hopes that he may in due course become one. One of *those* friends. Now do you follow me?'

He paused, allowing time for simpler minds to catch him up.

'He's from across the *park*, Nigel. Well, river now. They've moved, one hears. What was a park is now a river.'

Stormont had found his tongue. 'You mean the Friends are opening up a Station? Here in Panama? They can't be.'

'How interesting. Why not?'

'They left. They pulled out. When the Cold War ended they shut up shop and left the field to the Americans. There's a product-sharing deal, conditional on them keeping their distance. I sit on the joint committee that supervises the traffic.'

'And so you do, Nigel. With distinction, if I may say so.'

'So what's changed?'

'Circumstance, one assumes. The Cold War ended so the Friends went away. Now the Cold War is coming back and the Americans are going away. I'm only guessing, Nigel. I don't *know*. Any more than you do. They asked for their old slot. Our Masters decided to give it them.'

'How many?'

'One at present. No doubt if they're successful they'll ask for more. Perhaps we shall see the return of those heady days when the principal function of the Diplomatic Service was to provide cover for their activities.'

'Have the Americans been told?'

'No, and they're not to be. Osnard is to remain undeclared to anyone except ourselves.'

Stormont was digesting this when Francesca broke the silence. Fran was practical. Too practical sometimes.

'Will he work here in the Embassy? Physically, I mean.'

Maltby had a different voice for Francesca, as well as a different face. It hovered between instruction and caress.

'Indeed, yes, Fran. Physically and otherwise.'

'Will he have staff?'

'We are asked to make provision for one assistant, Fran.'

'Male or female?'

'To be determined. Not, one assumes, by the person selected, but these days one can't be sure.' Snigger.

'What's his rank?' Simon Pitt this time.

'Do the Friends have ranks, Simon? How amusing. I always see their condition as a rank of its own. Don't you? There's all of *us*. And after us, there's all of *them*. Presumably they see it differently. He's an Etonian. Odd, the things the Office tells one and the things it doesn't. Still we mustn't pre-judge him.'

Maltby had been educated at Harrow.

'Does he speak Spanish?' Francesca was back.

'Fluently, we are told, Fran. But I never see languages as a guarantee of anything, do you? A man who can make a fool of himself in three languages strikes me as a three-times-bigger fool than a man who is confined to one.'

'When does he arrive?' Stormont again.

'Friday the thirteenth, appropriately. That is to say, the thirteenth is the date on which I am *told* he will arrive.'

'That's eight days from now,' Stormont protested.

The Ambassador craned his long neck towards a calendar portraying the Queen in a feathered hat. 'Is it? Well, well. I suppose it is.'

'Is he married?' asked Simon Pitt.

'Not that one is aware of, Simon.'

'Meaning no?' – Stormont again.

'Meaning that I have not been informed that he is, and since he has asked for bachelor accommodation I assume that, whatever he has, he will come without it.'

Flinging out his arms to either side of him, Maltby folded them carefully in half until his hands came to rest behind his head. His gestures, though bizarre, were seldom without meaning. This one denoted that the meeting was about to close for golf.

'It's a full-term appointment, by the way, Nigel, not a temporary thing. Unless he gets thrown out, of course,' he added, brightening slightly. 'Fran. Dear. The Office is becoming testy about that draft memorandum we discussed. Could you possibly burn some midnight oil or is it all spoken for?'

And the wolfish smile again, as sad as old age.

*　　*　　*

'Ambassador.'

'Why, Nigel. How nice.'

It was quarter of an hour later. Maltby was putting papers into his safe. Stormont had caught him alone. Maltby was not pleased.

'What's Osnard supposed to be covering? They must have told you. You can't have given him a blank cheque.'

Maltby closed his safe, set the combination, cranked himself to his full height and glanced at his watch.

'Oh, I think I pretty much did. What's the point of not? They'll take what they want anyway. It isn't the Foreign Office's fault. Osnard's sponsored by some grand inter-ministerial body. One can't possibly resist.'

'Called what?'

'Planning & Application. It never occurred to me we were capable of either function.'

'Who heads them?'

'Nobody. I asked the same question. Personnel gave me the same answer. I should take him and be grateful. So should you.'

*　　*　　*

Nigel Stormont sat in his room, sifting incoming correspondence. In his day he had earned himself a name for coolness under pressure. When scandal broke over him in Madrid, his deportment was grudgingly held to be exemplary. It also saved his skin, for when Stormont submitted his obligatory letter of resignation, the Head of Personnel was all for accepting it until Higher Authority stayed his hand.

'Well, well. The cat with nine lives,' Personnel had murmured, from the depths of his great dark palace in the former India Office, not so much shaking Stormont's hand as noting its particulars for future treatment. 'So it's not the dole for you after all. It's Panama. Poor you. Enjoy Maltby. I'm sure you will. And we'll talk about you in a year or two, won't we? Something to look forward to.'

When Personnel buried the hatchet, said the wits in the Third Room, he took compass-bearings on the grave.

*   *   *

Andrew Osnard, Stormont repeated to himself. Bird. A brace of osnards flew over. Gully's just shot an osnard. Very funny. A Friend. One of *those* friends. A bachelor. A Spanish-speaker. A full-term sentence unless he gets remission for bad behaviour. Rank unknown, everything unknown. Our new Political Officer. Sponsored by a body that doesn't exist. A done thing, arriving in one week with unsexed assistant. Arriving to do what? To whom? To replace whom? One Nigel Stormont? He was not being fanciful, he was being realistic, even if Paddy's cough was stretching his nerves.

Five years ago it was unthinkable that some faceless upstart from the wrong side of the park, trained to hang around street corners and steam open mail, would be considered a suitable replacement for a pure-bred foreign servant of Stormont's class. But that was before the days of Treasury streamlining and the trumpeted recruitment of outside managerial skills to drag the Foreign Service by the scruff of the neck into the twenty-first century.

God, how he loathed this government. Little England, plc. Directed by a team of lying tenth-raters not fit to run an amusement arcade in Clacton-on-Sea. Conservatives who would strip the country of its last lightbulb to conserve their power. Who thought the Civil Service a luxury as expendable as world survival or the nation's health, and the Foreign Service the most expendable luxury of the lot. No. In the present climate of quack remedies and quick fixes, it was not at all unthinkable that the post of Head of Chancery,

Panama, should be voted redundant, and Nigel Stormont with it.

Why should we duplicate? he could hear the quangos of Planning & Application squawking from their one-day-a-week, thirty-five-thousand-a-year thrones. *Why have one chap doing the posh work and another chap doing the dirty work? Why not put both jobs under one hat? Fly the Osnard bird in. And as soon as he's got the lie of the land, fly the Stormont bird out. Save a job! Rationalise a post! And we'll all go out to lunch on the taxpayer.*

Personnel would love it. So would Maltby.

*　　*　　*

Stormont drifted round his room, poking at shelves. *Who's Who* contained not a single Osnard. Neither did *Debrett's*. Neither, he assumed, did *Birds of Britain*. The London telephone directory passed from Osmotherly to Osner without drawing breath. But it was four years old. He flipped through a couple of old Foreign Office redbooks, searching the Spanish-speaking embassies for a sign of former Osnard incarnations. None spotted. Not settled, not in flight. He looked up Planning & Application in the Whitehall Directory. Maltby was right. No such body existed. He called Reg the administration officer to discuss the vexed issue of the leak in the roof of his hiring.

'Poor Paddy's having to chase round the spare bedroom with pudding basins every time it rains, Reg,' he complained. 'And it rains a hell of a lot.'

Reg was locally employed and lived with a Panamanian hairdresser called Gladys. Nobody had met Gladys, and Stormont suspected she was a boy. For the fifteenth time they went over the history of the bankrupt contractor, the pending law suit and the unhelpful attitude of the Panamanian Protocol department.

'Reg, what are we doing about office space for Mr Osnard? Should we be discussing it?'

'I don't know what we should be discussing and what

we shouldn't, Nigel. I've been taking my orders from the Ambassador, haven't I?'

'And what orders has His Excellency been pleased to issue?'

'It's the east corridor, Nigel. All of it. It's brand new locks for his steel door, they came by courier yesterday, Mr Osnard to bring his own keys. It's steel cupboards in the old visitors' waiting room for his papers, combinations to be set by Mr Osnard on arrival, no record to be taken, as if we would. And I'm to make sure he's got lots and lots of points for his electronics. He's not a cook, is he?'

'I don't know what he is, Reg, but I'll bet you do.'

'Well, he sounds very nice on the telephone, Nigel, I will say. Like the BBC but human.'

'What do you talk about?'

'Number one was his car. He wants a hire car till he gets his own, so I'm to hire him one and he's sent me a fax of his driver's licence.'

'Say what sort?'

Reg giggled. 'Not a Lamborghini, he said, and not a three-wheeler. Something he could wear a bowler hat in if he wore a bowler hat because he's tall.'

'What else?'

'His flat, how soon we'd have it ready for him. We found him ever such a nice one, if I can get those decorators out in time. High up above the Club Unión, I told him. You can spit on their blue rinses and their toupees any time you like. It's only a lick of paint I'm asking. White, I said to him, broken to the colour of your choice, so what's your choice? Not pink, thank you, he says, and not daffodil. How about a nice warm camel-turd brown? I had to laugh.'

'How old is he, Reg?'

'My goodness, I've not a notion. He could be anything, really.'

'Still, you've got his driving licence there, haven't you?'

'*Andrew Julian Osnard,*' Reg read aloud, very excited. '*Date of Birth 01 10 1970 Watford.* Well I never, that's where my Mum and Dad got married.'

*   *   *

Stormont was standing in the corridor, drawing himself a coffee from the machine when young Simon Pitt sidled up to him and offered him a spy's eyeline of a passport photograph cupped into the hollow of his palm.

'What do you say, Nigel? Carruthers of the Great Game or an overweight Mata Hari in drag?'

The photograph was of a well-nourished Osnard with both ears showing, sent in advance so that Simon could arrange to have his diplomatic pass prepared by Panamanian Protocol in time for his arrival. Stormont stared at it and for a moment his whole private world seemed to slide out of his control: his ex-wife's alimony, too large but he'd insisted that she have it, Claire's university maintenance, Adrian's ambition to read for the Bar, his secret dream of finding a stone farmhouse on a hillside in the Algarve with its own olives and winter sun and dry air for Paddy's cough. And a full pension to make the fantasy come true.

'Looks a nice enough chap,' he conceded, as his innate decency asserted itself. 'Quite a lot behind the eyes. Could be fun.'

Paddy's right, he thought. I shouldn't have sat up the night with her. I should have got some sleep of my own.

*   *   *

On Mondays, by way of consolation after morning prayers, Stormont lunched at the Pavo Real with Yves Legrand, his opposite number at the French Embassy because they both loved a duel and good food.

'Oh, and by the way, we're getting a new man at last, I'm pleased to say,' said Stormont, after Legrand had entrusted him with a couple of confidences that were nothing of the kind. 'Young chap. Your sort of age. On the political side.'

'Will I like him?'

'Everyone will,' said Stormont firmly.

*   *   *

Stormont was scarcely back at his desk when Fran rang him on the internal telephone.

'Nigel. The most amazing thing. Can you guess what?'

'I don't expect so.'

'You know my *weird* half-brother Miles?'

'Not personally, but he is a concept to me.'

'Well, you know Miles was at Eton, obviously.'

'No, but I know now.'

'Well it's Miles' birthday today so I rang him. Can you believe, he was in the same house as Andy Osnard! He says he's absolutely *sweet*, a bit tubby, a bit *murky*, but frightfully good in the school play. And he was sacked for venery.'

'For *what?*'

'Girls, Nigel. Remember? Venus. It can't have been boys or that would be Adonery. Miles says it *may* have been for not paying his fees as well. He can't remember who got him first, whether it was Venus or the Bursar.'

In the lift Stormont met Gulliver carrying a briefcase and looking grave.

'Serious matters afoot tonight, Gully?'

'A mite *tricky*, this one, Nigel. A mite softly-softly-catchee-monkey frankly.'

'Well, watch yourself,' Stormont advised him, with appropriate gravity.

Gulliver had recently been sighted by one of Phoebe Maltby's bridge wives on the arm of a gorgeous Panamanian girl. She was twenty if a day, said the bridge wife, and *darling*, black as your hat. Phoebe proposed to warn her husband at an appropriate moment.

*   *   *

Paddy had gone to bed. Stormont could hear her coughing as he went upstairs.

Sounds as though I'll be going to the Schoenbergs alone, he thought. The Schoenbergs were American and civilised.

Elsie was a heavy-duty lawyer who kept flying back to Miami to fight dramatic court cases. Paul was CIA and one of the people who mustn't know that Andrew Osnard was a Friend.

CHAPTER EIGHT

'Pendel. To see the President.'

'Who?'

'His tailor. Me.'

The Palace of Herons stands at the heart of the Old City on a spit of land across the bay from Punta Paitilla. To drive to it from the other side of the bay is to be whisked from a developers' inferno to the filth and elegance of seventeenth-century colonial Spain. It is surrounded by appalling slums, but a careful selection of the route eliminates their existence. This morning, in front of the ancient porch, a ceremonial brass band played Strauss to a row of empty diplomatic cars and parked police motorcycles. The bandsmen wore white helmets and white uniforms, white gloves. Their instruments glistened like white gold. Torrents of rain flowed down their necks from the inadequate awning stretched above them. The double doors were guarded by bad charcoal suits.

Other white-gloved hands took Pendel's suitcase and passed it through an electronic scanner. He was beckoned to a scaffold. Standing on it he wondered whether spies in Panama were shot or hanged. The gloved hands returned the suitcase. The scaffold declared him harmless. The great secret agent had been admitted to the citadel.

'This way, please,' said a tall black god.

'I know,' said Pendel proudly.

A marble fountain played at the centre of a marble floor. Milk-white herons strutted in the spray, pecking at whatever caught their fancy. From floor-level cages in the wall more herons scowled at passers-by. And well they might, thought Pendel, remembering the story that Hannah insisted on hearing several times a week. In 1977 when Jimmy Carter came to Panama to ratify the new Canal Treaties, secret service men sprayed the Palace with a disinfectant that preserved presidents but killed herons. In a top-secret emergency operation the corpses were removed and live lookalikes flown down from Chitré under cover of darkness.

'Your name, please?'

'Pendel.'

'Your business, please?'

He waited, remembering railway stations when he was a child: too many big people hurrying past him in too many directions, and his suitcase always in the way. A kind lady was addressing him. Turning to her, he thought it must be Marta because of her beautiful voice. Then light fell across her face and it wasn't smashed, and he saw by the label on her Brownie suit that she was a presidential virgin named Helen.

'It is heavy?' she asked.

'Light as a feather,' he assured her courteously, rejecting her virginal hand.

Following her up the great stairs, Pendel exchanged the radiance of marble for the deep red dark of mahogany. More bad suits with earphones eyed him from pillared doorways. The virgin was telling him he had chosen a busy day.

'Whenever the President comes back we are *always* busy,' she said, raising her eyes to Heaven where she lived.

Ask about his missing hours in Hong Kong, Osnard had said. *Hell d'he get up to in Paris? Man screwing or conspiring?*

'As far as here, we are under Colombian rule,' the virgin was informing him, pointing her blameless hand at rows of early Panamanian governors. 'From here on, we are under the United States. Soon we shall be under ourselves.'

'Great,' said Pendel enthusiastically. 'High time too.'

They entered a panelled hall like a library without books. A honey smell of floor polish rose at him. A beeper sounded on the virgin's belt. He was alone.

Whole gaps in his itinerary. Find out about his missing hours.

*   *   *

And remained alone, and upright, clutching his suitcase. The yellow-covered chairs round the walls were too flimsy for a mere convict to sit on. Imagine breaking one. Bang goes remission. Days turn to weeks but if there's one thing Harry Pendel knows, it's how to do time. He'll stand here for the rest of his life if he must, suitcase in hand, waiting for them to call his name.

A great pair of doors was flung open behind him. A shaft of sunlight burst into the room, accompanied by a tattoo of busy footsteps and male voices of authority. Careful to make no disrespectful movement, Pendel sidled beneath a fat-faced governor from our Colombian period and druckened himself until he became a wall encumbered by a suitcase.

The approaching posse was a dozen strong and polyglot. Excited snatches of Spanish, Japanese and English resounded above the clatter of impatient shoes on parquet. The posse moved at politician speed: much bustle and circumstance, chattering like school kids freed from detention. Uniform was dark suits, the tone self-congratulatory, the formation, Pendel noticed as it thundered closer, arrowhead. And at its point, elevated a foot or two above the ground, floated a larger-than-lifesize embodiment of the Sun King himself, the All Pervading, the Shining One, the Divine Misser of Hours, dressed in a P & B black jacket, striped trousers and a pair of Ducker's black calf town with the toecaps.

A roseate glow, part-sanctity and part-gastronomy, suffused the presidential cheeks. The full head of hair was silvered, the lips were small and pink and moist, as if newly snatched from the maternal breast. The neat cornflower eyes were shining in the afterglow of conference achieved. Reaching Pendel, the posse pulled to a ragged halt and there was business and a bit of shoving in the ranks as some kind of order was pragmatically arrived at. His Sublimity strode forward, turned on his heel and faced his guests. An aide labelled Marco placed himself at his master's side. A virgin in Brownie costume joined them. Her name was not Helen but Juanita.

One by one the guests ventured forward to shake the Immortal One's hand and take their leave. His Radiance had a word of encouragement for each. If there had been gift-wrapped favours to take home to their mummies, Pendel would not have been surprised. Meanwhile the great spy is torturing himself with fears about the contents of his suit-case. What if the finishing hands have packed the wrong suit? He sees himself drawing back the lid to reveal Hannah's Bo-Peep costume that the Cuna women have run up for Carlita Rudd's fancy-dress birthday party: flowered bell skirt, frilly hat, blue pantaloons. He longs to take a reassuring look, but dare not. The farewells continued. Two of the guests, being Japanese, were small. The President was not. Some handshakes took place on the slope.

'It's a deal, then. Golf on Saturday,' His Supremacy promised, in the grey monotone so beloved of his children. A Japanese gentleman was promptly convulsed with laughter.

Other fortunates were singled out – 'Marcel, thank you for your support, we shall meet again in Paris then! Paris in the spring! – Don Pablo, be sure to give my greetings to your distinguished President and tell him I shall value the opinion of his National Bank –' until the last of the group had departed, the doors closed, the shaft of light vanished and there was no one in the room but His Immensity, one suave aide named Marco and the virgin named Juanita. And one wall with a suitcase.

Together, the trio turned and advanced down the room with the Sun King at its centre. Its destination was the presidential sanctum. The doors to it were not three feet from where Pendel stood. He hoisted a smile and, suitcase in hand, took a step forward. The silvered head lifted and turned in his direction, but the cornflower eyes saw only wall. The trio swept past him, the sanctum doors closed. Marco returned.

'Are you the tailor?'

'I am indeed, Señor Marco, and at His Excellency's service.'

'Wait.'

Pendel waited, as must all who only stand and serve. Years passed. The doors opened again.

'Make haste,' Marco ordered.

Ask about his missing hours in Paris, Tokyo and Hong Kong.

*   *   *

A carved gold screen has been erected in one corner of the room. Gilded gesso bows adorn each fretted corner. Gold roses tumble down the staves. Backlit by the window, His Transparency stands regally before it in his black jacket and striped trousers. The presidential palm is as soft as an old lady's but larger. Making contact with its silken cushions, Pendel has a memory of his Auntie Ruth chopping chicken for the Sunday soup while Benny sings 'Celeste Aida' at the upright piano.

'Welcome back, sir, after your arduous tour,' Pendel murmurs through a chicane of glottal obstructions.

But it is uncertain whether the World's Greatest Leader receives the full force of this strangled greeting because Marco has handed him a cordless red telephone and he is already speaking into it.

'Franco? Don't bother me with that stuff. Tell her she needs a lawyer. See you at the reception tonight. Catch my ear.'

Marco removes the red telephone. Pendel opens his suitcase. Not a Bo-Peep costume but a half-made tail suit with discreetly reinforced breast panels to bear the weight of twenty orders sleeps safely in its scented tissue coffin. The virgin makes a silent exit as the Master of the Earth takes up his post behind the gold screen with its mirrored interior.

It is an ancient artefact of the Palace. The silver head so beloved of its people vanishes and reappears as the presidential trousers are removed.

'If His Excellency would be so kind,' Pendel murmurs.

A presidential hand appears round the side of the gold screen. Pendel lays the basted black trousers over the presidential forearm. Arm and trousers disappear. More phones ring. *Ask about his missing hours.*

'It's the Spanish Ambassador, Excellency,' Marco calls from the desk. 'Wants a private audience.'

'Tell him tomorrow night after the Taiwanese.'

Pendel stands face to face with the Lord of the Universe: the Grand Master of Panama's political chessboard, the man who holds the keys to one of the world's two greatest gateways, determines the future of world trade and the balance of global power in the twenty-first century. Pendel inserts two fingers inside the presidential waistband while Marco announces another caller, one Manuel.

'Tell him Wednesday,' the President retorts over the top of the screen.

'Morning or afternoon?'

'Afternoon,' the President replies.

The presidential waistline is elusive. If the crotch is right, the trouser-length is wrong. Pendel raises the waist. The trousers rise above the presidential silk sockline, so that for a moment he looks like Charlie Chaplin.

'Manuel says afternoon is okay as long as it's only nine holes,' Marco warns his master severely.

Suddenly nothing stirs. What Pendel described to Osnard as a blessed truce amid the fray has descended over the sanctum. Nobody speaks. Not Marco, not the President nor his many telephones. The great spy is kneeling, pinning the presidential left trouser leg, but his wits do not desert him.

'And may I enquire of His Excellency with respect whether we were able to relax during our highly triumphant Far Eastern tour at all, sir? Some sport perhaps? A walk? A little shopping, if I may make so bold?'

And still no phone rings, nothing disturbs the blessed

truce while the Keeper of the Keys to Global Power considers his reply.

'Too tight,' he announces. 'You make me too tight, Mr Braithwaite. Why won't you let your President breathe, you tailors?'

*   *   *

'"Harry," he says to me, "those parks they've got in Paris, I'd do the same for Panama tomorrow if it wasn't for the property developers and the Communists."'

'Wait.' Osnard turned a page of his notebook, writing hard.

They were on the fourth floor of a three-hour hotel called the Paraiso in a bustling part of town. Across the road, an illuminated Coca-Cola sign turned off and on, now flooding the room with red flames, now leaving it in darkness. From the corridor came the stampede of arriving and departing couples. Through the adjoining walls, groans of chagrin or delight and the accelerating thump of eager bodies.

'He didn't say,' said Pendel cautiously. 'Not in as many words.'

'Don't paraphrase, mind? Just give it me the way he said it.' Osnard licked a thumb and turned a page.

Pendel was seeing Dr Johnson's summerhouse on Hampstead Heath, the day he went there with Auntie Ruth for the azaleas.

'"Harry," he says to me, "that park in Paris, I wish I could remember its name. There was a little hut there with a wood roof, just us and the bodyguards and the ducks." The President loves his Nature. "And it was there in that hut that history was made. And one day, if all goes according to plan, there'll be a plaque on the wooden wall telling the world that on this very spot the future prosperity, wellbeing and independence of the fledgling state of Panama was determined, plus the date."'

'Say who he was talking to? Japs, Frogs, Chinese? Didn't just sit there and talk to the flowers, did he?'

'Not as such, Andy. There were clues.'

'Give 'em to me –' licking his thumb again, a small slurp.

' "Harry, you'll have to protect me on this one, but the brilliance of the oriental mind is a total revelation to me, plus the French aren't far behind." '

'Say what kind of oriental?'

'Not as such.'

'Japanese? Chinese? Malaysian?'

'Andy, I fear you are trying to put thoughts into my head which were not there before.'

No sound except for the shriek of traffic, the clank and heave of air-conditioners, the canned music to drown the clank and heave. Latin voices yelling above the music. Osnard's ballpoint speeding over the pages of his notebook.

'And Marco didn't like you?'

'He never did, Andy.'

'Why not?'

'Palace courtiers don't like Turco tailors enjoying one-to-one pow-wows with their bosses, Andy. They don't like, "Marco, Mr Pendel and I haven't spoken for an age and we've got a lot to catch up with, so be a good lad and go and stand the other side of that mahogany door till I give you a shout –" do they?'

'Is he a poof?'

'Not so far as my knowledge extends, Andy, but I haven't asked him and it's not my business.'

'Take him out to dinner. Show him a time, give him a cut rate on a suit. Sounds like the sort o' chap we ought to have on our side. Anything about traditional anti-American feeling raising its head among the Japs?'

'Zero, Andy.'

'Japs as the world's next superpower?'

'No, Andy.'

'Natural leader o' the emerging industrial states? – still no? Jap–American animosity? – Panama's got to choose between the Devil and the Deep Blue Sea? – Pres feels like the ham in the sandwich – that type o' thing? – no?'

'Nothing above the normal in that regard, Andy, not on Japan, no. Well, there was just the one reference, Andy, now that it comes back to me.'

Osnard brightened.

'"Harry," he says to me, "all I pray is, that I never never *never* again have to sit down in a room with Japs one side of the table and Yanks the other because keeping the peace between them puts years onto my life, as you can see from my poor grey hairs," although I'm not sure that hair's all his own, to be frank. I think it's helped.'

'Chatty, was he?'

'Andy, it was pouring out of him. Once he's got that screen round him there's no holding him. And if he ever gets onto Panama as all the world's pawn, it's the morning gone.'

'How about his missing hours in Tokyo?'

Pendel was shaking his head. Gravely. 'I'm sorry, Andy. There we have to draw a veil,' he said, and turned his head towards the window in stoical refusal.

*   *   *

Osnard's pen had stopped in mid-caress. The Coca-Cola sign across the road switched him on and off.

'Hell's the matter with you?' he demanded.

'He's my third President, Andy,' Pendel replied to the window.

'So?'

'So I won't do it. I can't.'

'Can't do what, fuck's sake?'

'Reconcile it with my conscience. Grass.'

'Are you out o' your mind? This is gold-dust, man. We're talking major, major bonus. Tell me what Pres said to you about his missing Japanese hours while he was trying on his bloody knickers!'

It took Pendel much heart-searching to overcome his reticence. But he managed it. His shoulders fell, he loosened, his gaze returned to the room.

'"Harry," he says to me, "if your customers ever ask you why I had such a light schedule in Tokyo, you're please to tell them that while my wife was inspecting a silk factory with the Empress I was having myself my first ever piece of

Japanese tail" – which is not an expression I would use, Andy, as you know, neither in the shop, nor in the home – "because in that way, Harry, my friend," he says to me, "you will raise my stock in certain circles here in Panama, while putting other elements off the scent regarding the real nature of my activities and the highly secret talks I was conducting on the side, for the ultimate good of Panama despite what many may think."'

'Hell did he mean by that?'

'He was referring to certain threats that have been made against his person and suppressed in order not to alarm the public.'

'His *words*, Harry ol' boy, mind? Sound like the bloody *Guardian* on a wet Monday.'

Pendel was serene.

'There were no *words*, Andy. Not as such. *Words* were not needed.'

'Explain,' said Osnard while he wrote.

'The President wishes a special pocket inside the left breast of all his suits, to be added in total confidence. I'm to get the length of barrel from Marco. "Harry," he says, "don't think I'm being dramatic and never tell it to a living person. What I'm doing for the new emerging infant state of Panama which I love will cost me blood. I'm saying no more."'

From the street below, the jackass laughter of drunks rose at them like mockery.

'One king-sized bonus assured,' Osnard said, closing his notebook. 'What's the latest on Brother Abraxas!'

*   *   *

The same stage, a different setting. Osnard had found a flimsy bedroom chair and was sitting astride it with his podgy thighs spread and the backrest rising from his crotch.

'They're hard to define, Andy,' Pendel warned, pacing, hands behind his back.

'Who are, ol' boy?'

'The Silent Opposition.'

144

'I'll say they are.'

'They're holding their cards close to their chests.'

'Hell for? Democracy, isn't it? Why keep mum? Why not get up on their soapboxes, call out the students? Hell are they being silent *about*?'

'Let's just say Noriega taught them a sanitary lesson and they're not going to take the next one lying down. Nobody's ever going to put Mickie in prison again.'

'Mickie's their leader. Right?'

'Morally and practically, Mickie is their leader, Andy, though he'll never admit it and neither will his silent supporters, neither will his students that he's in touch with or his people on the other side of the bridge.'

'And Rafi stakes them.'

'All the way.' Pendel turned back into the room.

Osnard pulled his notebook from his lap, propped it on the back of the chair, resumed his writing. 'List o' members anywhere? Got a platform? Set o' principles? What bonds 'em?'

'They're for cleaning up the country, one.' Pendel paused to let Osnard write. He was hearing Marta, loving her. He was seeing Mickie, sober and reconstructed in a new suit. His breast was filling with loyal pride. 'They're for furthering Panama's identity as a single fledgling democracy when our American friends have finally upped sticks and left the scene if they ever do which is always doubtful, two. They're for educating the poor and needy, hospitals, improved university grants and a better deal for the poor farmers, rice and shrimp particularly, plus not selling off the country's assets to the highest bidder irregardless, including the Canal, three.'

'Lefties, are they?' Osnard suggested between bouts of composition while he sucked the plastic helmet of his ballpoint with his little rosebud mouth.

'Not more than is decent and healthy, thank you, Andy. Mickie is left-leaning, true. But moderation is his watchword plus he's got no time for Castro's Cuba or the Coms, no more has Marta.'

Osnard grimacing in concentration while he wrote. Pendel watching him with growing apprehension, wondering how to slow him down.

'I've heard quite a good joke about Mickie, if you want to know. He's *in vino veritas* but upside down. The more he drinks, the more he keeps silent in his opposition.'

'Tells you a whole lot when he's sober, though, doesn't he, our Mickie? You could hang him, some o' the stuff he's told you.'

'He's a friend, Andy. I don't hang my friends.'

'A *good* friend. And you've been a *good friend* to him. Maybe it's time you did something about it.'

'Like what?'

'Signing him up. Making an honest joe out o'him. Putting him on the payroll.'

'*Mickie?*'

'Not such a big deal. Tell him you've met this well-heeled Western philanthropist who admires his cause and would like to lend him a helping hand on the q.t. Don't have to say he's a Brit. Say he's a Yank.'

'*Mickie*, Andy?' Pendel whispered incredulously. ' "Mickie, would you like to be a spy?" Me go to Mickie and say that to him?'

'For money, why not? Fat man, fat salary,' Osnard said, as if stating an irrefutable law of espionage.

'Mickie wouldn't care for a Yank one bit,' said Pendel, wrestling with the enormity of Osnard's proposal. 'The invasion got right under his skin. State terrorism is how he calls it, and he's not referring to Panama.'

Osnard was using the chair as a rocking horse, coaxing it back and forth with his ample buttocks.

'London's taken a shine to you, Harry. Doesn't always happen. Want you to spread your wings. Put a fullscale network together, cover the board. Ministries, students, trade unions, National Assembly, Presidential Palace, Canal and more Canal. They'll pay you responsibility allowance, incentives, generous bonuses plus increased salary to set against your loan. Get Abraxas and his group aboard, we're home free.'

'*We*, Andy?'

146

Osnard's head remained gyroscopically still while the rump of him went on rocking, his voice sounded louder on account of being lowered.

'Me at your side. Guide, philosopher, chum. Can't handle it all alone. No one can. Too big a job.'

'I appreciate that, Andy. I respect it.'

'They'll pay subsources too. Goes without saying. Many as you've got. We could make a killing. You could. Long as it's cost effective. Hell's your problem?'

'I haven't got one, Andy.'

'So?'

So Mickie's my friend, he was thinking. Mickie's opposed enough already and he doesn't need to oppose any more. Silently or otherwise.

'I'll have to think about it, Andy.'

'Nobody pays us to think, Harry.'

'All the same, Andy, it's who I am.'

There was one more subject on Osnard's agenda for that evening but Pendel didn't grasp this at first because he was remembering a warder called Friendly who was a master of the six-inch elbow jab to the balls. That's who you remind me of, he was thinking. Friendly.

* * *

'Thursday's the day Louisa brings work home, right?'

'Thursdays is correct, Andy.'

Dismounting thigh by thigh from his rocking horse, Osnard fished in a pocket and extracted an ornate gold-plated cigarette lighter.

'Present from a rich Arab customer,' he said, handing it to Pendel where he stood at the centre of the room. 'London's pride. Try it.'

Pendel pressed the lever and it lit. He released the lever and the flame went out. He repeated the operation twice. Osnard took back the lighter, fondled its underparts, returned it.

'Now take a squiz through the lens,' he ordered with a magician's pride.

Marta's tiny flat had become Pendel's decompression chamber between Osnard and Bethania. She lay beside him, her face turned away from him. Sometimes she did that.

'So what are your students up to these days?' he asked her, addressing her long back.

'*My* students?'

'The boys and girls you and Mickie used to run with in the bad times. All those bomb-throwers you were in love with.'

'I wasn't in love with them. I loved you.'

'What happened to them? Where are they now?'

'They got rich. Stopped being students. Went into the Chase Manhattan. Joined the Club Unión.'

'Do you see any of them?'

'They wave at me from their expensive cars sometimes.'

'Do they care about Panama?'

'Not if they bank abroad.'

'So who makes the bombs these days?'

'No one.'

'I get a feeling sometimes there's a sort of Silent Opposition brewing. Starting at the top and trickling down. One of those middle-class revolutions that will flare up one day and take over the country when nobody's expecting it. An officers' putsch without officers, if you get me.'

'No,' she said.

'No what?'

'No, there is no Silent Opposition. There is profit. There is corruption. There is power. There are rich people and desperate people. There are apathetic people.' Her learned voice again. The meticulous bookish tone. The pedantry of the self-educated. 'There are people so poor they can't get poorer without dying. And there's politics. And politics is the biggest swindle of them all. Is this for Mr Osnard?'

'It would be if it was what he wanted to hear.'

Her hand found his and guided it to her lips and for a while she kissed it, finger by finger, saying nothing.

'Does he pay you a lot?' she asked.

'I can't supply him with what he wants. I don't know enough.'

'Nobody knows enough. Thirty people decide what will happen in Panama. The other two and a half million guess.'

'So what would your old student friends be doing if they *hadn't* joined the Chase Manhattan and *weren't* driving shiny cars?' Pendel insisted. 'What would they be doing if they'd stayed militant? What's logical? Given it's today, and they still wanted what they used to want for Panama?'

She pondered, coming slowly to what he was saying. 'You mean, to put pressure on the government? Bring it to its knees?'

'Yes.'

'First we produce chaos. You want chaos?'

'I might. If it's necessary.'

'It is. Chaos is a precondition of democratic awareness. Once the workers discover they are unled, they will elect leaders from their own ranks and the government will be scared of revolution and resign. You wish the workers to elect their own leaders?'

'I'd like them to elect Mickie,' said Pendel but she shook her head.

'Not Mickie.'

'All right, without Mickie.'

'We would go first to the fishermen. It was what we always planned but never did.'

'Why would you go to the fishermen?'

'We were students opposed to nuclear weapons. We were indignant that nuclear materials were passing through the Panama Canal. We believed such cargoes were dangerous to Panama and an insult to our national sovereignty.'

'What could the fishermen do about it?'

'We would go to their unions and their gang bosses. If they refused us, we would go to the criminal elements on the waterfront who are willing to do anything for money. Some of our students were rich in those days. Rich students with a conscience.'

'Like Mickie,' Pendel reminded her, but again she shook her head.

'We would say to them: "Get out every trawler and smack and dinghy that you can lay your hands on, load them up with food and water and take them to the Bridge of the Americas. Anchor them under the bridge and announce to the world that you mean to stay there. Many of the big cargo ships need a mile to slow down. After three days there will be two hundred ships waiting to pass through the Canal. After two weeks, a thousand. Thousands more will be turned away before they reach Panama, ordered to take different routes or go back to where they came from. There will be a crisis, the stock exchanges of the world will panic, the Yanquies will go crazy, the shipping industry will demand action, the balboa will collapse, the government will fail and no nuclear materials will ever again pass through the Canal.'

'I wasn't thinking about nuclear materials, to be honest, Marta.'

She raised herself on one elbow, her smashed face close to his.

'Listen. Panama today is already trying to prove to the world that it can run the Canal as well as the gringos. Nothing must interfere with the Canal. No strikes, no interruptions, no inefficiencies, no screw-ups. If the Panamanian government can't keep the Canal working properly, how can it steal the revenue, raise tariffs, sell off the concessions? The moment the international banking community starts to take fright, the *rabiblancos* will give us everything we ask. And we shall ask for *everything*. For our schools, our roads, our hospitals, our farmers and our poor. If they try to clear away our boats or shoot us or bribe us, we shall appeal to the nine thousand Panamanian workmen that it takes to run the Canal each day. And we shall ask them: which side of the bridge do you stand? Are you Panamanian men, or are you Yanqui slaves? Strikes are a sacred right in Panama. Those who oppose them are pariahs. There are people in government today who argue that the labour laws of Panama should not apply to the Canal. Let them see.'

She was lying flat upon him, her brown eyes so close to his that they were all he saw.

'Thank you,' he said, kissing her.

'My pleasure.'

CHAPTER NINE

Louisa Pendel loved her husband with an intensity understood only by women who have known what it is like to have
been born into the pampered captivity of bigoted parents,
and to have a beautiful elder sister four inches shorter than
you who does everything right two years before you do it
wrong, who seduces your boyfriends even if she doesn't go
to bed with them, though usually she does, and obliges you
to take the path of Noble Puritanism as the only available
response.

She loved him for his steady devotion to herself and to
the children, for being a striver like her father, and for
rebuilding a fine old English firm that everyone had given
up for dead, and for making chicken soup and *lockshen* on
Sundays in his striped apron, and for his *kibitzing*, which
meant his joking around, and for setting the table for their
special meals together, the best silver and china, cloth nap-
kins, never paper. And for putting up with the tantrums
which ran in her like conflicting impulses of hereditary electricity, there was nothing she could do about them till they
were safely over, or he had made love to her, which was by
far the best solution, since she had all her sister's appetites,
even if she lacked the looks and amorality to indulge them.
And she was deeply ashamed that she could never match

his jokes or give him the freed laughter he craved, because even with Harry to liberate it, her laughter still sounded like her mother's and so did her prayers, and her anger felt like her father's.

She loved the victim in Harry, and the determined survivor who had endured any privation rather than fall in with his wicked Uncle Benny and his criminal ways until the great Mr Braithwaite came along to save him, just as Harry himself had later come along to save her from her parents and the Zone, and provide her with a new, free, decent life away from everything that till then had held her down. And she loved him as the lonely decider, struggling with conflicting beliefs until Braithwaite's wise counsel led him to a non-denominational morality so like the Cooperative Christianity championed by her mother and preached throughout Louisa's childhood from the pulpit of the Union Church in Balboa.

For all these mercies she thanked God and Harry Pendel, and cursed her sister Emily. Louisa honestly believed she loved her husband in all his moods and varieties, but she had never known him like this and she was sick with terror.

*　　*　　*

If he would only hit her, if that was what he needed to do. If he would lash out, bawl at her, drag her into the garden where the children couldn't hear and say: 'Louisa, we're all washed up, I'm leaving you, I've got someone else.' If that was what he had. Anything, absolutely anything, was better than the bland pretence that their life together was fine, nothing had changed, except that he just had to pop out and measure a valued customer at nine o'clock at night and come back three hours later saying wasn't it time they had the Delgados to dinner? And why not have the Oakleys and Rafi Domingo as well? Which, as any fool in the world could have seen at a glance, was a recipe for catastrophe, but somehow the gap that had recently formed between herself and Harry didn't let her say this to him.

So Louisa held her tongue and duly invited Ernesto. One evening as he was on the point of going home she pressed the envelope into his hand and he took it cursorily, thinking it must be a reminder of some sort, Ernesto was such a dreamer and schemer, so wrapped up in his daily struggle against the lobbyists and intriguers that sometimes he hardly knew which hemisphere he was in, let alone what time of day it was. But next morning when he arrived he was courtesy itself, a real Spanish gentleman as always, and yes, he and his wife would be delighted, so long as Louisa would not be offended if they left early, Isabel his wife was concerned about their small son Jorge and his eye infection, sometimes he didn't seem to sleep at all.

After that she sent a card to Rafi Domingo, knowing that his wife wouldn't come because she never did, it was that sort of lousy marriage. And next day sure enough a huge bouquet of roses arrived, like fifty dollars' worth, with a racehorse on the card and Rafi saying in his own handwriting that he would be thrilled and enchanted, darling Louisa, but alas his wife would be somewhere or other. And Louisa knew exactly what the flowers meant because no woman under eighty was safe from Rafi's advances, the gossip said he had given up underpants in order to improve his time and motion ratio. And the shameful thing was, if Louisa was truthful with herself, which largely after a couple or three vodkas she was, she found him disconcertingly attractive. So finally she called Donna Oakley, a chore she had deliberately left till last, and Donna said, 'Oh shit, Louisa, we'd *love* to,' which was Donna's level exactly. What a group.

The dreaded day arrived and Harry came home early for once, armed with a pair of three hundred dollar porcelain candlesticks from Ludwig's, and French champagne from Motta's and a whole side of smoked salmon from somewhere else. And an hour later a team of fancy caterers showed up, led by a cocksure Argentine gigolo, and took over Louisa's kitchen because Harry said their own servants weren't reliable. Then Hannah raised a God-awful stink for no reason Louisa could fathom – aren't you going to be nice to Mr Delgado, darling? After all he's Mummy's boss and a close friend of the President of Panama. *And* he's going to save the Canal for us, and yes, Anytime Island too. And *no*, Mark, thank you, this is not an occasion for you to play 'Lazy Sheep' on your violin, Mr and Mrs Delgado might appreciate it but the other guests would not.

Then in walks Harry and says, oh Louisa, go on, let him play it, but Louisa is adamant, and gets into one of her monologues, they just pour out of her, she can't control them, she can only listen to them and groan: Harry, I do not understand why every time I give an instruction to my children you have to march in here and countermand it just to show you are master of the house. At which Hannah throws another screaming fit and Mark locks himself in his room and plays 'Lazy Sheep' non-stop till Louisa beats on his door and says, 'Mark, they'll be here *any minute*,' which was true because the doorbell rang just at that moment and in marches Rafi Domingo with his body lotion and his insinuating leer and sideburns and crocodile shoes – not all of Harry's tailoring wiles could save him from looking like the worst kind of stage dago, her father would have ordered him round to the back door on the strength of his hair oil alone.

And immediately after Rafi, enter the Delgados and the Oakleys all in short order, which proved just how unnatural the occasion was, because in Panama *nobody* shows up on time unless it's a stiff occasion, and suddenly it was all happening, with Ernesto sitting on her right side looking like the wise, good mandarin he was: just water, thank you, Louisa dear, I'm afraid I'm not much of a drinker, to which Louisa, who is by now the better for a couple of large ones taken in the privacy of her bathroom says to be truthful neither is she, she always thinks drink spoils a nice evening. But Mrs Delgado down the table on Harry's right overhears this and gives an odd, disbelieving smile as if she has heard better.

Meanwhile Rafi Domingo on Louisa's left is dividing his

time between clamping his stockinged foot on Louisa's whenever she lets him – he has slipped off one crocodile shoe for the purpose – and squinting down the front of Donna Oakley's dress which is cut on the lines of Emily's dresses, breasts pushed up like tennis balls and the cleavage pointing due southward to what her father when he was drunk had called the industrial area.

'You know what she means to me, your wife, Harry?' Rafi asks in mouthfuls of execrable Spanish-English, down the table to Harry. Lingua franca is English tonight for the Oakleys' benefit.

'Don't listen to him,' Louisa orders.

'She's my conscience!' Huge laugh with all his teeth and food showing. 'And I didn't know I got one till Louisa come along!'

And finds this so wonderfully funny that everybody has to toast his conscience while he cranes his neck for another helping of Donna's décolletage and wiggles his toes up and down Louisa's calf, which makes her furious and randy at the same time, Emily I hate you, Rafi leave me alone you sleazeball and take your eyes off Donna, and Jesus, Harry, are you finally going to fuck me tonight?

*   *   *

Why Harry had invited the Oakleys was another mystery to Louisa until she remembered that Kevin was floating some sort of speculation to do with the Canal, Kevin being something in commodities and otherwise what her father used to call a damned Yankee hustler, while his wife Donna worked out to Jane Fonda videos and jogged in vinyl shorts and wiggled her ass at every pretty Panamanian boy who pushed her trolley for her in the supermarket, and from all she heard not just her trolley.

And Harry from the first moment they sat down had been determined to talk about the Canal, first picking on Delgado who responded with dignified patrician platitudes, then pressing everybody else into the discussion whether or not they had anything to contribute. His questions of Delgado were so crude she was embarrassed. Only Rafi's roaming foot and the recognition that she was a tad over-sedated prevented her from telling him: *Harry, Mr Delgado is my fucking boss not yours. So why are you making such a horse's ass of yourself, you prick?* But that was Whore Emily talking, not Virtuous Louisa who never swore, or not in front of the children and never when she was sober.

No, Delgado replied politely to Harry's bombardment, nothing had been agreed during the presidential tour, but some interesting ideas had been put forward, Harry, there was a general spirit of cooperation, goodwill was of the essence.

Well done, Ernesto, thought Louisa, tell him where he gets off.

'Still I mean everyone knows those Japs are *after* the Canal, don't they, Ernie?' said Harry, branching into inane generalisations that he hadn't the knowledge to sustain. 'The only question is which way they're going to come at us, I don't know what *you* think, Rafi, at all?'

Rafi's silk stocking toes were jammed into the flesh of Louisa's knee joint and Donna's cleavage was opening like a barn door.

'I tell you what I think about Japs, Harry. You want to know what I think about Japs?' said Rafi in his rattly, auctioneer's voice, as he gathered in his audience.

'I would indeed,' said Harry unctuously.

But Rafi needed everyone.

'Ernesto, you want to know what I think about Japs?'

Delgado graciously expressed an interest in hearing what Rafi thought about the Japanese.

'Donna, you want to hear what I think about the Japs?'

'Just say it, for Christ's sake, Rafi,' Oakley said irritably.

But Rafi was still gathering them in.

'Louisa?' he asked wiggling his toes behind her knee.

'I guess we're all hanging on your words, Rafi,' said Louisa in her rôle of charming hostess and whore-sister.

So Rafi finally delivered himself of his opinion of the Japanese:

'I think those Jap bastards inject my horse Dolce Vita a

double dose valium before the big race last week!' he cried, and laughed so loudly at his own joke, to the glint of so many gold teeth, that his audience of necessity laughed with him, Louisa loudest and Donna after her by a short head.

But Harry was not put off. Instead, he launched himself on the subject that he knew upset his wife more than any other: the disposal of the former Canal Zone itself.

'I mean we've got to face it, Ernie, it's a nice little piece of real estate that you boys are carving up. Five hundred square miles of garden America, mown and watered like Central Park, more swimming pools than in the whole of the rest of Panama – it does make you *wonder*, doesn't it? I don't know whether the City of Knowledge idea is still a starter, Ernie? Some of my customers seem to think it's a bit of a dead duck, frankly, a university in the middle of a jungle. It's hard to imagine a learned professor seeing that as the summit of his career, I don't know if they're right.'

He was running low but nobody helped him out, so he forged on:

'I suppose it all depends on how many US military bases are going to be left vacant at the end of the day, doesn't it? Which requires the assistance of a crystal ball by all accounts. We'd have to tap the highly secret wires to the Pentagon, I dare say, to know the answer to *that* little conundrum.'

'It's bullshit,' said Kevin loudly. 'The smart boys have had the land all carved up among themselves for years, right, Ernie?'

A frightful emptiness set in. Delgado's fine face turned pale and stony. Nobody could think of anything to say except for Rafi who, indifferent to all atmosphere, was cheerfully interrogating Donna about the make-up she was wearing so that he could have his wife buy some. He was also trying to get his foot between Louisa's legs, which she had crossed in self-defence. Then suddenly Emily the Shrew found the words that Louisa the Immaculate was piously holding back and they came spilling out of her, first in a series of jerky statements of record, then in an unstoppable, alcohol-induced rush.

'Kevin. I do not understand what you are implying. Dr

Delgado is a champion of Canal conservation. If you are not aware of this, it is because Ernesto is too courteous and modest to tell you. You, on the other hand, are here in Panama with the sole intention of making money out of the Canal, a purpose for which it was not designed. The only way to make money out of the Canal is ruin it.' Her voice began sliding as she counted off the crimes that Kevin was contemplating. 'By cutting down the forests, Kevin. By depriving it of fresh water. By failing to maintain its structure and machinery to the standards required by our forefathers.' Her voice became harsh and nasal. She could hear it but not stop it. 'And so, Kevin, if you truly feel impelled to make money by selling off the achievements of great Americans, I suggest you go right back to San Francisco where you came from and sell the Golden Gate to the Japs. And Rafi, if you don't take your hand off my thigh I'm going to stick a fork in your knuckles.'

At which everybody seemed to decide they really ought to be getting back – to the ailing child, to the babysitter, to the dog, to whatever they had that was a safe distance from where they were right now.

*   *   *

But what does Harry do when he has soothed his guests, escorted them to their cars and waved goodbye to them from the doorstep? Deliver a Statement to the Board.

'It's expansion, Lou' – patting her back while he hugs her – 'that's all it is. Massaging the customers' – dabbing away her tears with his Irish linen handkerchief – 'It's expand or die, Lou, is what it is these days. Look what happened to dear old Arthur Braithwaite. First his business went, then he did. You wouldn't want that to happen to *me*, would you? So we expand. We open the Club. We socialise. We put ourselves about, because it's got to be. Eh, Lou? Right?'

But by now his patronising attentions have hardened her and she pulls free of him.

'Harry, there are other ways of dying. I wish you to think

about your family. I know of too many cases, and so do you, where men of forty have suffered heart attacks and other stress-related maladies. If your shop is not expanding I'm surprised since I recall a lot of stories recently of increased sales and output. But if you are truly worried about the future and not just using it as a pretext, we have the rice farm to fall back on and we would surely all prefer to live in reduced circumstances practising Christian abstinence than try to keep pace with your rich, immoral friends and have you die on us.'

At which Pendel grasps her to him in a fiery bearhug and promises to be home really early tomorrow – maybe take the kids to the funfair, do a movie. And Louisa cries and says, oh yes, let's do it, Harry! Really let's. But they don't. Because when tomorrow comes he remembers the reception for the Brazilian Trade Delegation – lot of important players, Lou – why don't we do it tomorrow instead? And when *that* tomorrow comes, I'm a liar, Lou, there's this dinner club I've gone and got myself elected to. They're throwing a jamboree for some heavy-hitters down from Mexico and did I see you had the new *Spillway* on your desk?

Spillway being the Canal newsletter.

*   *   *

And on Monday came the usual weekly phone call from Naomi. Louisa could tell at once from Naomi's voice that she had momentous news. She wondered what it was going to be this time. Guess who Pepe Kleeber took on his business trip to Houston last week, perhaps. Or, have you *heard* about Jaqui Lopez and her riding instructor? Or, who do you *think* Dolores Rodríguez goes to visit with when she tells her husband she's comforting her mother after her bypass operation? But this time Naomi didn't come on with any of that stuff, which was as well, because Louisa was of a mind to hang up if she did. Naomi just needed to catch up with all the lovely Pendels, and how was Mark making out with his exam work, and was it true Harry was buying Hannah her first pony? It was? Louisa, Harry is just the most generous man on earth, my wicked husband should take lessons from him! Not until, between them, they had painted a treacly picture of the entire deliriously happy Pendel family did Louisa realise that Naomi was commiserating with her:

'I'm so *proud* for you, Louisa. I'm proud you're all healthy, and the kids are progressing, and you love each other, and that God is kind to you and Harry appreciates what he has. And I'm *very* proud that I knew right off that what Letti Hortensas just told me about Harry could not *possibly* be true.'

Louisa remained frozen to the telephone, too scared to speak or ring off. Letti Hortensas, heiress and slut, wife of Alfonso. Alfonso Hortensas, Letti's husband, brothel owner, P & B customer and crook.

'Sure,' Louisa said, not knowing what she was agreeing to, except that by assenting to anything at all she was saying 'go on'.

'You and I know very well, Louisa, that Harry is not a person to visit some seedy downtown hotel where you pay by the hour. "Letti, dear," I said. "I think it's time you bought yourself a new pair of eye-glasses. Louisa is my friend. Harry and I have a long platonic friendship going way back which Louisa has always known about and understood. That marriage is built on *rock*," I told her. "It makes no difference your husband owns the Hotel Paraiso or you were sitting in the lobby waiting for him when Harry stepped out of the elevator with a bunch of whores. A lot of Panamanian women look like whores. A lot of whores do their business at the Paraiso. Harry has many customers from many walks of life." I want you to know I was loyal to you, Louisa. I supported you. I scotched the rumour. "Shifty?" I said to her. "Harry *never* looks shifty. He wouldn't know how. Have *you* ever seen Harry looking shifty? Of *course* you haven't."'

It took a long while for the feeling to return to Louisa's body. She was into serious denial. Her outburst at the dinner party had scared her stiff.

'Bitch!' she screamed through her tears.

But not till she had rung off and poured herself a large vodka from Harry's newly instated hospitality chest.

*   *   *

It was the new clubroom that had started it, she was convinced. The top floor of P & B had for years been the subject of Harry's most visionary fantasies.

I'm going to put the fitting room under the balcony, Lou, he used to say. I'm putting the Sportsman's Corner next to the boutique. Or: maybe I'll leave the fitting room where it is and put up an outside staircase. Or: I've got it, Lou! Listen. I'm going to throw out a cantilevered extension at the back, install a health club and sauna, open a small restaurant, P & B customers only, soup and catch of the day, how's that?

Harry had even had a model made and done the initial costing by the time that plan too was shelved. Thus the top floor had till now been a perennial armchair voyage that was enjoyed only in the planning. And anyway – where would the fitting room go? The answer, it turned out, was nowhere. The fitting room would stay right where it was. But the Sportsman's Corner, Harry's pride, would be squashed into Marta's glass box.

'So where will Marta go?' Louisa asked, half-hoping with the shameful side of her that go meant just that, because there were things about Marta's injuries that Louisa had never understood. Harry's sense of being responsible for them for instance, but then Harry felt responsible for everyone, it was part of what she loved about him. Things he let slip. Things he knew about. Radical students and how the poor lived in El Chorillo. And there was something about the power Marta could exert over him that was a little too like Louisa's own.

I'm jealous of everyone, she thought, fixing herself an essential dry martini cocktail to get her off the vodka. I'm jealous of Harry, I'm jealous of my sister and of my children. I'm practically jealous of myself.

*   *   *

And now the books. On China. On Japan. On the Tigers,

as he called them. Nine volumes in all. She counted. They had arrived without warning by night on the table in his den, and stayed there ever since, a silent, sinister, occupying army. Japan down the ages. Its economy. The rise and rise of the yen. From Empire to Imperial Democracy. South Korea. Its demography, economy and constitution. Malaysia, its past and future rôle in world affairs, collected essays of great scholars. Its traditions, language, lifestyle, destiny, cautious marriage of industrial convenience with China. China, whither Communism? The corruption of the Chinese oligarchy after Mao, human rights, the population time bomb, what's to be done? It's time I educated myself, Lou. I feel stuck. Old Braithwaite was right as usual. I should have gone to university. In Kuala Lumpur? In Tokyo? In Seoul? They're the coming places, Lou. They're the next century's superpowers, you'll see. Ten years from now, they'll be my only customers.

*　　*　　*

'Harry, I wish you please to define profit to me' – mustering the last of her courage – 'Who pays for the cold beers and the Scotches and wine and sandwiches and Marta's over-time? Do your customers buy suits from you because they keep you up talking and drinking until eleven o'clock? Harry, I do not understand you any more.'

She was going to throw the Hotel Paraiso at him as well but her courage had run dry and she needed another vodka from the top shelf in the bathroom. She couldn't see Harry very clearly and she suspected it was the same for him. There was a film of hot mist across her eyes and what she saw in place of Harry was herself made older by a lot of grief and vodka, standing here in the drawing room after he had walked out on her, and watching the children wave goodbye to her through the window of the four-track because it was Harry's turn to have them for the weekend.

'I'm going to make it all right for us, Lou,' he promised, patting her shoulder to console the invalid.

So what was wrong that had to be made right? And how the fuck did he propose to correct it?

*　　　*　　　*

Who was driving him? *What* was? If she was not enough for him, who was getting the rest of him? Who was Harry being, one minute pretending she didn't exist, the next showering her with gifts and going to ridiculous lengths to please the children? Putting himself about town as if his life depended on it? Accepting invitations from people he used to avoid like poison, except as customers – grubby tycoons like Rafi, politicians, entrepreneurs from the drug fringe? Pontificating about the Canal? Creeping out of the Hotel Paraiso with an elevatorload of hookers late at night? But the darkest episode of all was last night's.

It was a Thursday and on Thursdays she brought work home in order to be sure of clearing her office desk on Friday and having the weekend free for family. She had left her father's briefcase on her desk in her den, thinking she might grab an hour between putting the children to bed and cooking supper. But then she had a sudden intimation that the steaks had Mad Cow Disease, so she drove down the hill to get a chicken. Returning, she discovered to her pleasure that Harry had come back early: there was his four-track, crookedly parked as usual and no space in the garage for the Peugeot, so she had to leave it way down the hill, which she did willingly, and trudge back up the sidewalk with the shopping.

She was wearing sneakers. The house door was unlocked. Harry at his most forgetful. I'll surprise him, tease him about his parking. She stepped into the hall, and through the open doorway of her den she saw him standing with his back to her and her father's briefcase *open* on *her desk*. He had taken all the papers out of it and was flipping through them like someone who knows what he is looking for and isn't finding it. A couple of the files, confidential. Personal reports on people. A draft paper by a newly-joined member of Delgado's staff on services that could be provided for ships awaiting transit. Delgado was worried because the author had recently formed his own chandlering company and might therefore be trying to push contracts in its direction. Maybe Louisa would look it over and give him her opinion?

'*Harry,*' she said.

Or perhaps she yelled. But when you yell at Harry he doesn't jump. He just puts down whatever he's doing and waits for further orders. Which is what he did now: froze, then very slowly, so as not to alarm anybody, laid *her* papers on *her* desk. Then stepped one pace back from the desk and hunched himself in that self-effacing way he had, eyes on the ground six feet in front of him while he smiled a Librium smile.

'It's that bill, dear,' he explained in an under-dog voice.

'What bill?'

'You remember. From the Einstein Institute. Mark's extra music. The one they say they sent us and we haven't paid.'

'Harry, I paid that bill last week.'

'Now that's what I told them, you see. Louisa paid last week. She never forgets, I said. They wouldn't listen.'

'Harry, we have bank statements, we have cheque stubs, we have receipts, we have a bank that we can call and we have cash in the house. I do not understand why you have to ransack *my* briefcase in *my den* in search of a bill we have already paid.'

'Yes, well as long as we have, I won't bother, will I? Thank you for the information.'

And acting injured, or whatever he thought he was acting, he walked past her to his own den. And as he crossed the courtyard she saw him slip something into his trousers pocket and realised it was the revolting cigarette lighter that he had taken to carrying around with him these days – a present from a customer, he had said, waving it in her face, flicking it off and on for her, proud as a child with his new toy.

Then she panicked. Vision slipping, ears jangling, knees no good. Smell of burning, the children's sweat running down her own body, the whole scene. She saw El Chorillo in flames, and Harry's face as he came back into the house from the balcony, and the oily red light still glowing in his eyes. She saw him coming over to where she was cringing in the broom cupboard. And embracing her. Embracing Mark as well because she wouldn't let Mark go. Then stammering something to her that she had never understood or contemplated rationally until this minute, preferring to dismiss it as part of the demented exchange between traumatised witnesses to disaster:

'If I'd started one that size, they'd have put me away for ever,' he said.

Then he bowed his head and stared at his feet like a man praying standing up, the same gesture he had made just now but worse.

'I couldn't move my legs, you see,' he had explained. 'They were stuck. It was like a cramp. I should have run down there but I couldn't.'

Then worrying about what had happened to Marta.

Harry was about to torch the fucking house! she screamed at herself as she shivered and sipped her vodka and listened to his classy music from across the courtyard. *He's bought a lighter and he's going to incinerate his family!* He came to bed, she raped him and he seemed grateful. Next morning none of it had ever happened. In the mornings it never had. Not for Harry, not for Louisa. That was how they survived together. The four-track broke down and Harry had to borrow the Peugeot to drive the kids to school. Louisa went to work by taxi. The tile-cleaning maid found a snake in the larder and had hysterics. Hannah had a tooth out. It rained. Harry was not put away for ever, neither did he burn down the house with his new cigarette lighter. But he stayed out late, pleading yet another late customer.

*   *   *

'Osnard?' Louisa repeated, not believing her ears. '*Andrew Osnard?* Who in Heaven's name is Mr Osnard and why has he been invited to join us on our Sunday picnic on the island?'

'He's British, Lou, I told you. Joined the Embassy a couple of months ago. He's the ten-suit one, remember? He's all alone here. He was living in a hotel for weeks until he got his flat.'

'Which hotel?' she asked, thinking please God, let it be the Paraiso.

'The El Panama. He wants to meet a real family. You can understand that, can't you?' – the whipped hound, ever faithful, never understood.

And when she could think of nothing to say:

'He's fun, Lou. You'll see. Bouncy. Go down like a house on fire with the kids, I'll bet you.' His unhappy choice of phrase was followed by the new false laugh he had. 'It's my English roots raising their nasty little heads, I expect. Patriotism. Comes to us all, they say. You, too.'

'Harry, I do not understand what your love of country or mine has to do with inviting Mr Osnard to join us for an intimate family outing on Hannah's birthday when as we have all noticed you have little enough time for your children as it is.'

At which his head fell forward and he pleaded with her like an old beggar on the doorstep.

'Old Braithwaite made suits for Andy's dad, Lou, I used to tag along and hold the tape.'

*   *   *

Hannah wanted to go to the rice farm for her birthday. And so, for different reasons, did Louisa, because she couldn't understand why the rice farm had disappeared from Harry's conversational repertoire. In her worst moments she convinced herself he had installed a woman there – that greasy Angel would pimp for anyone. But as soon as she suggested the farm Harry turned all haughty and said big changes were afoot up there, best leave it to the lawyers till the deal was set.

So instead they rode in the four-track to Anytime, which was a house without walls perched like a wooden bandstand on its own round hazy island sixty yards across, in a vast sweltering flooded valley called Lake Gatún twenty miles inland from the Atlantic at the summit of the Canal's course, which is marked by a curling avenue of coloured buoys disappearing in pairs into the dripping haze. The island lay at the lake's western edge in a jigsaw of steaming jungle bays and inlets and mangrove swamps and other islands, of which Barro Colorado was the largest, and the least significant was Anytime, so named by the Pendel children after Paddington Bear's marmalade and rented by Louisa's father from his employers for a few forgotten dollars every year and now bequeathed to her in charity.

The Canal smouldered to the left of them and the mist coiled over it like an eternal dew. Pelicans dived through the mist and the air inside the car smelled of ship's oil and nothing in the world had changed or ever would, Amen. The same boats that had passed here when Louisa was Hannah's age passed now, the same black figures propped their bare elbows on the sweating railings, the same wet flags drooped from their masts and nobody in the world knew what they meant – her father used to joke – except for one blind old pirate in Portobelo. Pendel, strangely ill at ease in Mr Osnard's presence, drove in sulky silence. Louisa lounged beside him, which was what Mr Osnard had insisted upon, he swore he preferred it in the back.

Mr Osnard, she repeated drowsily to herself. *Portly* Mr Osnard. Ten years my junior at least, yet I'll *never* be able to call you Andy. She had forgotten, if she had ever known, how disarmingly polite an English gentleman could be when he put his insincere mind to it. Humour and politeness together, her mother used to warn her, make a dangerous heap of charm. So does being a good listener, Louisa reflected as she lay with her head back, smiling at the way Hannah pointed out the sights to him as if she owned them, and Mark letting her because it was her birthday – and besides, Mark in his way was quite as besotted by their guest as Hannah was.

One of the old lighthouses came into sight.

'Now why would *anybody* be such a silly ass as to paint a lighthouse *black* on one side and *white* on t'other,' Mr Osnard asked, having listened endlessly to Hannah on the horrendous appetite of alligators.

'Hannah, you're to be respectful to Mr Osnard now,' Louisa warned when Hannah hooted and told him he was a lemon.

'Tell her about old Braithwaite, Andy,' Harry suggested grudgingly. 'Tell her your childhood memories of him. She'd like that.'

He's showing him off to me, she thought. Why's he doing that?

But already she was slipping back into the mists of her own childhood, which was what she did whenever they drove to Anytime, an out-of-body experience: back into the deadly predictability of Zonian life from day to day, into the crematorium sweetness bequeathed to us by our dreaming forefathers, nothing left for us to do but drift amid the all-year-round flowers that the Company grows for us and the always-green lawns that the Company mows for us, and swim in the Company pools and hate our beautiful sisters and read the Company newspapers and fantasise about being a perfected society of early American Socialists, part-settlers, part-colonisers, part-preachers to the godless natives in the World Beyond the Zone, while never actually rising above our petty arguments and jealousies that are the lot of any foreign garrison, never questioning the Company's assumptions whether ethnic, sexual or social, never presuming to step outside the confinement allotted to us, but progressing obediently and inexorably, level by level, up and down the tideless narrow avenue of our preordained rut in life, knowing that every lock and lake and gully, every tunnel, robot, dam and every shaped and ordered hill on either side of them is the immutable achievement of the dead, and that our bounden duty here on earth is to praise God and the Company, steer a straight line between the walls, cultivate our faith and chastity in defiance of our promiscuous sister, masturbate ourselves to death and polish the brass on the Eighth Wonder of its Day.

*   *   *

Who gets the houses, Louisa? Who gets the land, swimming pools and tennis courts and hand-clipped hedges and plastic Christmas reindeer courtesy of the Company? *Louisa, Louisa, tell us how to raise revenue, cut costs, milk the gringos' sacred cow!* We want it *now*, Louisa! *Now* while we're in power, *now* while the foreign bidders are courting us, *now* before those dewy-eyed ecologists start preaching at us about their precious rainforests.

Whisperings of payoffs, manoeuvrings, secret deals, echoing down the corridors. The Canal will be modernised, widened to accommodate bigger shipping... they are planning new locks... multinational contractors are offering huge sums for consultancy, influence, commissions, contracts... And meanwhile: new files Louisa isn't allowed to handle and new bosses who stop talking when she walks into any room except Delgado's: her poor, decent, honourable Ernesto with his broom, vainly sweeping at the tide of their insatiable greed.

'I'm too damn *young*!' she yelled. 'I'm too *young* and too *alive* to see my childhood trashed before my eyes!'

She sat up with a jump. Her head must have rolled onto Pendel's uncollaborative shoulder.

'What did I say?' she demanded anxiously.

She had said nothing. It was diplomatic Mr Osnard from the back who had spoken. In his infinite politeness he was enquiring whether Louisa enjoyed watching the Panamanians taking over the Canal.

*   *   *

In Gamboa harbour Mark showed Mr Osnard how you got the tarpaulin off the motorboat and started the engine all by yourself. Harry took the helm long enough to navigate the wake of the Canal traffic, but it was Mark who beached the boat and made it fast, unloaded the luggage and, with a lot of help from jolly Mr Osnard, lit the barbecue.

*   *   *

Who is this glossy young man, so young, so handsome-ugly, so sensual, so amusing, so polite? What is this sensual man to my husband and what is my husband to him? Why is this sensual man like a new life for us – although Harry, having foisted him on us, seems to wish he never had? How come he knows so much about us, is so at ease with us, so family, talks so knowledgeably about the shop and Marta and Abraxas and Delgado and all the people in our lives, just because his father was a friend of Mr Braithwaite?

Why do I like him so much better than Harry does? He's Harry's friend, not mine. Why are my children all over him while Harry scowls and keeps his back turned and refuses to laugh at Mr Osnard's many jokes?

Her first thought was that Harry was jealous, and that pleased her. Her second thought was at once a nightmare and a terrible, shameful exultation: *oh Jesus, oh mother and father, Harry wants me to fall in love with Mr Osnard so that we're even.*

*　　　*　　　*

Pendel and Hannah cooking spare ribs. Mark preparing fishing rods. Louisa handing out beer and apple juice and watching her childhood chug away between the buoys. Mr Osnard asking her about Panamanian students – did she know any, were they militant? – and about people who lived the other side of the bridge.

'Well, we do have the rice farm,' says Louisa winsomely. 'But I don't think we know any *people* there!'

Harry and Mark sitting back to back on the boat. The fish, to quote Mr Osnard, giving themselves up in a spirit of voluntary euthanasia. Hannah lying on her tummy in the shade of the Anytime house, ostentatiously turning the expensive pages of the book on ponies that Mr Osnard has brought her for her birthday. And Louisa, under the influence of his gentle prompting and a secretive slug of vodka, regaling him with the story of her life this far, in the flirtatious language of her whore-sister Emily when she did her Scarlett O'Hara number before falling on her back.

'My problem – and I have to say this – is it *really* okay if I call you Andy? I'm Lou – though I love him dearly in *so* many ways, my problem – and thank God I only have the one, because almost every girl I *know* in Panama has a problem for every day of the *week* – my problem *has* to be my father.'

CHAPTER TEN

Louisa prepared her husband for his pilgrimage to the General in the same way that she got the children ready for Bible School, but with even more enthusiasm. Patches of attractive colour in her cheeks. Speaking with the greatest animation. A good deal of her enthusiasm taken from a bottle.

'Harry, we must wash the four-track. You are about to dress a modern living hero. The General has more medals for his rank and age than any general in the US Army. Mark, I want you to carry the buckets of hot water. Hannah, you will please take charge of the sponge and detergent and quit cursing *now*.'

Pendel could have run the four-track through the automatic car-wash at the local garage but Louisa needed godliness for the General today as well as cleanliness. She had never been so proud to be American. She said so repeatedly. She was so excited she tripped and almost fell. When they had cleaned the four-track she checked Pendel's tie. Checked it the way Auntie Ruth checked Benny's ties. Close to, then from a distance, like a painting. And she wasn't satisfied till he'd changed it for something quieter. Her breath smelt strongly of toothpaste. Pendel wondered why she cleaned her teeth so much these days.

'Harry, you are not so far as I know a co-respondent. It is therefore not appropriate that you *resemble* a co-respondent when you visit the United States General in charge of Southern Command.' Then in her best Ernie Delgado secretarial voice she rang the hairdresser for a ten o'clock appointment. 'No bulges and no sideburns, thank you, José. Mr Pendel will want it very short and tidy today. He is calling on the United States General in charge of Southern Command.'

After that she told Pendel who to be:

'Harry, you will not make jokes, you will be respectful' – fondly pressing down the shoulders of his jacket though they were perfect as they lay – 'and you will give the General my regards and you will be sure to tell him that *all* the Pendels and not just Milton Jenning's daughter are looking forward to the American Families' Thanksgiving Barbecue and Fireworks Display, the same as every year. And before you leave the shop you give those shoes another polish now. There wasn't a soldier born who didn't judge a man by his shoes and the General in charge of Southern Command is no exception. Drive very carefully, Harry. I mean it.'

Her strictures were unnecessary. Ascending the zigzag jungle road up Ancón Hill Pendel as usual meticulously observed the speed restrictions. At the US Army checkpoint he stiffened up and pulled a gritty smile for the sentry, for by then he was halfway to being a soldier himself. Passing the groomed white villas he observed how the stencilled rank of the occupants rose with him, and experienced a vicarious promotion on his way to Heaven. And as he walked up the noble steps to the front door of Number One Quarry Heights he assumed, despite his suitcase, the peculiar American military gait that keeps the upper body on a stately course while hips and knees perform their independent functions.

But from the moment he stepped inside the house, Harry Pendel was, as always when he came here, hopelessly in love.

*   *   *

176

This was not power. This was power's prize: a pro-consul's palace on a conquered foreign hill, manned by courteous Roman guards.

'Sir. The General will see you now, sir,' the sergeant informed him, depriving him of his suitcase in a single trained movement.

The glistening white hall was hung with brass plates for every general who had served here. Pendel greeted them like old friends even while he cast round nervously for unwelcome signs of change. He need not have feared. Some unfortunate glazing of the verandah, some unsightly air-conditioners. A few too many carpets. The General at an earlier stage in his career had subdued the Orient. Otherwise the house was much as Teddy Roosevelt might have found it when he came to inspect the progress of the moonshot of its day. Weightless, his own existence irrelevant, Pendel followed the sergeant through connecting halls, drawing rooms, libraries and parlours. Each window was a separate world for him: now the Canal, laden with shipping, winding grandly through the valley basin; now the layered mauve hills of forest draped with fever-mist; now the arches of the Bridge of the Americas bounding like the coils of a great sea monster across the bay, and the three far conical islands suspended from the sky.

And the birds! The animals! On this very hill – Pendel had learned from one of Louisa's father's books – more breeds existed than in all of Europe put together. In the branches of one great oak tree, full-grown iguanas basked and pondered in the midmorning sun. From another, brown and white marmosets came spinning down a pole to grab themselves a bit of mango put there by the General's jolly wife. Then up the pole again, hand over hand, trampling each other for the hell of it as they scampered back to safety. And on the perfect lawn, brown ñeques like great hamsters loped about their business. It was yet another house where Pendel had always wanted to live.

*   *   *

The sergeant was mounting the stairs, bearing Pendel's suitcase at the port. Pendel followed him. Old prints of warriors in uniform brandishing their moustaches at him. Recruitment posters demanding his involvement in forgotten wars. In the General's study a teak desk so brightly polished that Pendel swore he could see clean through it. But the summit of Pendel's levitation was the dressing room. Ninety years ago the finest American architectural and military minds had joined forces to create Panama's first sartorial shrine. In those days the tropics were not kind to gentlemen's clothes. The best-cut suits could gather mildew in a night. To confine them in small spaces compounded the humidity. Therefore the inventors of the General's dressing room devised, in place of wardrobes, a tall and airy chapel with upper windows ingeniously positioned to catch each passing breeze. And within it they worked their magic in the form of a great mahogany bar slung from pulleys to raise it to the apex or lower it to ground level. The lightest touch of woman was enough. And to the bar they attached the many day suits, morning coats, dinner jackets, tail suits, ceremonial and dress uniforms of the first general to command the Heights. So that they might hang free and rotate, wafted by zephyrs captured by the windows. In the whole world Pendel knew no more rousing tribute to his art than this.

'And you *preserve* it, General, sir! You *use* it!' he cried with passion. 'Which if I may say without disrespect is not what we British commonly associate with our respected American friends.'

'Well, Harry, we're none of us quite what we appear, are we?' said the General with innocent contentment as he studied himself in the mirror.

'No, sir, we are not. Though what will become of all this when it falls into the hands of our gallant Panamanian hosts, I suppose no man can determine,' he added craftily in his rôle of listening post. 'Anarchy and worse is what I hear from some of my more sensationally-minded customers.'

The General was young in spirit and liked frank speaking. 'Harry, it's a yo-yo. Yesterday they wanted us to go because we're bad colonial bears and they can't breathe while we're sitting on their heads. Today they want us to stay because we're the biggest employer in the country and if Uncle Sam walks out on them they'll suffer a crisis of confidence on the international money markets. Pack and unpack. Unpack and pack. Feels great, Harry. How's Louisa?'

'Thank you, General, Louisa is in the pink and will be all the more so for hearing that you enquired after her.'

'Milton Jenning was a fine engineer and a decent American. Sad loss to us all.'

They were trying a three-piece charcoal grey alpaca, single-breasted and priced at five hundred dollars, which was what Pendel had charged his first general a full nine years ago. He took a tuck in the waist. The General was fat-free and had the figure of an athletic god.

'I expect we'll be having a Japanese gentleman living up here next,' the listening post lamented, bending the General's arm at the elbow while they both watched the mirror. '*Plus* all his family and appendages and cook, I wouldn't wonder. You wouldn't think they'd heard of Pearl Harbor some of them. It depresses me, frankly, General, the way the old order changeth, if you'll pardon me.'

The General's answer, if he ever got as far as thinking of one, was drowned by the joyous intervention of his wife.

'Harry Pendel, you leave my husband alone this *minute*,' she protested gaily, sweeping in from nowhere with a great vase of lilies in her arms. 'He's all mine and you don't alter that suit by one gorgeous stitch. It's the sexiest thing I ever saw. I'm going to elope with him all over again right *now*. How's Louisa?'

*　　*　　*

They met in a neon-lit twenty-four-hour café beside the run down oceanic railway terminus that was now an embarkation point for day-trips on the Canal. Osnard sat slumped at a corner table wearing a Panama hat. An empty glass of something stood at his elbow. In the week since Pendel had last seen him he had put on weight and years.

'Tea or one o' these?'

'I'll take the tea, please, Andy, if you don't mind.'

'Tea,' Osnard told the waitress rudely, passing a hand heavily through his hair. 'And another o' these.'

'Thick night then, Andy.'

'Operational.'

Through the window they could contemplate the decaying hardware of Panama's heroic age. Old railway passenger cars, the upholstery ripped out of them by rats and vagrants, brass table lamps intact. Rusted steam engines, turntables, carriages, tenders left to rot like the toys of a spoilt child. On the pavement, backpackers huddled under awnings, fought off beggars, counted sodden dollars, tried to decipher Spanish signs. It had been raining most of the morning. It was raining still. The restaurant stank of warm gasoline. Ships' horns moaned above the din.

'It's a chance meeting,' Osnard said, through a suppressed burp. 'You were shopping, I was checking boat times.'

'Whatever was I buying?' Pendel asked, mystified.

'Fuck do I care?' Osnard took a swig of brandy while Pendel sipped his tea.

*   *   *

Pendel driving. They had agreed on the four-track because of the CD plates on Osnard's car. Wayside chapels marking places where spies and other motorists had been killed. Worried ponies with huge burdens driven by patient Indian families with bundles on their heads. A dead cow sprawled at a crossroads. A swarm of black vultures fighting for the best bits of it. A rear-wheel puncture announced by one deafening round of gunfire. Pendel changing the wheel while Osnard in his Panama hat squatted sullenly on the verge. A roadside restaurant out of town, hardwood tables under plastic awnings, chicken roasting on a barbecue. The rain stopped. Violent sunshine beat on an emerald lawn. Parrots screamed red-and-green murder from a bell-shaped aviary. Pendel and Osnard sat alone except for two heavy men in blue shirts at a table the other side of the wooden deck.

'Know 'em?'

'No, Andy, I'm pleased to say I don't.'

And two glasses o' house white to wash their chicken down – hang on, make it a bottle, then fuck off and leave us in peace.

*   *   *

'They're jumpy is what they are,' Pendel began.

Osnard had propped his head between the splayed fingers of one hand while he took notes with the other.

'There's half a dozen of them round the General all the time, so I'm not getting him alone. There was a colonel there, tall fellow, kept drawing him aside. Getting him to sign things, murmuring in his ear.'

'See what he signed?' Osnard moved his head slightly to relieve the pain.

'Not while I'm fitting, Andy.'

'Catch any murmurs?'

'No, and I don't think you'd have caught many either, not while you were down there on your knees.' He took a sip of wine. '"General," I said, "if it's not convenient or I'm hearing what I oughtn't, tell me is all I ask. I'll not be offended, I'll come back another day." He wouldn't have it. "Harry, you'll be pleased to stay right here where you belong. You're a raft of sanity in a stormswept sea." "All right, then," I said, "I'll stay." Then his wife comes in and nothing is said. But there are looks that are worth a million words, Andy, and this was one of them. What I call a highly meaningful and pregnant look between two people who know each other well.'

Osnard writing at no great speed. '"The General in charge o' Southern Command exchanged a pregnant look with his wife." *That* should put London on red alert,' he remarked sourly. 'General take a swipe at the State Department at all?'

'No, Andy.'

'Call 'em a bunch o' limp-wristed, over-educated faggots, bitch about the CIA college boys in their buttondown collars straight out o' Yale?'

Pendel collects his memories. Judiciously.

'He did a *bit*, Andy. It was in the air, I'll put it that way.'

Osnard writing with slightly more enthusiasm.

'Lament America's loss o' power, speculate about the future ownership o' the Canal?'

'There was tension, Andy. The students were spoken of, and not with what I call respect.'

'Just his words, mind ol' boy? I'll do the purple, you do the words.'

Pendel did his words as requested. ' "Harry," he says to me – very quiet, this is – I'm worrying about his collar from the front – "My advice to you is, Harry, sell your shop and your house and get your wife and family out of this hell-hole of a country while there's time. Milton Jenning was a great engineer. His daughter deserves better." I was numb. I didn't speak. I was too moved. He asked me how old our children were and he was highly relieved to discover they were not of university age, because he didn't like to think of Milton Jenning's grandchildren running in the streets with a lot of long-haired Commie bums.'

'Wait.'

Pendel waited.

'Okay. More.'

'Then he said I should take care of Louisa, and how she was a daughter worthy of her father on account of putting up with that duplicitous bastard Dr Ernesto Delgado of the Canal Commission, God rot him. And the General's not a man for language, Andy. I was shaken. So would you be.'

'*Delgado* a bastard?'

'Correct, Andy,' said Pendel, recalling that gentleman's unhelpful posture at dinner in his house, as well as several years of having him shoved down his throat as a latterday Braithwaite.

'Hell's he being duplicitous about?'

'The General didn't say, Andy, and it's not my place to ask.'

'Say anything about the US military bases staying or going?'

'Not as such, Andy.'

'Hell does that mean?'

'There were jokes. Gallows humour. Remarks to the effect that it won't be long before the toilets start to back up.'

'Safety o' shipping? Arab terrorists threatening to paralyse the Canal? Essential for the Yanks to stay and continue the war on drugs, control the arms boys, keep the peace?'

Pendel modestly shook his head to each of these suggestions. 'Andy, Andy, I'm a tailor, remember?' – and he bestowed a virtuous smile on a plume of ospreys swirling in a blue heaven.

Osnard ordered two glasses of aircraft fuel. Under its influence, his performance sharpened and specks of light re-entered his small black eyes.

'All right. Come-to-Jesus time. What did Mickie say? Does he want to play or not?'

*   *   *

But Pendel wouldn't be hurried. Not on the matter of Mickie. He was telling the story in his own time, about his own friend. He was cursing his own fluence and wishing very hard that Mickie had never put in an appearance at the Club Unión that night.

'He *may* want to play, Andy. If he does it'll be on terms. He's got to put his thinking-cap on.'

Osnard writing again. Osnard's sweat pattering on the plastic tablecloth. 'Where did you meet him?'

'At the Caesar's Park, Andy. In the long wide corridor outside the casino there. It's where Mickie holds court when he doesn't mind who he's with.'

Truth had briefly raised her dangerous head. Only the day before, Mickie and Pendel had sat in the very spot he described while Mickie had heaped love and invective on his wife and mourned the grief of his children. And Pendel his faithful cellmate sympathised, careful to say nothing that would push Mickie either way.

'Pitch him the eccentric millionaire philanthropist bit?'

'I did, Andy, and he took note.'

'Tell him a nationality?'

'I fudged, Andy. Like you said to. "My friend is Western, highly democratic but not American," I said. "And that's as far as I am prepared to go." "Harry boy," he said – which is what he calls me, Harry boy – "if he's English I'm halfway there. Kindly remember I'm an Oxford man and a former high officer of the Anglo-Panamanian Society of Culture." "Mickie," I said, "trust me, I can go no further. My eccentric friend has a certain quantity of money and he's prepared to put that quantity at your disposal provided he's persuaded of the rightness of your cause and I'm not talking loose change. If someone's selling Panama down the Canal," I said, "if it's the jackboots and salute the Führer in the streets again, and upsetting the chances of a small gallant young nation as she sets out on her maiden voyage towards democracy, then my eccentric friend is there to help any way he can with his millions."'

'How'd he take it?'

'"Harry boy," he said. "I've got to level with you. It's the money that talks to me at this moment because I'm running on empty. It's not the casinos have ruined me or what I give to my beloved students and the people who live the other side of the bridge. It's my trusted sources, it's the bribes I pay them, it's my out-of-pocket. Not just in Panama but Kuala Lumpur, Taipei, Tokyo and I don't know where else. I'm skint and that's the bare-cheeked truth."'

'Who does he have to bribe? Hell's he buying? Don't get it.'

'He didn't tell me, Andy, and I didn't ask. He went off at a tangent, which is his way. Gave me a lot of stuff about the carpetbaggers at the back door and the politicians filling their pockets with the Panamanian people's birthright.'

'How about Rafi Domingo?' Osnard asked with the belated petulance that comes over people when they offer money, then find their offer is accepted. 'Thought Domingo was staking him.'

'No longer, Andy.'

'Hell not?'

Truth once more came cautiously to Pendel's aid.

'As of a few days ago, Señor Domingo has ceased to be what you might call a welcome guest at Mickie's table. What was evident to all has finally become evident to Mickie too.'

'You mean he's rumbled his old lady and Rafi?'

'Correct, Andy.'

Osnard digested this. 'Buggers wear me out,' he complained. 'Plots here, plots there, talk o' the big sell-out, putsches round the corner, silent oppositions, students on the march. Hell are they *opposing*, Christ's sakes? What *for*? Why can't they come clean?'

'That's exactly what I said to him, Andy. "Mickie," I said, "my friend will not invest in an enigma. For as long as there's a very big secret out there which you know and my friend doesn't," I said, "his money's going to stay in his wallet." I was firm, Andy. With Mickie you have to be. He's iron. "*You* deliver your plot, Mickie," I said, "and *we'll* deliver our philanthropy." My words,' he added while Osnard puffed and wrote and the sweat went tap-tap on the table.

'How'd he take it?'

'He druckened himself, Andy.'

'He *what*?'

'Went all dark and nobody. I had to force the words out of him the same as an interrogator. "Harry boy," he says to me, "we're men of honour, you and me, so I won't mince my words either." He was fired up. "If you ask me *when*, I shall answer you *never*. Never *never*!"' The heat in Pendel's voice was very lifelike. You knew at once that he had been there, felt the Abraxas passion. '"Because *never* will I divulge the single slightest detail passed to me by my highly secret sources until I have cleared it with each and every one of them down the line."' His voice fell and became a solemn promise. '"I shall then furnish your friend with an order of battle of my Movement, plus a statement of its aims and dreams, plus a manifesto of intent should we ever win first prize in the great lottery of life, plus all requisite facts and figures regarding the secret machinations of this government which are in my view diabolical, subject to certain copper-bottomed assurances.'''

'Like what?'

'''Like treating my organisation with a high degree of circumspection and respect, such as clearing in advance via Harry Pendel all details however slight that bear upon my security or the security of those I am responsible for without exception.'' Period.'

There was silence. There was Osnard's fixed, dark stare. And there was muddled Harry Pendel's scowl, while he struggled to shield Mickie from the consequences of his miscalculated gift of love.

*　　*　　*

Osnard spoke first.

'Harry, ol' boy.'

'What is it, Andy?'

'You holding out on me by any chance?'

'I'm telling you what transpired, Mickie's words and mine.'

'This is the big one, Harry.'

'Thank you, I'm aware of that, Andy.'

'This is mega. This is what we were put on earth for, you and me. This is what London dreams of: a rampant middle-class radical freedom movement in place, up and running, ready to blaze away for democracy as soon as the balloon goes up.'

'I don't know where this is leading us actually, Andy.'

'This is no time for you to be paddling your own Canal. Get my meaning?'

'I don't think I do, Andy.'

'Together we stand. Divided we're screwed. You deliver Mickie, I deliver London, simple as that.'

An idea came to Pendel. A lovely one.

'There was one more stipulation he made, Andy, which I should just mention.'

'What's that, then?'

'It was so ridiculous, frankly, I didn't see the point of

passing it on to you. "Mickie," I told him, "it's a total non-starter. You've overplayed your hand. I don't think you'll be hearing from my friend again for rather a long while."'

'Go on.'

Pendel was laughing, but only inside himself. He had seen his way out, a doorway to freedom six feet wide. The fluence was rushing all over his body, tickling his shoulders, throbbing in his temples and singing in his ears. He took a breath and made another long paragraph:

'"It's regarding the method of payment of the cash that your mad millionaire proposes to pour into my Silent Opposition in order to bring it up to par and make it a worthy instrument of democracy for a small nation on the brink of self-determination and all that that entails."'

'So what is it?'

'The money to be paid up front, Andy. Cash or gold in toto,' Pendel replied with heavy apology. 'No credit, cheques or banks to be involved at any stage, owing to the security. For the exclusive use of his Movement, which includes both students and fishermen, down the middle and kosher, receipts and all the trimmings,' he concluded, with triumphant acknowledgements to his Uncle Benny.

But Osnard was not responding as Pendel had anticipated. To the contrary, his podgy features seemed to brighten as he heard Pendel out.

'I can see a case for that,' he said perfectly reasonably, after giving this interesting proposal the prolonged consideration it deserved. 'So should London. I'll run it by 'em, try it on for size, see what they come up with. Reasonable chaps, most of 'em. Keen. Flexible when necessary. Can't give cheques to fishermen. Makes no sense at all. Anything else I can help you with?'

'I'd have thought that was enough, thank you, Andy,' Pendel replied prissily, stifling his astonishment.

*   *   *

Marta stood at her stove making Greek coffee because she

knew he liked it. Pendel lay on her bed studying a complex chart of lines and bubbles and capital letters followed by numerals.

'It's an order of battle,' she explained. 'The way we used to do it when we were students. Codenames, cells, lines of communication, and a special liaison group to talk to the labour unions.'

'Where does Mickie fit in?'

'Nowhere. Mickie's our friend. It would not be appropriate.'

The coffee rose and settled again. She filled two cups.

'And the Bear rang.'

'What did he want?'

'He says he's thinking of doing an article about you.'

'That's nice then.'

'He wants to know how much the new clubroom cost you.'

'Why ever should that concern him?'

'Because he's evil too.'

She took the order of battle from him, handed him his coffee, sat close to him on the bed.

'And Mickie wants another suit. Houndstooth alpaca the same as you made for Rafi. I said not till he'd paid for the last one. Was that right?'

Pendel sipped his coffee. He felt afraid without knowing why.

'Give him what makes him happy,' he said, avoiding her eye. 'He's earned it.'

CHAPTER ELEVEN

Everyone was delighted with the way young Andy was working out. Even Ambassador Maltby, though not deemed capable of delight as others understood it, was heard to remark that a young man who played off eight and kept his mouth shut between strokes couldn't be all bad. Nigel Stormont had put aside his misgivings within days. Osnard staked no challenge to his position as Head of Chancery, showed due deference to the sensitivities of his colleagues, and shone, but not too brightly, on the cocktail and dinner round.

'Have you any suggestions about how I'm to explain you in this town?' Stormont asked him, none too kindly, at their first encounter. 'Not to mention here in the Embassy,' he added.

'How about Canal Watcher?' Osnard suggested. 'Britain's trade routes in the post-Colonial era. True, manner o' speaking. Just a question o' how you do your watching.'

Stormont could find no fault with this proposal. Every major Embassy in Panama had its Canal expert, except the Brits. But did Osnard know his stuff?

'So what's the bottom line as regards the US bases?' Stormont demanded, by way of testing Osnard's aptitude for his new post.

'Don't get you.'

'Will the US military stay or go?'

'Toss up. Lot o' Pans want the bases to stay as security for foreign investors. Short-termists. See it as a transition.'

'And the others?'

'Not one more day. Had 'em here as a colonial power since 1904, disgrace to the region, get the buggers out. US marines hit Mexico and Nicaragua from here in the 'twenties, put down Panamanian strikes in '25. US military's been here since the start o' the Canal. No one's comfortable with that except the bankers. Present time, US are using Panama as a base to hit the drug barons in the Andes and Central America and train Latin American soldiery in civic action against enemies yet to be defined. US bases employ four thousand Pans, give work to another eleven thousand. US troop strength officially seven thousand, but there's a lot hidden, lot o' hollow mountains full o' toys and funk holes. US military presence supposedly accounts for four point five per cent of the Gross National Product but that's horseshit when you reckon Panama's invisible earnings.'

'And the treaties?' said Stormont, secretly impressed.

'1904 treaty gave the Canal Zone to the Yanks in perpetuity, the '77 Torrijos-Carter treaty said the Canal and all its works had to be handed back to the Pans at the turn o' the century, free o' charge. Right-wing America still thinks it was a sell-out. Protocol allows for continued US military presence if both sides want it. Question o' who pays who how much for what when hasn't been addressed. Do I pass?'

He did. Osnard the official Canal Watcher duly settled into his flat, did his welcome parties, pressed the flesh and within weeks had become a pleasing minor feature of the diplomatic landscape. Within a few more he was an asset. If he played golf with the Ambassador he also played tennis with Simon Pitt, attended jolly beach parties with the junior staff and flung himself upon the diplomatic community's periodic frenzied efforts to raise conscience money for the underprivileged of Panama, of whom there was mercifully held to be an inexhaustible supply. An Embassy pantomime was in rehearsal. Osnard was unanimously voted Dame.

'Do you mind telling me something?' Stormont asked him

when they knew each other better. 'What's the Planning & Application Committee when it's at home?'

Osnard was vague. Stormont thought deliberately so.

'Not sure, actually. It's Treasury-led. Mixed bag o' people from across the board. Co-opted members from all walks o' life. Breath o' fresh air to blow out the cobwebs. Quangos plus God's anointed.'

'Any walks in particular?'

'Parliament. Press. Here and there. My boss sees it big but doesn't talk about it much. Chaired by a chap called Cavendish.'

'*Cavendish?*'

'First name Geoff.'

'*Geoffrey* Cavendish?'

'Freelancer o' some sort. Wheels and deals behind the scenes. Office in Saudi Arabia, houses in Paris and the West End, place in Scotland. Member o' Boodles.'

Stormont stared at Osnard in frank disbelief. Cavendish the influence-pedlar, he was thinking. Cavendish the defence lobbyist. Cavendish the self-styled statesman's friend. Ten per cent Cavendish, from the days when Stormont was doing a stint in the Foreign Office in London. Boom-boom Cavendish, arms broker. Geoff the Oil. Anybody finding himself in contact with the above-named will immediately report to Personnel Department before proceeding.

'Who else?' Stormont asked.

'Chap called Tug. T'other name unknown.'

'Not Kirby?'

'Just Tug,' said Osnard with an indifference that Stormont rather liked. 'Overheard it on the blower. My boss having lunch with Tug before the meeting. My boss paid. Seemed to be the form.'

Stormont bit his lip and asked no more. He already knew more than he wished and probably more than he ought. He turned instead to the delicate question of Osnard's future product, which they discussed in private conclave over lunch in a new Swiss restaurant that served kirsch with the coffee. Osnard found the place, Osnard insisted on paying the bill out of what he called his reptile fund, Osnard proposed they eat *cordon bleu* and gnocchi and wash it down with Chilean red before the kirsch.

At what point would the Embassy get a sight of Osnard's product? Stormont asked. Before it went to London? After? Never?

'My boss says no local sharing unless he gives the nod,' Osnard replied with his mouth full. 'Scared stiff o' Washington. Handling the distribution personally.'

'Are you comfortable with that?'

Osnard took a pull of red and shook his head. 'Fight it, my advice. Form an internal Embassy working-party. You, Ambass, Fran, me. Gully's Defence so he's not family, Pitt's on probation. Put together an indoctrination list, everyone signs off on it, meet out of hours.'

'Will your boss wear it, whoever he is?'

'You push, I'll pull. Name o' Luxmore, supposed to be a secret except everybody knows. Tell Ambass to beat the table. "Canal's a time bomb. Instant local response essential." That crap. He'll cave.'

'Ambass doesn't beat tables,' Stormont said.

But Maltby must have beaten something because after a stream of obstructive telegrams from their respective services, usually to be hand-decoded at dead of night, Osnard and Stormont were grudgingly permitted to make common cause. An Embassy working-party was set up with the harmless-sounding title of the Isthmus Study Group. A trio of morose technicians flew down from Washington and, after three days of listening to walls, pronounced them deaf. And at seven o'clock one turbulent Friday evening the four conspirators duly assembled round the Embassy rainforest-teak conference table and under the low light of a Ministry of Works lamp acknowledged by signature that they were privy to special material BUCHAN, provided by source BUCHAN under an operation codenamed BUCHAN. The solemnity of the moment was offset by a burst of humour from Maltby, afterwards ascribed to the temporary absence of his wife in England:

'From now on BUCHAN's likely to be an on-going thing,

sir,' Osnard declared airily as he collected the signed forms like a croupier raking in the chips. 'His stuff's coming in at quite a rate. Meeting once a week may not be enough.'

'A *what* thing, Andrew?' Maltby enquired, setting his pen down with a click.

'On-going.'

'On-going?'

'What I said, Ambass. On-going.'

'Yes. Quite so. Thank you. Well, from now on, if you please, Andrew, the *thing* – to use your parlance – is *on-gone*. BUCHAN may prevail. He may endure. He may persist, or at a pinch continue or resume. But he will never, as long as I am Ambassador, *on-go*, if you don't mind. It would be too distressing.'

After which, wonder of wonders, Maltby invited the whole team for bacon and eggs and swimming back at the Residence where, having raised a droll toast to 'the Buchaneers', he marched the guests into the garden to admire his toads, whose names he belted out above the din of passing traffic: 'Come on, Hercules, hop, hop! – don't *gawp* at her like that, Galileo, haven't you seen a pretty gal before?' And when they swam, deliciously in the half darkness, Maltby astonished everyone yet again by letting out a great glad cry of '*Christ*, she's beautiful!' in celebration of Fran. And finally, to round the night off, he insisted on playing dance music, and had his houseboys roll back the rugs, though Stormont couldn't help remarking that Fran danced with every man but Osnard, who ostentatiously preferred the Ambassador's books, which he patrolled with his hands behind his back in the manner of an English princeling inspecting a guard of honour.

'You don't think Andy's a bit left-handed, do you?' he asked Paddy over a nightcap. 'You never hear of him going out with girls. And he treats Fran as if she had the plague.'

He thought she was going to cough again, but she was laughing.

'*Darling*,' Paddy murmured, lifting her eyes to Heaven. '*Andy Osnard?*'

It was a view that Francesca Deane, had she heard it from

her recumbent position in Osnard's bed in his apartment in Paitilla, would have happily endorsed.

* * *

How she had got there was a mystery to her, though it was a mystery now ten weeks old.

'Only two ways to play this situation, girl,' Osnard had explained to her with the assurance he brought to everything, over lavish helpings of barbecued chicken and cold beer beside the pool of the El Panama. 'Method A. Sweat it out for six tense months then fall into each other's arms in a sticky coil. "Darling, why ever didn't we do this before, puff, puff?" Method B, the preferred one, bang away now, observe total *omertà* all round, see how we like it. If we do, have a ball. If we don't, chuck it and no one's the wiser. "Been there, didn't care for it, glad o' the information. Life moves on. *Basta.*"'

'There's also method C, thank you.'

'What's that?'

'Abstention, for one thing.'

'You mean me tie a knot in it and you take the veil?' He waved a well-cushioned hand at the poolside, where sumptuous girls of all sorts flirted with their swains to the music of a live band. 'Desert island out here, girl. Nearest white man thousands o' miles away. Just you and me and our duty to Mother England, till my wife comes out next month.'

Francesca was halfway to her feet. She actually yelled out, 'Your wife!'

'Haven't got one. Never did, never will,' Osnard said, rising with her. 'So now that obstacle to our happiness has been removed, hell's to say no?'

They danced very well while she struggled for an answer. She had never supposed that someone so generously built could move so lightly. Or that such small eyes could be so compelling. She had never supposed, if she was honest, that she could be attracted to a man who, to say the least, was several points short of a Greek god.

'I don't suppose it's occurred to you I might *hugely* prefer someone else, has it?' she demanded.

'In Panama? No way, girl. Checked you out. Local lads call you the English iceberg.'

They were dancing very close. It seemed the obvious thing to do.

'They call me nothing of the sort!'

'Want a bet?'

They were dancing even closer.

'What about at home?' she insisted. 'How do you know I haven't got a soulmate in Shropshire? Or London for that matter?'

He was kissing her temple but it could have been any part of her. His hand was perfectly still on her back and her back was bare.

'Not much good to you out here, girl. Don't get much satisfaction at five thousand miles, not in my book. Do you?'

It wasn't that Fran had been persuaded by Osnard's arguments, she told herself as she contemplated his replete and dozing figure beside her in the bed. Or that he was the best dancer in the world. Or that he made her laugh louder and longer than any man she had known. It was just that she couldn't imagine herself withstanding him for one more day, let alone three years.

She had arrived in Panama six months ago. In London she had spent her weekends with a frightfully handsome hunting stockbroker named Edgar. Their affair was mutually agreed to have run its course by the time she got her posting. With Edgar, everything was mutually agreed.

*   *   *

But who *was* Andy?

A believer in solidly-sourced material, Fran had never before slept with anyone she had not researched.

She knew he had been at Eton but only because Miles had told her. Osnard, who appeared to hate his old school, referred to it only as 'the nick' or 'Slough Grammar', and otherwise disdained all reference to his education. His intellect was widely based but arbitrary, as you would expect from someone whose school career had been abruptly curtailed. When he was drunk, he was fond of quoting Pasteur: *'chance favours only the prepared mind.'*

He was rich or, if he wasn't, he was spendthrift or extremely generous. Almost every pocket of his expensive locally-made suits – trust Andy to find himself the best tailor in town as soon as he arrived – seemed to be stuffed with twenty- and fifty-dollar bills. But when she pointed this out to him, he shrugged and told her it came with the job. If he took her to dinner or they stole a secret weekend in the country, he spent money like water.

He had owned a greyhound and raced it at the White City until – in his words – a bunch o' the boys invited him to take his doggie somewhere else. An ambitious project to open a go-karting stadium in Oman had met with similar frustrations. He had run a silver stall in Shepherd Market. None of these interludes could have lasted long, for he was only twenty-seven.

Of his parentage he declined to say anything at all, maintaining that he owed his immense charm and fortune to a distant aunt. He never referred to his previous conquests, though she had excellent reason to believe they were many and varied. True to his promise of *omertà* he never made the smallest claim on her in public, a thing she found arousing: to be one minute at the highest pitch of ecstasy in his extremely capable arms, the next sitting primly opposite him at a Chancery meeting and behaving as if they barely recognised each other.

And he was a spy. And his job was running another spy called BUCHAN. Or spies, since BUCHAN product seemed more diverse and exciting than anything one person could encompass.

* * *

And BUCHAN had the ear of the President and of the US General in charge of Southern Command. BUCHAN knew crooks and wheeler-dealers: just as Andy must have known them when he had his greyhound, whose name she had recently learned was Retribution. She attached significance to this: Andy had an agenda.

And BUCHAN was in touch with a secret democratic opposition that was waiting for the old fascists in Panama to show their true colours. He talked to militants in the students' movement and fishermen and secret activists inside the unions. He plotted with them, waiting for the day. He referred to them – rather glamorously, she thought – as people from the other side of the bridge. BUCHAN was on terms with Ernie Delgado too, the grey eminence of the Canal. And with Rafi Domingo, who laundered money for the cartels. BUCHAN knew Legislative Assembly members, lots of them. He knew lawyers and bankers. There seemed to be no one worth knowing in Panama that BUCHAN didn't know, and it was extraordinary to Fran, *eerie* in fact, that Andy in such a short time had succeeded in getting to the very heart of a Panama she never knew existed. But then he'd got to *her* heart pretty sharpish too.

And BUCHAN was sniffing a great plot, though nobody could quite work out what the plot consisted of: except that the French and possibly the Japanese and Chinese and the Tigers of South-East Asia were part of it or might be, and perhaps the drugs cartels of Central and South America. And the plot involved selling the Canal out of the back door, as Andy called it. But how? And how without the Americans knowing? After all, the Americans had effectively been running the country for most of the century, and they had the most amazingly sophisticated listening and monitoring systems all over the isthmus and Central America.

Yet the Americans mystifyingly knew nothing about it at all, which added hugely to the excitement. Or if they did, they weren't telling us. Or they knew but weren't telling one another, because these days when you talked about American foreign policy you had to ask which one, and which ambassador: the one at the US Embassy or the one up on Ancón Hill, because the US military still hadn't got used to the idea that it couldn't bang heads in Panama any more.

And London was extremely excited, and was digging up collateral from all sorts of odd places, sometimes from years ago, and making amazing deductions to do with whose ambitions for world power would dominate everybody else's because, as BUCHAN put it, all the world's vultures were gathering over poor little Panama and the game was guessing who was going to get the prize. And London kept pressing for *more, more*, all the time, which made Andy furious because overworking a network was like overworking a greyhound, he said: in the end you both pay for it, the dog and you. But that was all he told her. Otherwise he was secrecy itself, which she admired.

And all this in ten short weeks from a standing start, just like their love affair. Andy was a magician, touching things that had been around for years and making them thrilling and alive. Touching Fran that way too. But who was BUCHAN? If Andy was defined by BUCHAN, who defined BUCHAN?

*   *   *

Why did BUCHAN's friends speak so frankly to him or her? Was BUCHAN a shrink, a doctor? Or a scheming bitch, worming secrets out of her lovers with lascivious skills? Who was it who telephoned Andy in fifteen second bursts, ringing off almost before he could say, 'I'll be there'? Was it BUCHAN himself, or an intermediary, a student, a fisherman, a cutout, some special link-person in the network? Where did Andy go when, like a man commanded by a supernatural voice, he rose at dead of night, threw on his clothes, removed a wad of dollar bills from the wall-safe behind the bed and left her lying there without so much as a goodbye, to creep back again at dawn, chagrined or wildly elated, stinking of cigar smoke and women's perfume? And then to take her, still without a word, endlessly, wonderfully, tirelessly, hours, years on end, his thick body skimming weightlessly over her and round her, one peak after another, something that till now had only happened to Fran in her schoolgirl imagination?

And what great alchemy did Andy get up to when an

ordinary-looking brown envelope was delivered to the door and he disappeared to the bathroom with it and locked himself in for half an hour, leaving a stink of camphor behind or was it formaldehyde? What did Andy *see* when he reappeared from the broom cupboard with a strip of wet film no wider than a tapeworm, then sat at his desk coaxing it through a miniature editor?

'Shouldn't you be doing that at the Embassy?' she asked him.

'No dark room, no you,' he replied in the brown, dismissive voice she found so irresistible. What a perfect slob he was after Edgar! – so shifty, so unfettered, so *brave*!

She would observe him at the BUCHAN meetings: our chief Buchaneer, lounging potently at the long table, a dreamy forelock drifting over his right eye as he passed out his garishly-striped folders, then peered into the void while everybody except himself read them, BUCHAN's Panama, caught *in flagrante*:

Antonio So-and-so of the Foreign Ministry recently declared himself so infatuated by his Cuban mistress that he intends to use his best offices to improve Panama-Cuban relations in defiance of US objections...

Declared himself to whom? To his Cuban mistress? And she declared it to BUCHAN? Or declared it direct to Andy, perhaps – in bed? She remembered the perfume again and imagined it rubbed against him by bare bodies. Is Andy BUCHAN? *Nothing* was impossible.

So-and-so's other loyalty is to the Lebanese mafia in Colón, who are said to have paid twenty million dollars for 'favoured nation status' within Colón's criminal community...

And after Cuban mistresses and Lebanese crooks, BUCHAN takes a leap into the Canal:

The chaos inside the newly constituted Authority of the Canal is increasing on a daily basis as old hands are replaced by unquali-

fied staff appointed solely on nepotist lines, to the despair of Ernesto Delgado, the most blatant example being the appointment of José-María Fernandez as director of General Services after he acquired a thirty per cent holding in the Mainland Chinese fast-food chain Lee Lotus, Lee Lotus being forty per cent owned by companies belonging to the Rodríguez cocaine cartel of Brazil...

'Is that the Fernandez who made a pass at me at the National Day jamboree?' Fran asked Andy, deadpan, at a late evening session of the Buchaneers in Maltby's office.

She had lunched with him at his flat and made love to him all afternoon. Her question was inspired as much by afterglow as curiosity.

'Bandy-legged bald bloke,' Andy replied carelessly. 'Specs, spots, armpits and bad breath.'

'That's him. He wanted to fly me up to a festival in David.'

'When do you leave?'

'Andy, you're out of court,' said Nigel Stormont without looking up from his folder, and Fran had her work cut out not to burst out giggling.

And when the sessions ended, she would watch out of the corner of her eye as Andy piled together the folders and padded with them to his secret kingdom behind the new steel door in the east corridor, trailed by that creepy clerk of his who wore Fair Isle knitted waistcoats and slicked hair – Shepherd he called himself, always something in his hand like a spanner or a screwdriver or a bit of flex.

'What on earth does Shepherd *do* for you?'

'Cleans the windows.'

'He's not tall enough.'

'I lift him up.'

It was with a similarly low expectation that she now asked Osnard why he was once more getting dressed when everybody else was trying to sleep.

*   *   *

'See a chap about a dog,' he replied tersely. He had been on edge all evening.

200

'A greyhound?'

No answer.

'It's a very *late* dog,' she said, hoping to tease him from his introspection.

No answer.

'I suppose it's the same dog that featured so dramatically in the urgent decipher-yourself telegram you received this afternoon.'

In the act of pulling his shirt over his head, Osnard froze. 'Hell did you get that from?' he demanded, not at all pleasantly.

'I walked into Shepherd as I was getting in the lift to come home. He asked me whether you were still around so I naturally asked him why. He said he'd got a hot one for you but you were going to have to unbutton it yourself. I blushed for you, then realised he was talking about an urgent signal. Aren't you packing your pearl-handled Beretta?'

No answer.

'Where are you meeting her?'

'In a whorehouse,' he snapped, heading for the door.

'Have I offended you somehow?'

'Not yet. But you're getting there.'

'Perhaps you've offended me. I may go back to my flat. I need some serious sleep.'

But she stayed, with the smell of his round clever body still on her and the print of him in the bedclothes at her side and the memory of his watcher's eyes smouldering down at her in the half light. Even his tantrums excited her. So did his black side, in the rare moments when he let it show: in their lovemaking, when they were playing games and she brought him to the brink of violence, and his wet head would lift as if to strike, before he just, but only just, pulled back. Or at BUCHAN meetings when Maltby with customary perversity decided to needle him about a report – 'Is your source illiterate as well as omniscient, Andrew, or do we have you to thank for his split infinitives?' – and little by little the lines of his fluid face hardened and the danger light kindled in the depths of his eyes and she understood why he had christened his greyhound Retribution.

I'm losing control, she thought. Not of him, I never had it. Of me. More alarming still to the daughter of a terminally pompous Law Lord and the former partner of the immaculate Edgar, she was discovering a distinct appetite for the disreputable.

CHAPTER TWELVE

Osnard parked his diplomatic car outside the shopping complex at the foot of the tall building, greeted the security guards on duty and rose to the fourth floor. Under sickly strip-lighting the lion and unicorn boxed eternally. He typed a combination, entered the Embassy's reception lobby, unlocked an armoured glass door, climbed a staircase, entered a corridor, unlocked a grille and stepped into his own kingdom. A last door remained closed to him and it was made of steel. Selecting a long brass pipestem key from a bunch in his pocket, he inserted it the wrong way up, said fuck, removed it and inserted it the right way up. Alone, he moved a little differently to when he was observed. There was more rashness to him, something headlong. His jaw slumped, his shoulders hunched, his eyes looked out from under lowered brows, he seemed to be lunging at some unseen enemy.

The strongroom comprised the last two yards of corridor converted to a kind of larder. To Osnard's right lay pigeon-holes. To his left, amid a variety of incongruous articles such as fly spray and toilet paper, a green wall-safe. Ahead of him, an oversized red telephone reposed on a stack of electrical boxes. It was known in the vernacular as his digital link with God. A sign on the base said, 'Speech on this instrument costs £50.00 per minute.' Osnard had written beneath it the word 'Enjoy'. It was in this spirit that he now lifted the receiver and, ignoring the automatic voice commanding him to press buttons and observe procedures, dialled his London bookmaker, with whom he placed a couple of bets to the tune of five hundred pounds each on greyhounds whose names and appointments he seemed to know as well as he knew the bookmaker.

'No, you stupid tart, to win,' he said. When had Osnard ever backed a dog each way?

After this he resigned himself to the rigours of his trade. Extracting a plain folder from a pigeonhole marked TOP SECRET BUCHAN, he bore it to his office, switched on the lights, sat himself at his desk, belched and, head in hands, began to read again the four pages of instructions that he had received that afternoon from his Regional Director Luxmore in London and at considerable cost to his patience deciphered with his own hand. In a passable imitation of Luxmore's Scottish brogue, Osnard mouthed the text aloud:

'You will commit the following orders to memory' – suck of the teeth – 'This signal is not repeat not for Station files and will be destroyed within seventy-two hours of receipt, young Mr Osnard... You will advise BUCHAN forthwith of the following' – suck of the teeth – 'you may give BUCHAN the following undertakings only... you will administer the following dire warning... oh yes!'

With a grunt of exasperation, he refolded the telegram, selected a plain white envelope from a drawer of his desk, put the telegram inside it and fed the envelope into the right-hand hip pocket of the Pendel & Braithwaite trousers that he had charged to London as a necessary operational expense. Returning to the strongroom he picked up a shabby leather briefcase that was by intent the very opposite of official, set it on the shelf and with yet another key from his ring opened the green wall-safe, which contained a stiff-backed ledger and thick bundles of fifty-dollar bills – hundreds being by his own edict to London too suspect to negotiate without making yourself conspicuous.

By the bulkhead light in the ceiling above him he turned

up the current page of the ledger. It was divided into three columns of handwritten figures. The left-hand column was headed H for Harry, the right-hand column A for Andy. The centre column, which contained the largest sums, was headed Income. Neat bubbles and lines of the kind beloved of sexologists directed its resources to left and right. Having studied all three columns in aggrieved silence, Osnard took a pencil from his pocket and reluctantly wrote a 7 in the centre column, drew a bubble round it and added a line to the left of its circumference, awarding it to column H for Harry. Then he wrote a 3 and, in happier vein, directed it to column A for Andy. Humming to himself, he counted seven thousand dollars from the safe into the floppy bag. After it he tossed in the fly spray and other bits and pieces from the shelf. Disdainfully. As if he despised them, which indeed he did. He closed the bag, locked the safe, then the strongroom and finally the front door.

A full moon smiled on him as he stepped into the street. A starry sky arched over the bay, and was mirrored by the lights of waiting ships strung across the black horizon. He hailed a clapped-out Pontiac cab, gave an address. Soon he was rattling along the airport road, watching anxiously for a mauve-neon Cupid firing its penile arrow towards the bungalows of love it advertised. His features, discovered by the beam of an opposing car, had hardened. His small dark eyes, as they maintained their wary watch on the driver's mirrors, caught fire with every passing light. *Chance favours only the prepared mind,* he recited to himself. It was the favourite dictum of a science master at his prep school who, having flogged him black and blue, suggested they make up their differences by taking off their clothes.

*　　　*　　　*

Somewhere near Watford just north of London there is an Osnard Hall. To reach it you negotiate a hectic bypass, then swing sharply through a rundown housing estate called Elm Glade, because that was where the ancient elms once stood. The Hall has had more lives in its last fifty years than in its previous four centuries: now an old people's home, now an institute for young offenders, now a stable for racing greyhounds and most recently, under the stewardship of Osnard's gloomy elder brother Lindsay, a sanctuary of meditation for followers of an Eastern sect.

For a while, through each of these transformations, Osnards as far away as India and Argentina divided up the rent, argued over the upkeep and whether a surviving nanny should receive her pension. But gradually, like the house that had spawned them, they fell into disrepair or simply gave up the struggle to survive. An Osnard uncle took his bit to Kenya and lost it. An Osnard cousin thought he could lord it over the Australians, bought an ostrich farm and paid the price. An Osnard lawyer raided the family trust, stole what he had not already dissipated through incompetent investment, then put a bullet through his head. Osnards who had not gone down with the *Titanic* went down with Lloyd's. Gloomy Lindsay, never one for half-measures, put on the saffron robes of a Buddhist monk and hanged himself from the one sound cherry tree that remained in the walled garden.

Only Osnard's parents, self-impoverished, remained infuriatingly alive, his father on a mortgaged family estate in Spain, eking out the dregs of his fortune and sponging off his Spanish relatives; his mother in Brighton where she shared genteel squalor with a chihuahua and a bottle of gin.

*   *   *

Others, given such a cosmopolitan perspective upon life, might have headed for new pastures or at least the Spanish sun. But young Andrew had determined from an early age that he was for England and, more specifically, England was for him. A childhood of deprival and the odious boarding schools that had seared their imprint on him for all time had left him feeling at the age of twenty that he had paid more dues to England than any reasonable country was entitled to exact from him, and that from now on he would cease paying and collect.

The question was how. He had no craft or qualification, no proven skills outside the golf course and the bedroom. What he understood best was English rot, and what he needed was a decaying English institution that would restore to him what other decaying institutions had taken away. His first thought was Fleet Street. He was semi-literate and unfettered by principle. He had scores to settle. On the face of it he was perfectly cut out to join the new rich media class. But after two promising years as a cub reporter with the *Loughborough Evening Messenger* his career ended with a snap when a steamy article entitled 'Sex Antics of our City Elders' turned out to be based on the pillowtalk of the managing editor's wife.

A great animal charity had him and for a while he believed he had found his true vocation. In splendid premises handy for theatres and restaurants the needs of Britain's animals were thrashed out with passionate commitment. No gala première, white-tie banquet or foreign journey to observe the animals of other nations was too onerous for the charity's highly paid officers to undertake. And everything might have come to fruition. The Instant Response Donkey Fund (Organiser: A. Osnard), the Veteran Greyhound Country Holiday Scheme (Finance Officer: A. Osnard) had been widely applauded when two of his superiors were invited to account for themselves to the Serious Fraud Office.

After that, for a giddy week he contemplated the Anglican Church, which traditionally offered swift promotion to glib, sexually active agnostics on the make. His piety evaporated when his researches revealed to him that catastrophic investment had reduced the Church to unwelcome Christian poverty. Desperate, he embarked on a succession of ill-planned adventures in life's fast lane. Each was shortlived, each ended in failure. More than ever, he needed a profession.

'How about the BBC?' he asked the Secretary, back at

his university appointments board for the fifth or fifteenth occasion.

The Secretary, who was grey-haired and old before his time, flinched.

'That one's over,' he said.

Osnard proposed the National Trust.

'Do you like old buildings?' the Secretary asked, as if he feared that Osnard might blow them up.

'Adore them. Total addict.'

'Quite so.'

With trembling fingertips the Secretary lifted a corner of a file and peered inside.

'I suppose they might just take you. You're disreputable. Charm of a sort. Bilingual, if they like Spanish. Nothing lost by giving them a try, I dare say.'

'The National Trust?'

'No, no. The spies. Here. Take this to a dark corner and fill it in with invisible ink.'

*   *   *

Osnard had found his Grail. Here at last was his true Church of England, his rotten borough with a handsome budget. Here were the nation's most private prayers, preserved as if in a museum. Here were sceptics, dreamers, zealots and mad abbots. And the cash to make them real.

Not that his enlistment was a foregone conclusion. This was the new slimline Service, free of the shackles of the past, classless in the great Tory tradition, with men and women democratically hand-picked from all walks of the white, privately-educated, suburban classes. And Osnard was as hand-picked as the rest of them:

'This sad thing with your brother Lindsay – taking his own life – how do you think it affected you?' a hollow-eyed espiocrat asked him with a frightful writhe from across the polished table.

Osnard had always detested Lindsay. He pulled a brave face.

'It hurt a hell of a lot,' he said.

'In what way?' Another writhe.

'Makes you ask yourself what's valuable. What you care about. What you're put on earth to get on with.'

'And that – suppose you had your way – would be this Service?'

'No question.'

'And you don't feel – having skipped around the globe so much – family here, there and everywhere – dual passports – that you're as it were too un-English for this kind of service? Too much a citizen of the world, rather than one of *us*?'

Patriotism was a thorny subject. How would Osnard handle it? Would he react defensively? Would he be rude? Or worst of all emotional? They need not have feared. All he asked of them was a place to invest his amorality.

'England's where I keep my toothbrush,' he replied to relieved laughter.

He was beginning to understand the game. It wasn't what he said that mattered, but how he said it. Can the boy think on his feet? Does he ruffle easily? Does he finesse, is he scared, does he persuade? Can he think the lie and speak the truth? Can he think the lie and speak it?

'We have been perusing your list of Significant Others over the last five years, young Mr Osnard,' said a bearded Scot, wrinkling his eyes for greater shrewdness. 'It's eh, somewhat of a long list' – suck of the teeth – 'for a relatively short life.'

Laughter in which Osnard joined, but not too heartily.

'I guess the best way to judge a love affair is how it ends,' he replied with sweet modesty. 'Most of mine seem to have ended pretty well.'

'And the others?'

'Well, I mean Christ, we've all woken up in the wrong bed a few times, haven't we?'

And since this was patently unlikely of any of the six faces round the table and of his bearded questioner particularly, Osnard won another cautious laugh.

'And you're family, did you know that?' said Personnel, bestowing a knobbly handshake on him by way of congratulation.

'Well, I suppose I am now,' said Osnard.

'No, no, *old* family. One aunt, one cousin. Or did you really not know?'

To the huge gratification of Personnel, he didn't. And when he heard who they were, a riotous belly-laugh welled up inside him which he converted only at the last moment to an endearing smirk of amazement.

'My name's Luxmore,' said the bearded Scot, with a handshake strangely similar to Personnel's. 'I run Iberia and South America and a couple of other places along the way. You may also hear me spoken of in connection with a certain little matter in the Falklands. I shall be looking out for you as soon as you have profited from your basic training, young Mr Osnard.'

'Can't wait, sir,' said Osnard keenly.

* * *

Nor could he. The spies of the post-Cold War era, he had observed, were enjoying the best of times and the worst of times. The Service had money to burn but where on earth was the fire? Stuck in the so-called Spanish Cellar that could have doubled as the editorial offices of the Madrid telephone directory, cheek-by-jowl with chain-smoking, middle-aged débutantes in Alice bands, the young probationer jotted down an acerbic appraisal of his employers' standing in the Whitehall marketplace:

Ireland Preferred: Regular earner, excellent long-term prospects, but slim pickings when divided between rival agencies.
Islam Militant: Occasional flurries, basically underperforming. As a substitute for Red Terror, total flop.
Arms for drugs plc: A washout. Service doesn't know whether to play gamekeeper or poacher.

As to that vaunted commodity of the modern age, industrial espionage, he reckoned when you had broken a few Taiwanese codes and suborned a few Korean typists, there was really little more you could do for British industry than commiserate. Or so he had convinced himself until Scottie Luxmore beckoned him to his side.

*   *   *

'*Panama*, young Mr Osnard' – striding up and down his fitted blue carpet, snapping fingers, thrusting elbows, nothing still – 'that's the place for a young officer of your talents. It's the place for all of us, if the fools in Treasury could only see beyond their noses. We'd the same problem with the Falklands difficulty, I don't mind telling you. Deaf ears until the stroke of midnight.'

Luxmore's room is large and close to Heaven. Through its tinted armoured-glass windows the Palace of Westminster stands brave across the Thames. Luxmore himself is small. A sharp beard and brisk stride fail to bring him up to size. He is an old man in a young man's world, and if he doesn't run he's likely to fall down. Or so thinks Osnard. Luxmore gives a quick suck of the Scottish front teeth as if he has a boiled sweet permanently on the go.

'But we're making headway. We've the Board of Trade and the Bank of England beating down the doors. The Foreign Office, though not given to hysteria, has expressed cautious concern. I remember they expressed much the same emotion when I had the pleasure of advising them of General Galtieri's intentions regarding the misnomered Malvinas.'

Osnard's heart sinks.

'But sir –' he objects in the carefully tuned voice of breathless neophyte that he has adopted.

'Yes, Andrew?'

'What's the *British interest* in Panama? Or am I being stupid?'

Luxmore is gratified by the boy's innocence. Moulding the young for service at the sharp end has ever been one of his keenest pleasures.

'There is none, Andrew. In Panama as a nation, zero British interest in any shape or form,' he replies with an arch smile. 'A few stranded mariners, a few hundred millions of British investment, a dwindling bunch of assimilated ancient Britons, a couple of moribund consultative committees and our interest in the Republic of Panama is served.'

'Then what –'

With a wave Luxmore commands Osnard's silence. He is addressing his own reflection in the armoured glass.

'Phrase your question somewhat differently, however, young Mr Osnard, and you would receive a vastly different answer. Oh yes.'

'How, sir?'

'What is our *geopolitical* interest in Panama? Ask yourself that, if you will.' He was away. 'What is our *vital* interest? Where is the lifeblood of our great trading nation most at risk? Where, when we train our long lens upon the future wellbeing of these islands, do we recognise the darkest storm clouds gathering, young Mr Osnard?' He was flying. 'Where in the entire globe do we perceive the next Hong Kong living on borrowed time, the next disaster waiting to happen?' Across the river apparently, where his visionary gaze was fixed. 'The barbarians are at the gate, young Mr Osnard. Predators from every corner of the globe are descending upon little Panama. That great clock out there is ticking away the minutes to Armageddon. Does our Treasury heed it? No. They are hiding their ears in their hands yet again. Who will win the greatest Prize Possession of the new millennium? Will it be the Arabs? Are the Japanese sharpening their *katanas*? Of course they are! Will it be the Chinese, the Tigers, or a Pan-Latin consortium underpinned with billions of drug dollars? Will it be Europe without us? Those Germans again, those wily French? It won't be the British, Andrew. That's a racing certainty. No, no. Not our hemisphere. Not our canal. We have no *interest* in Panama. Panama is a *backwater*, young Mr Osnard. Panama is two men and a dog and let's all go out and have a good lunch!'

'They're mad,' Osnard whispers.

'No, they're not. They're right. It's not our bailiwick. It's the Back Yard.'

Osnard's comprehension falters, then leaps to life. The

Back Yard! How many times in his training course had he not heard it mentioned? The Back Yard! El Dorado of every British espiocrat! Power and influence in the American back yard! The special relationship revived! The longed-for return to the Golden Age when tweed-jacketed sons of Yale and Oxford sat side by side in the same panelled rooms, pooling their imperialist fantasies! Luxmore has again forgotten Osnard's presence, and is speaking into his own soul:

'The Americans have done it again. Oh yes. A stunning demonstration of their political immaturity. Of their craven retreat from international responsibility. Of the pervasive power of misplaced liberal sensitivities in foreign affairs. We'd the same problem with the Falklands imbroglio, I may tell you confidentially. Oh yes.' A peculiar rictal grimace came over him as he clasped his hands behind his back and rose on the balls of his little feet. 'Not only have the Americans signed a totally misbegotten treaty with the Panamanians – given away the shop, thank you very much Mr Jimmy Carter! – they're also proposing to *honour* it. In consequence, they are proposing to leave themselves and, what is worse, their allies with a *vacuum*. It will be our job to fill it. To persuade *them* to fill it. To show them the error of their ways. To resume our rightful place at the top table. It's the oldest tale of them all, Andrew. We're the last of the Romans. We have the knowledge, but they have the power.' A cunning glance towards Osnard now, but one that took in the corners of the room as well, lest a barbarian had crept in unobserved. 'Our task – your task – will be to provide the *grounds*, young Mr Osnard, the *arguments*, the *evidence* needful to bring our American allies to their senses. Do you follow me?'

'Not entirely, sir.'

'That is because as of now you lack the grand vision. But you will acquire it. Believe me, you will acquire it.'

'Yes, sir.'

'To a grand vision, Andrew, there belong certain components. Well-grounded intelligence from the field is but one of them. Your born intelligencer is the man who knows what he is looking for before he finds it. Remember that, young Mr Osnard.'

'I will, sir.'

'He intuits. He selects. He tastes. He says "yes" – or "no" – but he is not omnivorous. He is even – by his selection – fastidious. Do I make myself clear?'

'I'm afraid not, sir.'

'Good. Because when the time is ripe, all – no, not all, but a corner – will be revealed to you.'

'I can't wait.'

'You must. Patience is also a virtue of the born intelligencer. You must have the patience of the Red Indian. His sixth sense also. You must learn to see beyond the far horizon.'

To show him how, Luxmore once again directs his gaze upriver towards the stodgy fortresses of Whitehall and frowns. But his frown turns out to be directed at America:

'*Dangerous diffidence* is what I call it, young Mr Osnard. The world's one superpower restrained by puritan principle, God help us. Have they not heard of Suez? There are a few ghosts there that must be rising from their graves! There is no greater criminal in politics, young Mr Osnard, than he who shrinks from using honourable power. America must wield her sword or perish and drag us down with her. Are we to look on while our priceless Western inheritance is handed to heathens on a plate? The lifeblood of our trade, our mercantile power, ebbing through our fingers while the Jap economy zeroes out of the sun at us and the Tigers of South-East Asia tear us limb from limb? Is that who we are? Is that the spirit of the modern generation, young Mr Osnard? Maybe it is. Maybe we are wasting our time. Enlighten me, please. I do not jest, Andrew.'

'It's not *my* spirit, I know that, sir,' Osnard said devoutly.

'Good boy. Nor mine, nor mine.' Luxmore pauses, measures Osnard with his eyes, wondering how much more it is safe to tell him.

'Andrew.'

'Sir.'

'We are not alone, thank God.'

'Good, sir.'

'You say good. How much do you know?'

'Only what you're telling me. And what I've felt for a long time.'

'They told you nothing of this on your training course?'

Nothing of what? Osnard wonders.

'Nothing, sir.'

'A certain highly secret body known as the Planning & Application Committee was never mentioned?'

'No, sir.'

'Chaired by one Geoff Cavendish, a man remarkable for his far-reaching mind, skilled in the arts of influence and peaceful persuasion?'

'No, sir.'

'A man who knows his American as no other?'

'No, sir.'

'No talk of a new realism sweeping through the secret corridors? Of broadening the base of covert policy-making? Rallying good men and women from all walks of life to the secret flag?'

'No.'

'Of ensuring that those who have made this nation great shall have a hand in the saving of her, whether they be ministers of the Crown, captains of industry, press barons, bankers, ship-owners or men and women of the world?'

'No.'

'That together we shall *plan*, and having planned, *apply* our plans? That henceforth, through the careful importation of experienced outside minds, scruple shall be set aside in those cases where action may arrest the rot? Nothing?'

'Nothing.'

'Then I must hold my tongue, young Mr Osnard. And so must you. Henceforth it shall not be enough for this Service to know the size and strength of the rope that will hang us. With God's help we too shall wield the sword with which to cut it. Forget what I just said.'

'I will, sir.'

Church evidently over, Luxmore returns with renewed righteousness to the topic he has temporarily abandoned.

'Does it faintly concern our gallant Foreign Office or the high-minded liberals of Capitol Hill that the Panamanians are not fit to run a coffee stall, let alone the world's greatest gateway to trade? That they are corrupt and pleasure-seeking, venal to the point of immobility?' He swings round, as if to refute an objection from the back of the hall. 'Who will they sell themselves to, Andrew? Who will buy them? For what? And with what effect upon our vital interests? Catastrophic is not a word I use carelessly, Andrew.'

'Why not call it criminal?' Osnard suggests helpfully.

Luxmore shakes his head. The man is not yet born who can correct Scottie Luxmore's adjectives with impunity. Osnard's self-appointed mentor and guide has one more card to play and Osnard must watch him do it, since little that Luxmore ever does is real unless it is observed by others. Picking up a green telephone that links him with other immortals on Whitehall's Mount Olympus, he contrives a facial expression that is at once playful and significant.

'Tug!' he cries delightedly – and for a moment Osnard mistakes the word for an instruction rather than the nick-name it turns out to be. 'Tell me, Tug, am I correct in my belief that the Planners & Appliers are having themselves a little get-together next Thursday at a certain person's house? – I am. Well, well. My spies are not always so accurate, hem, hem. Tug, will you do me the honour of lunching you that day, the better to prepare you for the ordeal, ha, ha? And if friend Geoff were able to join us, may I take it you would not be averse? My shout, now, Tug, I insist. Listen, where would be congenial to us, I am wondering? Somewhere a wee bit apart from the mainstream, I was thinking. Let us avoid the more obvious watering-holes. I have in mind a small Italian restaurant just off the Embankment there – do you have a pencil handy, Tug?'

And meanwhile he pivots on one heel, rises on his toes, and lifts his knees in slow mark time in order to avoid falling over the telephone cable at his feet.

*　　　*　　　*

'*Panama?*' cried Personnel jovially. 'As a *first posting? You?* Stuck out there on your own at *your* tender age? All those gorgeous Panamanian *girls* to tempt you? Dope, sin, spies, crooks? Scottie must be off his head!'

And having had his fun, Personnel did what Osnard knew all along he was going to do. He posted him to Panama. Osnard's inexperience was no obstacle. His precocity in the black arts was well attested by his trainers. He was bilingual and in operational terms unsullied.

'Have to find yourself a head joe,' Personnel lamented as an afterthought. 'Apparently we've no one on the books down there. We seem to have left the place to the Americans. More fool us. You report direct to Luxmore, you understand? Keep the analysts out of this until otherwise instructed.'

*   *   *

Find us a banker, young Mr Osnard – suck of the Scottish front teeth inside the beard – *one who knows the world! These modern bankers put themselves about, not like the old sort at all. I remember we had a couple in Buenos Aires during the Falklands fracas.*

Assisted by a central computer whose existence has been roundly denied by both Westminster and Whitehall, Osnard calls up the file of every British banker in Panama but finds only a handful and nobody who on closer enquiry can be counted on to know the world.

Find us one of your state-of-the-art tycoons then, young Mr Osnard – wrinkle of the sagacious Scottish eyes – *someone with a finger in all the pies!*

Osnard calls up the particulars of every British businessman in Panama and though some are young, none has a finger in all the pies, much as he might like to have.

Then find us a scribbler, young Mr Osnard. Scribblers can ask questions without attracting interest, go anywhere, take risks! There must be a decent one somewhere. Seek him out. Bring him to me, if you please forthwith!

Osnard calls up the particulars of every British journalist known to take the odd swing through Panama and speak

Spanish. A well-dined, mustachioed man in a bow tie is held to be approachable. His name is Hector Pride and he writes for an unheard-of English language monthly called *The Latino*, published out of Costa Rica. His father is a wine shipper from Toledo.

Just the fellow we need, young Mr Osnard! – ferociously bestriding his carpet – *Sign him. Buy him. Money is no obstacle. If the skinflints of Treasury lock up their coffers, the counting houses of Threadneedle Street shall open theirs. I have that assurance from on high. It is a strange country, you may say, young Mr Osnard, that obliges its industrialists to pay for their intelligence, but such is the harsh nature of our cost-conscious world. . .*

Using an alias, Osnard puts on the guise of a Foreign Office research officer and invites Hector Pride to lunch at Simpson's and spends twice what Luxmore has allowed for the occasion. Pride, like many of his profession, speaks and eats and drinks a great deal, but does not care to listen. Osnard waits until the pudding to pop the question, then until the Gorgonzola, by which time Pride's patience has evidently run out, for to Osnard's dismay he abandons his monologue on the effect of Inca culture on contemporary Peruvian thought and explodes in ribald laughter.

'Why don't you make a pass at me?' he booms, to the alarm of diners either side. 'What's wrong with me? Got the girl in the bloody taxi, haven't you? So put your hand up her skirt!'

Pride, it transpires, is employed by a hated sister service of British Intelligence, which also owns his newspaper.

'There's this man Pendel I talked to you about,' Osnard reminds Luxmore, taking advantage of his gloom. 'The one with the wife in the Canal Commission. I can't help thinking they're ideal.'

*   *   *

He has been thinking it for days and nights, and thinking no one else. *Chance favours only the prepared mind.* He has drawn Pendel's criminal record, pored over Pendel's criminal photographs, full face and side view, studied his statements to the police though most were patently fabricated by his audience, read psychiatrists' and almoners' reports, records of his behaviour in prison, dug out whatever he could on Louisa and the tiny, inward world of the Zonian. Like an occult diviner, he has opened himself to Pendel's psychic intimations and vibrations, studied him as intently as would a medium his map of the impenetrable jungle where the plane is believed to have disappeared: I am coming to find you, I know what you are, wait for me, *chance favours only the prepared mind.*

*   *   *

Luxmore reflects. Only a week ago he has ruled this same Pendel unworthy of the high mission he has in mind:

As my head joe, Andrew? As yours? In a red hot post? A tailor? We'd be the laughing stock of the Top Floor!

And when Osnard again presses him, this time after lunch when Luxmore's mood tends to be more generous:

I am a stranger to prejudice, young Mr Osnard, and I respect your judgment. But those East End fellows end up stabbing you in the back. It's in their blood. Good heavens, we are not yet reduced to recruiting jailbirds!

But that is a week ago, and the Panamanian clock is ticking louder.

'You know I think we may be onto a winner here,' Luxmore declares as he sucks his teeth and leafs through Pendel's compendious file a second time. 'It was prudent of us to test the ground elsewhere first, oh yes. The Top Floor will surely give us marks for that' – the boy Pendel's implausible confession to the police flits by him, owning up to everything, incriminating no one – 'the man's first-class material once you look under the surface, just the type we need for a small criminal nation' – suck – 'we'd a fellow not unlike him working in the docks in Buenos Aires during the Falklands difficulty.' His eye settles for a moment on Osnard, but there is no suggestion in his glance that he considers his subordinate similarly qualified for criminal society. 'You'll have to ride him, Andrew. They've a hard mouth, these East End haberdashers, are you up to that?'

'I think so, sir. If you give me the odd tip here and there.'

'A villain is all to the good in this game provided he's *our* villain' – immigration papers of the father Pendel never knew – 'And the wife indubitably an asset' – suck – 'one foot in the Canal Commission already, my God. Daughter of an American engineer too, Andrew, I see a steadying hand here. Christian too. Our East End gentleman has done well for himself. No religious barriers to progress, we notice, eh-hem. Self-interest always firmly to the fore, as usual' – suck – 'Andrew, I begin to see shapes here forming before us in the sky. You'll have to look at his accounts three times, I'll tell you that for nothing. He'll graft, he'll have the nose, the cunning, but can you handle him? Who's going to run who? that'll be the problem' – a glimpse of Pendel's birth certificate bearing the name of the mother who ran away – 'these fellows certainly know how to get into a man's drawing room, too, no doubt of that, oh yes. *And* get their pound of flesh. We'll be throwing you in at the deep end, I fear. Can you handle it?'

'I believe I can, actually.'

'Yes, Andrew. So do I. A real hard customer, but *ours*, that's the point. A natural assimilator, prison-trained, knows the dark side of the street' – suck – '*and* the dirty underbelly of the human mind. There's jeopardy here, which I like. So will the Top Floor.' Luxmore slapped the file shut and started pacing again, this time in widths. 'If we can't appeal to his patriotism, we can put the frighteners on him and appeal to his greed. Let me tell you about head joes, Andy.'

'Please do, sir.'

The *sir*, though by tradition reserved for the Chief of Service, is Osnard's contribution to Luxmore's self-powered flight.

'You can take a *bad* head joe, young Mr Osnard. And you can stand him before the opposition's safe with the combination ringing in his stupid ears and he'll come back to you empty-handed. I know. I've been there. We'd one during the Falklands conflagration. But a *good* one, you can dump him blindfold in the desert and he'll sniff out his target in a week. Why? He's got the larceny' – suck – 'I've seen it many times. Remember that, Andy. If a man hath not larceny, he is nothing.'

'I really will,' says Osnard.

Another gear. Sits sharply to his desk. Reaches for telephone. Stays his hand. 'Call up Registry,' he orders Osnard. 'Have them pick us a random codename out of the hat. A codename shows intent. Draft me a submission, not above one page in length. They're busy men up there.' Takes up telephone finally. Taps number. 'Meanwhile I shall make a couple of private telephone calls to one or two influential members of the public who are sworn to secrecy and shall remain forever nameless' – suck – 'those amateurs from Treasury will put their spoke in anything. Think Canal, Andrew. Everything rides on the Canal.' Stops in tracks, replaces receiver on cradle. Eyes turn to smoked glass window where filtered black clouds menace the Mother of Parliaments. Beat. 'I shall tell them that, Andrew,' he breathes. *Everything rides on the Canal.* It shall be our slogan when we are dealing with people from all walks of life.'

But Osnard's thoughts remain on earthly things. 'We're going to have to work out quite a tricky pay structure for him, aren't we, sir?'

'Why's that? Nonsense. Rules are made to be broken. Didn't they teach you that? Of course they didn't. Those trainers are all has-beens. I see you have a point to press. Out with it.'

'Well, sir.'

'Yes, Andrew.'

'I'd like to get a reading on his financial situation as of now. In Panama. If he's making a pot of money –'

'Yes?'

'Well, we'll have to offer him a pot, won't we? A fellow netting quarter of a million bucks a year and we offer him another twenty-five thousand, we're unlikely to be tempting him. If you follow me.'

'So?' – playful, drawing the boy out.

'Well, sir, I wondered if one of your friends in the City

might get onto Pendel's bank under a pretext and find out the score.'

Luxmore is already on the telephone, spare hand thrust down the seam of his trousers.

'Miriam, dear. Find me Geoff Cavendish. Failing him, Tug. And, Miriam. It's urgent.'

*   *   *

It was another four days before Osnard was once more summoned to the presence. Pendel's wretched bank statements lay about on Luxmore's desk, courtesy of Ramón Rudd. Luxmore himself was standing stock still at his window, savouring a moment of history.

'He's appropriated his wife's savings, Andrew. Every penny. Can't resist usury. They never can. We've got him by the short-and-curlies.'

He waited while Osnard read the figures.

'A salary's no good to him then,' said Osnard, whose grasp on financial matters was a deal more sophisticated than his master's.

'Oh. Why not?'

'It'll go straight into his bank manager's pocket. We're going to have to bankroll him from day one.'

'How much?'

Osnard by now had a figure in his mind. He doubled it, knowing the virtue of starting as he meant to continue.

'My God, Andrew. As much as that?'

'It could be more, sir,' said Osnard bleakly. 'He's in up to his neck.'

Luxmore's gaze turned to the City's skyline for comfort.

'Andrew?'

'Sir?'

'I mentioned to you that a grand vision has certain components.'

'Yes, sir.'

'One of them is scale. Don't send me dross. No grapeshot. Not "Here, Scottie, take this bag of bones and see what your analysts make of it." Do you follow me?'

'Not quite, sir.'

'The analysts here are idiots. They don't make connections. They don't see shapes forming in the sky. A man reaps as he sows. Do you understand me? A great intelligencer catches history in the act. We can't expect some little nine-till-five fellow on the third floor who's worried about his mortgage to catch history in the act. Can we? It takes a man of vision to catch history in the act. Does it not?'

'I'll do my best, sir.'

'Don't let me down, Andrew.'

'I'll try not to, sir.'

*   *   *

But if Luxmore had chanced to turn round at that moment he would have found to his surprise that Osnard's demeanour lacked the meekness of his tone. A smile of triumph lit his guileless young face and sparks of greed his eyes. Packing, selling the car, swearing allegiance to each of half-a-dozen girlfriends and performing other chores associated with his departure, Andrew Osnard took a step not normally expected of a young Englishman setting out to serve his Queen in foreign climes. Through a distant relative in the West Indies he opened a numbered account on Grand Cayman, having first established that the compliant bank had a branch in Panama City.

CHAPTER THIRTEEN

Osnard paid off the clapped-out Pontiac and stepped into the night. The prickly quiet and low lighting reminded him of training school. He was sweating. In this bloody climate he usually was. Underpants nipping at his crutch. Shirt like a wet dishcloth. Hate it. Cars without lights crackled stealthily past him over the wet drive. High cropped hedges provided for extra discretion. It had rained and stopped again. Bag in hand, he crossed a tarmac courtyard. A naked six-foot plastic Venus, lit from somewhere inside her vulva, shed a sickly glow. He stubbed his foot against a plant-tub, swore, this time in Spanish, and came upon a row of garages with plastic ribbons dangling over their doorways and a low-powered candle bulb lighting each number. Reaching number eight, he shoved aside the ribbons, groped his way to a red pinlight on the far wall and pressed it: the fabled pushbutton. A genderless Voice from the Beyond thanked him for his visit.

'My name's Colombo. I booked.'

'You prefer a special room, Señor Colombo?'

'Prefer the one I booked. Three hours. How much?'

'You want to change to a special, Señor Colombo? Wild West? Arabian Nights? Tahiti? Fifty dollars more?'

'No.'

'One hundred and five dollars, please. Enjoy your stay.'

'Give me a receipt for three hundred,' Osnard said.

A buzzer sounded and an illuminated letterbox opened at his elbow. He posted one hundred and twenty dollars into its red mouth, which snapped shut. Delay while the notes were passed through a detector, the excess duly noted, the bogus receipt prepared.

'Come back and see us again, Señor Colombo.'

A shaft of white light half blinded him, a crimson welcome rug appeared at his feet, an electronic Tudor door clicked open. A fug of disinfectant fumes slapped him like a blast from an oven. An absent band struck up 'O Sole Mio'. Sweat pouring off him, he glared round for the air-conditioners at the same moment as he heard them crank themselves into action. Pink mirrors on the walls and ceiling. A convocation of Osnards glowering at each other. Mirrored bedhead, crimson flock counterpane shimmering under nauseous lighting. Freebie spongebag containing comb, toothbrush, three French letters, two bars of American milk chocolate. Television screen showing two matrons and a forty-five-year-old Latin man with hair on his arse cavorting naked in somebody's drawing room. Osnard looked for a switch to turn them off but the flex ran straight into the wall.

Jesus. Typical.

He sat on the bed, opened his shabby briefcase, set out his wares on the bedspread. One sheaf o' fresh carbon wrapped as locally-produced typing paper. Six reels o' subminiature film concealed in can o' fly spray. Why do Head Office concealment devices look as if they've been bought in Russian government-surplus stores? One subminiature tape recorder, undisguised. One bottle Scotch, head joes and their case officers for the use of. Seven thousand bucks in twenties and fifties. Pity to see it go but think of it as seed money.

And from his pocket, in all its undestroyed glory, Luxmore's four-page telegram, which Osnard laid out page by page for easy reading.Then he sat frowning at it with his mouth hanging open, selecting from it, memorising and rejecting simultaneously, the way a Method actor might read his lines: I'll say *this* but say it differently, I won't say *that* at all, I'll do *this* but my way not his. He heard the rumble of a car pulling into garage number eight. Rising, he tucked the four pages of the telegram back in his pocket and placed himself at the centre of the room. He heard the clunk of a tinny door and thought 'four-track'. He heard footsteps approaching and thought 'walks like a bloody waiter' while he tried to listen beyond them for sounds that might not be so friendly. Has Harry sold and told? Has he brought a bunch of heavies to arrest me? Of course he bloody hasn't, but the trainers said it was wise to wonder so I'm wondering. A knock at the door: three shorts, one long. Osnard slipped the lock and drew the door back, not all the way. Pendel, standing on the doorstep, clutching a fancy holdall.

'My goodness me, whatever are *they* up to, Andy? Reminds me of the Three Tolinos at Bertram Mills Circus when my Uncle Benny used to take me.'

'Christ's sake!' Osnard hissed as he bundled him into the room. 'You've got P & B plastered all over your bloody bag.'

*   *   *

There was no chair so they sat on the bed. Pendel was wearing a *panabrisa*. A week ago he had confided to Osnard that *panabrisas* would be the death of him: cool, smart and comfortable, Andy, and cost fifty dollars, I don't know why I bother. Osnard went into the routine. This was no chance encounter between tailor and customer. This was a full-scale, twenty-five-thousand-mile service conducted according to the classic spy-school handbook.

'Got any problems with being here?'

'Thank you, Andy, everything is hunkydory. How about you?'

'Got any materials that are better in my hands than yours?'

Groping in a pocket of his *panabrisa*, Pendel produced the ornamented cigarette lighter, delved again for a coin, unscrewed the base and shook out a black cylinder which he passed across the bed.

'There's only the twelve on there, Andy, I'm afraid, but I thought you'd better have them all the same. In my day we'd have waited till the film was finished before we took it to the chemist.'

'Nobody follow you, recognise you? Motorbike? Car? Nobody you didn't like the look of?'

Pendel shook his head.

'What do you do if we're disturbed?'

'I leave the explanations to you, Andy. I take my departure at my earliest convenience and I advise my subsources to get their heads down or take a foreign holiday and you wait for me to contact you when normal service is resumed.'

'How?'

'The emergency procedure. Callbox to callbox at the agreed times.'

Osnard obliged Pendel to recite the agreed times.

'How about if that doesn't work?'

'Well, there's always the shop, isn't there, Andy? We *are* somewhat overdue for a fitting on our tweed jacket, which provides us with a cast-iron excuse. It's a corker,' he added. 'I can always tell a nice jacket when I've cut one.'

'How many letters have you sent me since we last met?'

'Just the three, Andy. That was all I could manage in the time. Business is coming in you wouldn't believe. The new clubroom has really tipped the balance in my opinion.'

'What were they?'

'Two invoices and one invitation to a preview of new attractions in the boutique. They came out all right, did they? Because I worry sometimes.'

'You're not pressing hard enough. Writing gets lost in the print. You using ballpoint or pencil?'

'Pencil, Andy, like you told me.'

Osnard fished in the sump of his briefcase and came up with a plain wood pencil. 'Have a go with this next time. Double H. Harder.'

On the screen the two women had abandoned their man and were consoling themselves with one another.

*   *   *

Stores. Osnard handed Pendel the can of fly spray containing spare cassettes of film. Pendel shook it, pressed the top and grinned when it worked. Pendel expressed anxiety about the shelf-life of his carbons, whether they'd lost their fizz or anything, Andy? Osnard handed him a new set anyway and told him to sling whatever he had left of the old lot.

The network. Osnard needed to hear the progress of each subsource and record it in his notebook. Subsource Sabina, Marta's star creation and alter ego, dissident politics student with responsibility for the El Chorillo cadre of secret Maoists, was asking for a new printing press to replace her defunct one. Estimated cost five thousand dollars or maybe Andy knew where to put his hands on an old one?

'She buys her own,' Osnard ruled shortly as he wrote down 'printing press' and 'ten thousand dollars'. 'It's arm's length all the way. She still think she's selling her information to the Yanks?'

'Yes, Andy, until Sebastian tells her different.'

Sebastian, another Marta construct, was Sabina's lover, an embittered people's lawyer and retired anti-Noriega campaigner who, thanks to his impoverished clientele, provided snippets of deep background on such oddities as the underlife of Panama's Muslim Arab community.

'What's with Alpha Beta?' Osnard asked.

Subsource Beta was Pendel's own: a member of the National Assembly's Canal Consultative Committee and a part-time dealer in bank accounts looking for respectable homes. Beta's aunt Alpha was a secretary in the Panamanian Chamber of Commerce. In Panama everybody has an aunt working somewhere useful.

'Beta's up country stroking his constituency, Andy, which is why he's quiet. But he's got a nice meeting Thursday with the Chamber of Commerce and Industry of Panama and dinner with the Vice-President Friday, so there's light at the end of the tunnel. And London liked his latest, did they? He sometimes feels he's not appreciated.'

'It was okay. Far as it went.'

'Only Beta did rather wonder whether a bonus might be in order.'

Osnard seemed to wonder too, for he made a note and scribbled a figure and drew a circle round it.

'Let you know next time,' he said. 'What's with Marco?'

'Marco is what I'd call sitting pretty, Andy. We had a night on the town, I've met his wife, we've walked the dog together and gone to the pictures.'

'When are you going to pop the question?'

'Next week, Andy, if I'm in the mood.'

'Well, be in the mood. Starting salary five hundred a week, subject to review after three months, payable in advance. Bonus o' five thousand cash when he signs on the dotted line.'

'For Marco?'

'For you, you ass,' said Osnard, handing him a glass of Scotch in all the pink mirrors at once.

* * *

Osnard was making the kind of signals that people in authority make when they have something disagreeable to say. A pout of discontent settled over his rubbery features, he scowled at the cavorting acrobats on the television screen.

'You seem very sunny today,' he began accusingly.

'Thank you, Andy, and it's all down to you and London.'

'Lucky you've got the loan, then. Isn't it? I said, *isn't* it?'

'Andy, I'm thanking my Maker for it every day and the thought that I'm working it off puts a spring into my stride. Is there something wrong, then?'

Osnard had assumed his head prefect tone, though he had only ever been at the receiving end of it, usually before a beating.

'Yes. There is, actually. Quite a *lot* wrong.'

'Oh dear.'

'I'm afraid London are not quite as pleased with you as you appear to be with yourself.'

'Why's that then, Andy?'

'Nothing much. Nothing at all, really. They have merely decided that H. Pendel, superspy, is an overpaid, disloyal, grafting, two-faced con-artist.'

*   *   *

Pendel's smile underwent a slow but total eclipse. His shoulders fell, his hands, which till now had been supporting him on the bed, came obediently to rest at the front of his body, demonstrating to the officer that they meant no harm.

'Any particular reason at all, Andy? Or was it more the general overview they were taking?'

'Furthermore, they are not at *all* pleased with Mr Mickie bloody Abraxas.'

Pendel's head lifted sharply.

'Why? What's Mickie done?' he demanded with unexpected spirit – unexpected by himself, that was. 'Mickie's not in this,' he added aggressively.

'Not in *what*?'

'Mickie's done nothing.'

'No. He hasn't. That's the point. For too bloody long. Apart from graciously accepting ten thousand bucks cash up front as an act of good faith. What have *you* done? Also nothing. Contemplated Mickie contemplating his navel.' His voice had acquired the saw-edge of schoolboy sarcasm. 'And what have *I* done? Credited you with a very handsome bonus for *productivity* – joke – which, put into plain language, means recruiting a spectacularly *un*productive subsource, to wit one M. Abraxas, slayer of tyrants and champion o' the common man. London's having a bloody good laugh about that. Wondering whether the *officer in the field* – me – is a little too *green*, and a little too *gullible* to mix it with idle, money-grabbing sharks like M. Abraxas and you.'

Osnard's tirade had fallen on deaf ears. Instead of druckening himself, Pendel appeared to be enjoying an easing of the body, indicating that whatever he had feared was past, and whatever they were now dealing with was small beer by comparison with his nightmares. His hands returned to his sides, he crossed his legs and settled back against the bedhead.

'So what does London propose to do about him, we wonder, Andy?' he enquired sympathetically.

*　　*　　*

Osnard had abandoned his hectoring voice for one of puffy indignation.

'Bleating about his debts of honour. What about his debt of honour to *us*? Keeping us dancing on a string – "can't tell you today, tell you next month" – getting us all sexed up about a conspiracy that doesn't exist, bunch o' students only he can talk to, bunch o' fishermen who will only talk to the students, blah blah. Hell does he think he is, for Christ's sake? Hell does he think *we* are? Bloody idiots?'

'It's his loyalties, Andy. It's his delicate sources, same as you. All the people he's got to get the say-so from.'

'Fuck his loyalties! We've been waiting on his precious loyalties for three bloody weeks. If he's as loyal as all that he should never have bubbled his Movement to you in the first place. But he did. So you've got him over a barrel. And in our business, when you've got somebody over a barrel, you do something about it. You don't keep everybody waiting for the answer to the meaning o' the universe because some altruistic wino derelict needs three weeks to get his friends' permission to tell it to you.'

'So what *do* you do, Andy?' Pendel asked quietly.

And if Osnard had possessed that kind of ear or heart, he might have recognised in Pendel's voice the same undertow that had entered it at lunch a few weeks back when the question of recruiting Mickie's Silent Opposition was first raised.

'I'll tell you exactly what you do,' he snapped, once more donning his head prefect's gown. 'You go to Mr Bloody Abraxas and you say, "Mickie. Hate to break this to you. My mad millionaire chappie isn't going to wait any more. So unless you want to go back to the Panamanian slammer whence you came, on charges o' conspiring with persons unknown to do whatever the fuck you're conspiring to do, cough up. Because there's a bag o' money waiting for you if you *do*, and a very hard bed in a very small space if you *don't*.'' Is that water in that bottle?'

'Yes, Andy, I do believe it is. And I'm sure you'd like some.'

Pendel handed him the bottle, provided by the management for the resuscitation of exhausted customers. Osnard drank, wiped his lips with the back of his hand and the neck of the bottle with his podgy forefinger. Then he handed the bottle back to Pendel. But Pendel decided he wasn't thirsty. He was feeling sick, but it wasn't the kind of nausea that water cures. It had more to do with his close collegial friendship with his fellow prisoner Abraxas and Osnard's suggestion that he defile it. And the last thing in the world Pendel wanted to do at that moment was drink from a bottle that was wet with Osnard's spit.

'It's bits, bits, bits,' Osnard was complaining, still on his high horse. 'And what do they add up to? Flannel. Jam tomorrow. Wait-and-see. We're lacking the grand vision, Harry. The big one that's always just around the corner. London want it now. They can't wait any more. Nor can we. Are you reading me?'

'Loud and clear, Andy. Loud and clear.'

'Well good,' said Osnard in a grudging, half-conciliatory tone intended to restore their good relationship.

And from Abraxas, Osnard passed to a topic even closer to Pendel's heart, namely his wife Louisa.

*　　　*　　　*

'Delgado's on his way up in the world, see that?' Osnard kicked off breezily. 'Press made him up to lord high whoosit of the Canal Steering Committee, I see. Can't rise much higher than that without his toupee burning.'

'I read about it,' Pendel said.

'Where?'

'In the papers. Where else?'

'The newspapers?'

It was Osnard's turn to act the smiler, Pendel's to hold back.

'Wasn't Louisa who told you about it, then?'

'Not till it was public. She wouldn't.'

Stay away from my friend, Pendel's eyes were saying. Stay away from my wife.

'Why ever not?' Osnard asked.

'She's discreet. It's her sense of duty. I've told you already.'

'She know you're meeting me tonight?'

'Of course she doesn't. What am I? Daft?'

'She knows something's going on, though, doesn't she? Noticed your change o' life style, all that? Not blind.'

'I'm branching out. That's all she knows or needs to.'

'Lot o' ways o' branching out though, aren't there? Not all of 'em good news. Not for wives.'

'She's not bothered.'

'Wasn't the impression she gave me, Harry. Out there on Anytime Island. Struck me as being a mite exercised in her mind. Wasn't making heavy weather of it. Not her way. Just wanted me to tell her whether it was normal at your age.'

'What was?'

'Needing everybody's company. Twenty-four hours a day. Except hers. Scampering around town.'

'What did you tell her?'

'Said I'd wait till I was forty and let her know. Great woman, Harry.'

'Yes. She is. So stay off her.'

'Just occurred to me she might be happier if you were able to put her mind at ease.'

'Her mind's all right where it is.'

'Just wish we could step a bit closer to the well, that's all.'

'What well?'

'The well. The source. Fountain of all knowledge. Delgado. She's a fan o' Mickie's. Admires him. Told me. Adores Delgado. Loathes the idea of a backdoor sellout o' the Canal. Looks like a dead cert to me. Seen from here.'

Pendel's eyes were prison eyes again, sullen and locked in. But Osnard failed to notice Pendel's retreat into his own interior, preferring to muse aloud about Louisa in an inferential kind of way.

'One o' the absolute naturals of all time, if you ask me.'

'Who?'

' "Target the Canal," ' Osnard mused. ' "Everything rides on the Canal." Only thing London seems able to think about. Who's going to get it. What they'll do with it. Whole o' Whitehall wetting its striped pants to find out who Delgado talks to in the woodshed.' He closed his eyes reflectively. '*Marvellous* girl. One o' the world's best. Steady as a rock, grip like a limpet, loyal unto the grave. Fabulous material.'

'What for?'

Osnard let the Scotch slip down. 'Bit o' help from you, sold to her in the right way, proper use o' language, no problem,' he went on ruminatively. 'No direct action involved. Not asking her to plant a bomb in the Palace o' Herons, shack up with the students, go to sea with the fisher lads. All she has to do is listen and watch.'

'Watch what?'

'Don't have to mention your chum Andy. Didn't have to mention him to Abraxas or the others. Don't with her. Stress the marital tie, best thing. The old honour and obey. Louisa hands her stuff to you. You hand it to me. I bung it back at London. Doddle.'

'She loves the Canal, Andy. She's not about to betray it. That's not who she is.'

'She won't *be* betraying it, you ass! Saving it, Christ's sakes! She thinks the sun shines out o' Delgado's arse, right?'

'She's American, Andy. She respects Delgado but she loves America as well.'

'Not betraying America either, Christ's sakes! Holding Uncle Sam's nose to the grindstone. Keeping his troops *in situ.* Keeping the military bases. What more can she ask? She'll be helping Delgado by saving the Canal from the crooks, helping America by telling us how the Pans are screwing up and there's all the more reason for US troops to stay put. You speak? Didn't catch you.'

Pendel had indeed spoken, but his voice was so choked

that it was barely audible. So like Osnard he drew himself upright, then tried again.

'I think I must have asked you how much you thought Louisa was worth on the open market, Andy.'

Osnard welcomed this practical question. He had intended to raise it himself further down the line.

'Same as you, Harry. Even-Stevens,' he said heartily. 'Same basic, same bonuses. Absolute point o' principle with me. Gals are just as good as us. Better. Told London only yesterday. It's equal pay or there's no deal. We can double your money. One foot in the Silent Opposition, t'other in the Canal. Cheers.'

The film on the television had changed. Two cowgirls were undressing a cowboy in the middle of a canyon while tethered horses averted their gaze.

*   *   *

Pendel was speaking in his sleep, slowly and mechanically, to himself rather than to Osnard.

'She'd never do it.'

'Why not?'

'She's got principles.'

'We'll buy 'em.'

'They're not for sale. She's like her mother. The harder she's pushed, the more she stands still.'

'Why push her? Why not have her jump of her own free will?'

'Very funny.'

Osnard became declamatory. He flung up an arm and clasped the other to his breast. '"I'm a hero, Louisa! You can be another! March at my side! Join the crusade! Save the Canal! Save Delgado! Blow the whistle on corruption!" Want me to have a crack at her for you?'

'No. And you wouldn't be wise to try.'

'Why not?'

'She doesn't like the English, frankly. She puts up with me because I'm a highbred. But where the English upper classes are concerned she inclines to her father's opinion that they're a bunch of highly duplicitous bastards with no scruples of any sort or kind without exception.'

'Thought she took quite a shine to me.'

'Plus she wouldn't grass on her boss. Ever.'

'Not for a nice piece o' change? I wonder?'

But from Pendel, still the mechanical voice: 'Money doesn't speak to her, thank you. She thinks we've got enough as it is, plus there's quite a large part of her thinks it's evil and ought to be abolished.'

'So we'll pay her salary to her beloved hubby. Cash. No need to chalk it against the loan. You do the finances, she does the altruism. She need never know.'

But Pendel did not respond to this happy portrait of the spying couple. His face was stony, staring at the wall, ready for a long stretch.

*   *   *

On the screen, the cowboy lay supine on a horseblanket. The cowgirls, who had retained their hats and boots, stood one at either end of him, as if wondering which way to wrap him up. But Osnard was too busy delving in his briefcase to notice, and Pendel was still frowning at the wall.

'Christ – nearly forgot,' Osnard exclaimed.

And he brought out a wad of dollars, then another, until all seven thousand lay on the bed amid the fly spray and carbons and the cigarette lighter.

'Bonuses. Sorry about the delay. Clowns in Banking Section.'

With difficulty Pendel transferred his gaze to the bed. 'I'm not due bonuses. No one is.'

'Yes, you are. Sabina on preparedness among the older students. Alpha for Delgado's private business dealings with the Japs. Marco on the President's late night meetings. Bingo.'

Pendel shook his head in puzzlement.

'Three stars for Sabina, three stars for Alpha, one for Marco, seven grand in all,' Osnard insisted. 'Count it.'

'There's no need for that.'

Osnard pushed a receipt at him and a ballpoint pen. 'Ten grand. Seven down and three for your widows and orphans fund as usual.'

From somewhere deep inside himself, Pendel signed. But he left the money on the bed, to look at not to touch, while Osnard with the blindness of greed renewed his campaign for the recruitment of Louisa, and Pendel returned to the shadows of his private thoughts.

*　　　*　　　*

'Likes seafood, doesn't she?'

'What's that got to do with anything?'

'Isn't there some restaurant you take her to for treats?'

'La Casa del Marisco. Prawns mornay and the halibut. She never varies.'

'Tables good and wide apart, are they? Plenty o' privacy?'

'It's where we go for anniversaries and birthdays.'

'Special table?'

'Corner by the window.'

Osnard acted the fond husband, eyebrows raised, head fetchingly on the tilt. '"Something I got to tell you, darling. Thought it was time you knew. Public duty. Reporting the truth to people who can do something about it." Play?'

'It might. On Brighton Pier.'

'"So that your dear father can rest in his grave. Your mother too. For your ideals. Mickie's ideals. Mine as well, even if I've had to hide 'em under a bushel for security reasons."'

'What do I tell her about the children?'

'It's for their future.'

'Fine future they've got, with both of us sitting in the nick. Seen the arms stuck out of the windows, have you? I counted them once. You do that if you've been inside. Twenty-four to one window not including the washing, and it's one window to a cell.'

Osnard sighed as if this was going to hurt him more than Pendel.

'You're forcing me to play hardball, Harry.'

'I'm not forcing you. Nobody's forcing you.'

'I don't want to do this to you, Harry.'

'Then don't.'

'Tried to break it to you gently, Harry. Didn't work out, so I'm giving you the bottom line.'

'There isn't one, not with you.'

'Both your names are on the deeds. You and Louisa. You're both in the same hole. You want the deeds back – shop and farm – London will want a solid contribution from the pair o' you. If they don't get it, love will turn sour and they'll switch off the money supply and put you under the hammer. Shop, farm, golf clubs, four-track, kids, the whole catastrophe.'

Pendel's head took a while to lift, as if the judge's custodial sentence had taken a bit of time to sink in.

'That's blackmail, isn't it, Andy?'

'Market forces, ol' boy.'

Pendel rose slowly and stood motionless, feet together and head down, staring at the banknotes on the bed before tidying them into their envelope and putting the envelope in his bag, with the carbons and the fly spray.

'I'll need some days.' He was speaking to the floor. 'I've got to talk to her, haven't I?'

'Remedy's in your hands, Harry.'

Pendel shuffled towards the door, head down.

'So long, Harry. Next time, next place, okay? Go well now. Good luck.'

Pendel stopped, paused and turned, his face revealing nothing beyond a passive acceptance of his punishment.

'You too, Andy. And thank you for the bonus and the whisky and for sharing your suggestions with me regarding both Mickie and my wife.'

'My pleasure, Harry.'

'And don't forget to come and try your tweed jacket now. It's what I call tough but tasty. Time we made a new man of you.'

*   *   *

Locked an hour later in the cage at the furthest end of the strongroom Osnard spoke into the overlarge mouthpiece of the secret telephone and imagined his words being digitally recomposed in Luxmore's furry ear. In London Luxmore had arrived at his desk early in order to receive Osnard's call.

'Gave him the carrot, then waved the stick at him, sir,' he reported in the Boy Hero voice he kept for his master. 'Rather vigorously, I'm afraid. But he's still dithering. She will, she won't, she may. He's not saying.'

'Damn him!'

'That's what I felt.'

'So he's holding out for yet more money, eh?'

'Looks like it.'

'Never blame a shit for acting in character, Andrew.'

'Says he needs time to talk her round.'

'The clever monkey. Time to talk *us* round, more likely. What will buy her, Andrew? Give it me straight. My God, we'll keep him on a tight rein after this!'

'He hasn't mentioned a figure, sir.'

'I'll bet he hasn't. He's a negotiator. He's got us by the short-and-curlies and knows it. What's your guestimate? You know the fellow. What's your worst case?'

Osnard permitted a silence that denoted careful reflection.

'He's hard,' he said cautiously.

'I know he's hard! They're all hard! *You* know he's hard! The Top Floor knows he's hard. Geoff knows he's hard. Certain private investor friends of mine know he's hard. He's been hard from day one. He'll get harder as we come up to the post. My God, if I knew of a better hole, I'd go to it! There was a fellow in the Falklands contest took us for a fortune and never delivered a damn thing.'

'It's got to be on results.'

'Go on.'

'A bigger retainer will only encourage him to rest on his oars.'

'I agree. Totally. He'd laugh at us. That's what they do. Shylock us and laugh.'

'Bigger bonuses, on the other hand, wake him up. We've seen it before and we saw it tonight.'

'We did, did we?'

'You want to see him shovelling the stuff into his briefcase.'

'Oh my God.'

'On the other hand, he *has* given us Alpha and Beta and the students, he *has* put the Bear on a semi-conscious footing, he *has* recruited Abraxas to a point, and he *has* recruited Marco.'

'And we've paid him every inch of the way. Handsomely. And what have we had for it to date? Promises. Chickenfeed. "Stand by for the Big One." It makes me sick, Andrew. Sick.'

'I put that point to him fairly energetically, if I may say so, sir.'

Luxmore's voice softened immediately. 'I'm sure you did, Andrew. If I implied otherwise, I am truly sorry. Go on. Please.'

'My *personal* conviction –' Osnard resumed, with enormous diffidence –

'That's the only one that counts, Andrew!'

'– is that we work towards incentives only. If he delivers, we pay. The same goes, according to him, if he delivers his wife.'

'Holy Mother, Andrew! He *said* that to you? He *sold* his wife to you?'

'Not yet, but she's on the market.'

'Not in twenty years of this Service, Andrew. Not in all its history, has a man sold his wife to us for gold.'

Osnard had a special gear for talking money, a lower, more fluid engine-tone.

'I'm suggesting we put him on a regular bonus for every subsource he recruits, to include his wife. The bonus to be calculated as a proportion of the subsource's salary. A flat rate. If she earns a bonus, he earns a piece of it.'

'Additional?'

'Absolutely. There's also the unsolved question of what Sabina should pay her students.'

'Don't spoil them, Andrew! What about Abraxas?'

'If and when the Abraxas organisation delivers the conspiracy, the same commission is payable to Pendel, calculated as twenty-five per cent of what we pay Abraxas and his group by way of bonus.'

Now Luxmore made the silence.

'Did I hear *if and when*? What am I hearing there exactly, Andrew?'

'I'm sorry, sir. I just can't help wondering whether Abraxas isn't stringing us along. Or Pendel is. Forgive me. It's late.'

'Andrew.'

'Yes, sir.'

'Listen to me, Andrew. That's an order. There *is* a conspiracy. Don't lose heart merely because you're tired. Of *course* there is a conspiracy. You believe it, I believe it. One of the greatest opinion-makers in the *world* believes it. Personally. Profoundly. The best brains in Fleet Street believe it, or they very soon will. A conspiracy is out there, it is being cobbled together by an evil inner circle of the Panamanian élite, it centres on the Canal and we shall find it! Andrew?' Alarm, suddenly. 'Andrew!'

'Sir?'

'Scottie, if you don't mind. We've done with sir. Are you at peace in your heart, Andrew? Are you under strain? Are you comfortable? My goodness me I feel an ogre, never enquiring after your personal wellbeing amid all this. I am not without influence in the upper corridors these days, nor yet across the river. It saddens me when a diligent and loyal young man asks nothing for himself in these materialist times.'

Osnard gave the kind of embarrassed laugh that loyal and diligent young men give when they are embarrassed.

'I could do with some sleep if you've got any to spare.'

'Get some, Andrew. Now. As long as you like. That's an order. We need you.'

'Will do, sir. Good night.'

'Good morning, Andrew. I mean it now. And when you wake up, you'll hear that conspiracy loud and clear again, resounding like a hunting horn in your ears, and you'll spring from your bed and ride out in search of it, I know you will. I've been there. I've heard it too. We went to war for it.'

'Good night, sir.'

*   *   *

But the diligent young spymaster's day was far from over. *File while your memory is hot* the trainers had dinned into him *ad nauseam.* Returning to the strongroom he unlocked a bizarre metal casket to which he alone possessed the combination and extracted from it a red handbound volume similar in weight and portent to a ship's log, and encompassed by a kind of iron chastity belt, the two ends of which met in a second lock which Osnard also opened. Returning to his office he set the book on his desk beside his reading light, next to the bottle of Scotch, and his notes and tape recorder from the shabby briefcase.

The red book was his indispensable aid to creative reportwriting. In its hugely secret pages, areas of Head Office's outstanding ignorance, known otherwise as the analysts' Black Holes, were obligingly listed for the convenience of intelligence gatherers. And what analysts didn't know, in Osnard's simple logic, analysts couldn't check. And what they couldn't check they couldn't bloody well carp about. Osnard, like many new writers, had discovered he was unexpectedly sensitive to criticism. For two hours without a break Osnard reshaped, polished, honed and rewrote until BUCHAN's latest intelligence material fitted like perfectly-turned pegs into the analysts' Black Holes. A lapidary tone, an ever-watchful scepticism, an extra doubt raised here and there added to the air of authenticity. Till at last, confident of his handiwork, he telephoned his cypher clerk Shepherd, summoned him to the Embassy immediately and, on the principle that messages dispatched at unsociable hours are more impressive than their daytime fellows, presented him with a hand-coded TOPSECRET & BUCHAN telegram for immediate transmission.

'Only wish I could share it with you, Shep,' said Osnard in his We-Dive-At-Dawn voice, observing how Shepherd gazed wistfully at the unintelligible groups of numbers.

'Me too, Andy, but when it's need-to-know, it's need-to-know, isn't it?'

'Suppose it is,' Osnard conceded.

We'll send out old Shep, Personnel had said. Keep young Osnard on the straight and narrow.

*   *   *

Osnard drove but not to his apartment. He drove with purpose but the purpose lay out ahead of him, undefined. A fat wad of dollar bills was nudging against his left nipple. What will I have? Darting lights, colour photographs of naked black girls in illuminated frames, multi-lingual signs proclaiming LIVE EROTIC SEX. Respect it but not my mood tonight. He kept driving. Pimps, pushers, cops, bunch o' nancy boys, all looking for a buck. Uniformed GIs in threes. He passed the Costa Brava Club, young Chinese whores a speciality. Thanks, darlings, prefer 'em older and more grateful. Still he kept driving, his senses leading, which was what he liked his senses to do. The old Adam stirring. Taste everything, only way. Hell can you know whether you want a thing till you've bought it? His mind flitted back to Luxmore. *The greatest opinion-maker in the world believes in it...* Must be Ben Hatry. Luxmore had dropped his name a couple o' times in London. Punned with it. Our *Bene*fit Fund, ha ha. The *Beni*son of a certain patriotic media baron. *You didn't hear that, young Mr Osnard. The name of Hatry will never cross my lips.* Suck o' the teeth. What an arsehole.

Osnard swung his car across the road, hit the kerb, mounted it and parked on the pavement. I'm a diplomat so screw the lot o' you. *Casino and Club,* said the sign, and on the door ALL HANDGUNS TO BE CHECKED. Two nine-foot bouncers in capes and peaked hats guarded the entrance. Girls in mini-skirts and net stockings undulated at the foot of a red staircase. Looks my kind o' place.

*   *   *

It was six in the morning.

'Damn you, Andy Osnard, you had me scared,' Fran confessed with feeling as he climbed into bed beside her. 'What the hell happened to you?'

'She wore me out,' he said.

But his revival was already apparent.

CHAPTER FOURTEEN

The rage that had swept over Pendel with his departure from the pushbutton house of love did not subside as he climbed into the four-track or drove home badly through red mist or lay with a thumping heart on his side of the bed in Bethania, or woke next morning or the morning after. 'I'll need some days,' he had mumbled to Osnard. But it was not the days he was counting. It was the years. It was every wrong turning he had taken to oblige. It was every insult he had swallowed for the sake of the greater good, preferring to drucken himself rather than cause what Benny called a *gewalt*. It was every scream that had stopped in his throat before it reached the open air. It was a lifetime's worth of frustrated fury arriving uninvited among the host of characters who, for want of closer definition, traded under the name of Harry Pendel.

And it woke him like a bugle call, reviving and reproaching him in one huge blast, rallying his other emotions to its flag. Love, fear, outrage and revenge were among the first volunteers. It swept away the puny wall that had separated fact from fiction in Pendel's soul. It said 'Enough!' and 'Attack!' and tolerated no deserters. But attack what? And what with?

We want to buy your friend, Osnard is saying. *And if we can't, we'll send him back to prison. Ever been to prison, Pendel?*

Yes. And so's Mickie. And I saw him there. And he's hardly got the wind to say hullo.

We want to buy your wife, Osnard is saying. *And if we can't, we'll throw her onto the street and your kids with her. Ever been on the street, Pendel?*

It's where I came from.

And these threats were pistols, not dreams. Held to his head by Osnard. All right, Pendel had lied to him, if lying was the word. He had told Osnard what he wanted to hear and gone to extraordinary lengths to obtain it for him, including making it up. Some people lied because lying gave them a kick, made them feel braver or cleverer than all the lowly conformists who went on their bellies and told the truth. Not Pendel. Pendel lied to conform. To say the right things at all times, even if the right things were in one place and the truth was in another. To ride with the pressure until he could hop off and go home.

But Osnard's pressure hadn't let him hop off.

*   *   *

Berating himself, Pendel went through his usual materiel. As a practised self-accuser he tore his hair and called on God to witness his remorse. I'm ruined! It's a judgment! I'm back in prison! All life is a prison! It doesn't matter whether I'm inside or out! And I brought it all on myself! But his anger didn't go away. Eschewing Louisa's Cooperative Christianity, he resorted to the fearful language of Benny's half-remembered efforts at atonement, as chanted into his empty tankard at the Wink & Nod: *we have harmed, corrupted and ruined. . . We are guilty, we have betrayed. . . We have robbed, we have slandered. . . We have perverted and led astray. . . We have been false. . . We cut ourselves off from truth, and reality exists to entertain us. We hide behind distractions and toys.* The anger still refused to budge. It went wherever Pendel went, like a cat in a sick pantomime. Even when he embarked on a merciless historical analysis of his despicable behaviour from the beginning of time until the present day, his anger turned the sword away from his own breast and outward at the perverters of his humanity.

*   *   *

In the Beginning was the Hard Word, he told himself. It was applied by Andy when he barged into my shop and there was no resisting it because it was pressure, not only regarding the summer frocks but also one Arthur Braith-waite, known to Louisa and the children as God. And all right, strictly speaking Braithwaite did not exist. Why should he? Not every god has to exist in order to do his job.

And in consequence of the above, there was me under-taking to be a listening post. So I listened. And I heard a few things. And what wasn't heard as such was heard in my head, which was only natural, given the degree of pressure exerted. I'm a service industry so I served. What's so wrong about that? And after that there was what I would call a flowering at a certain level, which was hearing a lot more and getting better at it, because a thing you learn about spying is, it's like trade, it's like sex, it has to get better or it won't get anywhere.

So I entered what we might call the area of *positive hearing* in which certain words are put into people's mouths that they would have said if they'd thought of them at the time. Which is what everyone does anyway. Plus I photographed a few bits and pieces from Louisa's briefcase, which I did *not* like doing but Andy would have it and, bless him, he loves his photographs. But it wasn't stealing. It was looking. And anyone can look, is what I say. With or without a cigar-ette lighter in his pocket.

And what happened after that was Andy's fault com-pletely. I never encouraged him, I never even thought of it till he did. Andy required me to obtain *subsources*, your subsource being a bird of a very different feather from your unaware informant, and necessitating what I call a quantum leap, plus substantial returning as regards the purveyor's mental attitude. But I'll tell you something about sub-sources. Subsources, once you get into the way of them, are very nice people, a lot nicer than some I could name who had a somewhat larger place in reality, subsources being a secret family that doesn't answer back or have problems unless you tell them to. Subsources are about turning your friends into what they nearly were already, or would like to be, but strictly speaking never will be. Or what they wouldn't like to be at all, but rationally might have been, given what they are.

Take Sabina – whom Marta based loosely on herself, but not entirely – for example. Take your average fiery bomb-making student waiting to do his worst. Take Alpha and Beta and certain others who for reasons of security must remain nameless. Take Mickie with his Silent Opposition and his Conspiracy That Nobody Can Put His Finger On, which in my personal judgment was an idea of pure genius except that sooner rather than later I'm going to have to put my finger on it in a manner that will satisfy all parties, owing to Andy's highly remorseless pressure. Take the People Who Live the Other Side of the Bridge and the Real Heart of Panama that nobody can find except Mickie and a few students with a stethoscope. Take Marco who wouldn't say yes until I'd had his wife speak to him severely about the new deep freeze she wanted and the second car and getting their kid into the Einstein which I just *may* be able to arrange for them if Marco comes through on certain other fronts and maybe she ought to have another word with him in that regard?

All fluence. Loose threads, plucked from the air, woven and cut to measure.

*　　　*　　　*

So you build up your subsources and do their listening for them, and their worrying, and you research for them and read for them and listen to Marta about them, and you put them in the right places at the right times and generally set them off to their best advantage with all their ideals and problems and little ways, the same as I do in the shop. And you pay them, which is only proper. Part cash in their pockets and the rest put aside for a rainy day so that they don't flash it around and make themselves look silly and conspicuous and expose themselves to the full rigour of the Law. The only trouble being that my subsources can't have the cash in their pockets because they don't know they've earned it and some don't have the pockets as such, so I have to have it in mine. But that's only fair when you think about it because they *haven't* earned it, have they? I have. So I take the cash. Or Andy banks it for me in his widows and orphans. And the subsources are none the wiser, which is what Benny would have called a bloodless con. And what's life, if it isn't invention? Starting with inventing yourself.

Prisoners, it is well known, have their own morality. Such was Pendel's.

*   *   *

And having duly flailed himself and exonerated himself, he was at peace, except that the black cat was still glowering at him and the peace he felt was of the armed variety, a constructive outrage stronger and more lucid than any he had known in a lifetime peppered with injustices. He felt it in his hands, the way they tingled and muscled up. In his back, mostly across his shoulders. In his hips and heels as he strode about the house and shop. Thus exalted, he was able to clench his fists and hammer on the wooden walls of the prisoner's dock that always mentally surrounded him and roar out his innocence, or innocence as near as made no odds:

Because I'll tell you something else, Your Honour, while we're about it, if you'll wipe that Top Sheep's smile off your face: *it takes two to tango.* And Mr Andrew Osnard of Her Majesty's celestial whatnot *tangos.* I can feel it. Whether *he* can feel it is another matter, but I *think* he can. Sometimes people don't know they're doing things. But Andy's egging me on. He's making more of me than what I am, counting everything twice and pretending it's only the once, plus he's bent because I know bent, and London's worse than he is.

*   *   *

It was at this point in his deliberations that Pendel stopped addressing his Maker, His Honour or himself, and glared ahead of him at the wall of his workroom where he happened to be cutting yet another life-improving suit for Mickie Abraxas, the one that would win him back his wife. After so many of them, Pendel could have cut it with his eyes shut. But his eyes were wide open and so was his mouth. He seemed to be straining for oxygen, though his workroom, thanks to its high windows, had an adequate supply. He had been playing Mozart but Mozart was no longer his mood. With one hand he blindly switched him off. With the other he laid down his shears, but his gaze didn't flinch. It remained mooning at the same spot on the wall which, unlike other walls he had known, was painted neither millstone grey nor slime green but a soothing shade of gardenia that he and his decorator had taken pains to achieve.

Then he spoke. Aloud. One word.

Not as Archimedes might have spoken it. Not with any recognisable emotion. Rather in the tone of the I-speak-your-weight machines that had enlivened the railway stations of his childhood. Mechanically, but with assertion.

'*Jonah*,' he said.

Harry Pendel was having his grand vision at last. It floated before him at this very minute, intact, superb, fluorescent, complete. He'd had it from the start, he now realised, like a wad of money in his back pocket when all this time he'd been starving, thinking he was broke, struggling, aspiring, straining for knowledge he never quite possessed. Yet he possessed it! It had been sitting there, his very own to dispose of, his secret store! And he'd forgotten its existence until now! And here it was before him in glorious polychrome. My grand vision, pretending to be a wall. My conspiracy that has found its cause. The original uncut version. Brought to your screens by popular demand. And radiantly illuminated by anger.

And its name is Jonah.

*　　*　　*

It is a year ago but in Pendel's vaulting memory it is here and now and on the wall in front of him. It is a week after Benny's death. It is two days into Mark's first term at the Einstein and one day after Louisa has resumed gainful employment with the Canal. Pendel is driving his first-ever four-track. His destination is Colón, the purpose of his mission twofold: to pay his monthly visit to Mr Blüthner's textile warehouse, and to become a member of the Brotherhood at last.

He drives fast, as people do when they are driving to Colón, partly out of fear of highwaymen, partly in anticipation of the riches of the Free Zone ahead of them down the road. He is wearing a black suit that he has put on in the shop in order not to cause aggravation in the home and he has six days' worth of stubble. While Benny grieved for a departed friend, he gave up shaving. Pendel can do no less for Benny. He has even brought a black Homburg, though he intends to leave it on the back seat.

'It's a rash,' he explains to Louisa, who for her comfort and safety has not been informed of Benny's death as such, having been led to believe some years ago that Benny had died in alcoholic obscurity and accordingly presented no further threat. 'I think it's that new Swedish after-shave I was testing for the boutique,' he adds, inviting her concern.

'Harry, you will write to those Swedes and you will tell them their lotion is dangerous. It is not appropriate for sensitive skins. It is life-threatening for our children, it is inconsistent with Swedish notions of hygiene and if the rash persists you will sue the daylights out of them.'

'I've already drafted it,' says Pendel.

The Brotherhood is Benny's last wish, expressed in a failing scrawl that arrived at the shop after his death:

Harry boy, what you have been to me no question is a pearl of very great price except in one regard which is Charlie Blüthner's Brotherhood. A fine business you've got, two children and who

*knows what's in the pipeline. But the plum is still before you
and why you wouldn't pick it all these years is beyond me. Who
Charlie doesn't know in Panama is not worth knowing, plus
good works and influence have always gone hand in hand, with
the Brotherhood behind you you'll never want for business or
necessities. Charlie says the door's still open plus he owes me.
Though never as much as I'll owe you, my son, when I'm standing
in the corridor waiting for my turn, which in my private opinion
is a longshot but don't tell your Auntie Ruth. This place is all
right if you like rabbis.*

Blessings
Benny

* * *

Mr Blüthner in Colón rules over half-an-acre of open-plan
offices full of computers and happy secretaries in high-
necked blouses and black skirts and he is the second most
respectable man in the world after Arthur Braithwaite. Each
morning at seven he boards his company plane and has
himself flown for twenty minutes to Colón's France Field
airport where he is set down among the gaily-painted aircraft
of Colombian import-export executives who have dropped
by to do a little taxfree shopping or, being too busy, sent
their womenfolk instead. Each evening at six he flies home
again, except on Fridays when he flies home at three, and
at Yom Kippur when the firm takes its annual holiday and
Mr Blüthner atones for sins that no one knows about except
himself and, until a week ago, Uncle Benny.

'Harry.'

'Mr Blüthner, sir, always a pleasure.'

It's the same every time. The enigmatic smile, the formal
handshake, the waterproof respectability and no mention
of Louisa. Except that on this day the smile is sadder and
the handshake longer and Mr Blüthner is wearing a black
tie from stock.

'Your Uncle Benjamin was a great man,' he says, patting
Pendel's shoulder with his powdery little claw.

'A giant, Mr B.'

'Your business prospers, Harry?'

'I'm fortunate, Mr B.'

'You don't worry that the world gets warmer all the time? Soon nobody will buy your jackets?'

'When God invented the sun, Mr Blüthner, he was wise enough to invent air-conditioning.'

'And you would like to meet some friends of mine,' says Mr Blüthner, with a twinkly smile.

Mr Blüthner in Colón is several degrees racier than his familiar on the Pacific side.

'I don't know why I ever put it off,' says Pendel.

On other days they would have taken the back stairs to the textiles department for Pendel to admire the new alpacas. But today it's the crowded streets they take to, Mr Blüthner leading at a good snap until, sweating like stevedores, they arrive before an unmarked door. Mr Blüthner holds a key in his hand, but first he must give Pendel a roguish wink.

'You don't mind we sacrifice a virgin, Harry? Tarring and feathering a few *schwartzers* not going to be a problem to you?'

'Not if it's what Benny would have wanted for me, Mr Blüthner.'

Having darted a conspiratorial glance up and down the pavement, Mr Blüthner turns his key and gives the door a vigorous shove. It is a year ago or more, but it is here and now. On the gardenia wall in front of him Pendel sees the same door open, and the same pitch blackness beckon.

CHAPTER FIFTEEN

From bouncing sunlight Pendel followed his host into darkest night, lost him and stood still, waiting for his eyes to make the change, smiling in case he could be seen. Whom would he meet, in what weird attire? He sniffed the air but, instead of incense or warm blood, smelt old tobacco smoke and beer. Then gradually the instruments of the torture chamber came floating forward to present themselves: bottles behind a bar, a mirror behind the bottles, an Asian barman of great age, a cream-coloured piano with cavorting girls daubed on its raised lid, wooden fans puttering from the ceiling, a high window and a cord to open it, broken off short. And last, because they gleamed the least, Pendel's fellow-searchers for the Light, dressed, not in zodiacal robes and conical hats, but in the drab fatigues of Panamanian commerce: white short-sleeved shirts, buckled trousers under bricklayer bellies, loosened neck-ties patterned in red cauliflower.

Several faces were known to him from the humbler fringes of the Club Unión: Dutch Henk, whose wife had recently bolted to Jamaica with his savings and a Chinese drummer, tiptoeing gravely towards him with a frosted pewter tankard in each hand – 'Harry, our Brother, we are proud you have at last arrived among us' – as if Pendel had trekked across the polders to get to him. Olaf, Swedish shipping agent and drunk, with pebble spectacles and a wire-wool hairpiece, yelling in his cherished Oxford accent that wasn't one: 'I say, Brother Harry, old chap, good show, cheers.' Belgian Hugo, self-styled scrap-metal merchant and former Congo hand, offering Pendel 'something very special from your old country' out of a shaking silver hip flask.

No tethered virgins, no bubbling tar barrels or terrified *schwartzers*: just all the other reasons why Pendel had never joined till now, the same old cast in the same old play, with 'What's your poison, Brother Harry?' and 'Let's fill that up for you, Brother,' and 'What took you so long to come to us, Harry?' Until Mr Blüthner himself, adorned in a Beefeater's cape and mayoral chain, sounded two hoarse blasts on a dented English hunting horn, and a pair of double doors was kicked open to admit a column of Asian porters with trays above their heads marching into the room at punishment speed to a chant of 'Hold him down, you Zulu warrior' led by none other than Mr Blüthner himself who, as Pendel was beginning to understand, was retrieving certain elements that had gone missing from his early life, such as delinquency in adolescence.

For having summoned everyone to table, Mr Blüthner placed himself at the centre of it and Pendel at his side and remained standing happily at attention, as they all did, while Dutch Henk delivered himself of a long, incomprehensible grace, the drift of which being that the company would be even more virtuous than it already was if it ate the food before it – a premise Pendel was inclined to question as he took his first fatal mouthful of the most character-changing curry that had come his way since Benny last whisked him round the corner for a nice touch of Mr Khan's while your Auntie Ruth is doing her piety up the Daughters of Zion.

But no sooner had they sat than Mr Blüthner bounded to his feet again with two messages that were delightful to the company: our Brother Pendel making his first appearance among us here today – thunderous applause, interspersed with jocular obscenities, the company becoming by now mellow – and allow me to introduce a Brother who needs no introduction, so a big hand, please, for our wandering sage and longtime Servant of the Light, diver of the deep and explorer of the unknown, who has penetrated more dark places – dirty laughter – than any of us round this table today, the one and only, the irrepressible, the immortal Jonah, freshly returned from a triumphant wreck-raising expedition in the Dutch East Indies, of which some of you will have read. (Cries of 'Where?')

And Pendel, peering into his gardenia wall, could discover Jonah now as he did a year ago: crouched and cantankerous, with a yellowed complexion and lizard eyes, methodically provisioning his plate with the best of everything before him – red-hot pickles, spiced poppadoms and chapattis, chopped chili, nan bread, and an oozing speckled, red-brown lumpy substance that Pendel had already privately identified as unrefined napalm. Pendel could hear him too. Jonah, our wandering sage. The gardenia wall's sound-system is fault-less, even if Jonah has some difficulty making himself heard above the babel of smutty stories and fatuous toasts.

The next world war, Jonah was telling them, in thick Austra-lian accents, *would be played in Panama, the date had already been set, and you bastards had better bloody believe it.*

*   *   *

The first to challenge this assertion was an emaciated South African engineer named Piet.

'It's been done, Jonah, old boy. Little fellow we had here called Operation Just Cause. George Bush waved his wimp factor at us. Thousands dead.'

Which in turn provoked indistinct enquiries along the lines of 'What did *you* do in the invasion, Daddy?' and responses of an equally intellectual kind.

Here a firefight of charge and countercharge burst from several quarters at once, to the innocent pleasure of Mr Blüthner whose smile switched from one speaker to the next as keenly as if he were following a great tennis match. But Pendel heard little above the clamour of his intestines, and by the time he was restored to partial consciousness, Jonah had turned his attention to the shortcomings of the Canal.

'Modern shipping can't use the fucker. Ore containers, supertankers, container ships are too big for it,' he pronounced. 'It's a dinosaur.'

Olaf the Swede reminded the company that there was a plan to add more locks. Jonah treated this intelligence with the scorn it obviously deserved.

'Oh dead on, squire, great idea. More fucking locks. Fantastic. Incredible. What, I wonder, will science do next? Let's use the old French cut too, while we're about it. And take a slice through the Rodman Navy Base. And sometime around 2020, with God's grace and all the wonders of modernity, we'll have a very slightly wider Canal, and a *much* longer transit time. I drink to you, squire. I stand up and raise my glass to progress in the twenty-first fucking century.'

And probably beyond the smoke Jonah did exactly that, for Pendel, as he watches the replay on the gardenia wall, has a high-fidelity memory of Jonah leaping to his feet but remaining exactly the same height until, with exaggerated ceremony, he raises his tankard and ducks his yellowed face into it, lizard eyes and all, so that for a second Pendel wonders whether he will ever surface again, but these divers know their trade.

'Not that Uncle Sam gives a fart in a thunderstorm whether there's one fucking lock or six,' Jonah resumed in the same saw-edged tone of infinite contempt. 'The more the better as far as the Yanks are concerned. Our gallant Yankee friends have given up the Canal for dead long ago. I wouldn't be surprised if one or two of them were all for blowing the bugger up. Why should they want an efficient Canal? They've got their fast freightline from San Diego to New York, haven't they? Their *dry canal,* they're pleased to call it, run by decent moronic Americans instead of a shower of dagos. The rest of the world can go screw itself. The Canal's an outdated symbol. Let the other buggers use it – and bullshit to you, you dozy Kraut prick,' he added, to the somnolent Dutch Henk who had presumed to doubt his wisdom.

But elsewhere round the table weary heads were lifting,

fuddled faces turning towards Jonah's dubious sun. And Mr Blüthner, anxious not to miss one gem of repartee, was halfway out of his chair and across the table in his determination to catch Jonah's every word. The wandering sage was meanwhile rebuffing criticism:

'No, I am not talking through my fundament, you Mick nipple, I am talking *oil*, I am talking *Jap* oil. Oil that was once heavy and has now been made light. I am talking world domination by the Yellow Man, and the end of fucking civilisation as we know it, even in the Emerald fucking Isle.'

A wit asked whether Jonah meant the Japs were going to flood the Canal with oil, but he ignored him.

'The Japanese, my fine friends, were drilling their heavy oil long before they discovered how to use the stuff. They filled up kingsized storage tanks all over the country while their top scientists hunted day and night for a fucking formula to break it down. Well, now they've found it, so look out. Slap your hands over your appendages if you can find them, gentlemen, is my advice, and turn your arses to the rising sun before you kiss them goodbye. Because the Nips have *found* their magic emulsion. Which means that your tenure here in Paradise is scheduled to last about five minutes by the station clock. You pour it in, you shake it all about, and bingo, you've got oil like all the other boys. Fucking oceans of it. And once they've built their own Panama Canal, which is going to happen in the flick of a very small mayfly's dick, they will be in the happy position of being able to flood the fucking world with it. To the considerable rage of Uncle Sam.'

Pause. Growls of confused dissent from different corners of the table before the literal Olaf deputes himself to ask the obvious question.

'What are you meaning to say here, please, Jonah? – "once they have built their own Panama Canal"? Which orifice are you talking out of now, I would like to know, please? The idea of a new canal has been completely belly-up ever since the invasion. Perhaps you spend too much time under the water to hear what is going on upstairs. Before the invasion there existed a very high and intelligent tripartite

Commission to study alternatives to the Canal, including a new cut. The United States, Japan and Panama, all were members. Now this Commission is completely eliminated. The Americans are very pleased. They did not like the Commission at all. They pretended, but they did not like it. They like much better to have things stay as they are with some new locks, and have their heavy industry companies administer the terminal ports which will be very profitable. I know all this, thank you. It is my job. The matter is quite dead. So fuck you.'

But Jonah, far from crushed, was furiously triumphant.

Staring at the gardenia wall, Pendel, like Mr Blüthner, strains himself to catch every word of prophecy that falls from the great man's lips.

'Of course they didn't like the fucking Commission, you Nordic pedant! They hated it. And of course they want their own heavy construction companies bedded down in Colón and Panama City administering the terminal ports. Why do you think the Yanks boycotted the Commission once they'd joined it? Why do you think they invaded this stupid country in the first place? Pounded it to pieces any which way they could? To stop the naughty General flogging his cocaine to Uncle Sam? Bullshit! They did it to smash the Pan army and screw up the Pan economy so badly that the Japs couldn't buy the fucking country and build themselves a canal that works for them. Where do the Nips get their aluminium from? You don't know, so I'll tell you: Brazil. Where do they get their bauxite? Brazil again. Their clay? Venezuela.' He listed other substances Pendel had never heard of. 'Are you telling me the Nips are going to ship their essential industrial materials up to New York and fast-freight them to fucking San Diego, then cart them across to Japan just because the existing Canal's become too narrow and too slow for them? Are you telling me they're going to send their giant oil tankers round the fucking *Horn*? Pump their new oil across the fucking isthmus, which takes for fucking ever? Sit on their arses while five hundred bucks are slapped on the price of every fucking Jap compact that arrives in Philadelphia because the Canal can't fucking *carry* them any more? Who's the biggest user of the Canal?'

Hiatus while a volunteer is looked for.

'The Yanks,' said somebody bold, and paid the price:

'Bullshit, Yanks! Haven't you heard of flags of fucking convenience now sanctified by the delightful and harmless title of Open Registries? Who owns the convenience? The Japs and the Chinese. Which bastard's going to be building the next generation of Canal-going ships?'

'The Japs,' someone whispered.

A shaft of divine sunlight fights its way through the window of Pendel's cutting room and settles like a white dove on his head. Jonah's voice becomes sonorous. The fatuous expletives, like unneeded notes, fall away. 'Who's got the best high tech, the cheapest, fastest? Forget the American big boys. It's the Japs. Who's got the best heavy machinery, the wiliest negotiators? The best engineering brains, the best skilled labour and organisers?' he is declaiming in Pendel's ear. 'Who dreams night and day of commanding the world's most prestigious gateway? Whose surveyors and engineers are *at this very moment* boring for soil samples a thousand feet underneath the estuary of the Caimito River? You think they've given up just because the Yanks came in and pasted the place? You think they're going to kowtow to Uncle Sam, apologise for having had naughty thoughts about dominating world trade? The *Japs*? You think they're tearing their kimonos about the ecological mayhem of joining two incompatible oceans that have never been introduced to each other? The *Japs*, when their own survival's on the table? You think they're going to back *down* because they've been told to? The *Japs*? This isn't geopolitics, it's combustion. All we're doing is sitting here waiting for the bang.'

Somebody asks diffidently where the Chinese might figure in this scenario, Brother Jonah. It is Olaf again with his Oxford English undimmed: 'I mean, good Heavens, Jonah old chap, don't the Japanese hate the Chinese, and isn't it a two-way thing, actually? Why should the Chinese stand by while the Japs help themselves to all the power and glory?'

Jonah in Pendel's memory is by now nothing but toler-
ance and sweetness.

'Because the Chinks want the same as the Japs, Olaf, my
good friend. They want expansion. Wealth. Status. Recognition in the councils of the world. Respect for the yellow
man. What do the Japs want of the Chinese? you are asking
me. Allow me to explain. Firstly, they want them as their
neighbours. After that they want them as buyers of Japanese
goods. And after that again they want them as a source of
cheap labour to manufacture the said goods. The Japs think
the Chinks are a sub-species, you see, and the Chinese return
the compliment. But for the time being, the Chinks and the
Japs are blood brothers, and it is we, Olaf, the deluded
round-eyes, who are destined to suck on the hind tit.'

*   *   *

The rest of what Jonah said that afternoon came to Pendel
in garbled text. Not even the gardenia wall was equipped
to repair the damage done to his memory by a combination
of napalm and alcoholic substances. It took Benny's ghost,
standing at his elbow, to ad-lib the missing message:

*...Harry boy, I'll give it to you straight and haven't I always?
What we've got here is a very large con comparable to the boy who
flogged the Eiffel Tower to interested buyers, a five-star plot big
enough to send your friend Andy running to his bank manager,
no wonder Mickie Abraxas has been keeping shtumm for his friends
because it's dynamite plus he owes them. Harry boy, I've said it
before and I'll say it again, you've got more fluence in you than
Paganini and Gigli together and all you ever needed was the right
bus pulling up at the right stop on the right day and before you
knew it you'd be on your way there, no waiting in the corridor like
the rest of us, well this is the bus. We're talking a quarter-mile wide,
state-of-the-art, Japanese-built, sea-level canal from coast to coast,
Harry boy, planned in deepest secrecy while the Yanks are bleating
about new locks and having their heavy industrial mob muscling
in on the action, just like the old days except they're looking at the
wrong canal. And the Top Pan lawyers and politicos and Club
Unión as usual forming a tightly-knit group, up to their elbows in*

the till and thumbing their noses at Uncle Sam and milking the Japs rotten while they do it. Add in those wily Frogs Andy's always on at you about, plus a nice touch of your Colombian drug money for sinister and Harry boy, the Gunpowder Plot isn't in it, except who's going to catch you with the matches in your hand this time? Answer – nobody. You're asking me the price, Harry boy? You're telling me those Japs can't afford it? The Japs can't afford their own canal? How much did Osaka airport cost, then? Thirty billion used ones, Harry boy, is what I am reliably advised. A snip. Know how much a sea-level canal will cost? Three Osaka airports including legal fees and stamp duty. Harry, it's the kind of money those boys leave under the plate. Treaties, you ask? Binding obligations on the Pans not to spoil the Canal for Uncle Sam? Harry boy, that was the old Canal. And that's where the Pans will be depositing their binding obligations.

*   *   *

The gardenia wall has one last cameo for him.

Pendel and his host are standing on the doorstep of Mr Blüthner's emporium, saying goodbye to one another several times.

'You know something, Harry?'

'What's that, Mr B?'

'That Jonah fellow is the biggest bullshit artist in the world. He knows nothing about orimulsion and even less about Japanese industry. Their dreams of expansion: well, yes, there I agree. The Japanese have always been irrational about the Panama Canal. The problem is, by the time they're running it nobody will be using big ocean-going vessels any more, and nobody will be needing oil because we shall have better, cleaner, cheaper forms of energy. As to those minerals of his' – he shook his head – 'if they need them, they'll find them closer to home.'

'But Mr B, you were so happy in there!'

Mr Blüthner gave a rascally smile. 'Harry, I'll tell you. All the time I was listening to Jonah, I was hearing your Uncle Benny and thinking how he loved a con. Now then. How about you join our little Brotherhood?'

But Pendel for once cannot find it in him to say what Mr Blüthner wants to hear.

'I'm not ready for it, Mr B,' he replies earnestly. 'I've got to grow. I'm working on it and it will come. And when it does, and I'm ready, I'll be back to you like a hot cake.'

But he was ready now. His conspiracy was up and running, with or without the orimulsion. The black cat of anger was washing his paws for battle.

CHAPTER SIXTEEN

Days, Pendel had told Osnard. I'll need some days. Days of mutual thoughtfulness and marital renewal in which Pendel the husband and lover rebuilds the fallen bridges to his spouse and, concealing nothing, takes her with him into his most private realms, appointing her his confidante, helpmeet and fellow spy in the service of his grand vision.

As Pendel remade himself for Louisa, so he now remakes Louisa for the world. There are no more secrets between them. All is known, all is shared, they are together at last, head joe and subsource, conscious to one another and to Osnard, frank and bonded partners in a great endeavour. They have so much in common. Delgado their common source of intelligence on the destiny of gallant little Panama. London their common and exacting taskmaster. Anglo-Saxon civilisation at stake, children to protect, a network of brilliant subsources to nourish, a dastardly Japanese conspiracy to thwart, a common Canal to save. What woman worth her salt, what mother, what inheritor of her parents' wars, would not rally to the call, put on the cloak, take up the dagger, and spy the daylights out of the Canal's usurpers? From now on, the grand vision shall rule their lives entirely. Everything will be subordinated to it, every chance word and casual incident will be woven into the celestial tapestry. Perceived by Jonah, restored by Pendel, but with Louisa henceforth as its vestal. It is Louisa, with Delgado to assist her, who shall stand before it, bravely holding up the lamp.

And if Louisa is not in as many words aware of her new status, at least she cannot fail to be impressed by the harvest of little considerations that attends it.

Cancelling non-essential engagements and closing down the clubroom in the evenings Pendel hastens home to nurture and observe his agent-in-waiting, study her behaviour patterns and assemble the minutiae of her everyday existence in the workplace, most notably her relations with her revered, high-minded, adored and – to Pendel's jealous eye – grossly overvalued boss, Ernesto Delgado.

Till now, he fears, he has loved his wife as a concept only, as some standard of straightness that complemented his own complexity. Very well, from today he will put conceptual love aside and know her for herself. Till now when he was rattling at the bars of marriage he was trying to get out. Now he is trying to get in. No detail of her daily life is too slight for him: every comment about her peerless employer, his comings and goings, phone calls, engagements, conferences, fads and little ways. The smallest aberration in his daily routine, the name and standing of the most casual visitor to pass through Louisa's office on his way to an audience with the great man – all the trivia which till now Pendel has listened to politely with one ear – become matters of such close concern to him that he has actually to damp down his curiosity for fear of arousing her concern. For the same reason, his constant note-making takes place under operational conditions: crouched in his den – a few bills to deal with, dear – or in the lavatory – I don't know what I must have eaten, do you think it was the fish?

And a hand-delivered bill to Osnard in the morning.

Her own social life fascinates him almost as much as Delgado's. The lame get-togethers with other Zonians, now exiles in their own land, her membership of a Radical Forum that till now has seemed to Pendel about as radical as warm beer, a Cooperative Christian Fellowship Group that she attends out of loyalty to her late mother, become subjects of vast interest to him and to his tailoring notebook, where they are recorded in an impenetrable code of his own invention, a mixture of abbreviations, initials and deliberate bad writing comprehensible only to the trained eye. For unknown to Louisa, her life is now inseparably entwined with Mickie's. In Pendel's head if nowhere else, wife and friend link destinies as the Silent Opposition extends its secret frontiers to embrace dissident students, the Christian conscience and good-spirited Panamanians who live beyond the bridge. A lodge of former Zonians establishes itself in greatest secrecy, assembling by twos and threes in Balboa after dark.

Pendel has never been so close to her when they are apart, or so estranged from her when they are together. Sometimes he is shocked to feel himself superior to her, until he realises this is only natural since he knows so much more about her life than she does, is indeed the sole observer of her other, magical persona as intrepid secret agent inside the enemy's headquarters, targeted at the Monstrous Conspiracy to which the Silent Opposition with its network of devoted agents holds the key.

Sometimes, it is true, Pendel's mask slips and artistic vanity gets the better of him. He tells himself he is performing her a favour by touching everything she does with the wand of his secret creativity. Saving her. Shouldering her burden. Protecting her physically and morally from deceit and all its dire consequences. Keeping her out of jail. Sparing her the daily grind of many-stranded thinking. Leaving her thoughts and actions free to connect in a combined and healthy life together, instead of toiling in separate locked-off chambers like his own, never talking to each other except in whispers. But when the mask is replaced, there she is: his intrepid agent, his comrade-in-arms, desperately committed to the preservation of civilisation as we know it, if necessary by unlawful, not to say bent, means.

*   *   *

Seized with an overwhelming sense of his indebtedness towards Louisa, Pendel prevails on her to ask Delgado for a weekday off and takes her on an early-morning picnic: alone, just us, Lou, one-to-one, like before we had the kids. He arranges for the Oakleys to do the school run in place of him and drives her to Gamboa, to a beloved hilltop called Plantation Loop that dates back to their days in Calidonia, up a metalled US Army snake-road through dense forest to a ridge that is part of the Continental Divide between the Atlantic and Pacific Oceans. The symbolism of his choice does not escape him: the isthmus, ours to watch over, little Panama in our sacred care. It is an unearthly, changeful spot, buffeted by contrary winds and closer to the Garden of Eden than to the twenty-first century, despite the grimy sixty-foot-high cream-coloured golfball aerial that is the reason for the road in the first place: put there to listen to the Chinese or the Russians or the Japanese or the Nicaraguans or the Colombians, but now officially deaf – unless, that is, out of some surviving instinct for intrigue, it is able to recover its hearing in the presence of two English spies seeking solace from the tension of their daily sacrifice.

Above them, vultures and eagles swim in shoals through colourless, unmoving skies. Through a cleft in the trees, they can trace a valley of green hillsides all the way to the Bay of Panama. It is still only eight in the morning but the sweat pours off them as they return to the four-track for iced tea from a thermos and mince pies that Pendel has made the night before, her favourite.

'It's the best life, Lou,' he assures her gallantly as they sit side by side holding hands in the front of the four-track with the engine running and the air-conditioning on full.

'What is?'

'This one. Ours. Everything we've done has paid off. The children. Us. We're hunkydory.'

'As long as you're happy, Harry.'

Pendel decides that the moment is ripe to approach his great design.

'I heard a funny story in the shop the other day,' he says in a tone of amused reminiscence. 'About the Canal. That old Japanese plan that used to be talked about is back on the table, they tell me. I don't know if it's come your way at the Commission at all.'

'What Japanese plan?'

'A new cut. At sea level. Using the Caimito estuary. A figure of a hundred billion dollars is being bandied about, I don't know if I'm right.'

Louisa is not pleased. 'Harry, I do not understand why you bring me to the top of a hill in order to repeat rumours about a new Japanese canal. It's an immoral, ecologically destructive plan, it is anti-American and anti-Treaty. So I hope very much that you will go back to whoever told you this nonsense and advise them not to propagate rumours designed to make the future of our Canal even more difficult to adjust to.'

For a second a terrible sense of failure overtakes Pendel and he almost weeps. It is followed by indignation. I was trying to take her with me and she wouldn't come. She preferred her little rut. Doesn't she realise marriage is a two-way thing? Either you support someone or you fall over. He adopts a haughty tone.

'It's all highly hush-hush this time round, according to what I'm told, so it doesn't surprise me particularly that you haven't heard about it. There's top Panamanian brass involved, but they're keeping *shtumm* and meeting on the sly. Those Japs won't listen to argument, not where the Canal is concerned. Your very own Ernie Delgado's in on it too, they say, which doesn't surprise me quite as much as it ought, I expect. I never did manage to warm to Ernie the way you do. And Pres is in it up to his elbows. It's what his missing hours were all about on his Far Eastern tour.'

A long pause. One of her longest. At first he presumes that she is contemplating the enormity of his information.

'*Pres?*' she repeats.

'The President.'

'Of *Panama?*'

'Well, it's not the President of the United States, is it, dear?'

'Why do you call him *Pres?* That's what Mr Osnard calls

him. Harry, I do not understand why you are imitating Mr Osnard.'

*   *   *

'She's on the brink,' Pendel reported by telephone the same night, speaking very quietly in case the line was tapped. 'It's big. She's asking, is she up to it? There's things out there she doesn't want to know.'

'What sort o' things?'

'She's not saying, Andy. She's deciding. She's worried about Ernie.'

'Afraid he'll rumble her?'

'Afraid *she'll* rumble *him.* Ernie's got his hand out like the rest of them, Andy. That Mr Clean image of his is all a façade. "There's a side of me would rather not look," she told me. Her words. She's getting up her courage.'

The next night, in line with Osnard's advice, he took her to La Casa del Marisco for dinner, table by the window. She ordered lobster thermidor which astonished him.

'Harry, I am not made of stone. I have moods. I change. I am a sentient human being. Do you wish me to eat prawns and halibut?'

'Lou, I wish you to expand in every way that's comfortable for you.'

She's ready, he decided, watching her tuck into her lobster. She's grown into the part.

'Mr Osnard, sir, I'm very pleased to say I've got that second suit you've been hankering after,' Pendel announced next morning, telephoning this time from his cutting room. 'All folded and boxed up and wrapped in tissue paper, as long as it stays one to one. I shall be expecting your cheque shortly.'

'Great. When can we all get together? Adore to try it on.'

'We can't, I'm afraid, sir. Or not all of us. It isn't on offer. Like I said. I measure, I cut, I fit, I do it all myself personally.'

'Hell does that mean?'

'It means I also deliver. No one else is involved. Not as such. It's you and me and no direct involvement of third parties. I've talked and talked to them but they won't budge. It's deal through me or there's no deal. That's their firm policy, complain how we may.'

They met in Coco's Bar at the El Panama. Pendel had to yell above the band.

'It's her morality, Andy, like I said. She's adamant. She respects you, she likes you. But you're where she draws the line. Honour and obey her husband is one thing, spy on her employers for a British diplomat when she's American is another, never mind her employer is betraying a sacred trust. Call it hypocrisy, call it women. "Never mention Mr Osnard again," she says, and it's a breakpoint. "Don't bring him here, don't let him talk to my children, he'll pollute them. Never tell him I've agreed to do the awful thing you ask of me, or that I've joined the Silent Opposition." I'm giving it you straight, Andy, painful though it may be. When Louisa digs her toes in, it takes a Stealth bomber to shift her.'

Osnard helped himself to a fistful of cashews, put back his head, yawned and poured them into his mouth.

'London isn't going to like it.'

'Then they'll have to lump it, Andy, won't they?'

Osnard pondered this while he masticated. 'Yes. They will,' he agreed.

'And she's not going to be giving anything in writing either,' Pendel added as an afterthought. 'Nor's Mickie.'

'Wise girl,' said Osnard, still munching. 'We'll backdate her salary till the beginning of the month. And make sure you put in for her expenses. Car, heat, light, electricity, the date. Want another o' these or how about a short one?'

Louisa was recruited.

*　　　*　　　*

Next morning Harry Pendel rose with a sense of his own diversity stronger than any he had experienced in all his years of striving and imagining. He had never been so many people. Some were strangers to him, others warders and old lags known to him from previous convictions. But all were at his side, marching with him in the same direction, sharers of his grand vision.

'Heavy week coming up by the look of it, Lou,' he called to his wife through the shower curtain, firing the first shot of his new campaign. 'Lot of house calls, new orders in the pipeline.' She was washing her hair. She had taken to washing it a lot, sometimes twice a day. And cleaning her teeth five times at least. 'Playing squash tonight, dear?' he enquired with immense casualness.

She turned off the shower.

'Squash, dear. Are you playing tonight?'

'Do you want me to?'

'It's Thursday. Club night at the shop. I thought you always played squash on Thursdays. Standing date with Jo-Ann.'

'Do you *wish* me to play squash with Jo-Ann?'

'I was only asking, Lou. Not wishing. Asking. You like to keep fit, we know that. It shows, too.'

Count to five. Twice.

'Yes, Harry, tonight I intend to play squash with Jo-Ann.'

'Right. Great.'

'I shall come home from work. I shall change. I shall drive to the Club and play squash with Jo-Ann. We have a court booked from seven to eight.'

'Well, give her my love. She's a nice woman.'

'Jo-Ann likes two consecutive half-hour periods. One period to practise her backhand, one to practise her forehand. For her partner that routine is naturally reversed. Unless the partner is left-handed, which I am not.'

'Got you. Understood.'

'And the children will be visiting with the Oakleys,' she added in extension of her previous bulletin. 'They will eat fattening crisps, drink tooth-corroding cola, absorb violent television and camp on the Oakleys' insanitary floor in the interests of reconciliation between our two families.'

'Okay, then. Thanks.'

'Not at all.'

The shower started again and she went back to soaping her hair. The shower stopped.

'And after squash, it being Thursday, I shall devote myself to my work, planning and synthesising Señor Delgado's engagements for the forthcoming week.'

'So you said. And a very full schedule, I hear. I'm impressed.'

Rip aside the curtain. Promise her to be completely real from now on. But reality was no longer Pendel's subject, if it ever had been. On the way to school he sang the whole of 'My object all sublime' and the children thought he was joyously mad. Entering his shop he became an enchanted stranger. The new blue rugs and smart furnishings amazed him, so did the sight of the Sportsman's Corner in Marta's glass box and the shiny new frame round Braithwaite's portrait. Who on earth did that? I did. He was delighted by the aroma of Marta's coffee issuing from the clubroom upstairs and the sight of a fresh bulletin on student protest in the drawer of his work table. By ten o'clock the doorbell had already started ringing with promises of inspiration.

*   *   *

First to require his attention were the American Chargé and his pale aide, come to fit a new dinner jacket which the Chargé called a tux. Parked outside the shop stood his armoured Lincoln Continental manned by a stern driver with a crewcut. The Chargé was a droll, well-to-do Bostonian who had spent a lifetime reading Proust and playing croquet. His topic was the vexed matter of the American Families' Thanksgiving Barbecue and Fireworks Display, a subject of perennial anxiety to Louisa.

'We have no civilised alternative, Michael,' the Chargé insisted in his brahmin's drawl while Pendel chalked the collar.

'Right,' said the pale aide.

'Either we treat them like house-trained adults or we say they're bad kids we don't trust.'

'Right,' said the pale aide again.

'People respond to respect. If I did not believe that, I

would not have devoted my best years to the comedy of diplomacy.'

'*If* we could kindly bend our arm to the halfway mark, sir,' Pendel murmured, laying the edge of his palm in the crook of the Chargé's elbow.

'The military will hate us,' said the aide.

'Are these lapels going to bulge, Harry? They look kind of busty to me. Don't they to you, Michael?'

'One pressing, you'll never hear from them again, sir.'

'Look great to me,' said the pale aide.

'And our length of sleeve, sir? About so, or a trifle shorter?'

'I'm hesitating,' said the Chargé.

'About the military or the sleeves?' said the aide.

The Chargé flapped his wrists, watching them critically as he did so.

'So is fine, Harry. Do *so*. I have no doubt, Michael, that if the boys on Ancón Hill had their way we'd be seeing five thousand men in combat gear line the road and everybody bussed in and out in APCs.'

The aide gave a grim laugh.

'However we are not primitives, Michael. Nietzsche is not an appropriate rôle model for the world's only superpower as it enters the twenty-first century.'

Pendel turned the Chargé sideways so that he could better admire his back.

'And our jacket length, sir, overall? A suspicion longer or dare we say we're happy with what we see?'

'Harry, we are happy. It's tops. Forgive me for being a fraction *distrait* today. We're *trying* to prevent another war.'

'In which endeavour, sir, I'm sure we wish you all success,' said Pendel earnestly as the Chargé and his aide tripped down the steps with the crewcut driver sashaying alongside.

He could hardly wait for them to leave. Heavenly choirs were singing in his ears as he scribbled frantically in the clandestine back pages of his tailor's notebook.

Friction between US military and diplomatic personnel is reaching a highly critical flashpoint in the opinion of the US Chargé, the bone of contention being how to handle student insurrection if and when it raises its ugly head. In the words of the Chargé, spoken in total confidence to this informant...

What did they tell him? Dross. What did he hear? Glories. And this was only a rehearsal.

*   *   *

'Dr Sancho,' cried Pendel, opening his arms in delight. 'Long time no see, sir. Señor Lucullo, what a pleasure. Marta, where's that fatted calf then?'

Sancho a plastic surgeon who owned cruise ships and had a rich wife he hated. Lucullo a hairdresser with expectations. Both from Buenos Aires. Last time it had been mohair suits with double-breasted waistcoats for Europe. This time we just *have* to have white dinner jackets for the yacht.

'And all's quiet on the home front, then?' Pendel asked, artfully debriefing them over a glass upstairs. 'No big putsches planned at all? I always say South America's the only place where you can cut a gentleman his suit one week and see his statue wearing it the next.'

No big putsches, they confirmed with a giggle.

'But Harry, have you *heard* what *our* President said to *your* President when they thought nobody was listening?'

Pendel hadn't.

'There were these three Presidents all sitting in one room, right? Panama, Argentine, Peru. "*Well*," says the President of Panama. "It's all right for *you* boys. *You* get re-elected for a second term. But at home in Panama re-election is prohibited by our constitution. It simply isn't fair at all." So *our* President turns round and says, "Well, my dear, maybe it's because I can do twice what *you* can do once!" Then the President of Peru says –'

But Pendel never heard what the President of Peru said. Heavenly choirs sang again for him as he duly recorded in his notebook the backdoor efforts of the pro-Japanese President of Panama to extend his power into the twenty-first century, as confided by the devious and hypocritical Ernie Delgado to his trusted private secretary and indispensable assistant, Louisa also known as Lou.

*　　　*　　　*

'Those bastards in the opposition sent a woman to slap me at the meeting last night,' Juan Carlos of the Legislative Assembly announces proudly while Pendel chalks the shoulders of his morning suit. 'I never saw the bitch in my life. Steps out of the crowd, runs up to me all smiling. TV cameras, newspapers. Next thing I know she's given me a right hook. What am I supposed to do? Slap her one back in front of the cameras? Juan Carlos, the woman-beater? If I do nothing, they call me a poofter. You know what I do?'

'I can't imagine' – checking the waist and adding an inch to accommodate Juan Carlos's rise to fortune.

'Kiss her on the mouth. Put my tongue down her filthy throat. Got breath like a pig. They adore me.'

Pendel dazzled. Pendel levitated by admiration.

'Now what's all this I'm hearing about them putting you in charge of some very select committee, Juan Carlos?' he asks severely. 'I'll be dressing you for your presidential inauguration next.'

Juan Carlos let out a peal of coarse laughter.

'*Select?* The *Poverty* Committee? It's the lousiest committee in town. Got no money, no future. We sit and stare at each other, we say it's a pity about the poor, then we go have ourselves a decent lunch.'

In yet another intimate one-to-one conversation conducted with his highly trusted personal assistant behind closed doors, Ernesto Delgado, driving force of the Canal Commission and keen pusher of the top secret Japanese-Panamanian accord, remarked that a certain confidential file on the subject of the Canal's future would have to be slipped to the Poverty Committee for Juan Carlos to run his eye over. When asked what in the world the Poverty Committee had to do with Canal matters, Delgado gave a crafty smile and replied that not everything is what it seems in the world.

*　　　*　　　*

She was at her desk. He could see her exactly as he dialled

her direct line: the elegant upper corridor of the Head-quarters Building with its original louvre doors to keep the air moving; her tall airy room with its view of the old railway station desecrated by the McDonald's sign that drove her crazy every day; her super-modern desk with its computer screen and low-flush telephone. Her moment's indecision before she picks the receiver up.

'I wondered whether there was anything special you wanted to eat tonight, darling.'

'Why?'

'Thought I might drop in at the market on my way home.'

'Salad.'

'Something light after squash, right? Darling?'

'Yes, Harry. After squash, I shall require a light meal such as salad. As usual.'

'Busy day? Old Ernie on the stomp, is he?'

'What do you want?'

'I wanted to hear your voice, that's all, darling.'

Her laughter unnerved him. 'Well you'd better be quick because in two minutes this voice is going to be interpreting for a bunch of earnest harbourmasters from Kyoto who speak no Spanish and not a lot of English and only wish to meet the President of Panama.'

'I love you, Lou.'

'I hope so, Harry. Now excuse me.'

'Kyoto, eh?'

'Yes, Harry. Kyoto. Goodbye.'

KYOTO he wrote ecstatically in capitals. What a sub-source. What a woman. What a coup. *And only wish to meet the President*. And they shall. And Marco will be there to usher them to His Luminosity's secret chambers. And Ernie will hang up his halo and go with them. And Mickie will get to hear of it, thanks to his own highly paid sources in Tokyo or Timbuctoo or wherever he bribes them. And ace operator Pendel will report it word for word.

*   *   *

Intermission while Pendel, cloistered in his cutting room,

combs the local newspapers – these days he takes them all
– turns up a daily court circular entitled: *Today Your President
Will Receive.* No mention of earnest harbourmasters from
Kyoto, no Japanese on the menu at all. Excellent. The meeting was off the record. A secret, highly clandestine meeting,
Marco let them in at the back door, a bunch of tight-lipped
Japanese bankers pretending to be harbourmasters who
don't speak Spanish but they do. Add a second coat of magic
paint and multiply the result by infinity. Who else was there
– apart from wily Ernie? Of course! Guillaume was! The
crafty Frog himself! And here he is, standing before me,
shaking like a leaf!

'Monsieur Guillaume, sir, greetings, slap on time as usual!
Marta, a glass of the Scottish one for Monsieur.'

Guillaume comes from Lille. He is mousy and swift. By
profession he is a consultant geologist who samples soil for
prospectors. He has just returned from five weeks in Medellin in the course of which, he tells Pendel breathlessly, the
city has played host to twelve reported kidnappings and
twenty-one reported murders. Pendel is making him a fawn
alpaca single-breasted with a waistcoat and the spare
trousers. Artfully he steers the conversation towards the
topic of Columbian politics.

'I don't see how that President of theirs dare show his
face, quite frankly,' he complains. 'Not with all the scandals
and the drugs.'

Guillaume takes a gulp of Scotch and blinks.

'Harry, I thank God each day I live that I am a mere
technician. I go in. I read the soil. I make my report. I get
out. I go home. I have dinner. I make love to my wife. I
exist.'

'Plus you put in your very large fee,' Pendel reminds him
genially.

'In advance,' Guillaume agrees, nervously confirming his
survival with the aid of the long mirror. 'And first I bank it.
If they want to shoot me, they know they waste their money.'

*The only other participant to the meeting being the highly retiring
top French geologist and freelance international consultant with
close links to the Medellin cartel at the policy-making level, one*

Guillaume Delassus, esteemed in certain circles as a powerbroker without equal and the fifth most dangerous man in Panama.

And the other four prizes still to be awarded, he added to himself as he wrote.

*   *   *

Lunch-hour rush. Marta's tuna sandwiches in heavy demand. Marta herself everywhere and nowhere, deliberately avoiding Pendel's eye. Gusts of cigarette smoke and male laughter. Panamanians loving their fun, and doing it at P & B's. Ramón Rudd has brought a handsome boy. Beer from the ice bucket, wine wrapped in frozen wadding, newspapers from home and abroad, portable telephones used for effect. Pendel in his triple element of tailor, host and master spy skipping between fitting room and clubroom, pausing in midflight to dash off innocent memoranda in the back of his notebook, hearing more than he listens to, remembering more than he hears. The old guard with new recruits in tow. Talk of scandal, horses, money. Talk of women and occasionally the Canal. Crash of the front door, noise level falls then rises, cries of 'Rafi! Mickie!' as the Abraxas-Domingo show sweeps in with its customary panache, the famous playboy pair, reconciled once more, Rafi all gold chain, gold rings, gold teeth and Italian shoes, with a coat of many colours by P & B flung over his shoulders because Rafi hates dull, hates jackets unless they are outrageous, loves laughter, sunshine and Mickie's wife.

And Mickie sullen and unhappy but hanging onto his friend Rafi for dear life, as if Rafi is the only bit left to him after he has drunk and squandered all the rest away. The two men enter the fray and separate, the crowd draws to Rafi while Mickie heads for the fitting room and his umpteenth new suit that has to be finer than Rafi's, brighter than Rafi's, costlier, cooler, more seductive – Rafi are you going to win the First Lady's Gold Cup on Sunday?

Then suddenly the babel stops, whittled to one voice. It is Mickie's, booming and hopeless emerging from the fitting room, announcing to the assembled company that his new suit is a piece of shit.

He says it one way, then repeats it another, straight into Pendel's face, a challenge he would prefer to fling at Domingo but dare not, so he flings it at Pendel instead. Then he says it a third way because by now the gathering expects it of him. And Pendel not two feet from him, stone hard, waiting for him. On any other day Pendel would have side-stepped the onslaught, made a kindly joke, offered Mickie a drink, suggested he come back another time in a better mood, gentled him down the steps and poured him into a cab. The cellmates have played out such scenes before and Mickie has acknowledged them next day with expensive gifts of orchids, wine, precious huaca artefacts and craven hand-delivered notes of gratitude and apology.

But to expect this of Pendel today is to reckon without the black cat, which now bursts its leash and springs at Mickie with claws and teeth bared, ripping into him with a ferocity nobody dreamed Pendel could command. All the guilt he has ever felt about misusing Mickie's frailty, traducing him, exploiting him, selling him, visiting him in the pit of his blubbering humiliation, comes welling out of Pendel in a sustained salvo of transferred fury.

'*Why I can't make suits like Armani?*' he repeated, several times, straight into Mickie's astonished face. '*Why I can't make Armani suits?* Congratulations, Mickie. You just saved yourself a thousand bucks. So do me a favour. Go down to Armani and buy yourself a suit and don't come back here. Because Armani makes better Armani suits than I can. The door's over there.'

Mickie didn't budge. He was stultified. How on earth did a man of his mountainous dimensions buy himself an Armani suit across the counter? But Pendel couldn't stop himself. Shame, fury and a premonition of disaster were pulsing uncontrollably in his breast. Mickie my creation. Mickie my failure, my fellow prisoner, my spy, coming here to accuse me in my own safe house!

'You know what, Mickie? A suit from me, it doesn't advertise the man, it *defines* him. Maybe you don't want to be defined. Maybe there isn't *enough* of you to define.'

Laughter from the stalls. There was enough of Mickie to define anything several times over.

'A suit from me, Mickie, it's not a drunken scream. It's line, it's form, it's rock of eye, it's silhouette. It's the understatement that tells the world what it needs to know about you and no more. Old Braithwaite called it discretion. If somebody *notices* a suit of mine, I'm embarrassed because there must be something wrong with it. My suits aren't about improving your appearance or about making you the prettiest boy in the room. My suits are not confrontational. They hint. They imply. They encourage people to come to you. They help you improve your life, pay your debts, be an influence in the world. Because when it's my turn to follow old Braithwaite to the great sweatshop in the sky, I want to believe there are people down here in the street, walking around, wearing my suits and having a better opinion of themselves on account of them.'

Too much to keep inside me, Mickie. Time you shared the burden. He took a breath and seemed to want to check himself because he gave a kind of hiccough. He began again but Mickie mercifully got there first.

'Harry,' he whispered. 'I swear to God. It's the pants. That's all it is. They make me look like an old man. Old before my time. Don't give me all that philosophical horseshit. I know it already.'

Then a bugle must have sounded in Pendel's head. He looked round him at the astonished faces of his customers, he looked at Mickie staring at him, clutching the contested alpaca trousers, exactly as he had once clutched to himself the too big orange trousers of his prison uniform as if he were afraid somebody would snatch them from him. He saw Marta, motionless as a sculpture, her smashed face a patchwork of disapproval and alarm. He lowered his fists to his sides and drew himself to his full height as a prelude to standing comfortably.

'Mickie. Those trousers are going to be perfect,' he assured him in a gentler tone. 'I didn't want us in a houndstooth, but you would have it and you're not wrong. The entire world will love you in those trousers. The jacket too. Mickie, listen to me. Somebody's got to be in charge of this suit, you or me. Now who's it to be?'

'Jesus,' Mickie whispered, and slunk out on Rafi's arm.

*   *   *

The shop emptied and settled for its afternoon sleep, the customers withdrew. Money must be made, mistresses and wives placated, deals struck, horses backed, gossip traded. Marta too had disappeared. Her study time. Gone to put her head inside her books. Back in his cutting room Pendel switched on Stravinsky, cleared his tabletop of brown paper templates, cloth, chalk and scissors. Opening his tailor's notebook at the back pages he flattened it at the point where his coded jottings began. If he was chastened by his assault on his old friend he did not allow himself to know it. His muse was calling to him.

From a ring-backed invoice book he extracted a page of ruled paper with the nearly-royal crest of the house of Pendel & Braithwaite at its head, and below it in Pendel's copperplate hand an Account Rendered to Mr Andrew Osnard in the sum of two and a half thousand dollars at the address of his private apartment in Paitilla. Having set the invoice flat on the work surface, he took up an elderly pen attributed by mythic history to Braithwaite, and in an archaic hand that he had long cultivated for tailoring communications, added the words 'your early attention would oblige', which was a sign to say there's more to this bill than a demand for money. From a folder in the centre drawer of his desk he then drew a sheet of white, unruled, unwatermarked paper from the packet that Osnard had given him and sniffed it which he always did. It smelt of nothing he recognised except, very distantly, prison disinfectant.

Impregnated with magical substances, Harry. Carbon paper without carbon for one-time use only.

What do you do your end when you get it, then?

284

Develop it, you ass, what do you think?

Where, Andy? How?

Mind your own bloody business. In my bathroom. Shut up, you're embarrassing.

Laying the carbon gingerly over the invoice he took from his drawer the 2H pencil that Osnard had given him for the purpose and began writing to the resounding chords of Stravinsky, until Stravinsky suddenly annoyed him so he switched him off. The Devil always has the best tunes, Auntie Ruth used to say. He put on Bach but Louisa was passionate about Bach, so he switched off Bach and worked in friendless silence, which was unusual in him. Brows down, tip of tongue protruding, Mickie determinedly forgotten, the fluence beginning to rise in him. Listening for a suspicious footfall or the telltale shuffle of an enemy eavesdropper the other side of the door. Glancing constantly between the hieroglyphics in his notebook and the carbon. Inventing and joining. Organising, repairing. Perfecting. Enlarging out of recognition. Distorting. Making order out of confusion. So much to tell. So little time. Japs in every cupboard. The Mainland Chinese abetting them. Pendel flying. Now on top of his material, now under it. Now genius, now slavish editor of his imaginings, master of his cloud kingdom, prince and menial in one. The black cat always at his side. And the French as usual somewhere in the plot. An explosion, Harry boy, an explosion of the flesh. A rage of power, a swelling up, a letting go, a setting free. A bestriding of the earth, a proving of God's grace, a settling of debts. The sinful vertigo of creativity, of plundering and stealing and distorting and reinventing, performed by one transported, deliriously consenting, furious adult with his atonement pending and the cat swishing its tail. Change the carbon, screw up the old one, toss it in the wastebasket. Reload and resume firing on all guns. Rip the pages from the notebook, burn them in the grate.

'You want a coffee?' Marta enquired.

The world's greatest conspirator had forgotten to lock his door. Flames rising in the grate behind him. Charred paper waiting to be crushed.

'A coffee would be nice. Thank you.'

She closed the door behind her. Stiffly, not smiling at all.

'Do you need help?'

Her eyes were avoiding him. He took a breath.

'Yes.'

'What?'

'If the Japanese were secretly planning to build a new sea-level canal and had bought the Panamanian government on the sly and the students got to hear of it, what would they do?'

'*Today's* students?'

'Yours. The ones who talk to the fishermen.'

'Riot. Take to the streets. Attack the Presidential Palace, storm the Legislative Assembly, block the Canal, call a general strike, summon support from other countries in the region, launch an anti-colonial crusade across Latin America. Demand a free Panama. We would also burn all Japanese shops and hang the traitors, starting with the President. Is that enough?'

'Thank you. I'm sure that will be fine. And muster the people from the other side of the bridge, obviously,' he suggested as an afterthought.

'Naturally. Students are only the vanguard of the proletarian movement.'

'I'm sorry about Mickie,' Pendel muttered after a pause. 'I couldn't stop myself.'

'When we can't hurt our enemies we hurt our friends. As long as you know that.'

'I do.'

'The Bear rang.'

'About his article?'

'He didn't mention the article. He said he needs to see you. Soon. He's in his usual place. He made it sound like a threat.'

CHAPTER SEVENTEEN

The Boulevard Balboa on the Avenida Balboa was a low, sparse brasserie with a polystyrene ceiling and prison stri-plights boxed in with wooden slats. Some years ago it had been blown up, nobody remembered why. The big windows looked across the Avenida Balboa to the sea. At a long table, a heavy-jowled man protected by black-suited bodyguards in sunglasses was pontificating to a television camera. The Bear sat in his own space, reading his own newspaper. The tables around him were empty. He was wearing a P & B striped blazer and a sixty-dollar Panama hat from the boutique. His shiny pitch-black pirate beard looked as if it had just been shampooed. It matched the jet-black frames of his spectacles.

'You rang, Teddy,' Pendel reminded him after a minute of sitting unnoticed on the wrong side of the newspaper.

The newspaper reluctantly descended.

'What about?' the Bear asked.

'You phoned, I came. The jacket looks nice then.'

'Who bought the rice farm?'

'A friend of mine.'

'Abraxas?'

'Of course not.'

'Why of course not?'

'He's running out.'

'Who says?'

'He does.'

'Maybe you pay Abraxas. Maybe he works for you. You got some racket with Abraxas? You doing drugs together, like his father?'

'Teddy, I think you're out of your mind.'

'How did you pay off Rudd? Who's this mad millionaire you boast about without giving Rudd a piece of the action? That was most offensive. Why have you opened this ridiculous clubroom above your shop? Have you sold out to somebody? What's going on?'

'I'm a tailor, Teddy. I make clothes for gentlemen and I'm expanding. Are you going to give me some nice free publicity, then? There was an article in the *Miami Herald* not a long time back, I don't know if it came your way.'

The Bear sighed. His voice was inert. Compassion, humanity, curiosity had all drained out of it long ago, if they had ever been there in the first place.

'Let me explain the principles of journalism,' he said. 'I make money two ways. One way, people pay me to write stories, so I write them. I hate writing but I must eat, I must finance my appetites. Another way, people pay me not to write stories. For me, that's the better way because I don't have to write anything and I still get the money. If I play my cards right I get more for not writing than for writing. There's a third way I don't like. I call it my last recourse. I go to certain people in government and offer to sell them what I know. But that way's unsatisfactory.'

'Why?'

'I don't like selling in the dark. If I deal with somebody ordinary – with you – with him over there – and I know I can ruin his reputation or his business or his marriage, and he knows it too, then the story has its price, we can agree on something, it's normal commercial discourse. But when I go to the certain people in government' – very slightly, he shook his long head in disapproval – 'I don't know what it's worth to them. Some of them are smart. Some are donkeys. You don't know whether they're ignorant or they're not telling you. So it's bluff, it's counterbluff, it's time-consuming. Maybe they also threaten me with my own dossier in order to beat me down. I don't like wasting my life that way. You want to do business, you want to give me a quick answer and save me trouble, I'll give you a good price. Since you have a mad millionaire at your disposal, clearly he must be factored into any objective assessment of your means.'

Pendel had the sensation of putting his smile together by numbers, first one side then the other side, then the cheeks and, when he allowed them to focus, the eyes. Finally his voice.

'Teddy, I think what you're trying to pull here is a very old confidence trick. You're telling me "Fly, fly, all is known" and reckoning you'll move into my house while I'm on my way to the airport.'

'Are you working for the Americans? The certain people in government wouldn't like that. An Englishman trespassing on their preserves, they'd take a strong line. It's different if they do it themselves. They're betraying their own country. That's their choice, they were born here, it's their country, they can do what they like with it, they've worked their way. But for you to come here as a foreigner and betray it for them would be extremely provocative. There's no knowing what they might do.'

'Teddy, you are right. I'm proud to say I am working for the Americans. The General in charge of Southern Command likes a plain single-breasted with the extra trousers and what he calls the vest. The Chargé, he's a mohair tux and a tweed jacket for his holidays in North Haven.'

Pendel stood up and felt the backs of his knees trembling against his trousers.

'You don't know anything bad about me, Teddy. If you did, you wouldn't be asking. And the reason you don't know anything bad is that there isn't anything to know. And while we're on the subject of money, I'd be grateful if you'd pay for that nice jacket you're wearing so that Marta can clear her books.'

'How you can fuck that faceless halfbreed is beyond me.'

Pendel left the Bear as he had found him, head back, beard up, reading what he had written in his newspaper.

*   *   *

Arriving home, Pendel is pained to be greeted by an empty house. And this is my reward for a day's hard toil? he demands of the empty walls. A man with two professions, working himself to a shadow, must bring his own food home in the evenings? But there are consolations. Louisa's father's briefcase is once more lying on her desk. Popping it open, he takes out a hefty office diary with *Dr E. Delgado* done in black Gothic lettering on the cover. Next to it nestles a file of correspondence marked 'Engagements'. Ignoring distractions, including the imminent threat of exposure by the Bear, Pendel wills himself once more to become all spy. The overhead light is on a dimmer switch. He turns it to full. Pressing Osnard's cigarette lighter to one eye, he closes the other and squints through the tiny peephole while trying to keep his nose and fingers out of the way of the lens.

*   *   *

'Mickie rang,' Louisa said in bed.
    'Rang where?'
    'Me. At the office. He's going to kill himself again.'
    'Oh, right.'
    'He says you've gone mad. He says somebody's stolen your head.'
    'That's nice then.'
    'And I agreed,' she said, putting out the light.

*   *   *

It was Sunday night and their third casino but Andy still hadn't put God to the test which was what he had promised Fran he was going to do. She had barely seen him all weekend, apart from a few stolen hours of sleep and a bout of frenzied early-morning lovemaking before he hurried back to work. The rest of his weekend had been spent in the Embassy with Shepherd in his Fair Isle pullover and black plimsolls bringing hot towels and cups of coffee. Or so at least Fran had pictured it. It wasn't kind of her to put Shepherd in black plimsolls because she had never seen him wearing them. But she remembered a physical training instructor at boarding school who had worn them and Shepherd had the same servile enthusiasm.

'Heavy batch o' BUCHAN stuff,' Andy had explained cryptically. 'Got to knock it into report form. All a bit tense and get-it-to-us-by-yesterday.'

'When do the Buchaneers have the benefit?'

'London's pulled down the shutters. Too hot for local consumption till the analysts have run it through the sheep-dip.'

And so matters had rested till two hours ago when Andy had swept her off to an amazingly expensive restaurant on the waterfront where, over a bottle of expensive champagne, he had decided it was time to put God to the test.

'Picked up a legacy from an aunt last week. Piddling sum. No good to anyone. Get God to double it. Only way.'

He was in his hell-bent mood. Restless, questing eyes, flaring at anything, spoiling for collision.

'Do you take requests?' he yelled at the bandleader while they danced.

'Whatever Madame desires, Señor.'

'Then why not take the night off?' Andy suggested as Fran swung him smartly out of earshot.

'Andy, that's not tempting God, that's asking to get us killed,' she told him severely while he paid for dinner with damp fifty-dollar bills dragged from the inside pocket of a new linen jacket by his local tailor.

*   *   *

In the first casino he sat at the big table, watching but not playing, while Fran stood protectively behind him.

'Got a favourite colour?' he asked her over his shoulder.

'Isn't that for God to decide?'

'We do the colour, God does the luck. Rule o' the game.'

He drank more champagne but didn't place a bet. They know him, she thought suddenly as they left. He's been here before. She could tell by their faces and knowing smiles and come-again-soons.

'Operational,' he said curtly when she taxed him.

At the second casino a security guard made the mistake of trying to frisk them. Things would have turned ugly if Fran had not produced her diplomatic card. Once again Andy watched the play but took no active part, while two girls at the end of the table kept trying to catch his eye and one even called to him, 'Hi, Andy.'

'Operational,' he repeated.

The third casino was in a hotel she'd never heard of, in a bad part of town she had been told not to enter, in room 303 on the third floor, knock and wait. A huge bruiser patted Andy down and this time he did not object. He even advised Fran to let the man inspect her handbag. The croupiers stiffened as Fran and Andy entered the second room and a serious hush fell, turning heads and ending conversations: which was not surprising when you realised that Andy was asking for fifty thousand dollars' worth o' chips in five hundreds and thousands, don't need those little ones, thanks, you can put 'em back where they came from.

And the next thing Fran knew, Andy was sitting at the croupier's side and she was again standing behind him, and the croupier was a doughy, voluptuous whore with thick lips and a low halter-dress and small fluttery hands with red fingernails cut like claws and the wheel was spinning. And when it stopped Andy was ten thousand dollars better off because he was backing red. He played, so far as she could afterwards establish, eight or nine times. He had changed from champagne to Scotch. He doubled his fifty thousand dollars, which was apparently what he had set God as a target, then gave himself one last fling for a bit o' fun and picked up another twenty thousand. He asked for a carrier bag and a taxi at the door, because he thought it would be silly to walk down the road with a hundred and twenty thousand dollars in a bag and said Shepherd could fetch the bloody car tomorrow or give it away, he hated it.

But the sequence of these events remained disordered in Fran's mind because all she could concentrate on while they were unfolding was her very first gymkhana when her pony which like every other pony in the world was called Misty took the first fence perfectly then bolted four miles down the main road to Shrewsbury with Fran hanging onto its neck and the traffic going past in both directions and nobody seeming to give a damn except herself.

*   *   *

'The Bear came to my flat last night,' Marta said, having closed Pendel's cutting room door behind her. 'He brought a friend in the police.'

It was Monday morning. Pendel sat at his worktable, adding the finishing touches to an Order of Battle of the Silent Opposition. He put down his 2H pencil.

'Why? What are you supposed to have done?'

'They wanted to know about Mickie,'

'What about him?'

'Why he comes to the shop so much, why he calls you at such crazy hours.'

'What did you tell them?'

'They want me to spy on you,' she said.

CHAPTER EIGHTEEN

The arrival of the first material from Panama Station to bear the codename BUCHAN TWO had raised Scottie Luxmore, its originating genius in London, to unprecedented heights of self-congratulation. But this morning his euphoria had given way to a fretful nervousness. He paced at twice his usual speed. His hortatory Scottish voice had acquired a creak. His gaze veered restlessly across the river, northward and westward where his future now lay.

'*Cherchez la femme,* Johnny boy,' he advised a haggard youth named Johnson, who had succeeded Osnard in the ungrateful post of Luxmore's personal assistant. 'The female of the species is worth five men in this business any day.'

Johnson, who like his predecessor had mastered the essential art of sycophancy, leaned forward in his chair to show how keenly he was listening.

'They have the perfidy, Johnny. They have the nerve, they are born dissemblers. Why do you suppose she insisted on working exclusively through her husband?' His voice had the protest of a man pleading excuses in advance. 'She knew very well she would outshine him. Where would *he* be then? On the pavement. Dispensed with. Paid off. Why should she let that happen?' He wiped his open palms down the sides of his trousers. 'Swap two salaries for one and make a fool of her man while she's about it? Not our Louisa. Not our BUCHAN TWO!' His eyes narrowed, as if he had recognised someone at a distant window. But his peroration did not pause. 'I knew what I was doing. So did she. Never underrate a woman's intuition, Johnny. He's reached his ceiling. He's played out.'

'Osnard?' said Johnson hopefully. It was six months since he had been assigned to Luxmore's shadow and still no posting was in sight for him.

'Her husband, Johnny,' Luxmore retorted irritably, and drew the tips of his fingers in a clawing gesture down one side of his bearded cheek. 'BUCHAN ONE. Oh, his work was promising enough at first. But he'd no breadth of vision, they never have. No scale. No awareness of history. It was all tittle-tattle and warmed-up leftovers and covering his own backside. We could never have stuck with him, I see that now. She saw it too. She knows her man, that woman. Knows his limitations better than we do. And her own strength.'

'The analysts are a bit worried there's no collateral,' ventured Johnson, who could never resist a chance to chip at Osnard's pedestal. 'Sally Morpurgo called the BUCHAN TWO stuff overwritten and undersourced.'

The shot caught Luxmore on the turn, just as he was beginning his fifth length of the carpet. He smiled the broad, blank smile of an entirely humourless man.

'Did she now? And Miss Morpurgo is a most intelligent person, no question.'

'Well, I think she is.'

'And women are harsher on other women than we men are. Rightly.'

'It's true. I hadn't thought of it till now.'

'They are also subject to certain jealousies – envy is perhaps the better word here – from which we men are naturally immune. Are we not, Johnny?'

'I expect so. No. Yes, I mean.'

'What is Miss Morpurgo's objection precisely?' Luxmore asked in the tone of a man who can take fair criticism.

Johnson wished he had kept his mouth shut.

'She just says, well, there's no collateral. From the entire daily deluge, as she called it. Zero. No sigint, no friendly liaison, not a squeak out of the Americans. No travel int, no satellites, no unusual diplomatic traffic. It's Black-Hole stuff all the way. *She* says.'

'Is that all?'

'Well, not quite, actually.'

'Don't spare me, Johnny.'

'She said that never in the whole history of human intelligence had so much been paid for so little. It was a joke.'

If Johnson had hoped to undermine Luxmore's confidence in Osnard and his works, he was disappointed. Luxmore's breast swelled and his voice recovered its didactic Scottish pulse.

'Johnny.' A suck of the front teeth. 'Has it ever occurred to you that a proven negative today is the equivalent of yesterday's proven positive?'

'No, it hasn't, actually.'

'Then reflect for a moment, I beseech you. It takes a crafty mind indeed, Johnny, to hide his tracks from the ears and eyes of modern technology, does it not? From credit cards to travel tickets, telephone calls, fax machines, banks, hotels, you name it. We cannot buy a bottle of whisky at the supermarket these days without advising the world that we have done so. "No trace" in such circumstances comes close to proof of guilt. These men of the world understand that. They know what it takes to be unseen, unheard, unknown.'

'I'm sure they do, sir,' Johnson said.

'Men of the world do not suffer from the professional deformities which beset the more inward-looking officers of this Service, Johnny. They are not bunker-minded, bogged down in detail and superfluous information. They see the forest, not the trees. And what they see here is an East-South cabal of perilous dimensions.'

'Sally doesn't,' Johnson objected doggedly, deciding that he might as well be hanged for a pound as a penny. 'Nor does Moo.'

'Who is *Moo*?'

'Her assistant.'

Luxmore's smile remained tolerant and kindly. He too, it said, saw forests and not trees.

'Turn your own question inside out, Johnny, and I think you will have your answer. Why is there an underground Panamanian opposition if there is nothing in Panama to oppose? Why do clandestine dissident groups – not riff-raff, Johnny, but drawn from the concerned and affluent classes – wait in the wings, unless they know what there is to wait for? Why are the fishermen restive? – canny men, Johnny, never underrate your man of the sea. Why does the Panamanian President's man on the Canal Commission profess one policy in public while his private engagement book professes another? Why does he live one life on the surface and another below the waterline, hiding his tracks, conferring at unsociable hours with spurious Japanese harbourmasters? Why are the students restless? What is it they are sniffing in the air? Who has been whispering to them in their cafés and their discothèques? Why is the word *sell-out* passed from mouth to mouth?'

'I didn't know it was,' said Johnson, who of late had become increasingly puzzled to observe how raw intelligence out of Panama enhanced itself in transit across his master's desk.

But then Johnson wasn't cleared for everything – and least of all for Luxmore's sources of inspiration. When Luxmore was preparing his famous one-page summaries for submission to his mysterious planners and appliers, he first ordered up a heap of files from the Most Restricted archive, then locked the door on himself until the document was done – although the files, when Johnson ingeniously contrived to take a look at them, related to past events such as the Suez conflict of 1956 rather than to anything that was supposed to be happening now or in the future.

Luxmore was using Johnson as a sounding board. Some men, Johnson was learning, cannot think without an audience.

'It's the hardest thing for a Service like ours to put its finger on, Johnny: the human groundswell before it has stirred, the *vox populi* before it has spoken. Look at Iran and the Ayatollah. Look at Egypt in the run-up to Suez. Look at the *perestroika* and the collapse of the evil empire. Look at Saddam, one of our best customers. Who saw them coming, Johnny? Who saw them forming like black clouds upon the horizon? Not us. Look at Galtieri and the conflagration in the Falklands, my God. Again and again, our vast intelligence hammer is able to crack every nut except the one that matters: the human enigma.' He was pacing at his old speed, matching his footsteps to his bombast. 'But that's what we're cracking now. This time we can pre-empt. We have the bazaars wired. We know the mood of the mob, its subconscious agenda, its hidden flashpoints. We can forestall. We can outwit history. Ambush her –'

He grabbed his telephone so fast it scarcely had time to ring. But it was only his wife, asking whether he had yet again put the keys to her car in his pocket before he left for work. Luxmore tersely acknowledged his crime, rang off, tugged at the skirts of his jacket and resumed his pacing.

*   *   *

They chose Geoff's place because Ben Hatry said use it, and after all Geoff Cavendish was Ben Hatry's creature, though both men felt it prudent to keep this quiet. And there was rightness in it being Geoff's place because in a way the idea had been Geoff's from the beginning, in the sense that it was Geoff Cavendish who had produced the first game plan, and Ben Hatry had said fucking do it, which was how Ben Hatry chose to speak: as a great British media baron and employer of numberless terrified journalists he had a natural loathing for his mother tongue.

It was Cavendish who had fired Hatry's imagination, if that was what Ben Hatry possessed, Cavendish who had struck the deal with Luxmore, encouraged him, bolstered his budget and his ego, Cavendish who on Hatry's nod had given the first little lunches and informal briefings in expensive restaurants handy for the House, lobbied the right Members, though never in Hatry's name, unrolled the map, showed them where the damn place was and where the Canal went, because half of them were hazy, Cavendish who had sounded discreet alarm bells in the City and the oil companies, cuddled up to the imbecile Conservative right, which was no work of art for him, wooed its Empire-dreamers, Euro-haters, nigger-haters, pan-xenophobes and lost, uneducated children.

It was Cavendish who had conjured visions of an eleventh-hour crusade before the election, a phoenix risen from the Tory ashes and turned war god, of a leader clad in the suit of shining armour that till now had always seemed too big for him, Cavendish who made the same pitch in different language to the Opposition – don't worry, boys and girls, you don't have to oppose anything or take a position, just keep your heads down and say this is no time to rock the Loyal British Boat even if it's sailing slap in the wrong direction, piloted by lunatics and leaking like a colander.

It was Cavendish yet again who got the multis suitably worried, who stirred up murmurings about the devastating effect on British industry, commerce and the pound, Cavendish who made us *aware*, as he called it: which is to say turned rumour into received certainty by the ingenious use of arm's length columnists operating outside the Hatry empire and therefore notionally untainted by its frightful reputation; Cavendish who planted follow-up articles in learned shoestring journals with promises to keep, such articles in turn being puffed out of all proportion by bigger journals, and so up the ladder or down it to the inside pages of the tabloids, to editorials in the degraded so-called qualities and late-night public debate on television, not only on the Hatry-owned channels but on rival channels too – since nothing is more predictable than the media's parroting of its own fictions and the terror of each competitor that it will be scooped by the others, whether or not the story is true because quite frankly, dears, in the news game these days, we don't have the staff, time, interest, energy, literacy or minimal sense of responsibility to check our facts by any means except calling up whatever has been written by other hacks on the same subject and repeating it as gospel.

And it was Cavendish, this hulking, tweedy outdoor English *chap* with the voice of an upper-class cricket commentator on a sunny summer's afternoon, who had so convincingly propagated, always through well-dined intermediaries, Ben Hatry's treasured *If Not Now When?* doctrine that lay at the root of his trans-Atlantic arm-twisting and wire-pulling and intriguing, the thrust of which theory being that the United States cannot conceivably remain the world's one and only superpower for more than another decade at most, after which it was curtains, so if there was any heavy surgery that needed doing anywhere in the world, said the doctrine, however brutal and self-serving it might look from the outside or for that matter from the inside, then for our survival and our kids' survival and the survival of the Hatry empire and its evergrowing stranglehold on the hearts and minds of the Third and Fourth worlds: *do it now while we have the clout, for fuck's sake! Stop pussyfooting around! Take what you want, smash what you don't! But whatever you do or don't do, stop mollycoddling and conceding and apologising and wimping out.*

And if that put Ben Hatry into bed with the American Loony Right, as well as their blood brothers on this side of the pond, and made him the darling of the arms industry to boot – well, fuck it, he would say in his sweet mother tongue, he wasn't a politico, he hated the bastards, he was a realist, he didn't give a tinker's who he was allied to as long as they talked sense and didn't tiptoe around the international corridors saying to every Jap, nigger and dago: 'Pardon me for being a white middle-class liberal American, sir, and excuse us for being so big and strong and powerful and rich, but we believe in the dignity and equality of all God's people, and would you be so kind as to allow me to get down on my hands and knees and kiss your arse?'

Which was the image Ben Hatry painted tirelessly for the benefit of his lieutenants but always on the understanding that we keep it quiet among us boys and girls in the sacred interest of objective reporting of the news, which is what we are put on earth to do, or your fucking feet won't touch.

*   *   *

'Count me out,' Ben Hatry had told Cavendish the day before, in his toneless voice.

Sometimes he spoke without moving his lips at all. Sometimes he grew sick of his own machinations, sick of the whole human mediocrity.

'You two bastards handle them on your own,' he added viciously.

'As you wish, Chief. Pity, but there we are,' said Cavendish.

But Ben Hatry had come, as Cavendish knew he would, by cab because he didn't trust his chauffeur, and even arrived ten minutes early to read a summary of the shit that Cavendish had been sending to Van's people over the last few months – shit being his preferred term for prose – ending with a one-page red-hot report from those wankers across the river – unsigned, unsourced, unheaded – which Cavendish said was the clincher, the pure wine, the missing diamond, Chief, Van's people were going ballistic, hence today's get-together.

'Who's the bastard who wrote this?' Hatry enquired, ever anxious to give credit where it was due.

'Luxmore, Chief.'

'He the arsehole who screwed up the Falklands operation for us single-handed?'

'The same.'

'Didn't go through Rewrite Department, that's for sure.'

Nevertheless Ben Hatry read the report twice, a thing unknown in him.

'Is it true?' he asked Cavendish.

'True *enough*, Chief,' said Cavendish with the judicious moderation that characterised his judgments. 'True in *parts*. Not sure about its shelf-life. Van's boys may have to be a bit quick on the draw.'

Hatry tossed the report back at him.

'Well at least they'll know the fucking way this time,' he said with a mirthless nod for Tug Kirby, the third murderer, as Cavendish wittily dubbed him, who had just stormed into the room without wiping his great feet and was glowering round him looking for an enemy.

'Those Yanks arrived yet?' he roared.

'Any minute now, Tug,' Cavendish assured him soothingly.

'Buggers'll be late for their own funerals,' said Kirby.

*   *   *

A particular advantage of Geoff's place was its ideal position in the heart of Mayfair, handy for the side entrance to Claridges, in a gated and guarded cul de sac with a lot of heavy hitters and diplomats and lobbyists living there, and the Italian Embassy one end. Yet there was a pleasing anonymity about it too. You could be a cleaner, caterer, courier, butler, bodyguard, catamite or grand master of the universal galaxy. No one cared. And Geoff was a door-opener. He knew how to get to the power people, bring them together. With Geoff you could lean back and let it happen, which was what they were doing now: three Brits and their two American guests and everyone deniable as they tucked into a meal they agreed was not taking place, a help-yourself with no servants to witness it, consisting of salmon *tiède* flown down from the Cavendish estates in Scotland, quail's eggs, fruit and cheese, and all topped by a super bread-and-butter pudding made by Geoff's old nanny.

And to drink, iced tea and its stablemates, because in today's Born Again Washington, said Geoff Cavendish, alcohol at lunch was regarded as the Mark of the Beast.

And a round table so that nobody was dominant. Plenty of leg space. Soft chairs. The phones unplugged. Cavendish was great on people's comfort level. Girls galore if you wanted them. Ask Tug.

*   *   *

'Flight bearable, Elliot?' asked Cavendish.

'Oh, I'm in travel heaven, Geoff. I just *love* those bumpy little jets. Northolt was neat. I *love* Northolt. The chopper ride to Battersea, *epic. Beautiful* power station.'

With Elliot you never knew whether he was being sarcastic, or was he like this all the time? He was thirty-one years old, a Southerner from Alabama. He was a lawyer and a journalist, and floppy-droll except where he was on the attack. He had his own column in the *Washington Times* where he disputed ostentatiously with names that till recently had been bigger than his own. He was lank and cadaverous and dangerous and bespectacled. His face was all jaw and bone.

'Stopping over tonight or going home, Elliot?' Tug Kirby growled, implying that the second of these options was his preferred one.

'Tug, sadly we have to head right on back as soon as this party is over,' Elliot said.

'Not paying your respects to the Embassy?' said Tug with an oafish grin.

This was a joke. Tug didn't make a lot of them. The State Department were the last people on God's earth who should know of Elliot's visit or the Colonel's.

Seated at Elliot's side, the Colonel was chewing his salmon with the regulation number of bites.

'We don't have any *friends* over there, Tug,' he explained ingenuously. 'Just fairies.'

In Westminster Tug Kirby was known as the Minister with the Very Long Portfolio. Partly his sexual adventures had earned him this title, mostly it was his unrivalled collection of consultancies and directorships. There was not a defence company in the whole of the country or the Middle East, said the wits, that didn't own Tug Kirby, or Tug Kirby didn't own. Like his guests he was powerful and vaguely menacing. He had large fat shoulders and thick black eyebrows that looked stuck on. He had the mean, stupid eyes of a bull. Even while he was eating, his big curled fists stayed on the alert.

*   *   *

'Hey, Dirk – how's Van?' Hatry called gaily across the table.

Ben Hatry had switched on his legendary charm. No one

could resist it. His smile was just so much fun after so long in the clouds. The Colonel brightened immediately. Cavendish too was delighted to find his Chief suddenly in good spirits.

'Sir,' the Colonel barked, as if he were addressing a court martial, 'General Van sends his compliments, wishes to express his thanks to you, Ben, and your helpers for the invaluable practical support and encouragement you have given him over the past months and right up to this present moment in time.'

Shoulders back, chin in. *Sir.*

'Well, you tell him we're all disappointed as fuck he's not running for President,' said Hatry, with the same radiant smile. 'It's a damn shame the only good man in America hasn't got the balls to stand.'

The Colonel remained unaffected by Hatry's playful provocations. He was accustomed to them from previous meetings.

'General Van has youth on his side, sir. General sees things long. General's of a very strategic disposition.' He was nodding to himself between hushed, worried sentences while his eyes remained wide and vulnerable. 'General reads a lot. He's deep. Knows how to wait. Other men would have fired off their ammunition by now. Not the General. No, *sir.* When the time comes to swing the President, the General will be right there swinging him. Only man in America knows how, my opinion. Yes, *sir.*'

I obey, said the Colonel's spaniel eyes, but his jaw said get out of my damn way. His hair was cropped short. It was hard to remember as he sat to attention that he was not in uniform. It was hard not to wonder whether he was a little mad. Or whether they all were. The formalities were suddenly over. Elliot looked at his watch, raised his eyebrows rudely at Tug Kirby. The Colonel removed his napkin from his throat, primly dabbed his lips with it, then laid it on the table like an unwanted posy for Cavendish to clear away. Kirby was lighting a cigar.

'Do you mind putting that fucking thing out, please, Tug?' Hatry enquired politely.

Kirby stubbed it out. Sometimes he forgot that Hatry

owned his secrets. Cavendish was asking who took sweetener in his coffee and would anyone care for creamer? Now at last it was a meeting, not a feast. It was five men who cordially detested each other, seated round a well-polished eighteenth-century table and united by a great ideal.

*   *   *

'You boys going in or not?' said Ben Hatry, who was not famous for preamble.

'We'd sure as hell *like* to, Ben,' said Elliot, his face closed tight as a sea-door.

'So what's stopping you, for fuck's sake? You've got the evidence. You run the country. What are you waiting for?'

'Van would like to go in. So would Dirk here. Right, Dirk? All bands playing? Right, Dirk?'

'Sure would,' the Colonel breathed and shook his head at his linked hands.

'Then *do* it, for Christ's sake!' Tug Kirby cried.

Elliot affected not to hear this. 'The American *people* would like us to go in,' he said. 'They may not know it yet, but they soon will. The American people will want back what is rightfully theirs, and shouldn't have been given away in the first place. Nobody is *stopping* us, Ben. We have the Pentagon, we have the will, the trained men, the technology. We have the Senate, we have Congress. We have the Republican party. We write foreign policy. We have a firm hold on the media in battle conditions. Last time round it was absolute, this time it will be more absolute than that. Nobody is stopping us except ourselves, Ben. Nobody, and that's a fact.'

A moment's common silence descended. Kirby was the first to break it.

'Always takes a bit of courage to jump,' he said gruffly. 'Thatcher never wavered. Other chaps waver all the time.'

The silence returned.

'Which is how canals get lost, I suppose,' Cavendish suggested, but nobody laughed and the silence came back yet again.

'You know something Van said to me just the other day, Geoff?' said Elliot.

'What's that, old boy?' said Cavendish.

'Everybody who is not American has a rôle for America. Mostly they are people who have no rôle for themselves. Mostly they're jerking off.'

'General Van's deep,' said the Colonel.

'Get on with it,' said Hatry.

But Elliot took his time, resting his hands thoughtfully on his chest as if he were wearing a waistcoat and smoking a cheroot on his plantation.

'Ben, we have no damn *peg* for this thing,' he confessed, as one journalist to another. 'No *hook*. We have a *condition*. We do not have a smoking gun. No raped American nuns. No dead American babies. We have rumours. We have maybes. We have *your* spook reports, unsubstantiated by *our* spook agencies at this time, because that's the way we say it has to be. This is not the moment to turn out the State Department's bleeding hearts, or put billboards screaming Hands Off Panama! at the White House railings. This is a moment for decisive action and having the national conscience adapt retrospectively. The national conscience will do that. We can help it. You can help it, Ben.'

'I said I would. I will.'

'But what you cannot give us is a *peg*,' Elliot said. 'You cannot rape nuns. You cannot massacre babies for us.'

Kirby let out a misplaced guffaw of laughter. 'Don't you be so sure about that, Elliot,' he cried. 'You don't know our Ben the way we do. What? What?'

But all he got for applause was a pained frown from the Colonel.

'Of course you've got a fucking peg,' Ben Hatry retorted caustically.

'Name it,' Elliot said.

'The denials, for fuck's sake.'

'What denials?' said Elliot.

'Everyone's. The Panamanians will deny it, the Frogs will deny it, the Japs will deny it. So they're liars, the same as Castro was a liar. Castro denies his Russian rockets, so you go in. The Canal conspirators deny their conspiracy, so in you go again.'

'Ben, those rockets were *there*,' said Elliot. 'We had *pictures* of those rockets. We had a smoking gun. We have no smoking gun for this scenario. The American people got to see justice done. Talk doesn't do it. Never did. We need a smoking gun. The President will need a smoking gun. If he doesn't get one, he won't swing.'

'We don't happen to have a few happy snaps of Jap engineers in false beards digging a second canal by flashlight, do we, Ben?' Cavendish asked facetiously.

'No, we fucking don't,' Hatry retorted, never raising his voice but never needing to. 'So what are you going to do, Elliot? Wait till the Japs give you a photo call at lunchtime on the 31st of December in the year of Our Lord nineteen fucking ninety-nine?'

Elliot was unmoved. 'Ben, we don't have one emotive argument that will play on our television screens. Last time round we got lucky. Noriega's Dignity Battalions mishandled American women in the streets of Panama City. Until then we were grounded. We had drugs. So we wrote drugs big. We had Noriega's attitude problem. We wrote that big. We had his ugliness, and we wrote that big. Lot of people think ugly is immoral. We worked on that. We had his sexuality and his voodoo. We played the Castro card. But it wasn't till decent American women were harassed by disrespectful Hispanic soldiers in the name of dignity that the President felt obliged to send our boys in to teach them a little manners.'

'I heard you arranged that,' Hatry said.

'Wouldn't play twice, either way,' Elliot replied, brushing aside the suggestion as irrelevant.

Ben Hatry imploded. An underground test. There was no bang, he was fully tamped. Just a high-pressured hiss as he expelled air, frustration and fury in one burst.

'Jesus bloody Christ. That fucking Canal is *yours*, Elliot.'

'India was yours once, Ben.'

Hatry didn't bother to respond. He was staring through the curtained window at nothing that was worth his time.

'We need a peg,' Elliot repeated. 'No peg, no war. President won't swing. Final.'

* * *

It took Geoff Cavendish, with his polish and good robust looks to bring light and happiness back to the meeting.

'Well, gentlemen, it seems to me we have a great deal of common ground. We must leave the timing to General Van's judgment. Nobody disputes that. Can we talk around that a little? Tug, you're straining at the leash, I see.'

Hatry had made the curtained window his own. The prospect of listening to Kirby had only deepened his despondency.

'This Silent Opposition,' Kirby said. 'The Abraxas Group. Do you have a read on that, Elliot?'

'Should I?'

'Does Van?'

'He likes them.'

'Rather odd of him, isn't it?' said Kirby. 'Considering the fellow is anti-American?'

'Abraxas is not a puppet, he's not a client,' Elliot replied equably. 'If we're fielding a provisional Panamanian government till the country's safe for elections again, Abraxas is worth a lot of Brownie points. The libs can't scream colonial at us. Neither can the Pans.'

'And if he's no good you can always crash his plane, can't you,' said Hatry nastily.

* * *

Kirby again: 'My point being, Elliot, Abraxas is our man. Not yours. *Our* man by *his* choice. That makes his opposition ours too. Ours to control, ours to equip and advise. I think we should all remember that. Van should remember it particularly. It would look very bad for General Van if it were ever to turn out that Abraxas had been taking Uncle Sam's dollar. Or his chaps were equipped with American arms.

Don't want to stigmatise the poor fellow as a Yankee quisling from the start, do we?'

The Colonel had an idea. His eyes opened wide and shone. His smile was heavenly.

'Listen: we can do it false flag, Tug! We got *assets* out there! We can make it like Abraxas is getting stuff from Peru, Guatemala, Castro Cuba. We can make it *anything*. It's not any kind of problem!'

Tug Kirby only ever made one point at a time. 'We found Abraxas, we equip him,' he said stonily. 'We've got a first-class procurement man on the spot. You want to put up money, all offers gratefully received. But you put it up to *us*. Nothing local. Nothing direct. We run Abraxas, we supply him. He's ours. And his students and his fishermen and anybody else he's got. We supply the whole home side,' he ended, and rapped his huge knuckles on the eighteenth-century table in case they hadn't got the point.

'All that's if,' said Elliot after a while.

'If what?' Kirby demanded.

'If we go in,' said Elliot.

Abruptly Hatry unlocked his gaze from the window and swung round to face Elliot.

'I want exclusive first bite,' he said. 'My cameras and my scribes go in the first wave, my boys to run with the students and the fishermen, exclusive. Everyone else rides in the guard's van with the spares.'

Elliot was drily amused. 'Maybe you people should mount the invasion for us, Ben. Maybe that would solve your election problem for you. How about a rescue action to protect expatriate British citizens? Must be a couple of 'em down there in Panama.'

'Glad you raised that question, Elliot,' said Kirby.

A different axis. Kirby very tense and all eyes on him, even Hatry's.

'Why's that, Tug?' said Elliot.

'Time we talked about just what our man *does* get out of this,' Kirby retorted, blushing. Our man, meaning our leader. Our puppet. Our mascot.

'You want him sitting with Van in the Pentagon war room, Tug?' Elliot suggested playfully.

'Don't be bloody silly.'

'You want British troops on American gunships? Be my guest.'

'No we don't, thank you. It's your back yard. But we shall want *credit*.'

'How much, Tug? I'm told you drive a hard bargain.'

'Not that kind of credit. *Moral* credit.'

Elliot smiled. So did Hatry. Morality, their expressions implied, was negotiable.

'Our man to be visibly and loudly at the forefront,' Tug Kirby announced, counting off terms on his enormous fingers. 'Our man to wrap himself in the flag, your man to cheer him on while he does it, Rule Britannia and bugger Brussels. The special relationship seen to be up and running – right, Ben? Visits to Washington, handshakes, high profile, lot of kind words for our man. And your man to come to London as soon as you've swung him. He's overdue and it's been noticed. The rôle of British Intelligence to be leaked to the respectable press. We'll give you a text – right, Ben? The rest of Europe out of it and the Frogs in disgrace as usual.'

'Leave that shit to me,' Hatry said. 'He doesn't sell newspapers. I do.'

They parted like unreconciled lovers, worried they had said the wrong things, failed to say the right ones, not been understood. We'll run it by Van as soon as we get back, said Elliot. See what his sense is. General Van is long term, said the Colonel. General Van is a true visionary. The General has his eyes on the Jerusalem. The General knows how to wait.

'Give me a fucking drink,' said Hatry.

*   *   *

They sat alone, three Englishmen in withdrawal with their whiskies.

'Nice little meeting,' said Cavendish.

'Shits,' said Kirby.

'Buy the Silent Opposition,' Hatry ordered. 'Make sure it can speak and shoot. How real are the students?'

'They're iffy, Chief. Maoists, Trots, Peaceniks, a lot of 'em over age. They could jump either way.'

'Who the fuck cares which way they jump? Buy the sods and turn them loose. Van wants a peg. He's dreaming of it but doesn't dare to ask. Why d'you think the bastard sent his flunkies and stayed home? Maybe the students can supply the peg. Where's Luxmore's report?'

Cavendish handed it to him and he read it for the third time before pushing it back at him.

'Who's the bitch who writes our doom and gloom shit?' he asked.

Cavendish said a name.

'Give it to her,' Hatry said. Tell her I want the students larger. Link them with the poor and the oppressed, drop the Communism. And give us more about the Silent Opposition looking to Britain as a democratic rôle model for Panama in the twenty-first century. I want crisis. ''As terror walks the streets of Panama'', that shit. First editions, Sunday. Get onto Luxmore. Tell him it's time to get his fucking students out of bed.'

*   *   *

Luxmore had never been on such a dangerous mission. He was exalted, he was terrified. But then abroad always terrified him. He was desperately, heroically alone. An impressive passport in the jacket he must not remove enjoined all foreigners to grant the Queen's well-beloved messenger Mellors safe conduct across their borders. Piled on the First Class seat beside him were two bulky black leather briefcases sealed with wax, embossed with the royal crest and fitted with broad shoulder straps. The rules of his assumed office allowed him neither sleep nor drink. The briefcases must remain at all times within his sight and reach. No profane hand was permitted to defile the pouches of a Queen's Messenger. He was to befriend nobody, though out of operational necessity he had exempted a matronly British Airways stewardess from this edict. Halfway across the South Atlantic, he had unexpectedly needed to relieve himself. Twice he had risen to stake his claim, only to see himself anticipated by an unladen passenger. Finally, in the extreme of need, he had prevailed on the stewardess to stand guard over a vacant lavatory for him while he struggled crablike down the aisle with his burdens banging wildly against dozing Arabs, lurching into drinks trolleys.

'Must be ever such heavy secrets you've got in there,' the airhostess commented gaily as she saw him safely into dock.

Luxmore was delighted to recognise a fellow Scot.

'Where are you from then, my dear?'

'Aberdeen.'

'But how splendid! The silver city, my God!'

'How about you?'

Luxmore was about to respond with a generous description of his Scottish provenance when he remembered that his false passport had Mellors born in Clapham. His embarrassment deepened when she held the door back for him while he fought the pouches for floorspace to manoeuvre. Returning to his place he scanned the rows for potential hijackers and saw nobody he trusted.

The plane started its descent. My God, imagine! thought Luxmore as awe at his mission and a hatred of flying alternated with the nightmare of discovery – she crashes into the sea – the pouches with her. Rescue ships from America, Cuba, Russia and Britain race to the spot! Who was the mysterious Mellors? Why did his pouches plummet to the bottom of the ocean? Why were no papers found floating on the surface? Why will no one come forward to claim him? No widow, child, relative? The pouches are raised. Will Her Majesty's government kindly explain their extraordinary contents to a breathless world?

'Miami's your lot for this time then, is it?' the airhostess asked, watching him saddle up to disembark. 'I'll bet you'll be glad of a nice hot bath when you're shot of that lot.'

Luxmore kept his voice low in case Arabs overheard him. She was a good Scottish lass, and deserved the truth.

'Panama,' he murmured.

But she had already left him. She was too busy asking passengers to make sure their seats were in the upright position and their belts securely fastened.

CHAPTER NINETEEN

'They charge green fees according to one's rank,' Maltby explained, selecting a middle iron for his approach shot. The flag stood eighty yards away, for Maltby a day's journey. 'Private soldiers pay next to nothing. Achievers pay more as they go up the scale. They say the General can't afford to play at all.' He pulled a shaggy grin. 'I did a deal,' he confided proudly. 'I'm a sergeant.'

He lashed at the ball. Startled, it scurried sixty yards through sopping grass to safety, and hid. He loped after it. Stormont followed. An old Indian caddie in a straw hat was carrying a collation of ancient clubs in a mildewed bag.

The well-tended links of Amador are a bad golfer's dream and Maltby was a bad golfer. They lie in well-groomed strips between a pristine US Army base built in the vintage '20s, and the shore that runs beside the entrance to the Canal. There is a guard hut. There is a straight empty road protected by a bored American soldier and a bored Panamanian policeman. No one goes there much except the Army and its wives. On one horizon lies El Chorillo and beyond it the Satanic towers of Punta Paitilla, this morning softened by tiers of rolling cloud. Out to sea lie the islands and the causeway and the obligatory line of motionless ships waiting for their turn to pass under the Bridge of the Americas.

But for the bad golfer the most seductive feature of the place is the straight grass trenches that are sunk thirty feet below sea level and, having once been a part of the Canal works, serve as ducts for the imperfectly struck ball. The bad golfer may hook, he may slice. The trenches, for as long as he remains within their care, forgive him everything. All that is asked is that he connect and stay low.

'And Paddy's well and everything,' Maltby suggested, discreetly improving the lie of the ball with the toe of his cracked golf shoe. 'Her cough's better?'

'Not really,' said Stormont

'Oh dear. What do they say?'

'Not much.'

Maltby played again. The ball sped across the green and once more vanished. Maltby hurled himself after it. Rain fell. It was falling at ten-minute intervals but Maltby seemed unaware of it. The ball lay pertly at the centre of an island of sodden sand. The old caddie handed Maltby an appropriate club.

'You should get her away somewhere,' he advised Stormont airily. 'Switzerland or wherever one goes these days. Panama's so insanitary. You never know which side the germs are coming from. Fuck.'

Like some primeval insect his ball scuttled into a clump of rich green pampas. Through sheets of rain Stormont watched his Ambassador hack at it in huge arcs until it crept sullenly onto the green. Tension while Maltby performed a long putt. A peal of triumph as he holed out. He's snapped, thought Stormont. Mad. High time. A word, Nigel, if you'd be so good, Maltby had said on the telephone at one o'clock this morning, just as Paddy was getting off to sleep. Thought we might have it on the hoof, Nigel, if that's all right by you. Whatever you say, Ambassador.

'*Otherwise* the Embassy seems a rather *happy* spot these days,' Maltby resumed as they strode out towards the next trench. 'Barring Paddy's cough and poor old Phoebe.' Phoebe, his wife, neither so poor nor so old.

Maltby was unshaven. A ratty grey pullover, soaked through, hung from his upper body like a suit of chainmail of which he had mislaid the trousers. Why doesn't the bloody man treat himself to a set of waterproofs? Stormont marvelled as more rain seeped down his own neck.

'Phoebe's *never* happy,' Maltby was saying. 'I can't think why she came back. I loathe her. She loathes me. The children loathe us both. There seems absolutely no point in any of it. We haven't screwed for simply years, thank God.'

Stormont preserved an appalled silence. Not once in the eighteen months that they had known each other had Maltby confided in him. Now suddenly, for reasons unknown, there was no limit to their frightful intimacy.

'*You* got divorced all right,' Maltby complained. 'Yours was quite a public sort of thing too, if I remember. But you got over it. Your children speak to you. The Office didn't chuck you out.'

'Not quite.'

'Well, I do wish you'd have a word with Phoebe about it. Do her the world of good. Tell her you've been through it and it's not as bad as its reputation. She doesn't talk to people properly, that's part of the problem. Prefers to boss them about.'

'Perhaps it would be better if Paddy talked to her,' Stormont said.

Maltby was teeing up. He did this, Stormont noticed, without bending his knees. He simply folded himself in two, then unfolded himself, talking all the while.

'No, I think *you* should do it, quite honestly,' he went on while he addressed the ball with menacing feints. 'She worries about *me*, you see. She knows *she* can get on alone. But she thinks I'll be on the phone all the time asking her how to boil an egg. I wouldn't do any such thing. I'd move in a gorgeous girl and boil eggs for her all day long.' He drove and the ball shot upward, beyond the salvation of the trench. For a while it seemed content with its straight path. Then it changed its mind, turned left and disappeared into walls of rain.

'Oh *fart*,' said the Ambassador, revealing depths of language that Stormont had never guessed at.

The deluge became absurd. Leaving the ball to fend for

itself, they repaired to a regimental bandstand set before a crescent of married officers' mansions. But the old caddie didn't like the bandstand. He preferred the dubious shelter of a cluster of palm trees, where he stood with the torrent streaming off his hat.

'*Otherwise*,' said Maltby, 'as far as *I* know, we're rather a *jolly* crowd. No feuds, everyone chipper, our stock in Panama never higher, fascinating intelligence pouring in from all directions. What more can our masters ask? one wonders.'

'Why? What *are* they asking?'

But Maltby would not be hurried. He preferred his own strange path of indirection.

'Long chats with all sorts of people last night on Osnard's secret telephone,' he announced in a tone of fond reminiscence. 'Have *you* had a go on it?'

'I can't say I have,' said Stormont.

'Hideous red affair, wired up to a Boer War washing machine. You can say anything you like on it. I was terribly impressed. Such nice chaps too. Not that one has ever met them. But they *sounded* nice. A conference call. One spent one's entire time apologising for interrupting. A man called Luxmore is on his way to us. A Scottish person. We're to call him Mellors. I'm not supposed to tell you, so naturally I shall. Luxmore-Mellors will bring us life-altering news.'

The rain had stopped dead but Maltby didn't seem to have noticed. The caddie was still huddled under the palm trees, where he was smoking a fat roll of marijuana leaves.

'Perhaps you should stand that chap down,' Stormont suggested. 'If you're not playing any more.'

So they put some wet dollars together and sent the caddie back to the clubhouse with Maltby's clubs, and sat themselves on a dry bench at the edge of the bandstand and watched a swollen stream racing through Eden, and the sun like God's glory breaking out on every leaf and flower.

*　　*　　*

'It has been decided – the passive voice is not of my choosing, Nigel – it has been decided that Her Majesty's Government will lend secret support and aid to Panama's Silent Opposition. On a deniable basis, naturally. Luxmore whom we must call Mellors is coming out to tell us how to do it. There's a handbook on it, I understand. *How to Oust Your Host Government* or something of the sort. We must all dip into it. I don't know yet whether I shall be asked to admit Messrs Domingo and Abraxas to my kitchen garden at dead of night or whether this will fall to you. Not that I have a kitchen garden, but I seem to remember that the late Lord Halifax did, and met all sorts of people there. You look askance. Is askance what you're looking?'

'Why can't Osnard take care of it?' Stormont asked.

'As his Ambassador I have not encouraged his involvement. The boy has enough responsibilities as it is. He's young. He's junior. These Opposition people like the reassurance of a seasoned hand. Some are people like us, but some are hoary working-class chaps, stevedores, fishermen, farmers and the like. Far better we take the burden upon ourselves. We're also to support a shadowy body of bomb-making students, always tricky. We shall take over the students too. I'm sure you'll be very good with them. You seem troubled, Nigel. Have I upset you?'

'Why don't they send us more spies?'

'Oh, I don't think that's necessary. Visiting firemen perhaps, men like Luxmore-Mellors, but nobody permanent. We mustn't inflate the Embassy's numbers unnaturally, it would invite comment. I made that point also.'

'*You* did?' said Stormont incredulously.

'Yes, indeed. With two such experienced heads as yours and mine, I said, additional staff were quite unnecessary. I was firm. They would litter the place up, I said. Unacceptable. I pulled rank. I said we were men of the world. You would have been proud of me.'

Stormont thought he saw an unfamiliar sparkle in his Ambassador's eye, best compared with the awakening of desire.

'We shall need an *enormous* amount of stuff,' Maltby went on, with the enthusiasm of a schoolboy looking forward to a new train-set. 'Radios, cars, safe houses, couriers, not to mention matériel – machineguns, mines, rocket-launchers, masses of explosive, naturally, detonators, everything your heart has ever dreamed of. No modern Silent Opposition is complete without them, they assured me. And *spares* are frightfully important, one's told. Well you know how careless students are. Give them a radio in the morning, it's covered in graffiti by lunchtime. And I'm sure Silent Oppositions are no better. The weapons will all be British, you'll be relieved to hear. There's a tried and tested British company already standing by to supply them, which is nice. Minister Kirby thinks the world of them. They earned their spurs in Iran, or was it Iraq? Probably both. Gully thinks the world of them too, I'm pleased to say, and the Office has accepted my suggestion that he be advanced immediately to the rank and condition of Buchaneer. Osnard is swearing him in even as we speak.'

'*Your* suggestion,' Stormont repeated numbly.

'Yes, Nigel, I have decided that you and I are well cast for the business of intrigue. I once remarked to you how I yearned to take part in a British plot. Well, here it is. The secret bugle has sounded. I trust that none of us will be found wanting in our zeal – I do wish you could look a little happier, Nigel. You don't seem to realise the import of what I'm telling you. This Embassy is about to take an amazing leap forward. From a silted diplomatic backwater we shall become the hottest post in the ratings. Promotion, medals, notice of the most flattering kind will overnight be ours. Don't tell me you doubt our masters' wisdom? That would be very bad timing.'

'It's just that there seem to be rather a lot of stages missing,' Stormont said feebly, grappling with the acquisition of a brand new Ambassador.

'Nonsense. Of what sort?'

'Logic, for one.'

'Oh, really?' – coldly. 'Where precisely do you detect a want of logic?'

'Well I mean take the Silent Opposition. Nobody's even heard of it apart from us. Why hasn't it done something – leaked something to the press – spoken up?'

Maltby was already scoffing. 'But my dear chap! That's its name. That's its nature. It's silent. It keeps its counsel. Awaits its hour. Abraxas isn't a drunk. He's a bravura hero, a closet revolutionary for God and country. Domingo isn't a drug dealer with an oversized libido, he's a selfless warrior for democracy. As to the students, what is there to know? You remember how we were. Scatty. Inconstant. One thing one day, another thing the next. I fear you're becoming jaded, Nigel. Panama's getting you down. Time you took Paddy to Switzerland. Oh, and *yes*' – he went on, as if there were something he had omitted to say – 'nearly forgot. Mr Lux-more-Mellors will be bringing the gold bars,' he added, in the tone of someone tying a last administrative knot. 'One can't trust banks and courier services in these cases, not in the dark world of intrigue that you and I are entering, Nigel, so he's posing as a Queen's Messenger and bringing them by diplomatic bag.'

'The *what?*'

'Gold bars, Nigel. It seems they're what one gives to Silent Oppositions these days in preference to dollars or pounds or Swiss francs. I must say one can see the sense of it. Can *you* imagine running a Silent Opposition on pounds sterling? They'd devalue before one had mounted one's first abortive putsch. And Silent Oppositions don't come cheap, I'm told,' he added in the same throwaway tone. 'A few million is nothing these days, not if you're counting on buying a future government at the same time. Students, well, one can rein them in a bit, but do you *remember* how we used to get into debt? Good quartermastering will be essential on both fronts. But I think we're up to it, Nigel, don't you? I see it as a challenge myself. The sort of thing one dreams of in the midlife of one's career. A diplomatic El Dorado without the sweat of all that panning in the jungle.'

*　　　*　　　*

Maltby was musing. Stormont, tight-lipped at his side, had never known him so relaxed. Yet of himself he knew nothing at all. Or nothing he could explain. The sun was still radiant.

Crouched in the blackness of the bandstand, he felt like a life-prisoner who can't believe that the door of his cell stands open. His bluff was being called – but what bluff? Whom had he been fooling, except himself, as he watched the Embassy flourish under Osnard's spurious alchemy? 'Don't knock a good thing,' he had warned Paddy sharply when she had dared suggest that BUCHAN was a bit too gorgeous to be true, particularly when you got to know Andy a bit better.

Maltby was philosophising:

'An Embassy is not equipped to *evaluate*, Nigel. We may have a *view*, that's different. We may have local knowledge. Of course we do. And sometimes it appears to conflict with what is told us by our betters. We have our senses. We can see and hear and sniff. But we don't have acres of files, computers, analysts and scores of delicious young débutantes scampering up and down corridors, alas. We have no overview. No awareness of the world's game. Least of all in an Embassy as small and irrelevant as our own. We're bumpkins. You agree, I take it?'

'Did you tell them this?'

'Indeed I did, and on Osnard's magic telephone. One's words are so much more weighty when they're said in secret, don't you agree? We are *aware of our limitations*, I said. Our work is *humdrum*. From time to time we are granted glimpses of the bigger world. BUCHAN is such a glimpse. And we are *grateful*, we are *proud*. It is neither proper nor appropriate, I said, that a tiny Embassy, charged with reading the mood of the country and propagating the views of our own government, should be called upon to pass an objective judgment on matters too large for our horizons.'

'What made you say that?' Stormont asked. He meant to be louder, but something was catching his throat.

'BUCHAN, naturally. The Office accused me of being niggardly in my praise of the latest material. You too, by inference, were similarly accused. ''*Praise?*'' I said. ''You can have all the praise you want. Andrew Osnard is a charming fellow, conscientious to a fault, and the BUCHAN operation has provided us with enlightenment and food for thought. We admire it. We support it. It enlivens our little community. But we do not presume to award it a place in the grand scheme of things. That is for your analysts and our masters."'

'And they were content with that?'

'They devoured it. Andy is a very nice fellow, as I told them. Goes down a treat with the girls. Asset to the Embassy.' He broke off, leaving a note of question, and resumed on a lower key. 'All right, maybe he doesn't quite play to eight. Maybe he cheats a bit here and there. Who doesn't? My point is, it's absolutely nothing to do with you or me or anyone else in this Embassy, with the possible exception of young Andy, that the BUCHAN stuff is the most frightful tosh.'

*   *   *

Stormont's reputation for composure in crisis was deserved. He sat painfully still for a while – the bench was teak and he had a bit of a back, particularly in damp weather. He considered the line of sterile ships, the Bridge of the Americas, the Old City and its ugly modern sister across the bay. He uncrossed his legs and crossed them the other way. And he wondered whether, for reasons not yet revealed, he was witnessing the end of his career, or beginning a new one of which the outlines were unclear to him.

Maltby by contrast was basking in a kind of confessional ease. He was leaning right back, his long, goatish head propped against an iron pillar of the bandstand, and his tone was magnanimity itself.

'Now I don't *know*,' he was saying, 'and *you* don't know, which one of them makes it up. Is it BUCHAN? Is it Mrs BUCHAN? Is it the subsources, whoever they are – Abraxas, Domingo, the woman Sabina or that disgusting journalist one sees around the place, Teddy Somebody? Or is it Andrew himself, bless him, and all else is vanity? He's young. They *could* be fooling him. On the other hand, he's quick-witted and he's a rogue. No he's not. He's rotten through and through. He's a *major* shit.'

'I thought you liked him.'

'Oh, I do, I do, enormously. And I don't hold the cheating against him one bit. A lot of chaps cheat, but it's usually the bad players like me. I mean, I've known chaps apologise. I've *practically* apologised myself a couple of times.' He bestowed a shameful grin on a pair of big yellow butterflies who had decided to join the conversation. 'But Andy's a winner, you see. And winners who cheat *are* shits. How does he get on with Paddy?'

'Paddy adores him.'

'Oh my Lord, not too much, I hope? He's shagging Fran, I'm sorry to say.'

'Rubbish,' Stormont replied hotly. 'They barely talk to each other.'

'That's because they're shagging in secret. They've been at it for months. Seems to have turned her head completely.'

'How can you possibly know that?'

'My dear chap, I can't take my eyes off her, you *must* have noticed. I watch her every move. I've followed her. I don't *think* she spotted me. But then of course we prowlers rather hope they do. She left her flat and went to Osnard's. Didn't come out. Next morning, seven o'clock, I faked an urgent telegram and phoned her flat. No answer. You can't get it clearer than that.'

'And you haven't said anything to Osnard?'

'Whatever for? Fran's an angel, he's a shit, I'm a lecher. What would we possibly achieve?'

The bandstand started to crack and rattle with the next downpour, and they had to wait a few minutes for the sun.

'So what do you intend to do?' Stormont said gruffly, fending off all the questions he refused to ask himself.

'*Do*, did you say, Nigel?' It was Maltby as Stormont remembered him: arid, pedantic and aloof. 'Whatever about?'

'BUCHAN. Luxmore. The Silent Opposition. The students. The people beyond that bridge over there, whoever they are. Osnard. The fact that BUCHAN is a fiction. If he is. That the reports are tosh, as you call them.'

'My dear man. We're not being asked to *do* anything.

We're merely the servants of a higher cause.'

'But if London's swallowing it whole, and you think it's total crap –'

Maltby leaned forward in the way he would normally lean across his desk, fingertips together in an attitude of mute obstruction. 'Go on.'

'– then you've got to tell them,' said Stormont stoutly.

'Why?'

'To stop them being led up the garden path. Anything could happen.'

'But Nigel. I thought we had already agreed that we were not evaluators.'

A sleek olive-coloured bird had entered their domain and was quizzing them for crumbs.

'I've nothing for you,' Maltby assured it anxiously. 'I really haven't. Oh *damn*,' he exclaimed, plunging his hands into his pockets, patting them vainly for anything that would do. 'Later,' he told it. 'Come back tomorrow. No, the day after, about this time. We've got a top spy descending on us.'

*   *   *

'Our duty here in the Embassy, in these circumstances, Nigel, is to provide logistical support,' Maltby went on in a tight, businesslike tone. 'You agree?'

'I suppose it is,' said Stormont doubtfully.

'To assist, where assistance is helpful. To applaud, to encourage, to cool brows. To ease the burden on those in the firing seat.'

'Driving seat,' said Stormont absently. 'Or firing line, I suppose, if that's what you mean.'

'Thank you. Why is it that whenever I reach for a modern metaphor I come unstuck? I suppose I imagined a tank at that moment. One of Gully's, paid for in gold bars.'

'I suppose you did.'

Maltby's voice gathered power as if for the benefit of the audience outside the bandstand, but there was none. 'So it is in this spirit of wholehearted collaboration that I have made the point to London – and I am sure you will agree with me – that Andrew Osnard, whatever his sterling virtues, is too inexperienced to be handling very large sums of money, whether in the form of cash or gold. And that it is only fair, on him as well as the recipients of the money, that he be provided with a paymaster. As his Ambassador, I have selflessly volunteered for the task. London sees the wisdom of this. Whether Osnard sees it is to be doubted, but he can scarcely object, particularly since it is we – you and I, Nigel – who in due course will be taking over liaison with the Silent Opposition and the students. Money from secret funds is notoriously hard to account for and quite impossible to pursue once it has disappeared into the wrong hands. All the more important that it be scrupulously husbanded while it is in our care. I have asked that Chancery be provided with a safe of the type that Osnard has in his strongroom. The gold – and whatever else – will be stored there and you and I will be joint keyholders. If Osnard decides that he requires a large sum of money he may come to us and state his case. Assuming the sum is within the agreed guidelines you and I will jointly draw the cash and place it in the appropriate hands. Are you a rich man, Nigel?'

'No.'

'Nor I. Did your divorce effectively impoverish you?'

'Yes.'

'I would imagine so. And it will be no better when my turn comes. Phoebe is not easily satisfied.' He glanced at Stormont for confirmation of this, but Stormont's face, turned towards the Pacific, was set in iron.

'It's so very unreasonable of life,' Maltby went on by way of small talk. 'Here we are in middle age, healthy chaps with healthy appetites. We made a few mistakes, faced up to them, learned the lessons. And we've still got a few precious, wonderful years before the Zimmer frame. Only one blot spoils an otherwise perfect prospect. We're broke.'

From the sea Stormont's eyes had lifted to a range of cotton-wool clouds that had formed above the distant islands. And it seemed to him that he saw snow on them, and Paddy, cured of her cough, pottering cheerfully up the path to the chalet, bearing shopping from the village.

'They want me to sound out the Americans,' he said mechanically.

'Who do?' Maltby asked quickly.

'London,' said Stormont in the same toneless voice.

'To what end?'

'To find out how much they know. About Silent Oppositions. Students. Secret meetings with the Japanese. I'm to test the water and give nothing away. Fly kites, trail coats. All the fatuous things that people tell you to do when they're sitting on their arses in London. Neither State nor the CIA has seen Osnard's material, apparently. I'm to find out whether they have independent awareness.'

'Meaning: whether they know?'

'If you prefer,' said Stormont.

Maltby was indignant. 'Oh I do *detest* the Americans. They expect everyone to go to the devil at the same hectic pace as themselves. It takes hundreds of years to do it properly. Look at us.'

'Suppose the Americans know none of it. Suppose it's virgin. Or they are.'

'Suppose there's nothing to know. That's *far* more likely.'

'*Some* of it may be true,' said Stormont with a kind of stubborn gallantry.

'On the principle that a broken clock tells the truth once every twelve hours, yes, I grant you, some of it may be true,' said Maltby with contempt.

'And suppose the Americans believe it. Whether it's true or not,' Stormont went on doggedly. 'Fall for it, if you like. London did.'

'*Which* London? Not *our* London, that's for sure. And of *course* the Americans won't believe it. Not the real ones. Their systems are vastly superior to ours. They'll prove it's tosh, they'll thank us, say they've taken note and shred it.'

Stormont refused to be put off. 'People don't *trust* their own systems. Intelligence is like exams. You always think the chap sitting next to you knows more than you do.'

'Nigel,' said Maltby firmly, with all the authority of his appointment, 'allow me to remind you that we are not evaluators. Life has given us a rare opportunity to find fulfilment in our work and be of service to those whom we regard. A golden future stretches ahead of us. The crime in such cases is to waver.'

Still staring ahead of him but without the consolation of the clouds, Stormont sees his future until now. Paddy's cough eating her to nothing. The decaying British health service all they can afford. Premature retirement to Sussex on a pittance. The going-going-gone of every dream he has ever cherished. And the England that he used to love six feet under ground.

CHAPTER TWENTY

They lay in the room for finishing hands, on the floor, on a pile of rugs which the Cuna Indian women kept for the influx of cousins, aunts and uncles from San Blas. Above them hung ranks of tailored suits awaiting buttonholes. The only light came through the skylight, and it was pink from the city's glow. The only sound came from the traffic in the Vía España, and Marta's mewing in his ear. They were dressed. Her smashed face was buried in his neck. She was trembling. So was Pendel. They were one cold scared body together. They were children in an empty house.

'They said you were cheating on your taxes,' she said. 'I told them you paid your taxes. "I keep the books," I said. "I know."' She broke off in case he wanted to say something but he had nothing to say. 'They said you were cheating on your employer's insurance for the staff. I said, "I do the insurance. The insurance is in order." They said I shouldn't ask questions, they had a file on me and I needn't think that, because I had been beaten once, I was immune.' She moved her head against him. 'I hadn't asked any questions. They said they would write in the file that I had Castro and Che Guevara on my bedroom wall. They said I was going around with radical students again. I said I wasn't, which is true. They said you were a spy. They said Mickie was another.

They said his drunkenness was just a trick to hide his spying. They're mad.'

She had finished, but it took Pendel time to understand this, so there was a delay before he rolled onto her and with both hands pressed her cheek against his own, making their faces into a single face.

'Did they say what sort of spy?'

'What other sorts are there?'

'Real ones.'

The phone was ringing.

*   *   *

It rang above their heads, which telephones in Pendel's life didn't normally do, on an instrument that he always thought of as internal until he remembered that his Cuna women lived on the telephone, rejoiced in it, wept into it, hung on its every word as they listened to husbands, lovers, fathers, chiefs, children, headmen and an infinite number of relations with insoluble personal problems. And after the telephone had rung a while – for ever, in the arbitrary measurements of his personal existence, but in the rest of the world four times – he noticed that Marta was no longer in his arms but standing, buttoning her blouse for decency while she prepared to take the call. And that she wished to know whether he was here or somewhere else, a thing she always asked if a call appeared inconvenient. Then a stubbornness took hold of him and he stood up also, with the result that they were close again, as they had been when they were lying down.

'*I am here and you are not,*' he said emphatically into her ear.

Not a trick, not an affectation: just the protector in him speaking from the heart. As a precaution he then interposed himself between Marta and the telephone and by the pink glow of the skylight directly above him – a few stars had made it through the haze – he considered the instrument while it went on ringing, and tried to fathom its purpose. Think the worst threats first, Osnard had said in their training sessions. So he thought them and the worst threat seemed to be Osnard himself, so he thought Osnard. Then he thought the Bear. Then he thought the police. And then, because he had been thinking of her all along, he thought Louisa.

But Louisa wasn't a threat. She was a casualty he had created long ago, in collaboration with her mother and father and Braithwaite and Uncle Benny and the Sisters of Charity and all the other people who made up the person he himself had become. And she didn't threaten him so much as remind him of the mistaken nature of their relationship, and how it had gone so wrong in spite of all the care he had put into composing it, which was the mistake he had been thinking of: we shouldn't *compose* relationships, but if we don't, what else do we do?

So finally, when there was nothing much left to think about, Pendel reached for the telephone and picked it up at much the same moment that Marta picked up his other hand and held its knuckles to her lips and bared teeth, investing them with light, swift, reassuring bites. And her gesture roused him in some way for, with the phone to his ear he straightened instead of druckening himself, and spoke in a bold, clear, not to say playful Spanish voice designed to show that there was fight in him yet, not just an endless submission to circumstance.

'Pendel & Braithwaite here! Good evening and how can we be of service to you?'

But if his gay humour was subconsciously intended to draw his attacker's sting, it failed miserably because the shooting had already begun. The first incoming rounds reached him before he had finished speaking: a pattern of deliberate, ascending single explosions interspersed with the chatter of light machineguns, grenades and the short triumphant whine of ricochets. So for a second or two Pendel assumed it was the invasion all over again; except that this time he had agreed to keep Marta company in El Chorillo, which was why she was kissing his hand. Then over the sounds of shooting came the predictable whimpering of victims, echoing in a makeshift shelter of some kind, accusing and protesting and cursing and demanding, choked with horror and outrage, begging for everything from compensation to God's forgiveness, until gradually all these voices became one voice, and it belonged to Ana, *chiquilla* to Mickie Abraxas, childhood friend to Marta and the one woman left in Panama who would put up with him, and clean him when he was sick from too much of whatever he had been taking, and listen to his ramblings.

And from the moment Pendel recognised Ana he knew exactly what she was telling him despite the fact that, like all good storytellers, she kept the best bit till last. Which was why he didn't pass the telephone to Marta but kept it to himself, taking the beating on his own body instead of letting her take it on hers which was what had happened of necessity when the Digbats wouldn't allow him to stop them smashing her to pieces.

*   *   *

All the same, Ana's monologue had many paths and Pendel practically needed a map to get through it.

'It's not even my father's house, my father only lent it to me reluctantly because I lied to him, I told him I would be here with my girlfriend Estella and nobody else, Estella who me and Marta went to convent school with, which was a lie, certainly not Mickie, it belongs to a foreman at the fireworks factory called la Negra Vieja, Guararé is where the fireworks are made for all the festivals in Panama, but this is Guararé's own festival for itself, and my father is a friend of the foreman and was best man at his wedding, and the foreman said have my house for the festival while I go on my honeymoon to Aruba, but my father doesn't like fireworks so he said I could have it instead of him as long as I don't bring that slob Mickie so I lied, I said I wouldn't, I would bring my friend Estella, who was my friend at convent school and is currently the *chiquilla* of a timber merchant in David, because in Guararé for five days you see bullfights and dancing and fireworks like you don't see them anywhere else in Panama or anywhere else in the world. But I didn't bring

Estella, I brought Mickie and Mickie really needed me, he was so frightened and depressed and hilarious all at once, saying the police were fools, threatening him and calling him a British spy just like in the days of Noriega, all because he had got drunk at Oxford for a couple of terms and allowed himself to be talked into running some British club in Panama.'

And here Ana began laughing so loud that Pendel could only piece the story together patchily and with great patience, but the nub of it was clear enough, namely that she had never seen Mickie so high and low at once, one minute weeping and the next wild and full of fun, and God in Heaven, what made him do it? And God in Heaven again, what was she going to tell her father? Who was going to clear up the walls, the ceiling? Thank God it was a tiled floor, not floorboards, at least he'd had the decency to do it in the kitchen, a thousand dollars for a repaint was conservative, and her father a strict Catholic with views about suicide and heretics, all right he'd been drinking, they all had, what do you do at a festival except drink and dance and fuck and watch the fireworks which was what she was doing when she heard the bang behind her, where did he ever get it from, he never carried a pistol even though he talked a lot about blowing his brains out, he must have bought it after the police called on him and accused him of being this great spy and reminding him what had happened last time he went to gaol, and promising to make it happen again, never mind he wasn't a pretty boy any more, the old convicts weren't picky, she just screamed and laughed and ducked her head and closed her eyes and it wasn't till she turned round to see who'd thrown the rocket or whatever it was, that she saw the mess, some of it on her new dress, and Mickie himself upside down on the floor.

All of which left Pendel wondering strenuously which was the right side up for the exploded corpse of his friend, fellow prisoner and leader elect of Panama's now forever Silent Opposition.

He replaced the receiver and the invasion ended, the victims stopped complaining. Only mopping up remained. He had written down the address in Guararé with a 2H pencil from his pocket. A thin hard line but legible. Next he worried about money for Marta. Then he remembered the wad of Osnard's fifties in the right hand button-down hip pocket of his trousers. So he handed it to her and she took it, probably without knowing what she was doing.

'That was Ana,' he said. 'Mickie's killed himself.'

But of course she knew that. She'd had her face pressed against his face while they listened with the same ear, she'd recognised her friend's voice from the first moment and it was only the strength of Pendel's friendship with Mickie that had prevented her from snatching the receiver from his hand.

'It's not your fault,' she said fervently. She repeated it several times in order to drive it into his thick skull. 'He'd have done it anyway, whether you told him off or not, d'you hear? He didn't need an excuse. He was killing himself every day. Listen to me.'

'I am. I am.'

But he didn't say: yes, it *is* my fault, because there seemed no point.

Then she began shivering like a malaria victim and if he hadn't held her she'd have been on the floor like Mickie who was upside down.

'I want you to go to Miami tomorrow,' he said. He remembered a hotel that Rafi Domingo had told him about. 'Stay at the Grand Bay. It's in Coconut Grove. They do a marvellous buffet lunch,' he added idiotically. And the fallback, the way Osnard had taught him: 'If you can't get in, ask the concierge if you can collect messages there. They're nice people. Mention Rafi's name.'

'It's not your fault,' she repeated, weeping now. 'They beat him too hard in prison. He was a child. Adults you can beat. Not children. He was fat. He had sensitive skin.'

'I know,' Pendel agreed. 'We all have. We shouldn't do it to each other. No one should.'

But his concentration had wandered to the row of suits awaiting the finishing hand, because the biggest and most prominent of them was Mickie's houndstooth alpaca with a second pair of trousers, the ones he said made him look old before his time.

'I'll come with you,' she said. 'I can help you. I'll look after Ana.'

He shook his head. Vehemently. He grabbed her arms and shook his head again. I betrayed him. You didn't. I made him leader when you told me not to. He tried to say some of this, but his face must have been saying it already because she was recoiling from him, shaking herself free of him as if she didn't care for what she saw.

'Marta, are you listening? Listen and stop staring at me like that.'

'Yes,' she said.

'Thanks for the students and everything,' he insisted. 'Thanks for everything. Thanks. I'm sorry.'

'You'll need petrol,' she said and gave him a hundred dollars back.

After which they stood there, two people swapping banknotes while their world was ending.

'It was not necessary to thank me,' she told him, slipping into a stern, retrospective tone. 'I love you. Very little else is of consequence to me. Even Mickie.'

She seemed to have thought it through, for her body eased and the love had come back to her eyes.

*   *   *

It is the same night and the same hour exactly in the British Embassy in Calle 53 in Marbella, Panama City. The urgently convened meeting of the augmented Buchaneers has been running for an hour, though in Osnard's cheerless, airless, windowless barrack in the east wing Francesca Deane has constantly to remind herself that nothing has changed in the ordinary procedures of the world, it is the same time outside the room as it is in here, whether or not, in the calmest and most reasonable way, we are plotting the arming and financing of a group of super-secret ruling-class Panamanian dissidents known as the Silent Opposition, and the raising and recruitment of militant students, and the overthrow of the legitimate government of Panama and the installation of a Provisional Committee of Administration pledged to wrest the Canal from the scheming clutches of an East-South conspiracy.

Men in secret conclave enter an altered state, thought Fran, as the only woman present, discreetly examining the faces squeezed round the too-small table. It's in the shoulders, how they stiffen against the neck. It's in the muscles round the jaw and the dirty shadows round the faster, lustful eyes. I'm the only black in a roomful of whites. Her eyes skimmed past Osnard without seeing him and she remembered the look in the face of the woman croupier in the third casino: *So you're his girl,* it said. *Well I'll tell you something, darling. Your man and I get up to things you wouldn't know about in your dirtiest dreams.*

Men in secret conclave treat you like the woman they're saving from the flames, she thought. Whatever they've done to you, they expect you to think they're perfect. I should be standing on the doorstep of their croft. I should be wearing a long white dress and clutching their babies to my bosom as I wave them off to war. I should be saying: hullo, I'm Fran, I'm the first prize when you come home victorious. Men in secret conclave have a waxy guilt imparted by low white lighting and a weird grey steel cabinet on Meccano legs that hums like a tuneless house-painter up a ladder in order to protect our words from prying ears. Men in secret conclave give off a different smell. They are men on heat.

*　　*　　*

And Fran was as excited as they were, though her excitement made her sceptical, whereas the men's excitement made them erect and pointed them towards a fiercer god, even if the god of the moment was bearded little Mr Mellors who perched like a nervous lonely diner at the far end of the table from her and kept calling the meeting 'juntlemun' in a ripe Scottish brogue – as if, for tonight only, Fran had been upgraded to man's estate. He could not *believe*, juntlemun, he said, that he hadn't closed his eyes for twenty hours! Yet he swore he was game for twenty more.

'I cannot sufficiently emphasise, juntlemun, the immense national and dare I say geopolitical importance that is being accorded to this operation by the highest echelons of Her Majesty's Government,' he kept assuring them, between discussions of such divers matters as whether the rainforests of the Darién would provide an appropriate hideaway for a couple of thousand semi-automatic rifles, or should we be thinking of something a little more central for the home and office? And the men drinking it in. Swallowing it whole because it is monstrous but secret, therefore not monstrous at all. Shave off his stupid little Scottish beard, she advises them. Take him outside. De-bag him. Make him say it all again on the bus to Paitilla. Then see if you agree with a word of it.

But they didn't take him outside and they didn't de-bag him. They believed him. Admired him. Doted on him. Just look at Maltby, for instance! *Her* Maltby! – her louche, funny, pedantic, clever, married, unhappy Ambass, not safe in taxis, not safe in corridors, a sceptic to end all sceptics, he would have her think, yet he had yelled *Christ, she's beautiful!* when she dived into his pool: Maltby, sitting like an obedient schoolboy at Mellors' right hand, smirking unctuous encouragement, bucking his long crooked head back and forth like those pub birds that drink water out of dirty plastic mugs and urging a sulky Nigel Stormont to agree with him.

'*You'd* go along with that, wouldn't you, Nigel?' Maltby cried. 'Yes, he would. Done, Mellors.'

Or: '*We* give 'em the gold, *they* buy the guns through Gully. Far simpler than supplying them direct. *And* more deniable – agreed, Nigel? – yes, Gully? – done, Mellors.'

Or: 'No, no, Mr Mellors, thank you, no need for an extra body at all. Nigel and I are perfectly equal to a little skulduggery, aren't we, Nigel? And Gully here knows the ropes of old. What's a few hundred anti-personnel mines between friends, eh Gully? Made in Birmingham. You can't beat 'em.'

And Gully simpering and hammering his moustache with his handkerchief and jotting greedily in his order book while Mellors pushes what looks like a shopping list across the table at him, turning his eyes to Heaven so that he doesn't see himself do it.

'With the Minister's most *enthusiastic* approval,' he breathes, meaning: don't blame me.

'Our *only* problem here, Mellors, is keeping the circle of knowledge to an *absolute* minimum,' Maltby is saying keenly. 'That means corralling everybody who's likely to find out by mistake, like young Simon here' – a leer at Simon Pitt, who sits in a state of shellshock at Gully's side – 'and threatening them with penal servitude in the galleys for life if they blabber one indiscreet word. Right, Simon? Right? Right?'

'Right,' Simon agrees under torture.

A different Maltby, one Fran hasn't met before but always guessed at because he was so under-used and underappreciated. A different Stormont too, who frowns into a void every time he speaks, and endorses whatever Maltby says.

And a different Andy? Or is he the same model as before, only I never knew till now?

Covertly, she allows her eyes to focus on him.

*   *   *

A changed man. Not larger or fatter or thinner. Just further away. So far away in fact that she hardly recognised him across the table. His departure had begun in the casino, she now realised, and gathered speed with the dramatic news of Mellors' imminent arrival.

'Who needs the little shit?' he had demanded of her furiously, as if he held her responsible for summoning the wretched man. 'BUCHAN won't see him. BUCHAN TWO won't see him. She won't even see *me*. None o' them will see him. I've told him that already.'

'Then tell him again.'

'This is *my* fucking patch. Not his. *My* fucking operation. Fuck's it got to do with him?'

'Do you mind not swearing at me? He's your boss, Andy. He posted you here. I didn't. Regional heads have a right to drop in on their flock. Even in your Service, I presume.'

'Bullshit,' he retorted and the next thing she knew she was calmly packing up her possessions and Andy was telling her to make sure there were no nasty little hairs in the bath.

'What are you so afraid of him finding?' she demanded, ice cold. 'He's not your lover, is he? You're not sworn to chastity, are you? *Are* you? So you had a woman here. What's wrong with that? It doesn't have to have been me.'

'No. It doesn't.'

'Andy!'

He made a brief and graceless show of penitence.

'Don't like being spied on, that's all,' he said sulkily.

But when she broke out in relieved laughter at this good joke, he grabbed her car key from the sideboard, forced it into her palm and marched her with her luggage to the lift. All day long they had succeeded in avoiding each other until now, when they were obliged to sit across a table in this gloomy white jail with Andy glowering and Fran tightlipped, keeping her smiles for the stranger – who to her secret indignation was flattering Andy and deferring to him in the most nauseating way imaginable:

'But do these proposals make *sense* to you, now, Andrew?' Mellors insists, with a suck of his teeth. 'Speak up, now, young Mr Osnard. It's *your* achievement, good Heavens! You're the *man at the controls* here, the *star* – saving His Excellency's presence. Is it not better for the man in the field – at the front line, my God – to be unfettered by wearisome administration, Andrew, tell us frankly now? Nobody round this table wishes to impair your *exemplary* performance.'

To which sentiment Maltby then lends his enthusiastic support, seconded some moments later and with less enthusiasm by Stormont – the point at issue being the two-key system for controlling the Silent Opposition's finances, a task which, it is generally agreed, is best entrusted to senior officers.

So why is Andy down in the mouth at having such a heavy load lifted from his shoulders? Why isn't he grateful that Maltby and Stormont are falling over themselves to take the job off his hands?

'Up to you people,' he mumbles churlishly, with a sideways glower at Maltby. And goes back into deep sulk.

And when the question arises of how Abraxas and Domingo and the other Silent Opponents can be persuaded to deal directly with Stormont on matters of finance and logistics, Andy comes close to losing his temper altogether.

'Why don't you take over the whole bloody network while you're about it?' he flares, flushing crimson. 'Run it from Chancery in office hours, five days a week, be done with it. Help yourselves.'

'Andrew, Andrew, come, no hard words here please!' cries Mellors, tutting like an old Scottish hen. 'We are a team, Andrew, are we not? All that is being offered here is a helping hand– the counsel of wise heads – a steadying influence upon a brilliantly managed operation. Is it not, Ambassador?' Suck of the teeth, sad frown of troubled father, the placatory tone raised to entreaty. 'These Opposition fellows, they'll be driving a hard bargain, Andrew. Binding assurances will have to be given from the hip. Snap decisions of immense consequence will abound. Deep waters, Andrew, for a fellow of your tender years. Better to leave such matters in the capable hands of men of the world.'

Andy sulks. Stormont stares into his void. But dear, kind Maltby feels constrained to add a few comforting words of his own.

'My dear chap, you can't possibly hang on to the whole game, can he, Nigel? It's share and share alike in my Embassy – isn't it, Nigel? Nobody's taking your spies away from you. You'll still have your network to look after – brief, debrief, *pay* and so forth. All we want is your Opposition. What could be fairer than that?'

But still, to Fran's embarrassment, Andy refuses to accept the hand that is so courteously outstretched to him. His glittery little eyes switch to Maltby, then Stormont, then go back to Maltby. He mutters something nobody catches, which is probably as well. He pulls a bitter grin and nods to himself like a man cruelly cheated.

A last symbolic ceremony remains. Mellors stands, ducks beneath the table and reappears with two black leather shoulder bags of the sort Queen's Messengers cart about, one to each shoulder.

'Andrew, kindly open up the strongroom for us,' he commands.

Now everyone is standing. Fran stands too. Shepherd advances on the strongroom, unlocks the grille with a long brass key and pulls it back, exposing a solid steel door with a black dial at its centre. On Mellors' nod Andy steps forward and, with an expression of such pent-up venom that she is heartily glad she never saw it until now, swivels the dial this way and that until the lock yields. Even then, it takes an encouraging word from Maltby before Andy draws back the door and, with a mocking bow, invites his Ambassador and Head of Chancery to enter ahead of him. Still standing at the table, Fran makes out, beside an oversized red telephone attached to a kind of reconstructed vacuum cleaner, a steel safe with two keyholes. Her father the judge has one like it in his dressing room.

'One each now,' she hears Mellors pipe skittishly.

For a moment Fran is in her old school chapel, kneeling in the front pew and watching a huddle of handsome young priests as they chastely turn their backs to her and busy themselves with exciting things in preparation for her First Communion. Gradually her field of view clears and she sees Andy, under Mellors' parental eye, presenting Maltby and Stormont with one long-stemmed silver-plated key apiece. There is English amusement, which Andy does not share, while each man tries the other's keyhole before Maltby lets out a jolly '*Gotcha*' and the safe door clunks open.

But Fran by now is no longer looking at the safe. Her gaze is all upon Andy as he stares and stares at the gold bars that Mellors is taking one by one from his black shoulder bags and handing to Shepherd to be stacked criss-cross like spillikins. And it is Andy's sagging face that for the last time holds her in its spell because it tells her everything she ever did or didn't want to know about him. She knows he's been caught and she has a shrewd notion of what he's been caught at, though she has no idea at all whether those who have caught him know what they have done. She knows he is a liar, with or without the licence of his profession. She knows the source of the fifty thousand dollars he put on red. It is standing before her with its door open. She entirely understands why he is so angry that he has been forced to give away the keys. And after, that Fran can't watch any more, partly because her eyes have misted over in humiliation and self-disgust and partly because the ungainly frame of Maltby is bearing down on her with a pirate's grin, asking whether she would regard it as an offence against Creation if he took her to the Pavo Real for a boiled egg.

'Phoebe has decided to leave me,' he explains with pride. 'We're getting a divorce immediately. Nigel's plucking up his courage to break it to her. She'll never believe it if it comes from me.'

Fran took a moment to reply because her first instinct was to shudder and say no thank you very much. It was only when she kept thinking that she realised a number of things she might have realised earlier. Namely that for months she had been touched by Maltby's devotion to her, and grateful for the presence in her life of a man who longed for her so hopelessly. And that Maltby's sheepish adoration of her had become a source of priceless support as she wrestled with the knowledge that she was sharing her life with an amoralist whose lack of shame or scruple had at first attracted and now repelled her; whose interest in her had never been more than expedient and carnal; and whose net effect on her had been to instil a craving for the shambling devotion of her Ambassador.

And having thus rationally thought her way to this conclusion, Fran decided that it had been a long time since she had been so grateful for an invitation.

Marta sat hunched on the finishing hands' workbench looking down at the wad of money he had pressed on her and
thinking: his friend Mickie is dead, he believes he killed
him, and perhaps he did, the police are spying on him but
he wants me to sit on a beach in Miami and eat the buffet
lunch at the Grand Bay and buy clothes and wait until he
comes. And be happy and believe in him and get a tan and
have my face mended. And get a boy as well if I can, because
he would like me to have a handsome boy, a proxy Harry
Pendel, doing his loving for him while he stays faithful to
Louisa. That's who he is and you may call it complicated or
you may call it very simple. Harry has a dream for everyone.
Harry dreams all our lives for us, and gets them wrong every
time. Because number one I don't want to leave Panama. I
want to stay here and lie to the police for him and sit at his
bedside the way he sat at mine and find out what's gone
wrong for him and cure it. I want to tell him to get up and
hobble round the room because for as long as you stay lying
down all you can think of is getting another beating. But
when you stand up you start to be a *mensch* again, which is
his word for dignity. And number two I can't leave Panama
because the police have taken my passport by way of encouragement to spy on him.

Seven thousand dollars.

She had counted them onto the worktable by the glow
from the skylight above her. Seven thousand dollars from his
back pocket, pressed on her like guilt money the moment he
heard of Mickie's death – here, take this, it's Osnard's
money, Judas money, Mickie money, now it's yours. You'd
think a man setting out to do what Harry had to do would
keep his money in his pocket for eventualities. Undertaker
money. Police money. *Chiquilla* money. But Harry had
scarcely put the receiver down before he was pulling the
wad out of his back pocket, wanting to be shot of every dirty
dollar. Where had he got it from? the police had asked her.

'You're not stupid, Marta. You can read, study, make

bombs, make trouble, lead marches. Who gives him his money? Does Abraxas give it to him? Is he working for Abraxas and Abraxas is working for the British? What does he give Abraxas in return?'

'I don't know. My employer tells me nothing. Get out of my flat.'

'He fucks you, doesn't he?'

'No, he doesn't fuck me. He comes to see me because I have headaches and vomiting attacks and he is my employer and he was with me when I was beaten. He is a caring man and happily married.'

No, he doesn't fuck me, that at least was true, though it cost her more to tell them this precious truth than any number of easy lies. No, officer, he doesn't fuck me. No, officer, I don't ask him to. We lie on my bed, I put my hand in the heat of his crotch but only outside, he puts his hand inside my blouse, but one breast is all that he allows himself though he knows he can have the whole of me any time he wants, because he has the whole of me already, but the guilt owns him, he has more guilt than sins. And I tell him stories of who we might be if we were young and brave again in the days before they took my face off with their clubs. And that is love.

Marta's head was throbbing again and she felt sick. She stood up, clutching the money in both hands. She couldn't stand another minute in the Cuna work room. She walked down the corridor as far as the door to her office and, like a guided tourist a hundred years from now, stood at the threshold and looked in while she gave herself the commentary:

This is where the halfbreed Marta sat and did her accounts for the tailor Pendel. Over there in the shelves you see the books on sociology and history that Marta used to read in her spare time in an effort to raise herself in society and fulfil the dreams of her dead father the carpenter. As a self-educated man the tailor Pendel was concerned that all his staff but particularly the halfbreed Marta develop themselves to their maximum potential. This is the kitchen area where Marta made her famous sandwiches, all the prominent men of Panama would speak in bated breath of Marta's sandwiches, including Mickie Abraxas the famous suicidal spy, tuna was her speciality but in her heart she wished she could poison the whole pack of them except for Mickie and her employer Pendel. And over there in the corner behind the desk we have the very spot where in 1989 the tailor Pendel, having first closed the door, was sufficiently overcome to take Marta in his arms and protest his undying love for her. The tailor Pendel proposed they visit a pushbutton but Marta preferred to take him to her own apartment, and it was on the drive there that Marta incurred the facial injuries that left her permanently scarred, and it was the fellow student Abraxas who suborned the cowardly doctor into leaving his indelible imprint upon her – that doctor was so terrified of losing his rich practice that he couldn't keep his hands still. The same doctor afterwards had the wisdom to inform on Abraxas, an act that led effectively to his destruction.

Closing the door on her dead self, Marta continued down the corridor to Pendel's cutting room. I'll leave the money in his top left drawer. The door was ajar. Lights were burning inside the room. Marta was not surprised. Not long ago, her Harry had been a man of unearthly discipline but in recent weeks the stitching of his too-many lives had been too much for him. She pushed the door. Now we are in the tailor Pendel's cutting room, known to customers and employees alike as the Holy of Holies. Nobody was permitted to enter without knocking, or during his absence – except apparently for his wife Louisa, who was seated at her husband's desk with her spectacles on and a pile of his old notebooks at her elbow, and a lot of pencils and an order book, and a tin of fly spray in front of her, opened at the base while she played with the ornate cigarette lighter that Harry said a rich Arab had given him though P & B had no rich Arabs on its books.

*   *   *

She was dressed in a thin red cotton housecoat and apparently nothing else, because as she leaned forward she revealed her breasts in their entirety. She was clicking the lighter on and off and smiling at Marta through the flame.

'Where's my husband?' Louisa asked.

Click.

'He's gone to Guararé,' Marta replied. 'Mickie Abraxas killed himself at the fireworks.'

'I'm sorry.'

'So am I. So is your husband.'

'However it was not unexpected. We have had about five years' warning of the event,' Louisa pointed out quite reasonably.

Click.

'He was appalled,' Marta said.

'Mickie?'

'Your husband,' Marta said.

'Why does my husband keep a special invoice book for Mr Osnard's suits?'

Click.

'I don't know. It puzzles me too,' Marta said.

'Are you his mistress?'

'No.'

'Does he have one?'

Click.

'No.'

'Is that his money you're holding in your hand?'

'Yes.'

'Why?'

Click.

'He gave it me,' Marta said.

'For fucking?'

'For safekeeping. It was in his pocket when he heard the news.'

'Where does it come from?'

Click, and a flame that lit Louisa's left eye so close that Marta wondered why her eyebrow didn't catch fire and the flimsy red housecoat with it.

'I don't know,' Marta replied. 'Some customers pay cash. He doesn't always know what to do with it. He loves you.

He loves his family more than anything on earth. He loved Mickie too.'

'Does he love anybody else?'

'Yes.'

'Who?'

'Me.'

She was examining a piece of paper. 'Is this Mr Osnard's correct home address? Torre del Mar? Punta Paitilla?'

Click.

'Yes,' Marta said.

The conversation was over but Marta didn't realise this at first because Louisa went on clicking the lighter and smiling at the flame. And there were quite a few clicks and smiles before it occurred to Marta that Louisa was drunk in the way Marta's brother used to get drunk when life became too much for him. Not singing drunk or wobbly drunk, but crystal-headed, perfect-vision drunk. Drunk with all the knowledge she had been drinking to get rid of. And stark naked inside her housecoat.

CHAPTER TWENTY-ONE

It was one-twenty on the same morning when Osnard's front doorbell rang. For the last hour he had been in a state of advanced sobriety. At first, still raging from his defeat, he had revelled in violent methods of ridding himself of his hated guest: hurl him off the balcony to crash through the roof of the Club Unión a dozen floors below, ruining everybody's evening, drown him in the shower, put Jeyes Fluid in his whisky – 'Eh, well, Andrew, if you insist, but only the merest finger, if you please' – suck of the teeth as he expires. His fury was not confined to Luxmore:

Maltby! My Ambassador and golfing partner, Christ's sakes! Queen's own bloody representative, faded flower o' the British bloody Diplomatic Service and gyps me like a pro!

Stormont! Soul o' probity, one o' life's born losers, last o' the white men, Maltby's faithful poodle with the stomach ache, egging his master on with nods and grunts while my Lord Bishop Luxmore gives them both his blessing!

Was it conspiracy or cock-up? Osnard asked himself, over and over again. Was Maltby tipping a wink when he spoke of 'share and share alike' and 'can't hang on to the whole game'? *Maltby*, that smirking pedant, putting his fingers in the till? Bastard wouldn't know how. Forget it. And Osnard to a degree did indeed forget it. His natural pragmatism reasserted itself, he abandoned vengeful thoughts and applied himself instead to saving what remained of his great enterprise. The ship is holed but not sunk, he told himself. I'm still BUCHAN's paymaster. Maltby's right.

'Care for something different sir, or prefer to stay with the malt?'

'Andrew, please. I beseech you. *Scottie*, if you don't mind.'

'I'll try,' Osnard promised and, stepping through the open French doors, poured him another industrial-sized shot of malt whisky from the sideboard in the dining room and returned with it to the balcony. Jetlag, whisky and insomnia were finally taking their toll of Luxmore, he decided, clinically examining his master's semi-recumbent figure in the deckchair before him. So was the humidity – the flannel shirt soaked through, tracks of sweat streaming down the beard. So was his terror at being stuck out here in enemy territory with no wife to look after him – the haunted eyes flinching with every sudden clatter of footsteps or police siren or ribald shout that zigzagged up at them through the gimcrack canyons of Punta Paitilla. The sky was clear as water and strewn with brittle stars. A poacher's moon etched a lightpath between the anchored shipping in the mouth of the Canal, but no breeze came off the sea. It seldom did.

'You asked me whether there was anything Head Office might do to make life a bit easier for the Station, sir,' Osnard reminded Luxmore diffidently.

'Did I, Andrew? Well, I'm damned.' Luxmore sat up with a jolt. 'Fire ahead, Andrew, fire ahead. Though I'm pleased to see you've already done yourself pretty well out here,' he added, not entirely pleasantly, with an erratic swing of the arm that took in both the view and the grand apartment. 'Don't think I'm criticising you, mind. I drink to you. To your grit. Your acumen. Your youth. Qualities we all admire. Good health!' Slurp. 'You've a great career ahead of you, Andrew. Easier times than we had in my day, I may add. A softer bed. You know how much this costs at home now? Lucky if you see change out of a twenty pound note.'

'It's about this safe house I mentioned, sir,' Osnard

reminded him, in the manner of an anxious heir at his dying father's bedside. 'Time we weaned ourselves away from pushbuttons and three-hour hotels. Thought maybe one o' those conversions in the Old City would give us greater operational scope.'

But Luxmore was transmitting, not receiving. 'The way those stuffed-shirts backed you up this evening, Andrew. My God, it's not often you see respect like that lavished on a younger man. There's a medal in here somewhere for you when this is over. A certain little lady across the river may feel obliged to show her appreciation.'

A lull while he gazed in perplexity at the bay and seemed to confuse it with the Thames.

'Andrew!' – abruptly as he woke.

'Sir?'

'That fellow Stormont.'

'What about him?'

'Came a cropper in Madrid. Some woman he took up with, social tart. Married her, if I remember rightly. Beware of him.'

'I will.'

'And her, Andrew.'

'I will.'

'Do you have a woman here?' – peering round facetiously, under the sofa, at the curtains, acting bright. 'No hot-arsed Latin lovely tucked away at all? Don't answer that. Good health again. Keep her to yourself. Wise fellow.'

'I've been a bit too busy actually, sir,' Osnard confessed with a rueful smile. But he refused to give up. He had a notion he was printing things into Luxmore's subliminal memory for later. 'Only in my view, you see, in a perfect world we should be shooting for *two* safe houses. One for the network, which would obviously be my sole responsibility. Cayman Islands holding company's the best answer – and *another* house – available on an extremely limited, need-to-know basis and more representational in style – to service the Abraxas team, and eventually – provided always we can do it without creating interconsciousness, which at this stage I rather doubt – the students. And I think *probably* I should be handling that one too – as far as the purchase and cover details go – even if Ambass and Stormont have sole use at the end of the day. I don't think they have our expertise, frankly. It's a risk we just don't need to take. I'd love your view on this. Not now, necessarily. Later.'

A long-delayed suck of the teeth told Osnard that his regional director was still with him, if only just. Reaching out, Osnard removed the empty glass from Luxmore's hand and set it on the ceramic table.

'So what do you think, sir? An apartment like this one for the Opposition – fashionable, anonymous, handy for the financial community, nobody has to step out of his element – and a *second* house in the Old City to be run in tandem?' He had been thinking for some time of getting a foot on the ladder of Panama's booming property market. 'Basically, in the Old City you get what you pay for. It's location and location and location. A decent conversion at the moment – good duplex, architect-designed – sets you back give or take fifty grand. Top o' the range you get a twelve-room mansion, bit o' garden, rear access, sea view – offer them half a mil and they'll cut your arm off. Couple o' years from now, you've doubled your money, long as nobody does anything dramatic with the old Club Unión building that Torrijos turned into an Other Ranks Club out o' spite because the Club wouldn't have him as a member. Better get an update before we plunge. I can arrange that.'

'Andrew!'

'Right here.'

Suck of the teeth. Eyes close, then sharply reopen.

'Eh, tell me something, Andrew.'

'If I can, Scottie.'

Luxmore cranked his bearded head round until he was facing his subordinate. 'That prim Sassenach virgin with large attachments and come-hither eyes who graced our little gathering this evening –'

'Yes, sir?'

'Is she what in my young day we called a cock-teaser, by any chance? Because it seemed to me that if ever I saw a young woman who needed the undivided attention of a seven-foot tall – Andrew! For the love of God! Who the devil's that at this hour of the night?'

Luxmore's prescription for Fran was never revealed in its entirety. The ring of the front doorbell became a peal, then a blast. Like a scared rodent, Luxmore and his beard retreated to the furthest corner of the armchair.

* * *

The trainers had not been mistaken when they praised Osnard's aptitude in the black arts. A few measures of malt whisky in no way impaired his reactions and the prospect of being disagreeable to Fran sharpened them. If she had come to kiss and make up she had picked the wrong man and a worse moment. Which he now proposed to tell her in words of one Anglo-Saxon syllable. And she could take her foot off his bloody bell while she was about it.

Gratuitously instructing Luxmore to remain where he was, Osnard sidled across the dining room to the hall, closing doors along his way, and squinted through the fish-eye of his front door. The lens was coated with condensation. With a handkerchief from his pocket he wiped it clear on his own side, and made out one misty eye, its sex ambivalent, squinting back at him while the blast of the doorbell continued like a fire alarm. Then the eye pulled away and he recognised instead Louisa Pendel, wearing horn-rimmed glasses and precious little else, standing on one leg while she took her shoe off as a prelude to beating down the door with it.

* * *

Louisa did not remember which particular straw had broken her camel's back. Neither did she care. She had returned from squash to an empty house. The children were visiting with the Rudds and staying over. She rated Ramón one of the Great Unspeakables of Panama and detested letting them anywhere near him. It wasn't that Ramón hated women, it was the way he hinted that he knew more about

Harry than she did, and all of it bad. And the way that, just like Harry, he clammed up when she talked about the rice farm, although it was her money that had bought it.

But none of this accounted for how she felt when she came home from squash, or why she found herself weeping without a reason, when so often in the last ten years she had had a reason but refused to weep. So she supposed that what had happened to her was some kind of accumulation of despair, assisted by a large vodka on the rocks before her shower because she felt like it. Having showered, she examined herself naked, all six feet of her in the bedroom mirror.

Objectively. Forgetting my height for a moment. Forgetting my beautiful sister Emily with her golden tresses and *Playboy* centrefold ass and tits to kill for and list of conquests longer than the Panama City telephone directory. Would I or would I not, if I was a man, wish to sleep with this woman? She reckoned she might, but on what evidence? She only had Harry to go by.

She phrased her question differently. If I was Harry, would I still want to sleep with me after a dozen years of marriage? And the answer to that was: on recent evidence, not. Too tired. Too late. Too placatory. Too guilty about something. All right, he was always guilty. Guilt was his best thing. But these days he wore it like a placard: I am forfeit, I am untouchable, I am guilty, I don't deserve you, goodnight.

Brushing away her tears with one hand and clutching her glass in the other, she continued to parade back and forth across the bedroom, studying herself, pushing herself out and in, and thinking how for Emily everything came too easily, whether she was playing tennis or riding a horse or swimming or washing up, she couldn't make an ugly movement if she tried. Even as a woman, you practically had an orgasm watching her. Louisa tried writhing obscenely, the worst whore ever. A frost. Too knobbly. No flow. No hip movement. Too old. Always have been. Too tall. Fed up, she marched back to the kitchen and, still naked, determinedly poured herself another vodka, no ice this time.

And it was a real drink, not 'maybe I could do with a

drink,' because she had to open a new bottle and find a knife to cut round the seal before she could pour, which is not the sort of thing you do when, just casually, almost by accident, you pour yourself a little something to keep your spirits up while your husband's out screwing his mistress.

'Fuck him,' she said aloud.

The bottle came from Harry's new hospitality store. Chargeable, he said.

'Chargeable, who to?' she had demanded.

'Tax,' he said.

'Harry, I do not wish my house to be used as a tax-free bar.'

Guilty smirk. Sorry, Lou. Way of the world. Didn't mean to upset you. Won't do it again. Creep, cringe.

'Fuck him,' she repeated, and felt the better for it.

And fuck Emily too because without Emily to compete with I would never have taken the moral high road, never pretended to disapprove of everything, never kept my virginity so long it became a world record, just to show everyone how pure and serious I was by contrast with my fucking beautiful sister! I would never have fallen in love with every minister under the age of ninety who climbed into the pulpit in Balboa and told us to repent us of our sins and Emily's specially, never have set myself up as pious Miss Perfect and the arbiter of everyone's bad behaviour when all I really wanted was to be touched and admired and spoiled and fucked like all the other girls on the lot.

And fuck the rice farm too. *My* rice farm that Harry won't take me to any more because he's put his bloody *chiquilla* in it – here, darling, keep looking out of the window for me till I come back. Fuck you. Gulp of vodka. Another gulp. Then a great big gulp and feel it hit the parts that really count, oh boy. Thus fortified, she swept back to the bedroom to resume her gyrations with greater abandon – is *this* erotic? – go on, tell me! – is *this*? – all right, so get a load of *this*! But no one to tell her. No one to clap or laugh or get horny with her. No one to drink with her, cook for her, kiss her neck and talk her down. No Harry.

Breasts not bad for forty, all the same. Better than Jo-Ann's when she bares all. Not as good as Emily's but whose are? Here's to them. Here's to my tits. Tits, stand up, you're being toasted. She sat down abruptly on the bed, chin in hands, watching the phone ring on Harry's side.

'Go fuck yourself,' she advised it.

And to make her point more strongly, she lifted the receiver an inch, yelled 'Go fuck yourself' and put it down again.

But with kids, you always pick up in the end.

*   *   *

'*Yeah? So who is it?*' she yells, when it rings again.

It is Naomi, Panama's Minister of Misinformation, preparing to share some choice piece of scandal with her. Good. This conversation has been outstanding for too long already.

'Naomi, I am pleased to hear you because I have been meaning to write to you and now you have saved me a stamp. Naomi, I want you out of my fucking life. No, no, listen to me, Naomi. Naomi, if you happen to be passing through the Vasco Nuñez de Balboa Park and see my husband lying on his back enjoying oral intercourse with Barnum's baby elephant, I would be grateful if you would tell your twenty best friends and *never* tell me. Because I don't want to hear your fucking voice again till the Canal freezes over. Good night, Naomi.'

Tumbler in hand, Louisa puts on a red housecoat that Harry recently brought home for her, three big buttons and cleavage according to your mood, fetches a chisel and hammer from the garage and crosses the courtyard to Harry's den, which these days he keeps locked. Great sky. She hasn't seen a beautiful sky for weeks. Stars we used to tell our children about. That's Orion's belt with the dagger, Mark. And those are your Seven Sisters, Hannah, the ones you always dream of having. The new moon, pretty as a foal.

This is where he writes to her, she thought as she approached the door to his kingdom. To my darling *chiquilla*, care of my wife's rice farm. Through the misted window of her bathroom, Louisa has watched him for hours on end, silhouetted at his desk, head tilted to one side and tongue out while he writes his love letters though writing never came naturally to Harry, it is one of the things that Arthur Braithwaite, greatest living saint since Laurent, neglected in his fosterchild's education.

The door is locked as she has anticipated, but presents no problem. The door, when you really beat on it with a good heavy hammer, taking the hammer back as far as it will go, then smashing it down on Emily's head, which was what Louisa dreamed of doing all through her adolescence, is a piece of shit like most things in the world.

* * *

Having smashed the door, Louisa homed on her husband's desk and smashed open the top drawer with the hammer and chisel – three good heaves before she realised the drawer wasn't locked in the first place. She ransacked the contents. Bills. Architect's drawings for the Sportsman's Corner. Nobody's lucky first time. Not me anyway. She tried the second drawer. Locked, but surrenders at the first assault. The contents immediately more uplifting. Unfinished essays on the Canal. Learned journals, press cuttings, notes in Harry's flowery tailor's hand summarising the above.

Who is she? Who the fuck is he doing it all for? Harry, I am speaking to you. Listen to me, please. Who is this woman whom you have installed at *my* rice farm without *my* consent and whom you need to impress with your non-existent erudition? Who owns this dreamy, cowlike smile you have these days – I am chosen, I am blessed, I walk on water. Or the tears – oh shit, Harry, who owns those bloodcurdling tears that form in your eyes and never fall?

Rage and frustration welling in her again, she smashed open another drawer and froze. Holy shit! Money! Serious, real money! A whole drawer crammed full of fucking money. Hundreds, fifties, twenties. Lying loose in the drawer like old parking tickets. A thousand. Two, three thousand. He's been robbing banks. Who for?

For his woman? She does it for money? For his woman, to take her out to meals without it going through the house-keeping account? To keep her in the style she isn't accustomed to, at *my* rice farm, bought with *my* legacy? Louisa tried shouting his name several times, first to ask him politely, then to order him because he wouldn't answer, then to curse him because he wasn't there.

'Fuck you, Harry Pendel! Fuck you, fuck you, fuck you! Wherever you are. You're a fucking *cheat*!'

It was fuck everything from now on. It was her father's language when he'd had a skinful, and Louisa felt a daughter's pride that, having had a skinful herself or getting that way, she swore like her fucking father.

'*Hey, Lou, sweetheart, come over here. Where's that Titan?*' – he calls his daughter Titan after the giant German crane in Gamboa harbour – '*Don't an old man deserve a little attention from his daughter? Ain't you got a kiss for your old man? Call that a kiss? Fuck you! Fuck you, hear me? Fuck you!*'

Notes, mostly about Delgado. Distorted versions of things Harry had pumped her about over the dinners he liked to cook her. *My* Delgado. *My* beloved father-figure, Ernesto himself, probity on wheels, and *my* husband makes dirty notes about him. Why? Because he's jealous of him. He always was. He thinks I love Ernesto more than I love him. He thinks I want to fuck Ernesto. Headings: *Delgado's Women* – what women? Ernesto doesn't do that stuff! *Delgado and the Pres* – Mr Osnard's Pres again. *Delgado's Views on Japanese* – Ernesto's scared of them. Thinks they want his Canal. He's right. She exploded again. Aloud this time: 'Fuck you, Harry Pendel, I never *said* that, you're making it up! Who for? Why?'

A letter, not completed, not addressed. A scrap he must have meant to throw away:

I thought you would like to hear a rather interesting snippet Louisa overheard at work yesterday regarding our Ernie and saw fit to pass on to me –

Saw fit? I didn't *see fit.* I told him a piece of office gossip!

Why the fuck does a *wife* have to *see fit* before she tells her *husband* a piece of office gossip in their own home about a benign, upright man who wishes only to do right by Panama and the Canal? *Fuck* fit! Fuck *you* – you who would like to hear what we *see fit* to tell each other in our own home! You're a bitch. A foul-eared bitch who's stolen my husband and my rice farm.

You're *Sabina!*

*   *   *

Louisa had found the bitch's name at last. In trim tailor's capitals, because capitals came easiest to him, SABINA written small and loving with a balloon drawn round her. SABINA, followed by RAD STUD in brackets. You're Sabina and you're a rad stud and you know about other studs and you work for dollar signs from the US – or think you do, because *works for US* is between inverted commas and you get five hundred bucks a month plus a bonus when you put on a great performance. It was all there, laid out in one of Harry's flow-charts that he'd learned about from Mark. Flow-chart ideas don't have to be linear, Dad. They can float about like gas balloons on strings in any order you like. You can take them singly or together. They're really neat. The string from Sabina's gas balloon led straight as a die to H which was Harry's Napoleonic signature for himself when he was being grandiose. Whereas Alpha's string – because now she had discovered Alpha – led to Beta, then to Marco (Pres) and only then back to H. The Bear's string led to H too, but the Bear's balloon had tense wavy lines drawn round it as if it were about to explode at any moment.

And *Mickie* had a balloon all for himself and he was described as the *supremo of SO* and his string linked him to Rafi's balloon in eternity. *Our* Mickie? *Our Mickie* is the supremo of SO? And has a total of *six* strings leading out of him, to *Arms, Informants, Bribes, Communications, Cash, Rafi? Our* Rafi? *Our Mickie* who calls once a week in the middle of the night to announce his umpteenth suicide?

She began rummaging again. She wanted that bitch Sabina's letters to Harry. If she'd written letters Harry would have kept them. Harry couldn't throw away an empty matchbox or a spare egg yolk. It was his poor childhood again. She was turning everything over, hunting for Sabina's letters. Under her money? Under a floorboard? In a book?

Holy God, Delgado's diary. Kept by Harry, not Delgado. Not the real one, but a mock-up with the lines ruled in hard pencil, he must have copied it from my papers. Delgado's real engagements entered correctly. Unreal engagements entered in the spaces where he had none:

> *Midnight meeting with Jap 'harbourmasters', secretly attended by Pres... secret car-ride with Fr Ambassador, suitcase of money changes hands... meets emissary from Colombian drugs cartel 11 p.m. Ramón's new casino... Hosts private out-of-town dinner Jap 'harbourmasters' and Pan officials and Pres...*

My Delgado does all this? My Ernesto Delgado is on the take from the French Ambassador? Is fooling with the *Colombian drug cartels*? Harry, are you fucking mad? What filthy libels are you inventing about my boss? What dreadful lies are you telling? Who to? Who pays you for this filth?

'*Harry!*' she screamed, in outrage and despair. But his name came out as a whisper as the phone started ringing again.

*　　*　　*

Cunning this time, Louisa lifted the receiver, listened, said nothing, not even Get out of my fucking life.

'Harry?' A woman's voice, strangled, dragging, pleading. It's her. Long distance. Calling from the rice farm. Banging in the background. They must be breaking up the mill.

'Harry? Speak to me!' the woman's voice screams.

A Spanish bitch. Daddy always said don't trust them. Whimpering. It's her. Sabina. Needing Harry. Who doesn't?

'Harry, help me, I need you!'

Wait. Don't speak. Don't tell her you're not Harry. Hear what she says next. Lips pressed together. Receiver arm-locked to right ear. *Speak*, you bitch! Declare yourself! The bitch is breathing. Rasping breaths. Come on, Sabina, honey, *speak*. Say, 'Come and fuck me, Harry.' Say, 'I love you, Harry.' Say, 'Where's my fucking money, why do you keep it in a drawer, it's me, Sabina, rad stud, calling from the fucking rice farm and I'm lonely.'

More bangs. Crackle pop, like motorbikes backfiring. Wallop. Slap. Put down vodka glass. Holler at the top of my voice in my father's classical American Spanish.

'*Who is this? Answer me!*'

Wait. Zero. Whimpering but no words. Louisa changes to English.

'Get out of my husband's life, you hear me, Sabina, you fucking bitch! *Fuck you, Sabina!* Get out of my rice farm too!'

Still no words.

'I'm in his den, Sabina. I'm looking for your fucking letters to him, right *now*! Ernesto Delgado is *not* corrupt. Hear me? It's a lie. I work for him. It's other people who are corrupt, *not* Ernesto. Speak to me!'

More bangs and thumps in the earpiece. Jesus, what *is* this? The next invasion? Bitch sobs pitifully, hangs up. Vision of self, smashing receiver on cradle, as in any good movie. Sit down. Stare at phone, waiting for it to ring again. It doesn't. So I finally bashed my sister's head in. Or somebody else did. Poor little Emily. Fuck you. Louisa stands up. Steadily. Takes sobering swig of vodka. Head clear as a bell. Tough shit, Sabina. My husband's mad. Guess you're having a bad time too. Serves you right. Rice farms can be lonely places.

Bookshelves. Mind-food. Just the thing for bewildered intellects. Look in books for bitch's letters to Harry. New books in old places. Old books in new places. Explain. Harry, for the love of God, explain. *Tell* me, Harry. *Talk* to me. Who's Sabina? Who's Marco? Why are you making up stories about Rafi and Mickie? Why are you shitting on Ernesto?

A pause for study and reflection while Louisa Pendel in her red three-buttoned housecoat and nothing underneath patrols her husband's bookshelves, pushing out her breasts and buttocks. She is feeling extremely naked. Better than naked. Hot-naked. She would like another baby. She would like to have all of Hannah's Seven Sisters as long as none of them turns out to be an Emily. Her father's books on the Canal march past her, starting with the days when the Scots tried to form a colony in the Darién and lost half their country's wealth. She opens them one by one, shakes them so vigorously that the bindings creak, flings them carelessly aside. No love letters.

Books about Captain Morgan and his pirates who sacked Panama City and burned it to the ground except for the ruins where we take the kids picnicking. But no love letters from Sabina or anybody else. None from Alpha, Beta, Marcos or the Bear. Nor from some cute-arsed little rad stud with funny money from America. Books about the time when Panama belonged to Colombia. But no love letters, however hard she flings them at the wall.

*   *   *

Louisa Pendel, mother-to-be of Hannah's Seven Sisters, squats naked inside the housecoat he never fucked me in, calves to thighs and all the way back again, browsing through the construction of the Canal and wishing she hadn't screamed at that poor woman whose love letters she can't find and probably wasn't Sabina anyway and wasn't calling from the rice farm. Accounts of real men like George Goethals and William Crawford Gorgas, men who were solid and methodical as well as mad, men who were loyal to their wives instead of writing letters about seeing fit or blackening the reputation of her employer or hiding wads of banknotes in their locked desks, and wads of letters I can't find. Books that her father made her read, in the hope that she would one day build her own fucking canal.

'Harry?' Screaming at the top of her voice to scare him. 'Harry? Where did you put that sad bitch's letters? Harry, I wish to know.'

Books on the Canal Treaties. Books on drugs and 'Whither Latin America?' Whither my fucking husband is more like it. And whither poor Ernesto, if Harry has anything to do with it. Louisa sits down and addresses Harry quietly and reasonably in a tone calculated not to dominate him. Shouting doesn't do it any more. She is speaking to him as one mature human being to another from a teak-framed armchair her father used when he was trying to get her to sit on his knee.

'Harry, I do not understand what you are doing in your den night after night irrespective of what time you come home from whatever you have been doing before. If you are writing a novel about corruption or an autobiography or a history of tailoring, I think you should come out with it and tell me, since after all we are married.'

Harry druckens himself, which is how he describes it when he's joking about a tailor's false humility.

'It's the accounts, you see, Lou. You don't get the fluence, not during the daytime, not with the doorbell going all the time.'

'The *farm* accounts?'

She is being a bitch again. The rice farm has become a non-subject in the household and she is supposed to respect this: Ramón is restructuring the finances, Lou. Angel has got a bit of a question mark over him, Lou.

'The shop,' Harry mumbles, like a penitent.

'Harry, I am not ungifted. I took excellent grades in math. I can help you any time you wish.'

He is already shaking his head. 'They're not that sort of numbers, you see, Lou. It's more the creative side. Numbers out of the air.'

'Is this why you have notes scribbled all over the margins of McCullough's *Path Between the Seas*, so that no one will ever be able to read it except you?'

Harry brightens – artificially. 'Oh well, yes, you're right there, Lou, clever of you to notice it. I'm seriously thinking of having some of the old prints blown up, you see, giving more of a Canal tone to the Clubroom, maybe get hold of a few artefacts for the atmosphere.'

'Harry, you have always told me and I agree that Panamanians with certain noble exceptions like Ernesto Delgado do not care for the Canal. They didn't build it. We did. They did not even provide the labour. The labour came from China and Africa and Madagascar, it came from the Caribbean and India. And Ernesto is a good man.'

Jesus, she thought. Why do I speak like that? Why am I such a strident pious shrew? Easy. Because Emily is a whore.

*   *   *

She sat at his desk, head in hands, sorry she had split the drawers open, sorry she had bawled out that wretched weeping woman, sorry she had once more had wicked thoughts about her sister Emily. I'm never going to talk to anyone like that again in my life, she decided. I'm never going to punish myself again by punishing other people. I'm not my fucking mother or my fucking father and I am not a pious perfect God-fearing Zonian bitch. And I'm very sorry that in a stressful moment, under the influence of alcohol, I found it in me to abuse a fellow-sinner, even if she's Harry's mistress and if she is I'll murder her. Rummaging in a drawer that she had till now neglected, she came upon another unfinished masterpiece:

Andy, you will be very pleased to hear that our new arrangement is highly popular with all parties, especially the ladies. Everything being down to me, L is not compromised in her conscience as regards naughty Ernie plus it's safer regarding the family as a whole it being one to one.

Will continue this at shop.

And so will I, thought Louisa in the kitchen, giving herself one more for the road. Alcohol no longer affected her, she had discovered. What affected her was Andy alias Andrew Osnard who with her reading of this fragment had abruptly supplanted Sabina as the object of her curiosity.

But this was not new.

She had been curious about Mr Osnard ever since the trip to Anytime Island when she had concluded that Harry wished her to go to bed with him to ease his conscience, though from what Louisa knew of Harry's conscience, one fuck was unlikely to solve the problem.

She must have telephoned for a cab because there was one standing outside the door and the bell was ringing.

*   *   *

Osnard turned his back on the eyehole and walked through the dining room to the balcony where Luxmore sat in the same near-foetal position, too scared to speak or act. His bloodshot eyes were opened wide, fear stretched his upper lip into a sneer, two yellowed front teeth had appeared between his beard and his moustache and they must have been the ones he sucked when he wished to signal a happy turn of phrase.

'I am receiving an unscheduled visit from BUCHAN TWO,' Osnard told him quietly. 'We have a situation on our hands. You'd better get out fast.'

'Andrew. I'm a senior officer. My God, what's that hammering? She'll awaken the dead.'

'I'm going to put you with the coats. When you hear me shut the dining room door after her, take the lift to the lobby, give the concierge a dollar and tell him to get you a taxi to the El Panama.'

'My God, Andrew.'

'What is it?'

'Are you going to be all right? Listen to her. Is that a gun she's using? We should call the police. Andrew. One word.'

'What is it?'

'Can I trust the taxi driver? Some of these fellows, you hear things. Bodies in the harbour. I don't speak their Spanish, Andrew.'

Lifting Luxmore to his feet, Osnard led him to the hall, bundled him into the cloakroom and closed the door. He unchained the front door, slid the bolts, turned the key and opened it. The hammering stopped but the ringing continued.

'Louisa,' he said as he prised her finger from the bell

button. 'Marvellous. Where's Harry? Why don't you come on in?'

* * *

Transferring his grip to her wrist he heaved her into the hall and closed the door but did not bolt it or turn the key. They stood face to face and close while Osnard held her hand above their heads as if they were about to begin an old-fashioned waltz, and it was the hand that held the shoe. She let the shoe fall. No sound was coming out of her but he smelt her breath and it was like his mother's breath whenever he had to accept a kiss from her. Her dress was very thin. He could feel her breasts and the bulge of her pubic triangle through the red fabric.

'What the fuck are you playing at with my husband?' she said. 'What's this crap he's been telling you about Delgado taking bribes from the French and messing with the drugs cartels? Who's Sabina? Who's Alpha?'

But despite the force of her words she spoke uncertainly, in a voice neither loud enough nor convinced enough to penetrate the cloakroom door. And Osnard with his instinct for weakness sensed at once the fear in her: fear of himself, fear for Harry, fear of the forbidden, and the biggest fear of all, which was of hearing things so terrible she would never again be able not to hear them. But Osnard had heard them already. With her questions she had answered all his own, as they had gathered like unread signals in the secret rooms of his consciousness over recent weeks:

She knows nothing. Harry never recruited her. It's a con.

She was about to repeat her question or enlarge upon it or ask another, but Osnard could not risk this happening within Luxmore's hearing. Clamping one hand over her mouth, therefore, he lowered her arm, folded it behind her, turned her back to him and frogmarched her on one shoe into the dining room, at the same time as he banged the dining room door shut behind him with his foot. Halfway across the room he came to a halt, clutching her against him. In the flurry two of her buttons had come undone,

366

leaving her breasts uncovered. He could feel her heart thumping under his wrist. Her breathing had slowed to longer, deeper gasps. He heard the front door close as Luxmore took his leave. He waited and heard the ping of the arriving lift and the asthmatic sigh of electric doors. He heard the lift descend. He took his hand from her mouth and felt saliva in his palm. He cupped her bare breast in his hand and felt the nipple harden and nestle into his palm. Still standing behind her, he released her arm and saw it fall languidly to her side. He heard her whisper something as she kicked off her other shoe.

'Where's Harry?' he said, keeping his hold on her body.

'Gone to find Abraxas. He's dead.'

'Who's dead?'

'Abraxas. Who the fuck else? If Harry was dead he couldn't have gone to see him, could he?'

'Where did he die?'

'Guararé. Ana says he shot himself.'

'Who's Ana?'

'Mickie's woman.'

He put his right hand over her other breast and was treated to a mouthful of her coarse brown hair as she shoved her head hard into his face and her rump into his groin. He turned her halfway to him and kissed her temple and cheek bone and licked the sweat that was pouring off her in rivulets, and he felt her trembling increase until her lips and teeth locked over his mouth in a grimace, her tongue searched his, and he had a glimpse of her squeezed-up eyes and the tears seeping from the corners and he heard her mutter 'Emily.'

'Who's Emily?' he asked.

'My sister. I told you about her on the island.'

'Hell does she know about all this?'

'She lives in Dayton, Ohio and she fucked all my friends. Do you have any shame?'

'Afraid not. Had it out when I was a kid.'

Then one of her hands was hauling at his shirt tails, the other was delving clumsily in the waistband of his Pendel & Braithwaite trousers and she was whispering things to herself that he didn't catch and anyway were of no interest to him. He groped for the third button but she hit his hand impatiently aside and pulled the housecoat over her head in one movement. He stepped out of his shoes and peeled off his trousers, underpants and socks in a single damp roll. He pulled his shirt over his head. Naked and apart, they appraised each other, wrestlers about to engage. Then Osnard grabbed her in both arms and, lifting her clean off the ground, carted her across the threshold of his bedroom and dumped her on the bed where she at once began attacking him with great lunges of her thighs.

'Wait, Christ's sake,' he ordered, and pushed her off him.

Then he took her very slowly and deliberately, using all his skills and hers. To shut her up. To tie a loose cannon to the deck. To get her safely into my camp before whatever battle lay ahead. Because it's a maxim of mine that no reasonable offer should ever be passed up. Because I always fancied her. Because screwing one's friends' wives is never less than interesting.

*   *   *

Louisa lay with her back to him, her head under the pillows and her knees drawn up to protect her while she clutched the bedsheet to her nose. She had closed her eyes, more to die than to sleep. She was ten years old in her bedroom in Gamboa with the curtains drawn, sent there to repent her sins after slicing up Emily's new blouse with a pair of sewing scissors on the grounds that it was brazen. She wanted to get up and borrow his toothbrush and dress and comb her hair and leave, but to do any of those things was to admit the reality of time and place and Osnard's naked body in the bed beside her and the fact that she had nothing to wear except a flimsy red housecoat with the buttons torn off it – and where the hell was it anyway? – and a pair of flat shoes that were supposed not to show off her height – and what the hell had happened to *them*? – and her headache was so terrible that she had a good mind to demand to be taken to a hospital where she could begin last night again from the beginning, without vodka or smashing up Harry's desk if that was what she had done, without Marta or the shop or Mickie dying or Delgado's reputation being ripped to shreds by Harry, and without Osnard and all this. Twice she had gone to the bathroom, once to be sick, but each time she had crept back into bed and tried to make everything that had happened unhappen, and now Osnard was talking on the telephone and there was no way on earth she couldn't hear his hateful English drawl eighteen inches from her ear however many pillows she might pull over her head, or the sleepy bewildered Scottish accent from the other end of the line like last messages from a faulty radio.

'We've got some disturbing news coming through, I'm afraid, sir.'

'Disturbing? Who's disturbing?' The Scots voice waking up.

'About that Greek ship of ours.'

'Greek *ship*? What Greek ship? What are you talking about, Andrew?'

'Our flagship, sir. The flagship of the Silent Line.'

Long pause.

'Got you, Andrew! The Greek, my God! Point taken. Tricky how? Why tricky?'

'It seems to have foundered, sir.'

'Foundered? What against? How?'

'Sunk.' Pause for 'sunk' to sink in. 'Written off. Up west somewhere. Circumstances not yet established. I've sent a writer there to find out.'

More puzzled silence from the other end, reflecting Louisa's own.

'Writer?'

'A famous one.'

'Got you! Understood. The bestselling author from bygone times. Quite so. Say no more. Sunk how, Andrew? Sunk totally, you mean?'

'First reports say he'll never sail again.'

'God. *God!* Who did it, Andrew? That woman, I'll be bound. I'd put nothing beyond her. Not after last night.'

'Further details pending, I'm afraid, sir.'

'What about his crew? – his shipmates, dammit – his silent ones – have they gone down too?'

'We're waiting to hear. Best you go on back to London as planned, sir. I'll call you there.'

He rang off and yanked the pillow from her head where she was clutching it. Even with her eyes crammed shut she couldn't escape the sight of his replete young body stretched carelessly at her side or his idle, bloated penis half awake.

'I never said this,' he was telling her. 'All right?'

She turned resolutely away from him. Not all right.

'Your husband's a brave chap. He's under orders never to talk to you about it. Never will. Nor will I.'

'Brave how?'

'People tell him things. He tells 'em to us. What he doesn't hear he goes and finds out, often at some risk. Recently he stumbled on something big.'

'Is that why he photographed my papers?'

'We needed Delgado's engagements. There are missing hours in Delgado's life.'

'They're not missing hours. They're when he goes to Mass or looks after his wife and kids. He's got a kid in hospital. Sebastian.'

'That's what Delgado tells you.'

'It's true. Don't give me that bullshit. Is Harry doing this for England?'

'England, America, Europe. Civilised free world. You name it.'

'Then he's an asshole. So's England. So's the civilised free world.'

It took her time and effort but eventually she managed it. She climbed onto her elbow and turned to look down on him.

'I don't believe a fucking word you're telling me,' she said. 'You're a slimy English crook with a sackful of clever lies and Harry is out of his mind.'

'Then don't believe me. Just keep your big mouth shut.'

'It's bullshit. He makes it up. You're making it up. Everyone's jerking off.'

The phone was ringing, a different phone, one she hadn't

noticed, although it was on her side of the bed, linked to a pocket tape recorder next to the reading light. Osnard rolled roughly over her and grabbed the receiver, and she was in time to hear him say 'Harry' before she clapped her hands over her ears, squeezed her eyes shut and yanked her face into a rigid grimace of refusal. But somehow one of her hands didn't do its job properly. And somehow one ear heard her husband's voice above the babel of screaming and rejecting that was going on inside her head:

'Mickie was murdered, Andy,' Harry was announcing. His voice was deliberate and forearmed, but pressed for time. 'A professional shooting, by the sound of it, which is all I can say at the present time. However, I'm told there's more of the same on the way and precautions should therefore be taken by all interested parties. Rafi has already left for Miami, plus I'm getting word to the others in accordance with laid-down procedure. I'm worried about the students. I don't know how we're going to stop them calling out the flotilla.'

'Where are you?' Osnard asked.

And there was a spare moment after that when Louisa might have asked Harry a question or two on her own account – something on the lines of: 'Do you still love me?' – or 'Will you forgive me?' – or 'Are you going to notice the difference in me if I don't tell you?' – or 'What time will you be home this evening and shall I get food in so that we can cook together?' But she was still trying to select one of these when the line went dead and there was Osnard on his elbows above her, with his fluid cheeks hanging down and his little wet mouth open, but otherwise not apparently with any intention of making love to her because for the first time in their brief acquaintance he seemed to be at a loss.

'Hell was that?' he demanded of her as if she were at least in part responsible.

'Harry,' she said stupidly.

'Which one?'

'Yours, I suppose.'

At which he puffed and flopped onto his back beside her

with his hands behind his head as if he were taking a short break on a nudist beach. Then he picked up the phone again, not Harry's but the other one and, having dialled, asked for Señor Mellors in room something or other.

'It seems to have been murder,' he said without preamble, and she guessed he was speaking to the same Scottish man as before. 'Looks as though the students may break ranks... lot of emotion riding on the ball... much respected man... A professional wet job. Details still coming in. What do you mean, a peg, sir? Don't get you. Peg for what? No, of course. I understand. As soon as I can, sir. Straight away.'

Then for a while he seemed to go through a lot of things in his mind, because she heard him snorting and occasionally letting out a grim laugh, until he sat up sharply on the edge of the bed. Then stood up and walked to the dining room, to return with his rolled-up clothes. He fished out last night's shirt and pulled it on.

'Where are you going?' she demanded. And when he didn't answer, 'What are you doing? Andrew, I do not understand how you can get up, and dress, and walk out on me, and leave me here with no clothes and no place to go and no provision for my –'

She dried up.

'Well, sorry about that, ol' girl. Bit abrupt. Got to break camp, afraid. Both of us. Time to go home.'

'Home where?'

'Bethania for you. Merrie England for me. Rule one o' the house. Joe topped in the field, case officer gets out in his socks. Don't pass Go, don't collect two hundred quid. Hurry home to Mummy, shortest route.'

He was tying his tie in the mirror. Chin up, spirits revived. And for a passing moment and no longer, Louisa thought she sensed a stoicism about him, an acceptance of defeat that in a poor light could have passed for nobility.

'Say goodbye to Harry for me, will you? Great artist. My successor will be in touch. Or not.' Still in his shirt-tails he pulled open a drawer and chucked a tracksuit at her. 'Better have this for the cab. When you get home, burn it, then break up the ash. And keep your head down for a few weeks.

Chaps back home are getting out the war drums.'

*   *   *

Hatry the great press baron was at luncheon when the news
came through. He was sitting at his usual table at the Connaught, eating kidneys and bacon and drinking house claret
and refining his views on the new Russia, which were to the
effect that the more the bastards tore themselves apart, the
more Hatry was pleased.

And his audience by a happy accident was Geoff Cavendish, and the bringer of the news was none other than young
Johnson, Osnard's replacement in Luxmore's office, who
twenty minutes earlier had fished the crucial British Embassy
signal – penned by Ambassador Maltby himself – from the
pile of papers that had accumulated in Luxmore's in-tray
during his dramatic dash to Panama. Johnson, as an
ambitious intelligence officer, naturally made a point of
sifting through Luxmore's in-tray whenever a suitable
opportunity allowed.

And the wonderful thing was, Johnson had no one to
consult about the signal but himself. Not only was the entire
top floor out to lunch, but with Luxmore on his way home
there was no one in the building who was BUCHAN-cleared
apart from Johnson. Spurred by excitement and aspiration,
he at once telephoned Cavendish's office to be told that
Cavendish was lunching with Hatry. He telephoned Hatry's
office to be told that Hatry was lunching at the Connaught.
Risking all, he slapped a pre-emptive requisition on the only
car and driver available. For this act of hubris, as for others,
Johnson was later called to account.

'I'm Scottie Luxmore's assistant, sir,' he told Cavendish
breathlessly, selecting the more sympathetic of the two faces
peering up at him from their table in the bay. 'I've a rather
important message for you from Panama, I'm afraid, sir,
and I don't think it will keep. I didn't feel I should read it
to you over the telephone.'

'Sit down,' Hatry ordered. And to the waiter: 'Chair.'

So Johnson sat down and, having done so, was about to

hand Cavendish the full decoded text of Maltby's signal when Hatry snatched it from his hand and wrenched it open, so vigorously that other diners turned to stare and guess. Hatry read the signal cursorily and passed it to Cavendish. Cavendish read it, and so probably did at least one waiter, because by now there was a rush on to set a third place for Johnson and make him look more like an ordinary lunch guest and less like a perspiring young runner in a sports coat and grey flannels – attire that the Grill Room manager did not view with any favour, but it was a Friday after all and Johnson had been looking forward to a weekend in Gloucestershire with his mother.

'That's the one we want, isn't it?' Hatry asked Cavendish, through half-masticated kidney. 'We can go.'

'That's it,' Cavendish confirmed with quiet relish. 'That's our peg.'

'What about passing the word to Van?' said Hatry, wiping a piece of bread round his plate.

'Well, *I* think, Ben – the *best* thing in this case – is to let Brother Van read it in your newspapers,' said Cavendish in a series of dancing little phrases. '*Do* excuse me, I'm *so* sorry,' he added to Johnson, stepping over his feet. '*Must* just telephone.'

He said sorry to the waiter too and took his double damask napkin with him in his haste. And Johnson not long afterwards was sacked, nobody was ever quite sure why. Ostensibly, it was for riding around London with a decoded text that was complete with all its symbols and operational codenames. Unofficially, he was held to be a little too excitable for secret work. But probably it was barging into the Connaught Grill Room in a sports coat that was held to be the most grave of these offences.

CHAPTER TWENTY-TWO

To reach the firework festival at Guararé in the Panamanian province of Los Santos which forms part of a stunted peninsula on the south-west tip of the Gulf of Panama, Harry Pendel drove by way of Uncle Benny's house in Leman Street that smelt of burning coal, the Sisters of Charity orphanage, several East End synagogues and a succession of grossly overcrowded British penal institutions under the generous patronage of Her Majesty the Queen. All these establishments and others lay in the jungle blackness either side of him and on the pitted winding road ahead of him, on hilltops cut against a star-strewn sky and on the steel-grey ironing-board of the Pacific under a very clean new moon.

The difficult drive was made harder for him by the clamour of his children demanding songs and funny voices from the back of the four-track and by the well-meant exhortations of his unhappy wife which rang in his ears even on the most desolate parts of his journey: go slower, watch out for that deer, monkey, buck, dead horse, metre-long green iguana or family of six Indians on one bicycle, Harry, I do not understand why you have to drive at seventy miles an hour to keep an appointment with a dead man, and if it's the fireworks you're afraid of missing, you should please to know that the festival continues for five nights and five days and this is the first night and if we don't get there till tomorrow the children will entirely understand.

To this was added Ana's unbroken monologue of grief, the terrible forbearance of Marta asking him for nothing he wasn't able to give, and the presence of Mickie, slumped huge and morose in the passenger seat beside him, riding up against him with his spongy shoulder whenever they negotiated a bend or bounced over a pothole, and asking him in a glum refrain why he didn't make suits the way Armani did.

His feelings about Mickie were terrible and overwhelming. He knew that in all of Panama and in all his life he had only ever had one friend, and now he had killed him. He saw no difference any more between the Mickie he had loved and the Mickie he had invented, except that the Mickie he had loved was better, and the Mickie he had invented was some sort of mistaken homage, an act of vanity on Pendel's part: to create a champion out of his best friend, to show Osnard what grand company he kept. Because Mickie had been a hero in his own right. He had never needed Pendel's fluence. Mickie had stood up and been counted when it mattered as a reckless opponent of the tyranny. He had richly earned his beatings and imprisonment, and his right to be drunk for ever after. And to buy however many fine suits he needed to take away the scratch and stink of prison uniform. It was not Mickie's fault that he was weak where Pendel had painted him strong, or that he had given up the struggle where Pendel's fictions had painted him continuing it. If only I'd left him alone, he thought. If only I'd never fiddled with him, then chewed his head off because I had the guilts.

Somewhere at the foot of Ancón Hill he had filled the four-track with enough petrol to last him the rest of his life and given a dollar to a black beggar with white hair and one ear eaten off by leprosy or a wild animal or a disenchanted wife. At Chame, through sheer inattention, he shot a Customs roadblock, and at Penonomé he became aware of a pair of lynxes riding on his left tail-light – lynxes being young, very slim American-trained policemen in black leather who ride two to a motorcycle, carry submachine-guns and are famous for being polite to tourists and killing muggers, dopers and assassins – but tonight, it seemed, also murderous British spies. The lynx in front does the driving, the lynx on the pillion does the killing, Marta had explained to him, and he remembered this as they pulled alongside and he saw the fish-eye reflection of his own face floating among the streetlights in the liquid blackness of their visors. Then he remembered that lynxes only operated in Panama City and he fell to wondering whether they were on a jaunt of some kind or whether they had followed him out here in order to shoot him in privacy. But he never had an answer to his question because when he looked again they had returned to the blackness they had sprung from, leaving him the pitted, twisting road, the dead dogs in his headlights and the bush that was so dense to either side you saw no tree trunks, just black walls and eyes of animals and, through the open sunroof, heard the exchange of insults between species. Once he saw an owl that had been crucified to an electricity pole and its breast and the inside of its wings were white as a martyr's and its eyes were open. But whether it belonged to a recurring nightmare he had, or was the ultimate incarnation of it, remained a mystery.

After that Pendel must have dozed for a time and probably he took a wrong turning as well, because when he looked again he was on family holiday in Parita two years ago, picnicking with Louisa and the children on a grass square surrounded by one-storey houses with raised verandahs and stone mounting blocks for getting on and off your horse without spoiling your nice clean shoes. In Parita an old witch in a black hood had told Hannah that the people of the town put young boa constrictors under their roof tiles to catch mice, at which Hannah refused to enter any house in town, not for an ice cream, not for a pee. She was so scared that instead of attending Mass as they had planned they had to stand outside the church and wave at an old man in the white belltower who tolled the big bell with one hand while he waved back at them with the other, which they all afterwards agreed was better than going to Mass. And when he had finished with his bell he gave them an amazing slow-motion performance of an orang-utan, first swinging from an iron crossbar, then fleaing himself, armpits, head and crotch and eating the fleas between searches.

Passing Chitré Pendel remembered the shrimp farm where shrimps laid their eggs in the trunks of mangrove trees and Hannah had asked whether they got pregnant first. And after the shrimps he remembered a kind Swedish horticulturist lady who told them about the orchid called Little Prostitute of the Night, because by day it smelt of nothing but at night no decent person would let it into the house.

'Harry, it will not be necessary for you to explain this to our children. They are exposed to quite enough explicit material as it is.'

But Louisa's strictures made no difference because all week long Mark had called Hannah his *putita de noche* till Pendel told him to shut up.

And after Chitré came the battle zone: first the approaching red sky, then the rumble of ordnance, then the glow of flares as he was waved through one police checkpoint after another on his road to Guararé.

*   *   *

Pendel was walking, and people in white were walking beside him, leading him to the gallows. He was pleasantly surprised to find himself so reconciled to death. If he ever lived his life again, he decided, he would insist on a brand new actor in the leading rôle. He was walking to the gallows and there were angels at his side, and they were Marta's angels, he recognised them at once, the true heart of Panama, the people who lived the other side of the bridge, didn't take bribes or give them, made love to the people they loved, got pregnant and didn't have abortions, and come to think of it Louisa would admire them too, if only she could jump over the fences that confined her – but who can? We're born into prison, every one of us, sentenced to life from the moment we open our eyes, which was what made him so sad when he looked at his own children. But these children were different and they were angels and he was very glad to be meeting them in the last hours of his life. He had never doubted that Panama had more angels per acre, more white crinolines and flowered head-dresses, perfect shoulders, cooking-smells, music, dancing, laughter, more drunks, malign policemen and lethal fireworks than any comparable Paradise twenty times its size, and here they were assembled to escort him. And he was very gratified to discover bands playing, and competing folkdance teams with gangly romantic-eyed black men in cricket blazers and white shoes and flat hands that lovingly moulded the air round their partners' gyrating haunches. And to see that the double doors of the church were pulled open to give the Holy Virgin a grandstand view of the Bacchanalia outside, whether She wanted it or not. The angels were evidently determined She should not lose touch with ordinary life, warts and all.

He was walking slowly, as condemned men will, keeping to the centre of the street and smiling. He was smiling because everybody else was smiling, and because one discourteous gringo who refuses to smile amid a crowd of ridiculously beautiful Spanish-Indian *mestizo* revellers is an endangered species. And Marta was right, these were the most beautiful and virtuous and unsullied people on earth, as Pendel had already observed. To die among them would be a privilege. He would ask to be buried the other side of the bridge.

Twice he enquired after the way. Each time he was sent in a different direction. The first time a group of angels earnestly pointed him across the middle of the square, where he became the moving target for salvos of multi-warhead rockets fired at head height from windows and doorways on all four sides of him. And though he laughed and grinned and covered up and gave every sign of taking the joke in good part, it was actually a miracle that he reached the opposite bank with both eyes, ears and balls in place and not a burn on him, because the rockets were not a joke at all and there was no laughter to say they were. They were red-hot, high velocity missiles spewing molten flame, fired at short range under the guidance of a knobbly-knee'd, freckled, red-haired Amazon in frayed shorts who was the self-appointed mistress-gunner of a well-armed unit, and she was trailing her lethal rockets in a string like a tail behind her back while she lewdly pranced and gesticulated. She was smoking – what substance was anybody's guess – and between puffs she was screaming orders to her troops around the square: 'Cut his cock off, bring the gringo to his knees –' then another drag of cigarette smoke and the next command. But Pendel was a good chap and these were angels.

And the second time he asked the way he was shown a row of houses that lined one side of the square, with verandahs occupied by overdressed *rabiblancos* slumming it with their shiny BMWs parked alongside, and Pendel as he walked past one noisy verandah after another kept thinking: *I* know you, you're so-and-so's son, or daughter, my goodness how time passes. But their presence, when he thought about it more, did not concern him, neither did he care whether they spotted him in return, because the house where Mickie had shot himself was just a few doors along on his left, which was a very good reason to concentrate his thoughts exclusively on a sex-driven fellow-prisoner called Spider who'd hanged himself in his cell while Pendel was sleeping three feet away from him, Spider's being the only dead body Pendel had had to handle at close quarters. So it was Spider's fault in a way that Pendel in his distraction found that he had wandered into the middle of an informal police cordon consisting of a police car, a ring of bystanders and about twenty policemen who couldn't possibly have all fitted into the car but, as policemen are wont to in Panama, had collected like gulls around a fishing boat the moment there was a smell of profit or excitement in the air.

The point of attraction was a dazed old peasant seated on the kerb with his straw hat between his knees and his face in his hands, and he was roaring a lament in gorilla-like gusts of rage. Gathered round him were some dozen advisors and spectators and consultants, including several drunks who needed one another's support to remain upright, and an old woman presumably his wife who was loudly agreeing with the old man whenever he let her get a word in. And since the police were disinclined to clear a path through the group, and certainly not through their own ranks, Pendel had no option but to become a bystander himself though not an active participant in the debate. The old man was quite badly burned. Every time he took his hands from his face to make a point or rebut one it was easy to see he had been burned. A large patch of skin was missing from his left cheek and the wound extended southward into the open neck of his collarless shirt. And because he was burned, the police were proposing to take him to the local hospital where he would receive an injection which, as everyone agreed, was the appropriate remedy for a burn.

But the old man didn't want an injection and he didn't want the remedy. He would rather have the pain than the injection, he would rather get blood poisoning and any other evil after-effect, than go with the police to the hospital. And the reason was, he was an old drunk and this was probably the last festival of his life and everyone knew that when you had an injection you couldn't drink for the rest of the festival. He had therefore taken the conscious decision, of which his Maker and his wife were witness, to tell the police to shove the injection up their arses because he preferred to drink himself into a stupor, which would anyway take care of the pain. So he would be obliged if everyone got the hell out of his way please, including the police, and if they really wanted to do him a good turn, the best thing they could do was bring him a drink and another for his wife, a bottle of *seco* would be particularly welcome.

To all of which Pendel listened studiously, sensing the presence of a message in everything, even if its meaning was not clear to him. And gradually the police faded away, the crowd also. The old woman sat down beside her husband and put her arm round his neck and Pendel walked up the steps of the only house in the street with its lights out, saying to himself: I'm dead already, I'm as dead as you are, Mickie, so don't think your death can frighten me.

*   *   *

He knocked and no one came, but his knocking caused heads to turn in the street because who on earth knocks on anyone's door at festival time? So he stopped knocking and kept his face in the shadow of the porch. The door was closed but not locked. He turned the handle and stepped inside and his first thought was that he was back in the orphanage and Christmas was coming up and he was a Wise Man in the Nativity play again, holding a lantern and a stick and wearing an old brown trilby that someone had given to the poor – except that the actors inside the house he was now entering were in the wrong places and somebody had snatched the Holy Infant.

There was a bare tiled room for a stable. There was an aura of flickering light from the fireworks in the square. And there was a woman in a shawl watching over a crib and praying with her hands to her chin, who was Ana apparently feeling a need to cover her head in the presence of death. But the crib was not a crib. It was Mickie, upside down as she had promised, Mickie with his face flat on the kitchen floor and his arse in the air and a map of Panama one side of his head where one ear and one cheek should have been, and the gun he had done it with lying beside him pointing accusingly at the intruder, telling the world quite needlessly what the world already knew: that Harry Pendel, tailor, purveyor of dreams, inventor of people and places of escape, had murdered his own creation.

*   *   *

Gradually as Pendel's eyes became used to the fickle light of fireworks, flares and streetlights from the square he began to make out the rest of the mess that Mickie had left behind when he blew one side of his head off: the traces of him on the tiled floor and walls and in surprising places like a chest of drawers crudely daubed with rollicking pirates and their molls. And it was these that prompted his first words to Ana, which were of a practical rather than consoling kind.

'We ought to put something over the windows,' he said.

But she didn't answer, didn't stir, didn't turn her head, which suggested to him that in her way she was as dead as he was, Mickie had killed her too, she was contingent damage. She had tried to make Mickie happy, she had mopped him down and shared his bed, and now he had shot her: take this for all your trouble. So for a moment Pendel was angry with Mickie, accusing him of an act of great brutality, not just against his own body, but against his wife and mistress and children, and his friend Harry Pendel as well.

Then of course he remembered his own responsibility in the matter and his depiction of Mickie as a great resister and spy; and he tried to imagine how Mickie must have felt when the police dropped by to tell him he was going to do more prison; and the truth of his own guilt at once swept away any convenient reflections upon Mickie's irrelevant shortcomings as a suicide.

He touched Ana's shoulder and when she still didn't budge some residual sense of the responsibility of the entertainer sparked in him: this woman needs a bit of cheering up. So he put his hands under her armpits and hauled her to her feet and held her against him and she was as stiff and cold as he imagined Mickie was. Clearly she had been stuck for so long in one position keeping watch over him that his stillness and placidity had got into her bones somehow. She was a flighty, funny, skittish girl by nature, judging from the couple of occasions when Pendel had met her, and probably she had never in her life watched anything so motionless for so long. First she had screamed and ranted and complained – Pendel reckoned, remembering their telephone conversation – and when she had got all that out of her system, she'd gone into a kind of watching decline. And as she had cooled, she had set, which was why she was so stiff to hold and why her teeth were chattering and why she couldn't answer his question about the windows.

He looked for a drink to give her but all he could find was three empty whisky bottles and a half-drunk bottle of *seco* and he decided on his own authority that *seco* was not the answer. So he led her to a wicker chair and sat her in it, found some matches, lit the gas and put a saucepan of water on the flames, and when he turned and looked at her he saw that her eyes had found Mickie again, so he went to the bedroom and took the coverlet from the bed and put it over Mickie's head, smelling for the first time the warm rusty smell of his blood above the cordite and cooking smells and fire smoke that was rolling in from the verandah while the fireworks went on popping and whizzing in the square, and the girls screamed at the bangers that the boys held onto till the absolute last moment before chucking them at their feet. It was all there for Pendel and Ana to watch any time they wanted, they only had to lift their heads from Mickie and look out of the French windows to see the fun.

'Get him away from here,' she blurted from her wicker chair. And much, much louder: 'My father will kill me. Get him out. He's a British spy. They said so. So are you.'

'Be quiet,' Pendel told her, surprising himself.

And suddenly Harry Pendel changed. He was not a different man but himself at last, a man possessed and filled with his own strength. In one glorious ray of revelation he saw beyond melancholy, death and passivity to a grand validation of his life as an artist, an act of symmetry and defiance, vengeance and reconciliation, a majestic leap into a realm where all the spoiling limitations of reality are swept away by the larger truth of the creator's dream.

*   *   *

And some intimation of Pendel's resurrection must have communicated itself to Ana, because after a few sips of coffee she put down her cup and joined him in his ministrations: first to fill the basin with water and pour disinfectant into it, then to track down a broom, a squeegee mop, rolls of kitchen paper, dishcloths, detergent and a scrubbing brush, then to light a candle and place it low down so that its flame would not be visible from the square, where a fresh display of fireworks, fired this time into the air and not at passing gringos, was announcing the successful selection of a beauty queen – and there she was on her float with her white mantilla, her white pear-flower crown, her white shoulders and blazing proud eyes, a girl of such candescent beauty and excitement that first Ana and then Pendel paused in their labours to watch her pass with her retinue of princesses and prancing boys and enough flowers for a thousand funerals for Mickie.

Then back to work, scrubbing and slopping till the disinfected water in the handbasin was black in the half light, and had to be replaced and then replaced again, but Ana toiled with the goodwill Mickie always said she had – a good sport, he always said, as insatiable in bed as in a restaurant, and soon the scrubbing and the slopping became a catharsis for her and she was chattering away as blithely as if Mickie had just sidled out for a moment to fetch another bottle or have a quick Scotch with a neighbour on one of the lighted verandahs either side of them, where groups of revellers were this minute clapping and cheering at the beauty queen – and not lying face down in the middle of the floor with the bedspread over him and his arse in the air, and his hand still stretched towards the gun that Pendel had, unnoticed by Ana, slipped into a drawer for later use.

'Look, look, it's the Minister,' Ana said, all chat.

A group of grand men in white *panabrisas* had arrived at the centre of the square, surrounded by other men in black glasses. That's how I'll do it, Pendel was thinking. I'll be official like them.

'We'll need bandages. Look for a first aid box,' he said.

There wasn't one, so they cut up a sheet.

'I'll have to buy a new bedspread as well,' she said.

Mickie's P & B magenta smoking jacket hung over a chair. Pendel delved, pulled out Mickie's wallet and handed Ana a bunch of notes, enough for a new bedspread and a good time.

'How's Marta,' Ana asked, secreting the money in her bodice.

'Just great,' said Pendel heartily.

'And your wife?'

'Thank you, well too.'

To put the bandages round Mickie's head they had to sit
him in the wicker chair where Ana had sat. First they put
towels over the chair, then Pendel turned Mickie over and
Ana just made it to the lavatory in time, retching with the
door open and one hand up in the air behind her and her
fingers splayed in a gesture of refinement. While she was
retching Pendel stooped to Mickie and remembered Spider
again and giving him the kiss of life knowing that no amount
of kissing was going to enliven him in any way, however
much the guilty warders shouted at Pendel to bloody try
harder, son.

But Spider had never been a friend on Mickie's huge
scale, or a first customer, or a prisoner of his father's past,
or Noriega's prisoner of conscience, or had the conscience
beaten out of him while he was inside. Spider had never
been passed round the prison as new meat for the psycho-
paths to eat their fill of. Spider had gone loco because he
was accustomed to screwing two girls a day and three on
Sundays, and the prospect of five years without screwing a
single girl looked like slow starvation to him. And Spider
had strangled himself and messed himself and stuck his
tongue out while he did it, which made the kiss of life even
more ridiculous, whereas Mickie had obliterated himself,
leaving one good side to him, if you ignored the blackened
hole, and one really awful side that you couldn't ignore any
part of.

*   *   *

But as a cellmate and victim of Pendel's betrayal, Mickie
had all the stubbornness of his size. When Pendel got his
hands under his armpits, Mickie just made himself heavier,
and it took a huge heave on Pendel's part to get him going,
and another to prevent him from collapsing again when he
was already halfway up. And it needed a lot of padding and
bandaging before the two sides of his head looked anything

like even. But somehow Pendel managed all of it, and when Ana returned he put her straight to work pinching Mickie's nose so that he could wind the bandage above it and below it and leave Mickie room to breathe, which was as futile in its way as trying to make Spider breathe, but at least in Mickie's case it had a purpose. And by running the bandages at a slant Pendel was also able to leave one eye clear for Mickie to see through, because Mickie, whatever he had done while he was pulling the trigger, had finished up with his remaining eye wide open and looking very startled indeed. So Pendel bandaged round it, and when he had done that he mustered Ana's help to haul Mickie and the chair as far as the front door.

'The people in my home town have got a real problem,' Ana confided to him, evidently feeling a need for intimacy. 'Their priest is a homo and they hate him, the priest in the next town fucks all the girls and they love him. Small towns, you get these human problems.' She paused to catch her breath before renewing her exertions. 'My old aunt is very strict. She wrote to the bishop complaining that priests who fuck aren't proper priests.' She laughed engagingly. 'The bishop told her, "Try saying that to my flock and see what they do to you."'

Pendel laughed too. 'Sounds like a good bishop,' he said.

'Could *you* be a priest?' she asked, shoving again. 'My brother, he's *really* religious. "Ana," he says, "I think I'll be a priest." "You're crazy," I tell him. He's never had a girl, that's his problem. Maybe he's homo.'

'Lock the door after me and don't open it till I come back,' Pendel said. 'Okay?'

'Okay. I lock the door.'

'I'll give three light knocks, then a loud one. Got it?'

'Am I going to remember that?'

'Of course you are.'

Then, because she was so much happier, he thought he would complete the cure by turning her round and making her admire their great achievement: nice clean walls and floor and furniture and, instead of a dead lover, just another Guararé firework casualty in an improvised bandage, sitting stoically by the door with his good eye open while he waited for his old pal to bring up the four-track.

*   *   *

Pendel had driven the four-track at a snail's pace through the angels and the angels had slapped it as if it were a horse's rump, and shouted Gee-up, gringo! and thrown fireworks under it, and a couple of lads had jumped on the rear bumper, and there had been an unsuccessful effort to get a beauty princess to sit on the bonnet, but she was scared to get her white skirt dirty and Pendel did not encourage her because it wasn't a time to be giving lifts. Otherwise it had been an uneventful journey that gave him a chance to fine-tune his plan because, as Osnard had drummed into him in the training sessions, time spent in preparation is never time wasted, the great trick being to look at a clandestine operation from the point of view of everybody who was going to take part in it and ask yourself: what does *he* do? what does *she* do? where does everyone go when it's over? and so on.

He gave three light knocks and one loud one but nothing happened. He did it again and there was a gay call of 'Coming!' and when Ana opened the door – half way because of Mickie being behind it – he saw by the glow from the square that she had brushed her hair down her back and put on a clean blouse that left her shoulders bare like the other angels, and that the verandah doors were open to encourage the smells of cordite and get rid of the smells of blood and disinfectant.

'There's a desk in your bedroom,' he told her.

'So?'

'See if there's a sheet of writing paper in it. And a pencil or a pen. Make me a card saying ambulance that I can put on the facia of the four-track.'

'You're going to pretend you're an *ambulance*? That's really cool.'

Like a girl at a party she skipped away to the bedroom while he took Mickie's gun from its drawer and put it in his trouser pocket. He knew nothing about guns and this was not a big one, but it was fat for its size, as the hole in Mickie's head had testified. Then as an afterthought he selected from a drawer in the kitchen a knife with a serrated edge and wrapped it in paper towelling before hiding it. Ana came back triumphant: she had found a child's drawing book and some crayons and the only problem was that in her enthusiasm she had left out the 'I' at the end, so the sign read AMBULANCA. But it was otherwise a good sign so he took it from her and went down the steps to the parked four-track and laid the sign on the facia and switched on the winking emergency lights to quell the people who were stuck in the street behind him, hooting at him to get out of the way.

Here humour also came to Pendel's aid, for as he started to go back up the steps he turned to his critics and with a smile for all of them put his hands together in a praying gesture for their indulgence, then raised one finger to crave one minute, then pushed the door open and switched on the hall light to reveal Mickie with his bandaged head and one eye. At which most of the hooting and yelling subsided.

'Put his jacket over his shoulders when I lift him up,' he told Ana. 'Not yet. Wait.'

Then Pendel stooped into the weightlifter's crouch and remembered that he was strong, as well as treacherous and murderous, and that the strength was in his thighs and buttocks and stomach and across his shoulders, and that there had been enough occasions in the past when he had had to carry Mickie home and this was no different, except that Mickie wasn't sweating or threatening to be sick or asking to be taken back to prison, by which he meant his wife.

With these thoughts in his mind Pendel took a great arm-ful of Mickie's back and drew him to his feet, but there was not a lot of strength in the legs and worse there was no balance because in the humid heat of the night Mickie had done very little in the way of stiffening up. So the stiffening had to be all Pendel's as he helped his friend over the threshold and, with one arm on the iron balustrade and all the strength that his gods had ever given him, down the first of four steps to the four-track. Mickie's head was on his shoulder now, he could smell the blood through the strips of bedsheet. Ana had draped the jacket over Mickie's back and Pendel wasn't certain why he had told her to do that with the jacket except that it was a really good jacket and he couldn't bear to think of Ana giving it to the first beggar in the street, he wanted it to play a part in Mickie's glory, because that's where we're going Mickie – third step – we're going to our glory and you're going to be the prettiest boy in the room, the best-dressed hero the girls have ever seen.

'Go ahead, open the car door,' he told Ana, at which Mickie in one of his familiar, unpredictable assertions of free will decided to take over the proceedings, in this case by throwing himself towards the car in a free fall from the bottom step. But Pendel need not have worried. Two boys were waiting with their arms out, Ana had already mustered them, she was one of those girls who mustered boys automatically just by stepping into the street.

'Be gentle,' she ordered them severely. 'He may have passed out.'

'He's got his eyes open,' said a boy, making the classic false assumption that, because you can see one eye you know the other one is there.

'Lean his head back,' Pendel ordered.

But he leant it back himself while they looked on uncomfortably. He lowered the headrest of the passenger seat and propped Mickie's head against it, tugged the seat belt across his huge gut and fastened it, closed the door, thanked the boys, waved his gratitude at the waiting cars behind him and hopped into the driver's seat.

'Go back to the festival,' he told Ana.

But he had ceased to command her. She was her own self again and she was crying her heart out and insisting that Mickie had never in his life done anything that merited persecution by the police.

*　　　*　　　*

He drove slowly, which was his mood. And Mickie, as Uncle Benny would say, was deserving of respect. Mickie's bandaged head was rolling with the curves and bouncing with the pot-holes and only the seat belt kept him from falling onto Pendel's side of the car, which was very much the way Mickie had behaved on the journey up except that Pendel had not imagined him with one open eye. He was following the signs to the hospital, keeping his hazard lights winking and sitting bolt upright, the way the ambulance drivers sat when they sped down Leman Street. They didn't even lean with the bends.

So who are you *exactly*? Osnard was saying, testing Pendel's cover. I'm a gringo doctor attached to the local hospital, is what I am, he replied. I've got a highly sick patient in the car, so don't mess me around.

At checkpoints the policemen stood back for him. One officer even stopped the opposing traffic in order to show deference to the injured. The gesture proved unnecessary however, because Pendel ignored the turning to the hospital and drove straight on, northward along the road he had come, back towards Chitré where the shrimps laid eggs in mangrove trunks and Sarigua where orchids were little prostitutes. There had been a lot of traffic as he entered Guararé, he now remembered, but leaving it there was none. They rode alone under the new moon and a clear sky, just Mickie and himself. As he turned right towards Sarigua a running black woman with no shoes and a frantic expression on her face begged him for a lift and he felt lousy not taking her aboard. But spies on dangerous missions don't give lifts as he had already noted in Guararé, so he kept going, watching the ground turn white as he ascended.

He knew the very spot. Mickie, like Pendel, had loved the sea. Indeed, as Pendel surveyed his own life, it struck him belatedly that the sea had been the calming influence on his many warring gods, which was why Panama had been so peculiarly beneficial to him when he was living life before Osnard. 'Harry boy, you can have your Hong Kong, your London or your Hamburg, I don't care,' Benny had vowed, showing him the isthmus on a Philip's Pocket Atlas one visiting day: 'Where else in the world can you get on an eleven bus and see the Great Wall of China one way and the Eiffel Tower the other?' But Pendel from his cell window had seen neither. He had seen seas of different blues on either side of him, and escape in both directions.

A cow stood in the road with its head down. Pendel braked. Mickie slid stupidly forward and caught his neck under the seat belt. Pendel released him and let him slide to the floor. Mickie, I'm talking to you. I said I was sorry, didn't I? With an ill grace the cow sidled out of the way. Green signs directed him to a nature reserve. There was the ancient tribal encampment, he remembered, there were the high dunes, there were the white rocks that Hannah said were stranded seashells. Then there was the beach. The road became a trail, the trail ran straight as a Roman road with high hedges like walls to either side. Sometimes the hedges put their hands together above him and prayed. Sometimes they fell away and showed him the special quiet sky you get above still seas. The new moon was trying hard to be larger than it really was. A chaste white haze had formed between its points. There were so many stars, they looked like powder.

The trail ended but he kept driving. Marvellous what a four-wheel drive can do. Giant cactuses rose like blackened soldiers either side of him. Halt! Get out! Put your hands on the roof! Papers! He drove on, passing a notice telling him not to. He wondered about tyre prints. They'll trace the four-track. How? By looking at the tyres of every four-track in Panama? He wondered about footprints. My shoes. They'll trace my shoes. How? He remembered the lynxes. He remembered Marta. They said you were a spy. They said Mickie was another. So did I. He remembered the Bear. He remembered Louisa's eyes, too scared to ask the only question left: Harry, have you gone mad? The sane are madder than we'll ever know, he thought. And the mad are a lot more sane than some of us would like to think.

He stopped the car slowly, looking at the ground as he drew up. He wanted iron hard. He had it. White, porous rock like lifeless coral that hadn't shown a footprint for a million years. He got out, leaving the headlights on, went to the back of the four-track where he kept his tow-rope for wet weather. He hunted for the kitchen knife for long enough to panic, then remembered he had dropped it into the pocket of Mickie's smoking jacket. He cut four feet of rope, went round to Mickie's door, opened it, hauled him out and lowered him gently to the ground, upside down but no longer with his arse in the air because the journey had altered him, he preferred to lie more on his side and less on his great tummy.

Pendel took Mickie's arms and bent them behind his back and set to work tying his wrists together: a double granny but neater. Meanwhile for his sanity he was thinking only practical matters. The jacket. What would they have done with the jacket? He fetched the jacket from the four-track and laid it over Mickie's back, cape-like, the way he might have worn it. Then he took the gun out of his pocket and by the headlights established which position of the button was safe, and of course he had been carting it around all this time on 'fire' because that was how Mickie had left it, naturally enough. After blowing his brains out, he could hardly put the safety catch on.

Then he backed the car a short distance away from Mickie and wasn't at all sure why he did that except that he didn't want such a bright glare on what he was about to do, he wanted Mickie to have some privacy for the occasion and some kind of natural sanctity, even if it was of a primitive, you could say primeval kind, here in the centre of an eleven-thousand-year-old Indian encampment strewn with arrow-heads and cutting flints that Louisa said the children could collect but then put back, because there'd be none left if everybody who came here took one; here in a desert made by man and mangrove trees, so salinated that even the earth itself was dead.

*　　　*　　　*

Having moved the car he walked back to the body, knelt to it and tenderly unwound the bandages until Mickie's face looked much as it had looked on the kitchen floor except a little older, a little cleaner and, in Pendel's imagination at least, more heroic.

Mickie, boy, that face of yours is going to hang where it deserves, in the hall of martyrs in the Presidential Palace once Panama is freed of all the things you didn't like, he told Mickie in his heart. *Plus I'm very sorry, Mickie, that you ever met me, because no one should.*

He'd have liked to say something aloud but all his voices were internal. So he took a last look round and, seeing nobody who might object, he fired two shots as lovingly as if he were firing a humane killer into a sick pet, one shot below the left shoulder blade and one below the right. *Lead poisoning, Andy,* he was thinking, remembering his dinner with Osnard at the Club Unión. *The professional three shots. One to the head, two to the body, and what was left of him all over the front pages.*

*   *   *

With the first shot he was thinking: this is for you, Mickie.

And with the second he was thinking: this is for me.

Mickie had done the third for him already, so for a while Pendel just stood still with the gun in his hand, listening to the sea and the silence of Mickie's opposition.

Then he took Mickie's jacket off and returned to the car with it and drove about twenty yards before chucking the jacket out of the window, in the way any professional killer might when he finds to his irritation that, having bound his man and killed him and dumped him in your requisite deserted spot, he's still got his damned jacket in the car, the one he was wearing when I shot him, so he dumps that too.

Returning to Chitré, he drove the empty streets searching for a telephone box that wasn't occupied by drunks or lovers. He wanted his friend Andy to be the first to know.

CHAPTER TWENTY-THREE

The enigmatic depletion of the staff of the British Embassy in Panama in the days leading up to Operation Safe Passage raised a small storm in the British and international press and became an excuse for more general debate about Britain's behind-the-scenes rôle in the US invasion. Latin American opinion was unanimous. YANQUI STOOGE! screamed Panama's doughty *La Prensa*, over a year-old photograph of Ambassador Maltby sheepishly shaking hands with the General in charge of US Southern Command at some forgotten reception or other. Back in England opinion at first divided on predictable lines. While the Hatry press described the diplomatic exodus as a 'brilliantly masterminded Pimpernel operation in the best tradition of the Great Game' and 'a secret subtext we must never be allowed to know', its competitors cried COWARDS! and accused the government of base collusion with the worst elements of the American Right, of exploiting 'presidential frailties' in an election year, of pandering to anti-Japanese hysteria and aiding and abetting America's colonial ambitions at the expense of Britain's ties with Europe, all in the cause of bolstering a pitiful and discredited Prime Minister in the run-up to the general election and appealing to the most discreditable elements of the British national character.

While the Hatry press favoured front page colour photographs of the Prime Minister shuttling his way to glory in Washington – MODEST BRITISH LION SHOWS TEETH – its competitors challenged Britain's 'vicarious imperial fantasies' under the double banner of THE FACTS AND THE FALLACY and WHILE THE REST OF EUROPE BLUSHES and compared the 'trumped-up charges against the Panamanian and Japanese governments' with deliberate contrivances published by the Hearst press in order to justify an aggressive American posture in what became the Spanish-American war.

But what *was* Britain's rôle? How, if at all – to quote a *Times* leader headed NO COLLUSION – had the British got their trotters in the American trough? Once again all eyes turned to the British Embassy in Panama, and its relationship or alleged lack of one with a sometime Oxford student, Noriega victim and noted scion of Panama's political establishment, Mickie Abraxas, whose 'mutilated' body was found dumped on waste land outside the town of Parita after he had been 'tortured and ritually assassinated', purportedly by a special unit attached to the presidential staff. The Hatry press broke the story. The Hatry press gave it its spin. Hatry television networks spun it a bit harder. Soon every British newspaper across the spectrum had its own Abraxas story, from OUR MAN IN PANAMA to DID SECRET HERO SHAKE HANDS WITH QUEEN? and CHUBBY BOOZER WAS BRITAIN'S 007. A more sober and therefore largely unregarded report in a struggling independent broadsheet said that Abraxas' widow had been spirited out of Panama within hours of the discovery of her husband's body, and was now purportedly recovering at a safe address in Miami under the protection of one Rafael Domingo, a close friend of the dead man and prominent Panamanian.

A hasty refutation put out by three Panamanian pathologists claiming that Abraxas was an inveterate alcoholic who had shot himself in a fit of depression after drinking a quart of Scotch whisky was greeted with the derision it deserved.

A Hatry tabloid summed up public reaction: WHO DO YOU THINK YOU'RE FOOLING, SEÑORES? An official statement by the British Chargé, Mr Simon Pitt, to the effect that 'Mr Abraxas had no formal or informal ties with this Embassy or any other official British representation in Panama' was made to look particularly absurd when it was discovered that Abraxas had been sometime President of the Anglo-Panamanian Society of Culture. His tenure had been curtailed 'for health reasons'. An expert on espionage matters explained the hidden logic of this for the benefit of the uninitiated. Having been 'spotted' by local intelligence operatives as a potential British agent, Abraxas would for cover reasons have been ordered to sever all overt ties with the Embassy. The proper way to do this would have been to concoct a 'dispute' with the Embassy in order to 'alienate' Abraxas from his controllers. No such dispute was acknowledged by Mr Pitt, and Abraxas may have paid dearly for this want of imagination on the part of British intelligence. Informed sources reported that the Panamanian security authorities had for some while been interested in his activities. A Shadow Minister on the opposition benches who had the temerity to paraphrase Oscar Wilde to the effect that one man dying for a cause did not make that cause valid was duly pilloried by the tabloids with one Hatry organ promising its readers shocking revelations about the man's luckless sex life.

Then one morning as if to order the spotlight turned to THE PANAMA HAT-TRICK, as they were henceforth dubbed, namely the three British diplomats who in the words of one commentator had 'sneaked their goods, women and wagons out of the Embassy compound on the very eve of the ferocious US air assault'. The fact that they were four and one was herself a woman was not allowed to spoil a good headline. A luckless Foreign Office spokesperson's explanation for their departure was met with hilarity:

'*Mr Andrew Osnard was not a regular member of the Foreign Service. He was temporarily engaged for his expertise on matters related to the Panama Canal in which he was highly qualified.*'

The press was delighted to note his high qualifications: Eton, greyhound-racing and go-karting in Oman.

Q: Why did Osnard leave Panama in such a hurry?

A: Mr Osnard's usefulness was deemed to have expired.

Q: Was this because Mickie Abraxas had expired?

A: No comment.

Q: Is Osnard a spook?

A: No comment.

Q: Where's Osnard now?

A: We have no knowledge of Mr Osnard's whereabouts.

Poor woman. Next day the press was proud to enlighten her with a photograph of Osnard making no comment on the ski slopes of Davos in the company of a society beauty twice his age.

'*Ambassador Maltby was recalled to London for consultations shortly before Operation Safe Passage was launched. The timing of his recall was coincidental.*'

Q: How shortly?

A: (the same unfortunate spokesperson) Shortly.

Q: Before he disappeared or afterwards?

A: That is a ridiculous question.

Q: What was Maltby's relationship with Abraxas?

A: We know of no such relationship.

Q: Panama was a pretty humble posting, wasn't it, for a man of Maltby's intellectual calibre?

A: We have great respect for the Republic of Panama. Mr Maltby was considered the right man for the job.

Q: Where is he now?

A: Ambassador Maltby is on indefinite leave of absence while he attends to matters of a personal nature.

Q: Can you define the nature?

A: I just did. Personal.

Q: What sort of personal?

A: We understand that Mr Maltby has come into an inheritance and may be contemplating a new career. He's a distinguished scholar.

Q: Is that another way of saying he's been sacked?

A: Certainly not.

Q: Paid off?

A: Thank you for coming to this press conference.

Discovered at her home in Wimbledon, where she was a renowned bowls player, Mrs Maltby wisely declined to comment on her husband's whereabouts:

'No, no. Off you go, all of you. You'll get nothing out of me. I know you press-johnnies of old. You're leeches and you make it up. We had you in Bermuda when the Queen came. No, haven't heard a word from him. Don't expect to. His life's his own, nothing to do with me. Oh I expect he'll ring in one day, if he can remember the number and get his coins together. That's all I'm going to say. *Spy?* Don't be utterly ridiculous. Do you think I wouldn't know? *Abraxas?* Never heard of him. Sounds like a health club. Yes, I have. He was the brute who was sick all over me at the Queen's birthday bash. Dreadful person. What do you mean, you silly man, romantically linked? Haven't you seen their photographs? She's twenty-four, he's forty-seven and that's an understatement.'

I'LL SCRATCH LAW LORD'S DAUGHTER'S EYES OUT SAYS JILTED ENVOY'S WIFE. One intrepid reporter claimed to have traced the couple to Bali. Another, famed for his secret sources, had them living in the lap of luxury in a hilltop mansion in Montana which the CIA puts at the disposal of 'assets' who have earned its special thanks.

'*Miss Francesca Deane resigned voluntarily from the Foreign Service while en poste in Panama. She was a capable officer and we regret her decision, which was taken on entirely personal grounds.*'

Q: Same grounds as Maltby's?
A: (the same spokesperson, bloodied but unbowed) Pass.
Q: Does that mean no comment?
A: It means pass. It means no comment. What's the difference? Can we please give up this topic and return to something serious?

(A Latin American journalist through her interpreter):
Q: Was Francesca Deane the lover of Mickie Abraxas?
A: What *are* you talking about?
Q: Many people in Panama are saying she was responsible for the break-up of the Abraxas marriage.

A: I cannot conceivably comment on what many people in Panama are supposed to be saying.

Q: Many people in Panama are also saying that Stormont, Maltby, Deane and Osnard were a cadre of highly-trained British terrorists tasked by the CIA to infiltrate the democratic Panamanian government and bring it down from inside!

A: Is this woman accredited? Has anyone ever set eyes on her before? Excuse me! Would you kindly show your press card to the janitor?

*　　*　　*

The case of Nigel Stormont caused little stir. FO LOTHARIO GOES WALKABOUT and a rehash of his much publicised love affair with a former colleague's wife while serving at the British Embassy in Madrid failed to survive the early editions. Paddy Stormont's admission to a Swiss cancer clinic and Stormont's deft handling of the press put a blight on further speculation. As the days went by, Stormont was arbitrarily dismissed as a minor player in what was now seen as a vast and impenetrable British coup that in the words of Hatry's highest paid leader-writer had 'saved America's bacon and proved that Britain under a Tory leadership is capable of being a willing and welcome partner in the grand old Atlantic Alliance, whether or not her so-called European partners choose to waver on the touchlines'.

The participation of a minuscule British token force in the invasion, unnoticed outside the United Kingdom, was a cause for national rejoicing. The better churches flew the flag of St George and schoolchildren not already truant were awarded a day's holiday. Regarding Pendel, the very mention of his name was the subject of a grand-slam gagging order observed by every patriotically-minded newspaper and television network in the land. Such is the fate of secret agents everywhere.

CHAPTER TWENTY-FOUR

It was night and they were sacking Panama again, setting fire to its towers and hovels, terrifying its animals and children and womenfolk with cannon fire, cutting down the men in the street and getting it all over by morning. Pendel stood on the balcony where he had stood the last time, watching without thinking, hearing but not feeling, druckening himself without stooping, atoning without moving his lips, just as his Uncle Benny had atoned into his empty tankard, word for sacred word:

Our power knows no limits, yet we cannot find food for a starving child, or a home for a refugee... Our knowledge is without measure and we build the weapons that will destroy us... We live on the edge of ourselves, terrified of the darkness within... We have harmed, corrupted and ruined, we have made mistakes and deceived.

From inside the house Louisa was yelling again but Pendel wasn't really bothered. He was listening to the shrieks of the bats that were wheeling and protesting in the darkness above him. He loved bats and Louisa hated them and it always scared him when people hated things unreasonably because you never knew where it would end. A bat is ugly, therefore I hate it. You are ugly, therefore I will kill you. Beauty, he decided, was a bully, and perhaps that was why, although he was by trade a beautifier, he had always regarded Marta's disfigurement as a force for good.

'*Come inside,*' Louisa was screaming. 'Come inside *now,* Harry, for the love of God. Do you think you're invulnerable or something?'

Well, he would have liked to come inside, he was a family man at heart, but the love of God was not on Pendel's mind tonight, neither did he consider himself invulnerable. Quite the reverse. He considered himself wounded without cure. As to God – He was as bad as anyone else at not being able to end what He had started. So instead of coming inside, Pendel preferred to hang around on the balcony, away from the accusing glances and too-much knowledge of his children and the scolding tongue of his wife, and the unleavable memory of Mickie's suicide, and watch the neighbours' cats charging in tight order from left to right across his lawn. Three were tabby, one was ginger and by the daylight of the magnesium flares that burned without getting any lower – you could see them in their natural colours instead of the black that cats should be at night.

There were other things that interested Pendel intensely amid the mayhem and the din. The way Mrs Costello in number twelve went on playing Uncle Benny's piano, for example, which was what Pendel would have done if he could play and had inherited the piano. To be able to hold onto a piece of music with your fingers when you're terrified out of your wits – that must be a truly wonderful way of keeping a grip on yourself. And her concentration was amazing. Even from this distance he could see how she closed her eyes and moved her lips like a rabbi to the notes she was playing on her keyboard, the way Uncle Benny used to while Auntie Ruth put her hands behind her back and pushed her chest out and sang.

Then there was the Mendozas' enormously cherished metallic blue Mercedes from number seven, which was rolling down the hill because Pete Mendoza had been so glad to get home before the attack that he had left the car in neutral with the handbrake off, and the car had gradually woken up to this. I'm sprung, it said to itself. They've left the cell door open. All I have to do is walk. So it started walking, first lumbering like Mickie and, like Mickie perhaps, hoping very much for the chance collision that would change his life but, in its despair, running at full gallop, and Heaven alone knew where it would finish up or at what speed, or what collateral damage it might cause before it stopped, or whether by some freak of German over-engineering the pram sequence from some Russian film that Pendel had forgotten the name of had been programmed into one of its sealed units.

All of these fiddly details were of immense importance to Pendel. Like Mrs Costello, he could get his mind round them, whereas the shelling from Ancón Hill and the hovering gunships cranking themselves round and coming in again were wearyingly familiar to him, part of everyday reality if that was what everyday reality was: a poor tailor boy lighting fires to please his friend and betters, then watching the world go up in smoke. And all the stuff you thought you cared about, ill-placed levity on the way there.

No, Your Honour, I did not start this war.

Yes, Your Honour, I grant you, it is possible I wrote the anthem. But allow me to point out with due respect that the one who writes the anthem does not necessarily start the war.

'Harry, I do not understand why you remain outdoors when your family is begging you to join them. No, Harry, not in a minute. *Now.* We wish you to come inside please, and protect us.'

Oh Lou, oh Christ, I wish so much, so very much, that I could join them too. But I have to leave the lie behind, even if, hand on heart, I don't know what the truth is. I have to stay and go at the same time, but at this moment, I can't stay.

There had been no warning but then Panama was under warning all the time. Behave your little self or else. Remember you are not a country but a canal. Besides, the need for such warnings was exaggerated. Does a runaway blue Mercedes pram without a baby in it give a warning before it bounces down a couple of flights of snake-road and crashes into a bunch of fugitives? Of course it doesn't. Does a football stadium give a warning before it collapses killing hundreds? Does a murderer warn his victim in advance that the police will call on him and ask whether he's a British spy, and whether he would like to spend a week or two with a few hard cases in Panama's best stocked nick? As to a specific warning of human intent – 'We are about to bomb you' – 'We are about to betray you' – why alarm everyone? A warning wouldn't help the poor since there was nothing they could do about it, except what Mickie did. And the rich didn't need a warning because it was by now an established principle of invading Panama that the rich were not at risk, which was what Mickie always said, whether he was drunk or sober.

So there was no warning and the helicopter gunships came in from the sea as usual but this time there was no resistance because there was no army, so El Chorillo had taken the wise course of giving itself up before the planes got there, which was a sign that the place was finally coming to heel, and that Mickie in taking the same pre-empting line of action was not mistaken either, even if the results were messy. A block of flats similar to Marta's fell to its knees of its own accord, reminding him of Mickie upside down. A makeshift primary school set fire to itself. A sanctuary for geriatrics blew a hole in its own wall almost the exact size of the hole in Mickie's head. Then it turfed half its inmates into the street so that they could help deal with the fire problem, the way people had dealt with it in Guararé, mainly by ignoring it. And a whole lot of other people had sensibly started running before they could possibly have anything to run from – as a sort of fire drill – and screaming before they had been hit. And all this, Pendel noticed over Louisa's yelling, had taken place before the first edge of troubled air reached his balcony in Bethania or the first tremors shook the broom cupboard under the stairs where Louisa had taken the children.

'Dad!' Mark this time. 'Dad, come inside. Please! Please!'

'Daddy, Daddy, Daddy.' Hannah now. 'I love you!'

No, Hannah. No, Mark. Of love another time, please, and alas I cannot come inside. When a man sets fire to the world and kills his best friend into the bargain, and sends his non-mistress to Miami to spare her the further attentions of the police, though he had known from her turned away eyes that she wouldn't go, he does his best to abandon any ideas he has of being a protector.

'Harry, they have it all worked out. Everything is pinpoint. Everything is high-tech. The new weaponry can select a single window from a distance of many miles. They do not bomb civilians any more. Kindly come indoors.'

But Pendel could not have gone indoors although in many ways he wanted to because once again his legs wouldn't work. Each time he set fire to the world, or killed a friend, he now realised, they ceased to function. And there was a big blaze forming over El Chorillo, with black smoke coming out of the top of the blaze – though, like the cats, the smoke wasn't black all over, being red underneath from the flames and silver on the top from the magnesium flares in the sky. This gathering blaze held Pendel fixed in its stare and he couldn't move his eyes or legs an inch in any other direction. He had to stare it back and think of Mickie.

'Harry, I wish to know where you are going, please!'

So do I. Nevertheless her question puzzled him until he realised that he was after all walking, not towards Louisa or the children but away from her, and away from the shame of them, that he was on a hard road going downhill in long strides following the path that Pete's Mercedes pram had taken when it set off on its own, although with the back of his head he was longing to turn round, run up the hill and embrace his children and his wife.

'Harry, I love you. Whatever you've done wrong, I've done worse. Harry, I do not mind what you are or who you are or what you've done or who to. Harry, stay here.'

He was walking in long steps. The steep hill was hitting the heels of his shoes, making him jolt, and it's a thing about going downhill and losing height that it gets harder and harder and harder to turn back. Going downhill was so seductive. And he had the road to himself because generally during an invasion those who aren't out looting stay indoors and try to telephone their friends, which was what the people were doing in their lighted windows as he strode past. And sometimes they got through to them because their friends, like themselves, inhabited areas where normal services are not disturbed in time of war. But Marta couldn't telephone anybody. Marta lived among people who, if only spiritually, came from the other side of the bridge, and for them war was a serious and even fatal obstruction to the conduct of their daily lives.

He kept walking and wanting to turn back but not doing it. He was distracted in his head and needed to find a way of turning exhaustion into sleep, and maybe that was what death was useful for. He would have liked to do something that would last, like have Marta's head in his neck again, and her other breast in his hand, but his trouble was, he felt unsuited to companionship and preferred his own society to anybody else's on the grounds that he caused less havoc when he was safely isolated, which was what the judge had told him and it was true, and was what Mickie had also told him and it was even truer.

Definitely he no longer cared about suits, his own or anyone else's. The line, the form, the rock of eye, the silhouette, were of no concern to him any more. People must wear what they liked and the best people didn't have a choice, he noticed. A lot of them got by perfectly well with a pair of jeans and a white shirt or a flowered dress that they washed and rotated all their lives. A lot of them had not the least idea of what rock of eye meant. Like these people running past him, for instance, with bleeding feet and wide-open mouths, shoving him out of the way and shouting 'Fire!' and screaming like their own children. Screaming 'Mickie!' and 'You bastard, Pendel.' He looked for Marta among them but didn't see her, and probably she had decided he was too sullied for her, too disgusting. He looked for the Mendozas' metallic blue Mercedes in case it had decided to change sides and join the terrified mob, but he saw no sign of it. He saw a fire hydrant that had been amputated at the waist. It was gushing black blood all over the street. He saw Mickie a couple of times but didn't get so much as a nod of recognition out of him.

He kept walking and he realised that he was quite far into the valley and it must be the valley into town. But when you are walking alone in the middle of a road that you drive every day, it becomes difficult to recognise familiar landmarks, specially when they are lit with flares and you are being jostled by frightened people running away. But his destination was not a problem to him. It was Mickie, it was Marta. It was the centre of the orange fireball that kept its eye firmly on him while he walked, ordering him forward, talking to him in the voices of all the new good Panamanian neighbours it was not too late for him to get to know. And certainly in the place that he was headed for, nobody would ever again ask him to improve on life's appearance, neither would they mistake his dreaming for their terrible reality.

Acknowledgments

Nobody who helped me with this novel is responsible for its failings.

In Panama I must first thank the distinguished American novelist Richard Koster who, with great generosity of spirit, went out of his way to open doors for me, and provided me with much wise counsel. Alberto Calvo gave handsomely of his time and support. Roberto Reichard was ever helpful, and hospitable to a fault. And when the book was done he revealed the eye of a natural editor. The lion-hearted Guillermo Sanchez, scourge of Noriega and to this day *La Prensa*'s vigilant champion of the decent Panama, did me the honour of reading the finished manuscript and gave it his nod, as did Richard Wainio of the Panama Canal Commission, who was able to laugh where lesser men would have blanched.

Andrew and Diana Hyde sacrificed hours of their precious time, despite the twins, never sought to know my purposes and saved me from some embarrassing bloomers. Dr Liborio García-Correa and his family took me to their collective bosom and guided me to places and people I would not otherwise have reached. I shall always be grateful to Dr García-Correa's tireless researches on my behalf and for the splendid trips we made together – notably to Barro Colorado. Sarah Simpson, manager and owner of the Pavo Real restaurant, provided me with much good nourishment. Hélène Breebaart, who makes beautiful clothes for beautiful Panamanian ladies, kindly advised me on how I might set up my gentlemen's tailoring establishment. And the staff of the Smithsonian Tropical Research Institute gave me two unforgettable days.

My portrait of the staff of the British Embassy in Panama is the sheerest fantasy. The British diplomats and their wives whom I met in Panama were uniformly able, diligent and honourable. They are the last people on earth to hatch wicked conspiracies or steal gold bars and they have nothing in common, thank Heaven, with the imaginary characters described in this book.

Back in London, my thanks go to Rex Cowan and Gordon Smith for their advice on Pendel's partly-Jewish background, and to Doug Hayward of Mount Street W who allowed me my first misty glimpse of Harry Pendel the tailor. Doug, if you ever drop by to be measured for a suit, is likely to receive you sitting in his armchair beside the front door. There's a cosy old sofa to sit on, and a coffee table strewn with books and magazines. No portrait of the great Arthur Braithwaite hangs, alas, on his wall, neither does he tolerate much in the way of chit-chat in his fitting room, where the mood is brisk and businesslike. But if you close your eyes one quiet summer's evening in his shop, you may just hear the distant echo of Harry Pendel's voice extolling the virtues of alpaca cloth or buttons made of tagua nut.

For Harry Pendel's music I am indebted to another great tailor, Dennis Wilkinson of L. G. Wilkinson of St George Street. Dennis, when he cuts, likes nothing better than to turn his key upon the world and play his favourite classics. Alex Rudelhof admitted me to the intimate mysteries of measuring.

And lastly, without Graham Greene this book would never have come about. After Greene's *Our Man in Havana*, the notion of an intelligence fabricator would not leave me alone.

John le Carré